Return to the Lake House

The Scottish Highlands Series

Winter in the Scottish Highlands

The Secrets of the Glen

Return to the Lake House

The Boathouse by the Loch

AUTHOR'S NOTE

This series is best read sequentially to enjoy the story arc as it was intended.

Return to the Lake House is the third book.

Return to the Lake House

The Scottish Highlands Series

Book III

ELISE DARCY

Penny Lane Press

ISBN 978-1-913147-30-3

"Your life does not get better by chance, it gets better by change."–*Jim Rohn*

1

Jake stirred and opened his eyes to see Faye gently lifting her daughter.

Half-asleep, Natty clung to Jake's neck. 'No, I want Daddy,' she protested.

'It's alright, Faye – I'll take her up to bed.' They'd fallen asleep on the sofa downstairs. Jake awkwardly hoisted himself up from the settee with the child still clinging to his neck.

'I don't wanna go upstairs,' a sleepy voice said, muffled against Jake's neck.

'Sorry, kiddo. The boss has spoken.' He winked at Faye.

She did not return his smile, he noticed. She switched the TV off as he crossed the lounge and headed for the stairs.

Jake tucked Natty into bed. She'd fallen asleep again and didn't stir. Before he returned downstairs, he made sure there were no chinks of light filtering through the curtains. It wasn't even five in the morning, but the sun was already up. June had been a very warm, sunny month, and Jake thought they might be in for a lovely summer.

He checked she was still asleep before pulling the door until it was slightly ajar and heading downstairs.

Faye was in the lounge, opening the curtains. Jake was about to step into the room when Faye approached. She didn't say a word as she walked past him and out of the room.

Jake followed her into the small kitchen next door. 'Faye?'

She switched the strip light on in the kitchen and put the kettle on.

Jake stood in the kitchen doorway. He closed his eyes and rubbed the back of his stiff neck. In his experience – and he reckoned most people would agree – the couch never made for a good night's sleep.

'I'm making coffee. Do you want some?'

Jake opened his eyes. There was something in her tone of voice that said she was cheesed off. 'I heard Natty get up. I know I should have put her straight back to bed, but she'd had a nightmare, and I didn't want to wake you upstairs,' Jake explained. 'So, I brought her down for a glass of milk, and we watched some TV.' He was getting the distinct impression he had done the wrong thing.

Faye didn't turn around.

Jake watched her open a cupboard and get out two mugs. He held out his hand in a conciliatory gesture. 'Look, I get it. I was out of line.'

Faye spooned two teaspoons of coffee into the mugs and filled them with boiling water.

'Faye?'

She turned to face Jake, holding a mug of coffee in each hand. 'She called you *Daddy*.'

Jake sighed and shuffled into the kitchen, still rubbing his sore neck. He pulled out a chair and motioned Faye to sit. He sat down opposite her as she passed him a mug of coffee. Jake smiled and looked at his watch. 'In a couple of hours, over breakfast, why don't you ask your daughter who she thinks I am? You know what she's going to say?'

Faye sipped her coffee in silence.

'She's going to say that I'm just Jake, her mum's friend, who watches over her while her mum is at her evening classes.' Jake frowned. 'Words to that effect.' It was way too early in the morning to think coherently, let alone string a sentence together.

Faye hadn't been at an evening class this time. She'd been gone the whole day on a course, and had got stuck in a long traffic jam on the way home.

Faye listened.

'Natty was half-asleep and confused when she woke up. I mean, how often do I crash here, Faye?'

Faye didn't answer. It was a rhetorical question. Despite the numerous times he'd babysat, it was the first time he hadn't gone home once she returned. He'd stayed the night on the couch rather than take the tube across London to his own place late at night.

'How's the course going?' he asked.

Faye was on an eighteen-month course, studying for a higher qualification to become a headteacher. Some of her classes were held in the evenings locally, but some were at a college outside London, which meant she didn't get back until late. Either way, she needed a sitter – Natty was nine; too young to be left on her own.

Faye didn't have any close relatives living nearby that she could leave Natty with, which meant she relied on babysitters. But lately, this had not worked out. Faye desperately wanted to further her career. Currently a deputy head, she was good at her job and wanted to eventually run her own school.

The previous evening, Jake had kept an eye on the time,

getting worried when she didn't arrive home. Natty had become exhausted, and by the time Faye did get back, he'd already put her to bed.

Whilst this was the first time he'd crashed at Faye's, by the look of things, it would also be the last. He raised his mug and drank his coffee, waiting for Faye to say something – anything.

'You're right. I don't know where she'd get a crazy idea like that from.'

Jake nodded in agreement. 'Besides, Faye, you know what a bright kid you've got there. She's really on the ball, always asking questions. I swear she's going to be a lawyer or something when she grows up.'

'Yeah, how crazy if she becomes a lawyer just like you … were.' Faye dropped her eyes to her coffee mug. It had developed over time, this unspoken understanding they shared. Talk revolved around the job – Jake was a teacher too – and around Natty, which he knew was fine by Faye. She'd told him that as a deputy head, some colleagues – and she wasn't naming any names – talk incessantly about any and every problem they had, as if her office was some sort of confessional box. They seemed to forget that they were colleagues. *I'm not at work to make friends*, Faye had said.

Jake had wondered why none of Faye's female colleagues had offered to help with babysitting. Perhaps that was what Faye was afraid of – striking up a friendship which would result in endless hours of listening to their problems once she returned home.

With Jake, there was no chance of that. He wouldn't talk about his past life – or his problems – and she knew it.

Faye had a life outside of teaching. Jake knew that she loved her job – but Natty was her priority. Work was work; that was all, even if she did have career ambitions. And Jake understood this, even if he had stepped into her private life on occasion – on several occasions now; too many to count. The trouble was that he was enjoying Faye and Natty's company. The last thing he wanted was for Faye to end his babysitting duty.

❖

She glanced at Jake, thinking *this was a mistake*. Jake staying over was innocent enough, considering the circumstances. But the rule, their rule, was bending before her very eyes, and she was the one bending it. She wanted him to stick around. What she couldn't figure out was why.

They both finished their coffee in silence. Jake got up and put his coffee mug in the sink. Faye turned in her chair, feeling like some sort of apology was in order. She shouldn't have mentioned his past. She wouldn't like Jake to think she had been looking into his personal history. 'I didn't Google you or anything like that, Jake.'

'I know that, Faye.'

'It's just common knowledge. God, that sounds awful.'

'It is awful. But when you come from a background like mine, everything is out there, on the news, on social media, for Joe Public to see.'

Faye cringed. She recalled one of the standard questions at the job interview for the first teaching position he'd applied for, which had happened to be at her school. As the deputy head, she had been one of the interviewers asking him about his previous work experience.

She remembered when they'd been shortlisting for the position and discussing the candidates. They were all intrigued as to why Jake had left his lucrative position as a high-flying corporate lawyer working in the Ross Corporation. They knew about his background with the Rosses. She had read about him in the papers; about how he'd been taken in by the Rosses when he was a young child after his parents had tragically died, and had married Eleanor Ross.

Of course, they wouldn't bring that up in an interview, nor the tragic skiing accident in the Cairngorms the previous Christmas that had taken his young wife. But they had asked about his previous career – it was a standard question – and why he'd decided to apply for the Initial Teacher Training course to become a maths teacher in an inner-city school.

Even while the head was asking that question, Faye had already had a good idea why Jake had made such a drastic change. She imagined that after losing his wife, he wanted a completely fresh start away from the company; away from the life that reminded him of her. And perhaps the life, the career he'd had in the Ross Corporation, wasn't for him anyway. As sad as it was that he had lost his wife, the career he was now forging, training on the job to teach, was a better fit. From Faye's perspective, she certainly thought he'd made the right decision; Jake showed great promise, was a natural in the classroom, and had a fantastic rapport with the classes he taught.

'I'm sorry, Jake. I didn't mean to bring up your past.'

'So am I.' Jake walked out of the kitchen.

Faye cursed under her breath. She got up from the table and put her cup in the sink.

'By the way,' Jake called out as he headed for the sofa, 'whoever her father is, he doesn't know what he's missing.'

'Yes, he does.' Faye stared miserably into the sink.

'What was that?' Jake turned to see Faye emerging from the kitchen. She crossed the lounge and sat in the single armchair.

'I said he does know what he's missing.'

Jake sat on the sofa and leaned forward, resting his elbows on his knees. He sighed. 'The past is always following you around like a permanent hangover just itching to spoil your day.'

Faye had the sudden urge to show Jake he wasn't the only one with unresolved personal issues; he wasn't the only one hurting. 'Do you know, my father doesn't see my daughter – his only grandchild?' She anticipated his shocked response: *How could he? What's wrong with the man?* Instead, she was the one in for a shock.

'I know,' Jake answered nonchalantly. 'He blames you for leaving Natty's father and thinks that as you took it upon yourself to be a single parent, you shouldn't expect family members to step in.'

Faye was stunned. 'Who told you that?'

'Your daughter – who else?'

'Oh.' *Serves me right for having such an outspoken nine-year-old*, Faye thought. She wondered about the last time she had spoken with Natty's grandfather, when he had made a rare visit to their house. Had their raised voices woken Natty? Had she got out of bed and sat on the stair, listening to that blazing row?

Jake held up two hands. 'Look, I didn't ask, okay? One day she just started talking about the grandfather that she rarely sees, and I guess she must have overheard some adult conversations she shouldn't have.'

Faye leaned back in her chair to look through the open doorway into the hall, expecting to see Natty sitting on the stair, listening. Of course, she wasn't there; she was tucked up in bed, fast asleep. All the same, the next time she spoke, Faye lowered her voice. 'I didn't tell her the truth, you know.'

'About her father?'

Faye nodded. 'I did leave her father, it's true.' She paused. 'Her grandfather got on really well with him.'

'Oh, I see – so your father sort of sided with him when you broke up?'

'Yeah, he couldn't understand why I'd ditch such a lovely bloke, but our relationship, it just wasn't working out. We wanted different things. It was just as well we never married. He was a foreign student over here doing a PhD at a London university. We met when I was doing my Master's in education. I got pregnant. He kept asking to marry me.'

'He was a foreign student?'

'From the Middle East; Oman. He wanted me and Natty to live with him in his country. But my life was here. Perhaps if we hadn't had a baby together, we'd have parted ways a lot sooner.'

Jake nodded. 'I'm so sorry to hear things didn't work out.'

Faye smiled. 'I wouldn't change a thing, because I have a beautiful little girl. As you've gathered, she takes after my ex in the looks department, with those big brown eyes, glossy dark hair, and olive skin.'

'But she's got her mother's features, and she's going to break some hearts someday,' Jake blurted.

Faye stared at him.

In the awkward silence that followed, she noticed him looking around the room, avoiding eye contact, until his attention settled on a cushion beside him on the sofa. She watched him pick it up, put it on his lap, and examine the pattern intensely. He seemed embarrassed; she thought he was probably wondering what on earth had made him say such a thing.

She imagined he was beginning to feel that it had been a bad idea to crash at hers. She suddenly felt self-conscious in her silk pyjamas, with her blonde bob, normally straightened, all askew. He'd never seen her in casual clothes before, let alone in her pyjamas. She always looked professional, choosing to wear suits for work, even when she attended her evening classes.

'Now that sounded like a really bad chat-up line,' Faye joked.

Jake looked up and smiled weakly. She caught him looking at his watch, which reminded her that if she returned to bed straight away, she might get an extra hour before Natty woke up.

2

Faye decided she did fancy another hour in bed, although she imagined she wouldn't get back to sleep.

'Where are you going?' Jake asked.

'Back to bed.'

'Faye. Tell me what happened between you and your father.'

Faye struggled with indecision. She shouldn't tell him. She was breaking her own rules, and she knew she would regret it. Once the precedent was set, once the door was closed on a purely professional relationship, she didn't know where it would lead and how it would affect their working relationship. But had that line already been crossed when she had let him into her private life to babysit? Of course it had. Completely against her better judgement, Faye sat down. 'She's only got her grandfather, you know.'

'I know,' Jake tossed the cushion to one side.

Faye looked at him a long moment. 'I guess she tells you everything.'

'Pretty much.' Jake shrugged. 'She …'

'… talks a lot.' Faye glanced at him. 'I suppose you're wondering why my dad and I can't get along enough so that she can at least see him.'

Jake listened.

Faye studied her fingernails intently. 'My father, Patrick, thinks I should let Natty's father see her. He doesn't agree with my decision to cut him out of our lives completely.' Faye wondered what Jake would think of that.

'So, this is his rather grown-up way of emphasising that point, is it – shutting you out of his life?' Jake shook his head. 'The stupidity of some people. Sorry, I shouldn't call your father stupid. I don't even know the man. But I know one thing – he has a fantastic daughter, and granddaughter, and he should take you in his arms, and hold you both tight, because you never know—' Jake stopped and swallowed.

'Jake?'

'You never know if … when something might happen, and you never get that chance again to hold someone you love in your arms.'

Faye sat forward in her chair and realised the conversation had stopped being about her and Natty. She knew who Jake was talking about – Eleanor.

She reached out and touched his hand. 'We're not going anywhere, Natty and I.'

Jake placed a gentle hand on top of hers. 'You'd better not.'

'I'm making sure of it – especially where my daughter is concerned.'

Jake was studying her hand. 'What do you mean?'

Faye withdrew her hand and stood up.

'Are you off back to bed?'

She shook her head, and walked over to close the lounge door. 'I swear my daughter's hearing is superhuman. I just want to make sure she doesn't wake up and hear what I say next. I don't want to scare her.'

'Scare her?' Jake frowned. 'Is everything okay?'

'Yes – it is now, since I left Yousaf – or rather, ran away and took Natty with me. You see, my father does not know why I walked out on him. We seemed so happy. We were so happy, until—' Faye took a breath.

Jake leaned forward in his chair. 'What is it – tell me! Did he hurt you?' Jake swivelled his head to the door. 'Did he hurt—'

'Oh, no, nothing like that. Yousaf was the gentlest soul you could ever imagine.'

'Then why did you walk out?'

'As I said before, when we finished our courses, and Natty was born, he wanted us to return with him to Oman.'

'But you didn't want to go.'

Faye shook her head. 'I just couldn't imagine leaving England and bringing up my daughter there. I begged Yousaf to stay here, but he was torn. I think he came from a wealthy family in Oman, but there was still the pressure as the eldest son to look after his extended family. When I said I wasn't going to go with him, at first he stayed, but then I think he was being pressured by his family to go back.'

'Did he tell them about you and Natty?'

'Yes. He told them I didn't want to go and live in Oman. Then he asked if he could take Natty for a holiday to Oman.'

'He what?'

'I would have gone with him during the holidays, to meet his family, but he didn't want to wait until the school holidays. He wanted to show them his beautiful daughter.'

'Did he take her?'

'I didn't know how to be away from her for a week, and voiced my concerns to my father, but he said to let him take her to meet the family. He said it might be one of the few chances Yousaf's family got to see her. So I agreed.' Faye swallowed. 'I nearly lost her, Jake.'

'What are you talking about?'

'If I hadn't overheard him on the phone …'

Jake got up and walked over, kneeling in front of her chair. 'What happened?'

I was home early from work. There had been an incident at school, a burst pipe flooding several classrooms. The school had to close for the afternoon. Yousaf had been due to collect her from the nursery that afternoon and go straight to the airport. I wanted … needed to say goodbye to her before they left, but he'd said it was the only flight time he could find, and that meant I'd be at work when they left. It was not ideal at all. I'd also been so, so worried about her going all that way without me. I was getting seriously cold feet. The flood at school, getting off work early, just seemed to be fated. I raced back home, and before I even opened the front door, I could hear my little Natty's chatter. They were still there.'

Faye took a breath before she continued. 'I crept indoors, wanting it to be a surprise. I knew Yousaf wouldn't be happy if I changed my mind about Natty going. The flights were booked. But I had checked online and discovered there was still availability on a flight during the next school holiday – he'd said there wasn't, and I'd believed him. It didn't sit right with me that he'd lied about it. Although I didn't think that at the time; I just thought he'd made an innocent error when he'd searched for the flights.'

'That wasn't the case?'

Faye vehemently shook her head. 'When I walked in, he was on his mobile in the lounge, calling for a taxi to pick them up and take them to the airport. I glanced in the lounge. He didn't see me, but I saw Natty sitting happily on his knee, playing with a doll. I saw the plane tickets on the sideboard. I picked them up, and was about to walk into the lounge to tell him he'd better not forget the tickets. Then I happened to notice something odd. They were not return tickets.'

'What do you mean?'

'They were one-way tickets.'

Faye could tell by the bemused look on Jake's face that he didn't get it.

'He was leaving for Oman, and he wasn't coming back.'

'But he was taking your daughter.'

'Exactly.'

It took a moment for Jake to take this in, Faye could tell. She watched his expression.

'Are you saying he was going to kidnap her?'

'I suppose *kidnap* is a strong word. After all she was … is his daughter. But he'd planned it all along, to leave and take Natty with him. He must have made a decision that he was returning to Oman and never coming back. He already knew I wouldn't go with him, so he'd decided he was taking her without me. He knew I'd never, ever let that happen, so that's why he'd planned the trip, supposedly just a visit to take Natty to meet his relatives.'

Jake looked dumbfounded. 'So, why did he tell you? He could have just collected her from nursery one day and left.'

'My father was a police officer. He's retired now, but he still has connections on the force. Yousaf obviously realised he risked the possibility that if I discovered she was missing, someone might catch up with him and Natty before he could board a flight.'

Faye swallowed. 'He'd obviously thought it through and planned to leave when I was at work, just in case I got cold feet and didn't want Natty to go with him. To be honest, I don't know why I let him talk me into it.'

They fell silent until Jake said, 'How long ago was that?'

'Five years ago.' Faye shuddered. 'Even now, it turns my stomach – the thought that if I hadn't left work early that day because of a burst pipe, I might never have seen my daughter again.'

Jake said in a small voice, 'What about if he comes back?'

'We moved house. I changed schools. I took Natty out of her nursery and put her with a childminder instead until she started school.'

Jake nodded.

'I'm always looking over my shoulder, afraid he'll return.'

'That's terrible.'

'I know. The worst part was that he was such a lovely, gentle man. I think he was pressured by his family. I realised they'd always come first. Natty asks after her father from time to time. She was too young when he left to remember him. But he can't be a part of her life. You understand that – don't you?'

'Of course I do.' Jake reached for her hand. 'So, what happened – did you confront him?'

Faye remembered to breathe. 'No, I did not. I remembered standing in the doorway, watching him cradling Natty affectionately, thinking that I must have it all wrong. But then when he saw me in the doorway, I knew. He didn't smile, or ask me what had happened, why I'd returned from work early. All he did was just sit there, looking guilty.' Faye sighed. 'I just handed him his ticket, and took Natty in my arms. I didn't have to say anything. He knew I knew. The taxi turned up. I said goodbye. He promised he'd be back, said it was just a visit. But I saw his eyes flicker to his daughter when he said he'd be coming back. Of course he would. To fetch what was his. As soon as he got in the taxi, I was already planning to leave the house, my job, Natty's nursery and move on somewhere that he and his family wouldn't find us.'

'Why didn't you tell your father all this?'

'I did. He just said I was being paranoid and that there was no way Yousaf would do that.'

'He said that?'

'Yes. I even told him about the phone conversation I'd overheard between Yousaf and his father. In hindsight, I realised what they were talking about. Of course, I could only hear one side of the conversation – but I heard him say: *Yes, of course I'm bringing her with me. Do you think I'd leave her behind?*' Faye stared at Jake. 'I thought, after several years together, he was staying in England for good.' Faye rubbed her tired eyes. 'Sorry, I shouldn't have told you all this.'

'Actually, I think you most definitely should have.'

Faye looked at him questioningly.

Jake continued, 'What if some guy turns up at your house, god forbid, claiming to be Natty's father, while I'm babysitting?'

Faye saw his point. She said softly, 'I think you remind Natty of him.'

'Who – Yousaf?'

'Yes – in a good way. I know I said she doesn't really remember him. She was too young when he left. But you are gentle and caring towards her just like he was.'

'I'm sorry she can't see her father.'

'You do understand?'

'Of course I do. I'm just sorry that your father doesn't.'

'So am I. Of course, it didn't help that some time later, Yousaf wrote to me. I wasn't interested in getting any communication from him, but because he didn't have my address, he had written care of my father.'

'Oh dear.'

'Yes, precisely. My father passed on the letter. And I gave him strict instructions not to tell Yousaf my new address.' Faye sighed. 'Of course, the fact that my father found out I hadn't told Yousaf my new address didn't help our relationship either. I did read the letter, though. It was basically one long apology. Yousaf said he didn't know what he had been thinking, and it had been all his overbearing parents' idea, which was obviously no excuse for him going through with it, but he wanted desperately to make things right.'

They fell silent again. Faye didn't think there was any point going back to bed now. She stood up. 'I'm going to get dressed.'

Jake was already dressed. He had slept on the couch in his clothes. He said, 'Yes, I'd better head off.' He paused. 'It is a shame you can't patch things up with your dad – for Natty's sake. She's a great kid, and they're both missing out.'

Faye was at the lounge door with her hand on the doorknob. She turned to look at him across the room.

He quickly added, 'Not that it's down to you to repair the relationship. Your father is being completely unreasonable.'

Faye breathed a heavy sigh. 'Actually, there is probably some truth in what he said about me being paranoid.'

'I don't agree at all. The guy was going to take your kid. I know

Natty is his too, but it's clear what his intentions were, to take her away from you, forever. You'd probably never have seen her again.'

'The thought of that … it's why I cut my father out of her life too.'

Jake looked at her, bemused. 'But you said—'

'Yeah, it's not the case that he doesn't want to see her. My father really liked Yousaf, and he still doesn't believe that Yousaf wanted to take Natty back to Oman with him for good. I've always been afraid that Yousaf might contact my father, and …' She trailed off.

Jake frowned. 'And …?' he prompted.

Faye sighed. 'Sometimes I do think I'm paranoid. I had all sorts of crazy scenarios go round in my head, like what if Yousaf came back to England, and they agreed to meet up behind my back with Natty. I know it sounds crazy and far-fetched, but I couldn't risk it.'

'Faye, I understand completely.' Jake stared at her solemnly. 'It'll never happen again, Faye – not on my watch.'

Faye held Jake's gaze. She said, 'He still gets in contact, leaves me phone messages.'

'Your father?'

Faye nodded. 'It's always the same, suggesting we could still go back to the way things are, with him seeing Natty, if only I'd stop being so silly. He just doesn't get it. Until he accepts my side of the story, I can't do that.'

'I need a drink,' Jake said suddenly.

'Bit early for alcohol.'

Jake laughed at the joke.

Faye said, 'You want your coffee strong and black.'

He smiled. 'You can read me like an open book.'

Not quite, Faye thought. He hadn't opened up about his late wife, and she didn't expect him to. I'll go and make that coffee.'

3

Jake opened his eyes. He could hear whispering coming from the kitchen. He sat up and stretched. Thankfully, the stiffness in his neck was gone. He noted the two coffee cups on the coffee table: one empty, the other full. Jake guessed he must have fallen asleep while Faye was making the second cup. Jake picked up the blanket from the floor and glanced at Faye's empty mug. She must have sat there and drank it while he slept. The thought of Faye watching him sleep gave him a twinge of embarrassment. He hoped he hadn't snored. He wondered why it should bother him.

He glanced at his watch and raised his eyebrows. It was nine in the morning. He couldn't believe that he'd gone back to sleep for four hours. He had not slept well in nearly six months; not since the accident in the Cairngorms. His sleeping pattern – the new normal for him – was waking up at four in the morning after a nightmare in which he was trying to chase after Eleanor on the ski slopes, yelling at her: *Stop! Slow down! You're going too fast!* And then he'd wake up and remember what had happened to her.

The past few months, throwing himself into teacher training and meeting Faye and Natty, had literally saved him from a downward spiral involving a big bottle of Jack Daniels. He was glad that Faye didn't have any alcohol in the house. Not that he really needed that now. Jake realised another thing; for the first time, he had gone back to sleep and not had that godawful nightmare.

Jake stood up, picked up his shirt from the back of the chair and put it on over his white vest. He'd changed into casual clothes – he was wearing jeans – for babysitting duty the previous night. He found his trainers under the sofa. He was just sitting on the sofa, slipping them on, when Natty ran into the room. 'Jake! You're awake!' She ran into his arms.

'Hey there. You should have woken me up.'

'I wanted to, but Mummy said I had to let you sleep.'

'Really?' That explained the whispers he'd heard from the kitchen on waking.

'It's lucky it's Saturday,' Jake commented, 'otherwise I would have been late for work.'

'I asked Mummy if you could spend the day with us, but she said you were probably busy. Can you stay today, Jakey?'

Jake smiled at her. She was the only person he'd ever known who called him by a pet name.

'Can you? Please say yes.'

Jake wanted to. Of course he'd say yes. But it wasn't up to him. Jake cast his gaze over to the door, wondering where Faye was. Then he heard someone padding around upstairs and the sound of a shower.

'Mummy will be cross if she thinks I woke you up when she went to shower.'

Jake smiled. 'Don't worry. I'll tell her I was awake already.' He looked at her. 'Have you had breakfast?'

Natty shook her head.

'Come on. Let's give your mum a surprise.' Jake grinned.

So did Natty. She stopped at the stairs on the way to the kitchen. 'I need a wee!'

Jake watched her run up the stairs. 'Mum! I need a wee!'

Jake heard Faye's muffled voice from behind the bathroom door upstairs. 'I've just got in the shower!'

'Please, I'm desperate!'

'Why do you do this every time?!'

'I don't know!'

'Will you please keep your voice down! Jake is sleeping.'

'No, he's awake now.'

'I'm not surprised. How many times have I told you, indoor voices!'

Jake glanced up the stairs as Faye stepped out of the bathroom in nothing but a white towel that only covered her torso and left her shoulders and her legs up to the thigh bare. Her skin was glistening with water.

Jake drew a sharp breath, catching her there at the top of the landing. She hadn't spotted him staring up at her, but at any minute, she might. Jake retreated to the kitchen, feeling rather hot under the collar, and busied himself making breakfast, trying his utmost not to think of Faye in nothing but a towel.

Jake opened a kitchen cupboard and found a bottle of Worcestershire sauce. 'This will come in handy,' he muttered with a grin on his face. He found a frying pan. As he cracked some eggs into a glass bowl, he heard Faye and Natty padding around upstairs. He could hear their monotone voices through the ceiling and occasionally heard them very clearly indeed.

'Will you please get out of the bathroom!'

Jake paused, listening to Faye's raised voice.

'Will you please have some patience!' Natty shot back.

Jake smiled up at the ceiling. 'Women!' He shook his head and turned his attention to the cooker, moving the omelette gently around the pan.

Faye and Natty emerged, looking suitably cross with each other. He wondered if they went through the same routine every morning. He tried to hide the smile on his face as Natty ran over.

Faye dragged a seat from under the table and sat down. 'What's cooking?'

Natty said, 'See? I told you there would be a surprise when you came downstairs, Mummy.'

Jake looked sheepishly at Faye. He avoided eye contact, feeling embarrassed that he'd been eyeing her up while she was standing there, half-naked, in a towel. But by god, she had looked gorgeous.

Jake undid his top shirt button. 'Is it me, or is it hot in here?'

Faye said, 'I don't think it's hot in here, but then again, my hair is still wet.'

Jake gave her a sideways glance. She was combing it through. All he could picture was her in that infernal towel.

'Why don't you go upstairs and blow-dry your hair?' Jake suggested, hoping she would.

'Nah, I'm going to let it dry au naturelle.'

Jake would rather she hadn't used the words *au naturelle*. It only served to make him picture the towel falling to her feet, leaving her standing there naked.

He winced. *For god's sake, get a grip!* he told himself silently.

'Everything all right, Jake?' Faye asked.

'Oh, er … yes … fine.' He avoided looking at her until the omelettes and hash browns were cooked.

'What's that smell?' Natty asked.

Jake glanced over his shoulder at Natty, who was sitting with her mum at their small Formica table in the kitchen. 'This omelette is my own speciality. It has a little something added – hope you like it.'

'What is it?' Natty said enthusiastically.

'Omelette a la Lea & Perrins.' Jake slipped a portion on to a plate in front of Natty.

Natty sniffed the air. 'Smells yummy.'

'It is yummy,' said Jake as he served Faye a portion.

'Thanks, Jake.'

'You're welcome.' Jake sat down at the table next to Natty.

They ate.

Natty hummed and ate.

'Don't hum while you eat, honey,' said Faye.

'I wasn't humming.'

Natty hummed and ate.

Jake smiled across the table at Faye.

Faye glanced at Jake, giving him a silent warning not to encourage Natty. Jake didn't say a word, although he did find the humming quite funny, and rather endearing. Jake wondered what his and Eleanor's child would have been like, and how their lives would have changed as first-time parents.

Jake always did his best not to dwell on the past. There lay bad things – a life with Eleanor and his child that would never be. He tried his best to stay in the here and now, which was always a hell of a lot easier when he was round Faye and Natty. It was why he volunteered to babysit at every opportunity.

Faye turned to her daughter. 'Natty? Can you remember what you said to Jake last night?'

Jake turned to look at Natty. She was concentrating intently on moving her fork towards her mouth without losing the large piece of omelette that was balanced on top.

'Natty?' Faye said sharply.

Natty quickly turned her head. 'No, I don't remember.' She turned her attention back to her fork. There was no omelette.

Jake looked at Faye. He shrugged his shoulders, as if to say, *See? I told you she wouldn't remember calling me Daddy*. He turned back to Natty. 'Is the omelette nice?'

'Oh, yes. It's the best omelette I've ever had.'

There was a sigh from the other side of the table.

Jake caught Faye rolling her eyes at her daughter. 'I thought my omelettes were the best.'

Natty just shrugged.

'Well, seeing as you like it so much,' said Jake, rather enjoying the praise and the little bit of well-intentioned banter, 'I could pop round another day and make breakfast again.' There was none of this banter at his own home, where he'd moved for a fresh start. He lived alone and missed this sort of thing. When he closed his front door, the silence was overwhelming. He still hadn't got used to it, and had realised, after several months, that he probably never would.

'Would you like that?' he asked Natty, before immediately realising he was asking the wrong person. 'Um, Faye, would you mind awfully if I popped in another time to make Natty my speciality omelette?'

Natty put her fork down. 'Mummy, can Jakey stay the night again? Then he'd be here in the morning to make breakfast.'

Jake noticed that Faye didn't answer. He stepped into the awkward silence. 'This was just a one-off, sweetheart.'

'Why?'

Jake resisted a smile. He'd never heard that word so much in his life before he'd met Natty. He answered her question while Faye finished her omelette. 'Mummy was home very late last night from her course because she got held up in traffic.'

'So?'

That was another word he heard quite a bit at Faye's house, most often when Natty didn't like the answer to her question.

Natty said, 'Are you and Mummy getting back together?'

Jake didn't understand the question, 'I'm sorry – what?' He caught Faye looking at her daughter quizzically. She said, 'What do you mean?'

'My friend Annabelle said her dad is coming back to live with her mum.'

Faye dropped her fork.

Jake stole a furtive glance at Faye. Her eyes were closed, and she was furiously rubbing her temples with her fingertips as though she had a sudden migraine.

'Er … Natty,' Jake turned in his chair to look at her. She was still quite happily tucking into her breakfast, unaware of the furore her innocent question had the potential to unleash. 'What makes you think I used to live with your mum?' Jake chose his words carefully.

'Well, Annabelle's dad sees Annabelle at the weekends over at his house,' said Natty, 'and now he is moving back in with her mummy.'

'Honey, I haven't ever … er … lived here.' Jake looked over at Faye.

'We moved house,' Natty said matter-of-factly.

'Natty.' Faye sat forward in her chair. 'Jake didn't live with us in the last house. You must remember.'

Jake stared at Natty. By the sound of things, when her real dad had left, she had only been three years old. Faye had said herself that Natty didn't really remember him.

'But you see me at the weekend.'

'Yes, when I'm babysitting. You know that your mum and I are teachers. Actually, I'm a student teacher – but do you understand what that means – that we're work colleagues?' Jake wasn't sure he was explaining himself very well.

'And you're my friend.'

'That's right,' Jake said triumphantly.

'Just like Annabelle and her special friend.'

'Who is Annabelle's special friend?' asked Jake.

'Her daddy.'

Jake heard Faye sigh heavily. She closed her eyes, slowly shaking her head from side to side.

Jake put his fork down. 'Natty, do you think I'm your daddy?'

'Of course you are.' Natty laughed. 'What a silly question.' She turned to Faye. 'May I leave the table now?'

'Huh?' Faye opened her eyes.

'Mummy, I'm leaving the table now,' she said in a sing-song voice, and slid the chair away from the table. She gave Jake a kiss on the cheek and ran up the stairs.

'Don't forget to clean your teeth,' Faye called after her in a deadpan voice. 'I hope you haven't forgotten your trip today.'

'Oh, no.'

Natty wasn't the only one who'd forgotten all about her trip today. Jake had forgotten about it too, probably because it was Saturday, and it wasn't a school trip. Natty was in a swimming club.

'Do I have to go?'

Faye shouted back, 'Yes. Your bag is all packed, remember?'

'Will Jake be here when I get back?'

Jake had just lost his appetite. He slid his plate along the table and stole a glance at Faye. Things had just got complicated. And Jake had Monday to look forward to, being cooped up in a classroom with someone who was going to be very cheesed off indeed.

It was the end-of-term assessment for his teacher training course. Faye was his mentor and would be sitting in on his lessons for the entire day, taking notes. It was important that he passed these assessments. But if he didn't sort things out with Natty, having his mentor in a foul mood would not bode well for the next week at work. Even though Faye was extremely professional, and all this wasn't really his fault, he knew they both sensed that things between them had crossed a line. He was afraid it would mean the end of his babysitting role for good.

Ten minutes later, the kitchen was cleared – in silence – and Natty was struggling into her coat.

Outside, the minibus had turned up to collect her. The driver tooted.

Jake and Faye stood side by side at the front door as Natty skipped down the steps and along the pathway to the waiting bus.

Halfway down the path, Natty skidded to a stop, as though she had forgotten something. She turned around and waved. Faye and Jake waved back. She stood looking at them for a brief moment, a grin erupting on her little face, then turned and ran to the bus.

Jake and Faye exchanged glances. Faye's was distinctly cool. She picked up her summer jacket from the coat hook behind the front door. She was off out. She didn't say where, Jake noticed.

Although Jake wanted to take a shower himself, and put on a

clean set of clothes, he didn't want to go home just yet and stare at four blank walls – quite literally. He had lived in his new place for months, and yet he'd barely even unpacked his boxes, let alone hung a picture from his extensive collection of art. In fact, in the spirit of doing something charitable – he was thinking of Eleanor and all those good causes she used to belong to – he was planning to hand them all to Sotheby's, auction them off to the highest bidder, and then give the money away.

He didn't see the point of hanging them on the walls. The place wasn't a home. All he had brought was one sofa, a large TV screen, which was standing on the floor, and a large double bed. There was a clothes rack on wheels in the bedroom that the previous tenants had left behind, along with some hangers.

Jake thought that perhaps if he'd bought himself a house, instead of renting, there would have been the impetus to turn the house into a home, put his own stamp on it, and actually unpack all his boxes. But he hadn't. He suspected that even if he had bought a place, it would have made little difference. It wasn't the furniture, or the things hung on the walls, that made a house into a home for Jake. It was the people – the family. If you were lucky.

That didn't mean that someone who was single couldn't have a proper home, but for Jake personally, no matter where he lived, there would always be something – someone – missing. He'd discovered after losing Eleanor that it had helped tremendously to change his career and sever ties with the Ross Corporation, but when he went home at night, after work, it had made little difference that he had moved out of the top-floor flat in the Ross Corporation building.

The only room that was fully furnished, and had pictures on the wall, and cupboards and drawers overflowing with stuff, feeling lived-in and occupied, was the spare bedroom he'd set up for the times he'd looked after Natty at his place.

He thought of Faye as he trudged out of the door. She was in a rented house too. She'd moved around. But she'd made hers a home. She also had Natty, and a meaning to her life outside of work. Jake turned around and looked at Faye standing at the door. He couldn't, wouldn't lose them, even if it was just babysitting.

'Faye.'

She shot him a look that said, *Don't talk*.

Jake clamped his mouth shut, dismissing any notion of having a civilised conversation before he left.

He turned around and shuffled off down the street. Some young children ran past him, on their way to the local park around the corner, their parents calling to them to slow down and wait for them to catch up.

He imagined that Faye probably thought he was going to mention the faux pas at the breakfast table. He wouldn't have done so. Besides, what could he do about it? In fact, if he admitted it, he felt chuffed that Natty considered him father material, not to mention the fact that she'd suggested he was her best friend, just like her friend Annabelle's father was to his daughter.

I would have made a good father, he thought.

Of course he knew there was still time; oodles of it, in fact. Just a few days earlier, he had been reading about some actor becoming a father again at the age of eighty. The thought hadn't made Jake feel any better, though.

He sighed, stealing a glance over his shoulder at Faye as she walked to her car. He slowed his pace, hoping she might change her mind and decide not to leave things on this note. But she did not look back.

Any thought of spending the day with Faye evaporated.

4

It was Monday morning. Jake spotted Faye driving into the school car park just as he was trying to fasten his tie. He was standing by his bike and noticed she chose a parking spot as far away from the push bike stand as possible. Jake sighed. She knew he cycled into work every morning. He hadn't heard from her for the rest of the weekend. They still weren't talking about what had happened on Saturday morning.

She walked in the direction of the school building. Jake hurried after her and discovered that any attempt to fasten his tie on the go was futile. For somebody who didn't want to be a suit anymore, Jake wondered at the irony of changing his career to one where he felt obligated, in order to make a good impression with his students, to still wear a blasted tie.

He caught up with her in the lift. Fortunately, the school day hadn't officially started, so no children had arrived. They had the lift, which travelled up to the floor where the staff room was located, to themselves.

Faye stood with her arms folded across her chest, watching Jake's increasingly frustrated attempts to fasten his tie. Finally, he held out both ends at her in an *I could do with some help here* gesture.

He caught a look on her face and decided he wouldn't be surprised if she had the impulse to tell him to go and hang himself with it. He gave up and turned away. She was still annoyed over what had happened on Saturday morning.

If Faye had talked to Natty about her father, then the situation on Saturday would never have arisen. She obviously didn't believe what Yousaf had written in his letter, even though Jake thought he had sounded genuinely contrite, and very sorry for what his family had talked him into doing. Jake didn't want to take sides, but he did understand, coming from a wealthy, influential family like the Rosses, how much control they could have over your life. It did make Jake wonder whether, if his parents hadn't died, and he'd never been taken in by the Rosses, he would have gone straight into teaching. It was a career he felt much more in tune with, and it came with a life he enjoyed – staying put in one place and forging links with a school community. He'd never had that in the past. The cliché of living in an ivory tower was not lost on Jake in relation to his life with the Rosses.

❖

The lift shunted to a stop on the first floor and the lift door opened. Jake and Faye both sighed, aware that the lift stopped at every floor, whether someone pressed the button for the lift or not.

The door closed and the lift started up again.

Faye turned to Jake and rolled her eyes. He was still having trouble with his tie. 'Do you need help with that?'

Jake turned to face her. 'I thought you weren't speaking to me?'

'I'm not,' she said, taking both ends of his tie. It was unfair of her to blame him for what had happened on Saturday – she knew that. She'd been mulling things over and had realised the mistake was hers. She had a golden rule, and it was quite simple – Natty was not going to pay for her mistakes. Natty had friends whose mothers were single parents like herself. One mother seemed to change boyfriends as often as she changed her wardrobe, which, on her substantial spousal maintenance, was often. To be fair, some boyfriends did last longer than a 'season', but sadly, the longer they lasted, the more unfair it became on Natty's friend to sever the ties with her potential new daddy. So, Faye's golden rule had translated quite simply into no dating until Natty was eighteen. She hadn't told her friends this. They had already been after her joining a dating website. If they'd known why she hadn't, they'd have told her that she was mad – ten years would make her in her early forties, and as time went on, it would only become harder to meet someone, start a relationship, find her soulmate.

Of course, she knew all this, but Natty came first. That was why she had found a way round her own golden rule, so she could enjoy some adult company after work and maybe even start a relationship. Her intention to remain celibate for years just hadn't worked out.

It had started innocently enough – a drink after work with her single female friends, sometimes a girls' night out at the movies; but where there were single women, there were single men. A compliment – surprisingly welcome – had led to a little flirtatious patter, goaded on by her friends, and before she knew it, her friends had ditched her, and she was on a live date. Although that particular date hadn't worked out, dating had not just been a one-off occurrence. She'd got back into the dating game.

She had not broken the golden rule; there was no instant family about to happen. This was strictly a Natty-free zone. And

Natty accepted this arrangement. They were Mummy's grown-up friends – she had thought this explanation through carefully beforehand. Just as Natty wouldn't expect her mum to go and play with her and Annabelle at Annabelle's house, Natty had to accept being babysat when Mummy wanted to go to a friend's house to 'play'. And just as she had anticipated, this arrangement had worked surprisingly well for the handful of guys she had dated so far. The trouble was that as soon as she had any notion that things might be getting more serious than a casual fling, that was always the end of it.

She did make Natty's existence known from the start – how else could she explain her house being out of bounds? Of course, they all said they'd like to meet her daughter; it was only polite. When she refused point blank, only one had asked why. She imagined that a single young woman with a child was probably not what most single guys were expecting. She came with baggage.

But she wasn't looking for commitment.

She was having fun.

She was having sex.

And she wasn't hurting anybody.

No relationship had become serious enough to raise the issue of moving in together, which was just as well. She wouldn't let things get that far. Love was never part of the plan. But if she were to cross paths with her soulmate, then she would have a dilemma on her hands.

Now, Faye had detected a flaw in this seemingly simple babysitting arrangement, and it was standing right in front of her. She had let someone into her little family, and into her heart. Faye was falling in love before she had even realised what was happening.

Jake attempted to look down at what she was doing.

'Chin up,' said Faye pushing his chin up perhaps a little too hard.

Jake lowered his eyes instead to look at Faye's bent head. Her face was a mass of concentration as she flicked the ends of the tie this way and that. She wasn't wearing make-up, and her face was scrubbed clean, but her cheeks were slightly flushed in the hot confines of the lift. Her hair was still a little damp from her morning shower, and he thought he could smell lavender.

A mental image of Faye in the shower crept up on him, forcing him to avert his gaze – this was his colleague, his mentor, he was thinking about, and it was inappropriate. Still, he couldn't get the image out of his head of how she'd looked when he'd seen her on Saturday morning, fresh out of the shower.

The lift door opened on another floor.

'Good morning!'

They both recognised the headteacher's voice. Faye and Jake, standing in very close proximity to one another, Faye's hands on Jake's tie. They both turned to look at the head.

Faye and Jake both mumbled an awkward good morning, Faye instantly dropping the ends of Jake's tie and stepping back.

The head eyed them as he got in the lift. 'Good weekend?'

Jake and Faye immediately nodded their heads, 'Yeah, good thanks,' said Faye, hoping she sounded convincing. Jake echoed her sentiments. They both avoided eye contact with each other.

Faye noticed the head's eyes lingering on them both. She hoped he didn't think there was something going on between them. It didn't help that the lift door had happened to open just as she was helping Jake with his tie. She hoped the head didn't mention seeing them together in the lift on Monday morning to anybody else. It was all innocent enough, unless he read something into it, and the last thing she wanted was tongues wagging at their expense on a Monday morning at work.

The head got out at the next floor.

Faye sighed in relief and turned to Jake, surprising him when she reached for the tie.

Faye turned down the collar of his shirt. 'There.' She brushed the tie against Jake's chest as he looked down at her handiwork.

'Thanks.'

She studied the tie.

'Still not speaking?'

She thought a moment, then shook her head.

They both turned to face the front of the lift. Faye thought back to the first time Jake had babysat Natty.

❖

The sitter had unexpectedly cancelled. She wouldn't have asked any of her other colleagues – they had enough commitments after work with their own families, and didn't have time to look after someone else's child. The young, single teachers had better things to do at the weekend than look after Natty – apart from Jake. She'd overheard a snippet of a conversation between another student teacher they'd recruited and a newly qualified teacher – both single, attractive young woman talking about Jake.

It was unprofessional, talking about a colleague behind his back. As the deputy head, she really should have reprimanded them on the spot when she'd realised who they were talking about. But Faye's curiosity had got the better of her. It sounded as though they'd both tried some friendly banter with Jake when they'd discovered he was single. Faye wasn't surprised by this. Jake was a good-looking guy. However, it sounded as though he was steering clear of them, to the point of being rude.

How could he not be interested? one had said with a flick of her hair. She was clearly under the impression she was god's gift, Faye thought, which Faye decided was fair enough. They were both very attractive women. The other one had explained that Jake had lost his wife. They had both decided that they didn't want that sort of baggage. Besides, they'd concluded he clearly wasn't ready for another relationship, otherwise how could he have resisted either of them?

That was Faye's take on the situation too, so she had approached him to see if he wouldn't mind babysitting – just for one night while she went out on a date.

From the start of his employment, Jake had taken a genuine interest in Natty's welfare during Faye's conversations with him. So, despite some initial reservations – namely how Natty was going to get on with her new sitter – Faye had picked up the phone and dialled his home number. She'd rehearsed it. She was going on a dinner date, she'd be back by eleven-thirty at the latest, and it was an absolute one-off. Did she sound desperate? She hoped not. The meal had been planned for two weeks, and the sitter had let her down at the last moment. Thirty minutes later, Natty was ensconced on the sofa, cuddled up to Jake, listening to a story. She hardly gave a rather bemused Faye a second glance as she headed out of the door.

And that was how it had started. More dates had followed, but then she had started her headteacher training, and she'd no longer had time for pseudo-relationships.

Jake had become the back-up sitter, and then, before she knew it, the original sitter had become the back-up sitter, as she found herself reaching – at Natty's insistence – for Jake's number first.

And that was how, Faye had realised that morning, she had unwittingly let into Natty's life that which she sought to keep out; namely a man who would in all probability not be around in the foreseeable future. At some point, he would meet someone, whether he was ready to start a new relationship or not, and understandably he would have other priorities. Looking after someone else's child would go out of the window.

The question she was now asking herself was: should she wait for that to happen and let Natty's obvious attachment to Jake grow? Or should she end the arrangement straight away?

The lift jerked to a halt unexpectedly, throwing Faye into Jake's arms. She quickly extricated herself from his embrace. Not that she wanted to. And there was the crux of the problem. Natty wasn't the only one whose attachment to Jake had grown over the course of the last few weeks.

5

Jake had been waiting impatiently for the lift doors to open. He'd begun to sweat. Despite appreciating Faye sorting his tie, he'd had to loosen it. He hated confined spaces, and had done ever since the skiing accident the previous Christmas.

Jake did not want to think about that. He'd followed Faye into the lift that morning without thinking; he always took the stairs. The lift jerking to a stop on the floor below hadn't helped, although he had appreciated the unexpected upside – Faye being thrown into his arms. He could have held her in his embrace all day.

Free of the lift, Jake headed straight for his desk in the staff room, while Faye hung back, removing her coat and placing it on the rack behind the door. Jake sat down and glanced out of the window at the early summer morning.

Mondays were good.

Work was good.

He reached for the first exercise book, ready to start marking the ever-increasing pile. Faye sat down opposite him. He wondered why she hadn't gone straight to her office, although the Monday morning staff meeting was due to take place in the staff room, so he imagined that was why she'd followed him in.

For a long moment, he watched her looking out of the window and wondered what was on her mind. Something about her demeanour told him he'd better not ask. Besides, he knew she wouldn't tell him – they weren't speaking. At least, she wasn't speaking to him.

He sighed and turned his attention to the exercise book. He glanced at the clock on the wall. Time was limited; they were due to start lessons soon after the staff meeting, and he always endeavoured to return the previous day's work to his students marked. He had never spared a thought for how much paperwork was actually involved in teaching, with every lesson bringing a deluge of paperwork. He had honestly thought he had left his desk-bound, pen-pushing days behind him.

Jake reached for his pen. He looked up. It wasn't there. He drew the plastic pen-holder closer and peered into the little rounded compartments; the pencils, eraser, sharpener and ruler were all there in their appropriate places, but somebody had borrowed his silver Parker. Jake looked around the staff room. It hadn't been long, and the room had quickly filled up with teaching staff. They all had their heads down and were quietly catching up on their paperwork, preparing for another working week.

At the far end of the room, a young male teacher caught his attention. Jake watched him whisper something to his colleague, a woman who, like Jake, had started Initial Teacher Training. They both looked in Jake's direction. He caught their eyes flickering to Faye, and then they whispered something else, clearly about them.

Jake sighed. With Faye sorting out Jake's tie in the lift, one could easily mistake them for a couple who had come into work together. Everyone knew they weren't together – didn't they? Had the head said something? He couldn't imagine it, but then perhaps because of the many times he'd babysat over the last few weeks, it was giving them something to talk about, like the possibility that babysitting was just a euphemism for something else – an excuse to spend time together.

One of them, the young man, gave him a thumbs-up. The young woman saw the gesture and frowned.

Jake sighed heavily.

'What is it?' hissed Faye across the table.

Hoping Faye hadn't seen the little exchange, Jake tipped up his pen-holder for Faye to see. 'Somebody stole my pen!'

Faye whipped a biro from her pen-holder and held it up. 'Will this do?'

'That's not my Parker.'

Faye leaned forward and slammed the pen down on top of Jake's desk. She held it there. 'It's a pen. Do you want it?'

'Yes,' he said meekly.

She lifted her hand from the pen, sat back in her seat and resumed looking out of the window.

Jake stared at her for a long moment before reaching for the pen. It was quite a nice biro, as biros went, but he still wanted his Parker. Jake took another look around the staff room only to find more heads were now turned his way, more eyes were on them both. The two members of staff who had been talking about them exchanged a glance, raising their eyebrows. Jake imagined they were going to have a field day now it appeared that they were lovers who were having a little tiff.

Jake made one more sweep of the staff room, wondering which sneaky person had stolen his pen, before starting to mark the exercise book with the biro. No sooner had he put pen to paper than his mobile phone rang. Jake looked at his watch. He couldn't imagine who would be phoning him on a Monday morning – or any morning, for that matter. He'd stopped working with the Ross Corporation, and anybody trying to get in touch with him should know that by now. Either that, or it was the wrong number. In any case, he chose to ignore it. He got the phone out of his pocket and swiped the decline icon. Whatever it was, he was no longer their man. Besides, he needed to get his marking done before the school day began. He knew he should have taken the exercise books home with him at the weekend.

His phone rang again. This time there were murmurs of disapproval in the staff room. Jake wasn't the only one furiously catching up with work before the start of the school week.

Faye took a file from her in-tray, throwing him a *Well, aren't you going to answer that?* look.

Jake answered his phone. He didn't bother leaving the staff room because he knew he wouldn't be on the phone long.

'Yes – who is it?' he said curtly. He did not recognise the number. But he should have.

Jake listened and sighed heavily; he could well do without the call.

'No, I haven't seen him, Lydia.'

Faye looked up from her paperwork.

'Just calm down and tell me what happened.' Jake glanced at Faye, then leaned back in his chair and swivelled it to face the window. He closed his eyes and listened.

'I'll call you back as soon as I know anything, Lydia.' Jake turned his chair round to his desk.

Faye looked up from her paperwork as Jake put his phone in his pocket and stood up. 'I've got to go out.'

'What – now?'

'Yes.'

'But Jake, what about the staff meeting?'

Every Monday morning at eight-thirty was the time the staff all met the head for a briefing.

Jake closed the exercise book and tossed it back on the pile. He looked at his watch. He didn't have to be in work so early. Officially, the working day hadn't begun yet. 'I'll be back for the staff meeting, I promise.'

Jake plucked his jacket from the back of his chair.

'But where are you going?'

'I've got to find someone.'

'Who?'

'It's personal,' said Jake without thinking.

Faye returned her attention to her paperwork without comment.

Jake hovered for a moment, wishing he hadn't said that. He didn't have time for this. He headed for the door, fishing in his pockets for the key to his padlock. 'Damn!' Jake halted abruptly – there was no key. He checked both jacket pockets and his trouser pockets, then cast a glance over to his desk. *What did I do with it when I hurried after Faye?* he wondered.

He glanced over his shoulder at Faye; she was still at the desk, studying a file. Jake reluctantly retraced his steps. He leaned on the back of his chair, staring intently at his mentor.

Faye didn't look up. 'I thought you were off out?'

'Faye, I can't find the key to my padlock.'

She shrugged. 'Maybe you left the key in your padlock.'

'I never do that.'

They both turned to look out of the window, even though

they wouldn't be able to tell from where they were whether Jake had put the padlock on his bike and then left the key in it. It was very unlikely; it was an expensive bike, and Jake was fastidious with locking it up.

As that moment, they both saw someone in a hoodie riding Jake's very expensive bike out of the entrance gates.

'Is that your bike?' Faye asked evenly.

'Oh, you have got to be kidding me!' Jake exclaimed.

They weren't the only ones staring out of the window. Someone else commented, 'I think someone stole Jake's bike.'

'Well, that's what happens when you ride a bike like that in a neighbourhood like ours.'

Jake slapped his forehead. Of course, they were right.

She looked at him. 'Aren't you going to call the police?'

Jake didn't care about his bike – or rather, he did, but just then he had a far more urgent situation to deal with.

'Faye, can I borrow your car?'

'If you need a ride, call a taxi.'

'There isn't time.'

Faye put her pen down, and said in a hushed voice, 'What is it? What's going on?'

'All right, people,' a loud voice interrupted them. 'As you're all here, I thought we might as well start the meeting early, which will give you a bit more time for lesson preparation before the day begins.' The head clapped his hands. 'Let's gather round.'

Faye closed her file and got up as everyone else started to take a seat at the large oval table towards the front of the staff room.

Jake didn't make a move.

Faye shrugged her shoulders and headed for the table.

Jake glanced at the car keys on Faye's desk. He looked up to see the other teachers filing past him and Faye already seated at the table, staring his way. On a push bike, he could have cut through the traffic, but with his bike gone, as he'd told Faye, he didn't have time to wait for a taxi.

Jake looked back at the car keys.

'And that means you too, Jake.' The head was standing at the table, watching Jake.

'Damn,' said Jake under his breath. He quickly helped himself to a coffee from the machine in the corner, like everybody else, and then reluctantly took a seat.

'Right, people – are we finally all here?' Jake was aware that the comment was specifically directed at him.

'Okay, folks, let's look at the minutes of the last meeting.' He ruffled some papers and looked at his deputy, who was sitting next to him.

Faye passed him the minutes.

Jake hoped the meeting would be over quickly; then he might have time to nip out before the school day officially started at nine.

The head scanned down the minutes from the previous week and then tossed the sheet aside. 'We'll come back to that later,' he said. 'The first thing I would like to talk about is professional development days.'

There was a collective sigh.

'Yes, I know you don't want to hear it, but some of you are not exploring all the available opportunities for improving your skills and abilities in the classroom, and I realise most do not want to be away from the chalkface even for a day, but if it carries on, and you don't make use of them, you'll have saved up so much you could retire on it.'

It was a joke, but nobody laughed.

The head continued, 'I can't have two-thirds of the school disappearing at the same time if you all decide to pursue the same course, so by the end of the week, I want all required professional course days applied for. Do I make myself clear?'

'Crystal,' somebody said from the back.

The head gave him a second look, unsure whether he was being sarcastic.

Jake was relieved the professional days didn't apply to him as a trainee. Taking time off away from work was not Jake's favourite topic.

'And remember,' the head continued as he picked up the meeting minutes again, 'not more than one day at a time.'

'And not at the same time as others in your year group,' the staff all chanted in unison, having heard it a million times before.

The head looked up in surprise. 'Well, not that you'd actually go off with your colleagues.'

There was a snigger behind Faye.

Faye turned and looked at the young man who Jake was positive had been talking about him and Faye earlier. Jake looked at his shoes.

'But you all know your year groups and who you cover for, so when one's away …'

'The other stays,' somebody said wearily.

'That's right,' the head said to no one in particular. 'Now, let's get down to business.' He held up a piece of paper. 'Before we get into the minutes from last week, has anybody got anything new to raise since last Monday?'

Someone raised their hand and said, 'Jake's bike was stolen a few minutes ago.'

Jake had been staring out of the window. He fixed an annoyed gaze on the colleague who'd spoken. He did not want the meeting going on any longer than necessary, and certainly did not want the issue of his stolen bike raised.

The head looked at Jake. 'Is that right?'

'Yeah.'

'Have you phoned the police?'

Jake shook his head.

'Why ever not?' He held up an exasperated hand, indicated the door. 'Go.'

Jake said, 'Pardon me?'

'Go – make that call. Do what you have to do.'

Jake slowly got out of his seat. Was the head seriously letting him go early from the meeting?

'Right now!'

Jake sighed in relief as he closed the staff room door on the head, who was looking at the minutes and saying, 'Let's start with absenteeism …'

Jake swiped Faye's car keys from her desk as he passed by, ensuring nobody was looking. Then he made a show of getting out his phone as he left the room, just in case the head was eyeing him as he walked out. But he wasn't calling the police – he was calling Lydia to say he was on his way.

6

Jake was standing by the lift, tapping his foot impatiently, when Faye joined him.

He looked at her, surprised. 'I thought you were in the meeting?'

She folded her arms.

Jake sighed and held out her keys. 'I'd better phone for a taxi.'

She took the keys. 'Don't bother. I'm coming with you.'

'But I don't know when I'll be back!' Jake blurted without thinking.

Faye nodded. 'I guessed that. I just called our supply teacher. I've booked him in today, to cover for you, just in case.'

'I could hug you,' Jake said. Then he realised that he'd better not. He was still treading carefully after the weekend, although he was very pleased that Faye wasn't giving him the silent treatment anymore.

'What did you tell the head?' Jake asked anxiously.

'That if you end up down at the station, giving a statement, you might be some time. And that as I was a witness, I should go with you.'

'You said that?'

'Well, it's true – isn't it?'

Jake nodded.

'As I don't have any teaching commitments this morning, and I can catch up with paperwork when I get back, I decided I'd accompany you. As I said, I told the head we might be some time at the station.'

Jake looked at her sheepishly. It might be true, if he had phoned the police.

'So, you've phoned the police.'

'Not exactly.'

'What does that mean?'

'There's something I need to do first.'

'Is it something to do with that phone call earlier?'

The lift doors opened. Faye followed him inside.

'I have to find someone.' Jake kept his eye on the red digits above the door that were counting down to *G*.

'Can't it wait until after work?'

'No,' said Jake firmly.

The lift door opened, and they made their way to the car park.

'Look, if we take a detour to my house—'

'Is that where you'll find this person you're looking for?'

'No, but if you just drop me home, I can collect my car.' Jake pursed his lips, avoiding further conversation about the phone call as they got in her car and Faye drove out of the school gates.

'Who's Lydia?'

Jake turned to Faye in surprise. 'You were listening in on my conversation.'

'Well, I couldn't help overhearing somebody who was sitting directly opposite me,' she said testily. She turned her attention back to the road ahead.

'That doesn't mean you have to *listen*,' Jake emphasised the last word. He could hear the irritability in his voice and knew he was being unreasonable.

Faye glanced his way. 'It's family, isn't it?'

In the cold light of day, he was beginning to regret the previous night. Faye was obviously not happy about the amount of time he was spending with her daughter, and he was not happy that Faye, who had shared with him the details of some familial woes, may expect him to do the same.

He gave in – a little. 'Lydia is my brother-in-law Marcus's fiancée.'

'What happened to him?'

'I don't know.' Jake sighed heavily. 'They probably had another fight.' Jake rubbed his temples; he could feel the early stages of a tension headache coming on.

'Another fight?' Faye repeated. 'Doesn't sound like a match made in heaven.'

He stole a glance at Faye. By the look on her face, he guessed she was silently cursing herself for what she'd just said.

'You're right – it isn't.' He voiced his thoughts. 'The thing is, I can never figure out why. On paper they should be … what did you call it?'

Faye hesitated. 'A match made in heaven?'

'Yeah.'

'You're good friends with Lydia?'

'What makes you say that?'

'She rang you for help. I mean, she could have gone to …' Faye paused. 'Oh, any number of people. What about Marcus's parents, his father?'

'It's not that straightforward, Faye.'

'What do you mean?'

'She rang me because it's probably my fault.'

'What's your fault?' Faye said indignantly. 'They had a row. What's that got to do with—' Faye stopped abruptly.

Her wide eyes gave away exactly what she was thinking, and Jake found it genuinely amusing. Despite the circumstances, he laughed out loud. 'It's got nothing to do with Lydia and me, if that's what you're thinking. We are not having an affair or anything like that.'

Jake thought that if Faye met Lydia, she'd understand. Lydia, a six-foot, sultry stunner, privately educated on the East Coast of America and a Harvard law graduate, was a formidable corporate lawyer. On paper, she was a good match for Marcus, who was an Eton-educated Oxbridge graduate corporate executive and heir to a business empire.

Jake had nothing against educated, career-orientated women. But what he had against Lydia was her condescending attitude towards anybody who didn't reach her dizzying heights of perfection, and, in Jake's personal experience, towards some who had; if you didn't come from the *right stock* – meaning money – it didn't matter what you achieved; you were still nobody.

She was a snob through and through.

Her one redeeming quality, as far as Jake was concerned, was her relationship with Marcus. It was obvious to anybody that she loved the guy, and it was obvious to Jake that Marcus didn't deserve it – he treated her like a doormat. His habit of disappearing was causing her immense embarrassment, not to mention emotional pain – and was causing Jake a huge headache. He didn't know why Lydia didn't just end it.

They pulled up in front of Jake's house.

Faye switched the engine off and turned to Jake. 'So, why did she call *you*?'

It was the same reason she called last time and the time before that; Lydia might love Marcus, but her love of the high society circles she moved in came an extremely close second. She was ambitious. Jake had a feeling Lydia didn't want anything tarnishing the 'golden couple' image she was carefully cultivating. She didn't want tawdry pictures of her wrecked fiancé, collapsed in some putrid doorway, splashed over some sleazy tabloid blowing away those perfectly orchestrated pictures in *Hello!* magazine. She didn't want the police arresting Marcus with some prostitute hanging on his arm. Above all, she didn't want to know any details. That was where Jake came in.

How many times had it happened in the past month? Jake had lost count, and this worried him. And there was something else. On the phone, Lydia – who was normally Ms Ice – had lost her cool completely. She was actually pleading with him to patch it up with Marcus, as though it was all his fault. She'd said, *Can't you just talk to him? Just one kind word?* Jake had never seen this side of Lydia – the ice maiden thawed – which in any other context would have delighted him no end. But her small voice on the other end of the line, and her words, *He misses you*, had thrown Jake completely.

Had Lydia been trying to tell him this all along by ringing him up and asking him to find Marcus in the hope that Jake would see what he had caused and forgive him? Had she finally lost patience today and spelled it out: that Marcus's increasingly erratic behaviour was his fault? Had he hurt him that much? But then, thought Jake, the truth does hurt.

'What is it?' Jake felt Faye's hand on his arm.

'Have you ever said something …' Jake searched for the right words and decided to change tack. 'If someone can't handle the truth, do you tell them anyway or do you let them continue believing they are the one in the right?'

Jake wasn't sure if that made any sense.

Faye stared at Jake a long moment.

'This is me you're talking to, remember? You know exactly what I'm going to say.'

Jake nodded. 'The truth.'

7

Taking out the house keys, Jake turned them over in his hand and walked up the front path. He reached the front door and heard the clunk of a car door behind him. He turned briefly to see Faye standing beside the car. Guessing she was anxious to get back to school, he called out, 'You don't have to wait.' He had told her he'd report the stolen bike later. That wasn't his priority right now – finding Marcus was.

'It's fine. I'll hang around just to make sure you've got your car keys.' Faye pointed at the car that was sitting outside his house.

Jake entered the house. The car keys were in the kitchen drawer, next to the sink.

Jake found the keys, shut the drawer and looked up. 'That's odd,' he said, looking out of the kitchen window into the garden. The kitchen had patio doors that looked over the walled garden at the back of the house. It wasn't very large – just a small patio, a grassed area and some borders – but he did appreciate the outside space. Over the past month, once the weather had finally turned summery, he had taken to throwing the patio doors open and wandering outside to sit on the patio.

Despite the bright morning, the patio was floodlit by the

security light. Jake imagined that a cat must have set it off the night before, but it should have timed out after a sufficient interval. Jake walked out of the kitchen, making a mental note to fix the light.

He opened the front door. Faye must have been watching for him. Jake held up his car keys, dangling them in front of his face.

It started to rain.

Jake ducked back into the hall and reached for a coat; past experience told him he'd be out searching for Marcus for hours, probably finding him in some bar or pub, passed out.

Quickly throwing it over his shoulders, Jake stopped. Something had caught his attention; he could have sworn there was water on the dining room floor, visible through the open doorway.

'Now, that's typical. I'm away one night, just one bloody night, and I get a burst pipe.' Jake sighed and went to investigate.

Jake didn't have a leaking pipe.

There was no water.

A small pane of glass in the back door was broken, and shards of glass littered the floor. *Break-in*, Jake thought, but he tried the back door, and it hadn't been forced; it was still locked. He guessed his would-be intruders had given up and moved on to easier pickings.

Burglary – it was random, it was opportunistic, but he hadn't imagined that one day a crime statistic would come knocking on his own door.

Staring at the glass, lost in thought, Jake suddenly became aware of a dark mass obscuring the bottom half of his door; something or someone had been on the other side the whole time he had been standing there.

Jake raced down the hall and reached for a cricket bat that was propped inside the umbrella stand by the front door. He'd kept the bat for sentimental reasons, as a memento from his school days.

Grabbing the handle, he swung the bat above his head, feeling more confident that if this was an intruder, he had some protection. He slowly unlocked the back door.

'Is everything okay?'

Jake spun round. Faye was standing in the front doorway, looking down the hallway at him, concerned. Jake had forgotten he'd left his front door open.

'I thought you were going back to school?'

'I guessed you'd nipped back inside to grab a coat. I switched my car engine on to leave, then noticed you hadn't come out to your car. For someone who was in a hurry to find Marcus, I thought it odd.'

'I think somebody attempted a break-in,' said Jake.

'Oh, Jake. How unlucky can you be? First your bike, then your house.'

'I know,' Jake said through gritted teeth. As if he didn't have enough on his plate with finding Marcus.

'Is anything missing?'

'I don't know, but I think there's somebody still outside.' Jake pointed towards the dining room.

'Is there an access pathway around the back?'

'Yes, at the end of the row of terraces, just three doors down.'

Faye disappeared outside before Jake had a chance to tell her to stay put. He knew he should call the police, but how long would they take to get there? And he still had to find Marcus.

Jake slowly unlocked the back door. He turned the handle clockwise. It clicked open. Jake stepped backwards into the hall. Distracted by the crunching underfoot, he turned awkwardly away from the door. His foot slipped on the glass, and he lost his footing, toppling forward onto the hall floor as the back door swung open.

The cricket bat fell out of his hand, and he could only watch helplessly as it spun out of reach on the polished wood floor. He landed with both hands palm down on the glass. The next thing he heard was footsteps behind him as he was trying to get up. Then someone landed on him. Flat on his front with somebody pinning him down, Jake wished that the bat was in his hand; if he could get himself out of this predicament, he might need it. Jake tried to hoist himself up from the floor, but the broken glass under his hands made using them to push himself up impossible.

A man's arm reached round from behind him. He anticipated this, making a grab at his assailant but the pain in his hand was immense, and he couldn't get a grip. Jake elbowed the man hard. He heard a grunt, the arm disappeared, and the weight shifted. Jake took the opportunity to struggle to his feet, thinking quickly whether to stand and defend himself or make a grab for the bat. He decided to stand his ground and turned on his assailant, surprised to find him still hunched on the floor with his back to Jake.

'God, that hurt.' Clutching his stomach, the man coughed and sat up. 'I slipped over on the glass, and fell on you. I was only trying to help you up. What did you have to go and do that for, Jake?'

'Marcus? What the hell—?'

'What the hell am I doing here?' Marcus struggled to his feet. 'I needed a place to stay.'

Jake stared at his bloodied hands.

'That looks nasty,' Marcus said.

Jake's hands were dripping blood over his polished wooden floor. 'You're not welcome here.'

'I know that, but last night I was so out of it I couldn't check into a hotel, and I didn't want to sleep on a park bench, so I thought …'

'You thought you'd come here and break into my house! For god's sake, Marcus, what were you thinking? You've got a home to go to, haven't you?'

It was becoming routine, the call from Lydia, the trawl around the sleazy parts of London, the hotel room for Marcus to sleep it off. And it was becoming intolerable; this was the last straw. Jake held up both hands in exasperation. 'Look at what you did!' He turned his hands palm up to Marcus so he could see.

'Where were you last night?' said Marcus, ignoring Jake's bloody hands.

'Last night?' Jake realised that the previous night had been the first time he hadn't been there for Marcus. Nobody had known where Jake was. Jake imagined there were several messages on his answer phone – all from Lydia. A nasty thought occurred to him; was all this for his benefit? Surely not! What had Lydia said on the phone about Marcus missing him? These were the only occasions they saw each other. Was Marcus doing this on purpose?

'Turn around very slowly!'

Marcus was standing in the doorway, his back to the garden, obscuring Jake's view. 'Who is that?' Marcus turned to see who had shouted out.

Jake looked past Marcus at Faye.

If it wasn't for the circumstances, the sight of Faye marching up the garden towards the house carrying a large five-pronged garden fork in front of her would have been quite funny. The trouble was that he suddenly realised this wasn't just at empty threat – Faye was prepared to use it.

He quickly understood the gravity of the situation. Faye had approached the back of the house. She'd seen two men in the house; Jake facing her direction, his bloody hands held up high to a man standing directly in front of him, his back to Faye. She could have drawn only one conclusion.

'Whatever you've got in your hand, put the weapon down!' Her voice thundered authoritatively.

Jake put his hands down immediately. 'It's alright, Faye,' he shouted out.

Marcus turned back to look at Jake, a bemused expression on his face.

Jake could see Faye moving down the garden, still holding the garden fork out in front of her.

Marcus didn't move. He just stood in front of Jake, gaping at the woman moving towards him.

Faye started to run towards Marcus.

'Faye – stop!' Jake shouted out as he launched himself at Marcus, pulling him away from the door and plummeting to the floor with him as Faye charged toward them.

'What in hell?' said Marcus.

'Sorry.' They'd fallen quite hard. 'Are you hurt?'

'I … no … I'm okay.'

Jake looked up to see Faye approaching the door, garden fork at the ready. He scrambled around Marcus to position himself between Marcus and the door. 'Stay down.' Jake kept one hand on Marcus's chest and the other held up towards the back door, where he expected Faye to enter.

She didn't.

'Faye?'

Marcus said, 'You know this lunatic?'

'Shut up,' said Jake. 'Faye?' he said to the doorway.

Faye cautiously moved into view, the fork at the ready.

'You can put the fork down now, Faye,' he said calmly.

Faye looked from the dark-haired, dark-eyed man to Jake.

'I've got it covered, literally,' Jake reassured her.

Faye lowered her weapon.

Jake lowered his bloody hand and gestured behind him, 'Faye, meet Marcus.'

For a brief moment, Faye looked bewildered. 'Bloody hell, Jake, why didn't you tell me?'

Jake sighed. 'I did yell out.'

Marcus got quickly to his feet, keeping a wary eye on Faye.

Faye propped the fork by the door and stepped inside. Broken glass splintered beneath her feet.

Jake was having difficulty getting up from the floor without using his hands. Marcus caught his arm at the elbow and helped him up. Once on his feet, Jake roughly pulled his arm from Marcus's grasp.

'Hey!' Marcus took a step back in surprise. 'I was only trying to help.'

'I think you've helped enough for one day, don't you?' Jake said. Holding his hands out in front of him, he headed for the kitchen.

Marcus frowned. 'What's that supposed to mean?' He took off after Jake.

Faye shut the back door, trying to avoid treading on more broken glass. 'Shall I clear this mess up?'

'No, thanks,' Jake called back to her. 'I'm used to picking up the pieces,' he added sarcastically, throwing Marcus a black look over his shoulder.

Jake reached the kitchen; the door was shut. He stood helplessly in front of it.

Marcus caught up. 'So, you need my help now,' he said, sounding smug.

'Don't be petty. Just open the damn door; I'm bleeding all over my hallway.'

Marcus drew in a sharp breath in mock horror. 'Heaven forbid you should get a stain on that rug – never mind if you bleed to death.'

'I'd rather bleed to death in the kitchen, if it's all the same to you.' Jake was rather fond of the rug.

'Linoleum; easy to clean,' Marcus shook his head. 'There's nothing like getting your priorities straight.'

'Oh, that's a good one coming from you. Lydia was frantic. She phoned me in a panic this morning.'

❖

Faye wandered up the hallway, listening to Jake and Marcus bicker. She stopped at the rug and looked at the cricket bat. She knelt down to pick it up and placed the bat in the umbrella stand, where she guessed Jake kept it. Then she noticed a blood stain on the rug.

Jake and Marcus continued to bicker outside the kitchen door. Faye decided now was probably not a good time to mention the soiled rug.

Faye walked up behind Jake and Marcus and stood there, shaking her head. She found it slightly amusing; neither would back down. This was a side of Jake she had never seen before. They were both behaving like kids in a playground.

After a short time, Faye decided she had heard enough. She said loudly, 'If you two children would excuse me …' She barged between them to open the kitchen door.

'What did she just call us?' Marcus said to Jake as they followed her into the kitchen.

'Losers,' said Jake knowing exactly what Faye had been thinking; they were behaving like idiots. What was it about Marcus that brought out the worst in him? It hadn't always been this way. Now, when he was around Marcus, Jake could feel his capacity for rational adult judgement giving way to a child's raw emotion. That was why he needed to stay away from him; there were times he wondered just what he might be capable of doing. There was a very real possibility that one day he would just lose it and lash out. He sighed. He felt like he should have let Faye poke Marcus in the ribs with the garden fork.

Jake sat at the kitchen table and watched Marcus take a seat opposite. He wanted Marcus to get the hell out of his house.

Every call from Lydia signalled the start of a waking nightmare. The same picture went through his mind when he got the call: Marcus, still dressed for work, expensive suit, long wool coat, Gucci watch, and completely out if it – a walking beacon in the wrong neighbourhood, a death waiting to happen. Could he bear the thought of finding Marcus beaten, mugged, and dead in the gutter? No. And yet still he went looking, every time.

Jake thought about how many times William had asked him why he and Marcus weren't friends anymore. William didn't understand why they couldn't just patch up their differences. William was under the impression that it was all because Jake had left the company. Jake wasn't about to tell anybody what had really caused this deep, bitter rift between them – least of all William. If William knew what had really happened, there was a strong possibility that Marcus would not only have lost his sister and his best friend, but his father as well. Jake couldn't be that cruel.

He had to face the fact that he still loved the guy. He'd known Marcus most of his life; that friendship hadn't just vanished overnight. But on top of losing Eleanor, he was seriously beginning to doubt whether he could take much more. If Marcus couldn't clean up his act, Jake knew that for his own sanity, he needed to cut Marcus out of his life.

There was a solution; Marcus could return to America. Without Jake to torment, maybe these episodes would stop. Perhaps Marcus and Lydia could get back to some sort of normality. Lydia would be up for it – returning home to America. Marcus could do with just taking himself off to an island, relaxing on a beautiful beach and getting himself together. Marcus's father owned the whole company. Financially speaking, Marcus really didn't have to lift a finger. His father wasn't one of those types who'd cut off his children if they didn't work. Marcus could have just sat on some exotic beach, waiting for it all to pass to him some day.

Jake stole a glance at Marcus as they both took a seat at the kitchen table, and knew it wasn't that simple. Life never was. Marcus wouldn't return of his own volition. He'd been promoted to COO, Chief Operating Officer, the role just below the CEO of the company. He now oversaw the daily operations of the company, reporting to his father, William Ross, the CEO. To everybody's surprise, William had effectively stepped down. He was still the CEO, but these days he was more likely to be found whiling away his time on a golf course than in a board meeting.

Marcus was now the head of the Ross Corporation in all but name. To do that job, Marcus was based primarily in London. Of course, he hadn't had to take on that role. In fact, Jake really had no clue how anyone could hold down such a position while carrying on the way he was after work.

A move to America would amount to Marcus giving up his position, and that would mean a serious demotion. Jake looked at the state of him and thought that perhaps such a move would not be a bad thing.

But Marcus lived for work. He had never taken a day off school or work in his life. Jake could forget any idea that these binge-filled drinking sessions would lead him to screw up at work; it was a nice thought, but it was unlikely to happen. And if it did, and he was sent to America with Lydia, this posed a more serious scenario – although Marcus might be safer in America, away from the pressures of work, away from Jake, would he be safer from the risk he posed to himself? Jake stared across the kitchen table at Marcus. He didn't believe that he would.

8

There was an alternative to finding a way to get Marcus to move to America. Jake thought of moving away himself, somewhere Marcus couldn't find him. Although he knew there would be a permanent position waiting for him at his current school when he had completed his Initial Teacher Training and qualified, he also knew that he could apply to another local authority for a teaching post. He could start over. After all, he was free and single, with no responsibilities; nothing to keep him there. So why wasn't he seriously considering it?

Jake's attention wandered over to Faye. He watched her as she opened several kitchen cupboards before turning his way and throwing her hands up in exasperation. 'Where do you keep the first aid kit?'

'It's in the cupboard under the sink unit.' Jake cocked his head in that direction.

Faye found the box and sat down beside Jake. She spread the contents of the little white box on the table. Antiseptic cream, gauze and bandages.

Jake moved his right hand towards her.

Marcus peered across the table at Jake's wound.

Faye gagged.

'What is it?' Jake searched her face.

Faye got up from the table. 'I'm sorry, I …' she crossed the room and stood by the patio doors, her back to him, and took deep breaths. 'I just can't stand the sight of blood.'

Marcus started to laugh. 'And you call yourself a friend?' He turned in his chair to look at her. 'Actually, who are you?' Marcus looked at Jake and then back at Faye. 'Wait – are you together?'

Jake knew what he meant by *together*. The look of shock on Marcus's face at the possibility that he had moved on from Eleanor already was obvious.

Jake quickly said, 'We're just friends, okay?'

Faye added, 'We're also work colleagues.'

'Colleagues? Then what are you doing here? Aren't you both meant to be at school, or something?'

Before Jake had a chance to answer, Marcus asked, 'Where were you last night, Jake?'

Jake's eyes flickered to Faye. This was awkward. 'I was out babysitting for a friend.'

'And you stayed over?'

'They were caught out in traffic and didn't get home until late. I slept on their couch, if you must know.' Jake avoided Faye's gaze.

Marcus got up from the table and took the chair beside Jake that Faye had just vacated, and looked at Jake's hands.

Faye turned around. 'Jake, shouldn't you go to the hospital to have that treated.'

Marcus looked at Jake.

Jake knew that taking a trip to casualty meant that Faye would have to inform the head where he was, and that might mean dragging his personal life – meaning Marcus – into it.

Jake looked at Marcus and rolled his eyes at that thought. He'd already put his career on the line by going in search of Marcus. He was meant to be at work.

Jake glanced at Faye. They were meant to be visiting the police station to report his stolen bike. He didn't want to get Faye into trouble with the head. He didn't want to get into trouble himself and put his teaching qualification on the line. As it was, Jake knew he was taking liberties, making an excuse to leave work ostensibly to visit the police station to report a stolen bike when both he and Faye knew it wasn't necessary. He could report it over the phone. It was only a bike – albeit a stupidly expensive one.

Jake thought it served him right. He'd been so preoccupied with thinking about Faye that he'd forgotten to lock it. It was just bad luck that an opportunist had noticed it. Faye must have seen the look on his face when he'd answered the phone to Lydia. She'd gone with him out of concern. Jake knew that now.

He nodded at Marcus to get on with it.

Marcus got out the antiseptic, some gauze and some bandages, and proceeded to dab the cuts, cleaning the wounds. 'The bleeding is stopping, so that's good,' Marcus commented. Jake winced. Faye turned back to the patio door and focused on the view out into the garden.

Jake turned his attention on Faye.

She hadn't asked why Marcus had attempted to break into his home yet – but he could tell by her expression that she was waiting for an explanation. Faye turned around as Marcus was bandaging Jake's hands.

Jake asked, 'Are you okay, Faye?'

Faye nodded. 'I feel so silly that I can't stand the sight of blood.'

'Not at all. I knew someone just like you.'

Marcus looked up.

'What?'

'You said you knew someone. What you should have said was …'

'Oh, just get on with bandaging my hands, will you?' Jake said testily. He did not want to get into another argument with Marcus. He wished he hadn't brought up Eleanor.

'Are you done yet?' It hadn't taken long, and he wanted Marcus to leave.

Marcus finished wrapping the last piece of bandage around Jake's wrist and taped it. Jake grudgingly acknowledged that Marcus hadn't done a bad job. He held up his bandaged hands at Faye. 'You can come over now. Look, no blood!' He couldn't resist a little joke at her expense.

Marcus said seriously, 'She's right, you know. You really should go to the hospital and have your hands looked at by a professional.'

'Why? Don't you think I trust you to do the right thing, Marcus?'

Faye looked at Jake; the comment seemed strangely out of context.

Marcus stood up abruptly, knocking the chair over. 'I see you're back to your old self.'

'Why wouldn't I be? Has something changed since last we met?'

Marcus stormed out of the kitchen and slammed the door.

Jake returned his attention to his newly bandaged hands. He glanced at Faye, and caught her expression. 'What?'

'You didn't thank him.'

'And what precisely should I be thanking him for?' Jake's

patronising tone continued, 'Breaking into my house? Cutting my hands to shreds? What would you suggest?'

'I suggest,' Faye interjected, 'you start by thanking me for not informing the head.' She folded her arms. 'Yet.'

She walked to the kitchen door and opened it.

'Where are you going?' Jake asked, suddenly worried.

❖

Faye walked out, slammed the door behind her and stood on the other side, breathing hard. His sarcastic tone of voice had riled her, but she wasn't really angry with Jake. After all, he was right; all this wasn't his fault. She was angry with herself for not listening to her instincts. She knew she should have left right away and taken Jake to hospital to have his injury looked at. After all, he was still her student and her responsibility during official school hours. So why hadn't she? She thought Jake might be surprised to learn that she wasn't thinking of herself, and of getting into trouble with the head for taking him home in the first place, aware that he had not left work to sort out his stolen bike but his personal problems. She knew instinctively that Jake would not want the head to know that.

'He's got blood on his beloved rug, you know.'

Faye looked up to see Marcus sitting on one of the chairs in the hallway. There were two small wooden chairs set against the wall either side of a compact telephone table. . He was leaning forward, elbows on his knees, examining the rug.

She frowned at him. 'I know.'

He looked up at Faye. 'He's going to be angry.'

She shrugged. A bit of blood on a rug was the least of her concerns right now, and she imagined Jake's too. Marcus sat back in the chair. He motioned to the phone on the side table next to him. 'I'm waiting for a cab.'

Faye noticed a small overnight bag at Marcus's feet.

Marcus followed her gaze. He kicked at the bag. 'Are you looking at that?'

Faye wasn't really all that interested in hearing about Marcus's spats with his fiancée. 'It's none of my business.'

'Oh, I think it is. I'm sure you've got better things to do with your time than spend it searching for me.'

'How did you know Jake was looking for you?'

He sighed and rolled his eyes. 'Lydia, of course.' Her name rolled off his tongue like the word disgusted him. 'She knows I have an … um … what does she call it? A substance problem.'

'Alcohol,' Faye said bluntly. *The first way to kick it is to admit it*, she thought. That was what various counsellors had chanted, anyway. Her father had had a stressful job in the police, and his alcohol problem had got out of hand. He'd been stone-cold sober since he'd retired. But that was the reason she never had a drop in the house – that and the fact that she'd had her own issues in the past, which she didn't want to think about. Now she never kept a drop of alcohol in her flat; not even wine.

Marcus didn't respond. He avoided eye contact.

Faye looked at him.in surprise. She gleaned that it wasn't alcohol, but something more serious. It was no wonder he was keeping quiet.

Faye stood there and studied Marcus intently. She wasn't surprised he wouldn't talk about it. He'd be taking a risk admitting he might be in possession of an illegal substance, never mind what it was. She could easily have called the police and had him arrested, especially as he had tried to break into Jake's house.

There was the sound of a cupboard door closing in the

kitchen. Faye glanced in that direction. 'Does Jake know about your … substance issue?'

Marcus studied his hands.

Faye guessed not.

'Issue – I prefer that word to Lydia's. I'm not the one with the problem.'

Faye rolled her eyes. *Spoken like a true addict*, she thought, guessing he was putting all his issues at Lydia's door, and perhaps at Jake's too.

'So, I expect you know I had a row with my fiancée,' said Marcus, changing the subject. 'I keep an overnight bag at work to take to a hotel, just in case we have what Lydia calls *one of our little crises*.'

If he had just been staying at a hotel, Faye wondered, then what was all the fuss about? Why the urgency to find him? She got the impression that Marcus was not telling her the whole story. And why should he? It really was none of her business. Still, it did intrigue her.

There was a crash in the kitchen. Marcus and Faye turned towards the door. It sounded like a china mug hitting the floor. 'Damn and blast it!' Jake's voice thundered.

'Jake's trying to make himself a drink,' Faye stated.

'Not having much luck, is he?' Marcus added.

They could hear the kettle boiling in the kitchen. Faye wanted to pop her head in the kitchen and ask him if he was okay, but she didn't want another sarcastic retort. She thought it best to give him some space just for the moment. This must have come as a shock, finding Marcus there, and then getting hurt into the bargain. However, she didn't much care for waiting around in the hall with the person who had caused all this.

Faye's gaze shifted to the glass on the dining room floor. She turned back to Marcus, glaring at him. 'Why did you come here last night?

'Someone stole my wallet. I needed a place to crash for the night. I didn't expect Jake would be out.'

Faye pursed her lips. She hoped Marcus didn't ask which friend Jake had been babysitting for. She said, 'Did you report it to the police?'

'What – in the state I was in last night? I'd more likely have been arrested.' He cocked his head to one side. 'Besides, there's not a lot I could tell them. It could have happened in Timbuktu for all I was aware.'

'Ah.'

'It's not all that surprising. I got what I deserved. I don't exactly frequent the most salubrious places in town when I'm in search of some stuff.' Marcus immediately shut is mouth, staring at her, wide-eyed.

Faye realised he'd forgotten himself and hadn't intended to say that. A silence ensued as Faye imagined this smartly dressed corporate exec wandering around some sink estate in search of *some stuff*. Of course she was making assumptions – she had no clue where in London he went in search of drugs, or what sort of people dealt them. But she could imagine it wasn't Chiswick on a Saturday evening.

She had an idea that Jake knew more than Marcus gave him credit for. Part of his teaching training would include ways of detecting substance abuse among his students. He knew the signs. It explained Jake's behaviour that morning after Lydia's call.

Faye breathed a heavy sigh. Marcus was going to get himself into some serious trouble. Losing a wallet was one thing, but this guy could find himself losing something a whole lot more precious in pursuit of his next fix – his life.

9

Faye listened to the sounds coming from the kitchen. *What now?* she thought. Should she return to work alone, and make some excuse for Jake? He shouldn't really teach so soon after an accident. He needed to rest. And if the head saw him, she'd have to come up with some explanation.

She heard the kettle boil again, and this time the unmistakable sound of Jake stirring a teaspoon in a mug. He must have successfully got a mug out of the cupboard without dropping it this time. She imagined that he was now sitting at the kitchen table, drinking coffee. How did she know this with certainty?

She thought back to their first day together – another student teacher to take through their paces. They always had that same bewildered expression on their faces during their first day in the real world of teaching. The noisy corridors, playgrounds and classrooms. The endless paperwork and demands on their time. She could see the reality of their new jobs hitting them like a brick. At least Jake was more mature than the fresh-faced university graduates who were completing their postgraduate training on the job. Although he had been thrust straight in the deep end on Initial Teacher Training, rather than spending three years at university getting a degree, at least training primarily on the job meant he'd be under no illusions about what he was getting himself into when he qualified.

Jake might not have been so fresh-faced, but she had treated him just the same as the others. The day always started with a hot drink and a chance to sit and acclimatise in the staff room before facing the reality of the classroom. Jake always chose a cup of coffee.

'I only had a tenner and some loose change in my pocket,' said Marcus. 'It was just enough to get a cab here last night. Jesus, what was I thinking?' He stared up at the ceiling.

Faye looked at Marcus. 'So you smashed the pane to try and get inside his house?' Faye promptly switching back to the topic in hand, which was Jake's broken back door.

'Can the police arrest someone for breaking, not entering?'

Yes, it's called criminal damage. She didn't think it was a joking matter.

'Ignore me. That was a stupid question. I don't remember what I did, to be honest. It's a blank. I must have attempted to get in.' He looked down at his hands. 'I'm surprised that I didn't cut myself trying. Mind you, I'm sure some people would have been quite happy to see me bleed to death on their back doorstep.' Marcus's gaze settled on the kitchen door.

Faye ignored the strange comment. 'You slept on his doorstep?' Faye didn't know why she was acting so surprised. It was obvious that was what he'd done.

'Didn't have much choice, did I? He didn't come home at all last night.' He lowered his voice. 'I thought he was with a woman. God knows, he hasn't been getting any—' Marcus halted. 'Sorry. I have a tendency to run off at the mouth.'

Faye knew Jake wasn't in a relationship, but it sounded as though he'd had some dates since he lost his wife. Faye only knew this because she'd overheard him a couple of times when he'd answered his mobile, confirming restaurant reservations for two.

Marcus continued, 'The next thing I know, I'm woken up by the back door suddenly opening, and then a mad woman running towards me, waving a garden fork at me. Just your typical Monday morning.' Marcus grinned at Faye. 'Do you accept my apology?'

'Is that what you've been doing – apologising? I don't think I heard one.'

'Touché!' exclaimed Marcus obviously enjoying the banter.

Touché? Faye looked at him, bemused. Did people really still use that word? She imagined they did in the sort of circles that Marcus moved in – his wealthy friends and family. Her thoughts deviated to Jake, alone in the kitchen. 'You know what? I don't think it's *me* you should be apologising to.'

'No way!' Marcus stood up. He eyed her warily.

'Maybe if you talked to him …' Faye gestured to the kitchen, her voice sounding reasonable.

Marcus returned to his seat. 'Talking about it is no good, Faye; it won't change things.'

She wanted to ask, *change what?* But it was none of her business. Instead she said, 'It might.'

'You have no idea what I'm talking about – do you?'

Faye shook her head. Whatever was going on between them, Marcus was probably pleased to hear that Jake hadn't spoken about it.

Marcus asked, 'So, if you don't talk about your personal lives, what do you talk about all day?'

Faye shook her head at that question. Marcus made it sound

as though they spent all day in the staffroom drinking coffee. In reality, they had little time for idle chit-chat about their personal lives in between team meetings, classroom teaching and preparation and planning of lessons – not to mention all the paperwork. What little down time they did have was often spent talking about Natty, a subject they were both interested in and comfortable with.

'I have a daughter.'

'I know. Natasha, isn't it?'

Faye was surprised. 'How did you …?'

'Jake of course. He talks about her. You know when he was with Eleanor, he wanted kids.' He paused. 'You did know he was married – to my sister?'

'Yes.'

Marcus studied her. 'He doesn't talk to you, does he?'

'Not really.' She thought about the previous night, and Jake opening up just a little; it was rare. He'd done so before, just a little too, mentioning his wife, and touching on his reasons for changing his life, his career, so drastically.

'He should. He needs to talk to someone.'

It sounded to Faye like Marcus was ready to make that apology. She got up.

'Where are you going?'

'To tell Jake you're ready to talk.'

'No – don't!' Marcus sprang out of his seat and grabbed her arm.

Faye turned slowly towards Marcus. 'Let go.' She might only be a slender five foot two, but as her martial arts instructor had drummed into them at the karate lessons she had enrolled in when she was in her early twenties, you should never underestimate your opponent. It was the golden rule.

Marcus did the right thing. He let go.

Faye didn't have time for those lessons anymore. They had been a bit of a phase. At the time, she'd been dating a guy who was into martial arts. He had persuaded her to go along to some classes. She had enjoyed it.

Natty had enrolled too, intrigued when she'd found a photo of her mum at a dojo, taking lessons. Those lessons had been as short lived as that relationship, but she had walked away with a few self-defence moves, which had actually come in handy in the place she'd least expected – not out on the streets, being accosted by a stranger, but in the classroom with teenagers.

Faye didn't want to think about the poor behaviour of some of the students, and what some of her teachers had to put up with on a daily basis. So far, Jake had been lucky with his classes. She was aware that some never made it through Initial Teacher Training, put off by the stresses of the job. She hoped Jake wasn't one of them. She did not want to lose a talented teacher.

Faye looked at Marcus. She decided that whatever was going on between him and Jake, it was best to leave well alone and not get involved. Besides, she had no way of knowing whether she would be helping Jake or making matters worse. If Jake had wanted her to know about Marcus, he would have enlightened her.

Faye backed off. She reluctantly sat back down in the other seat at the small wooden table deciding she'd give Jake a few more minutes to finish his drink and gather his thoughts. Then she was leaving – with or without him.

Satisfied that she wasn't going anywhere, Marcus re-took his seat and looked at his watch. 'Where is that damn taxi?' He continued to study his watch, avoiding Faye's gaze, although he did ask, 'Haven't you got somewhere to be?'

She stared at him for a long moment before speaking. 'We were meant to be stopping off at the police station.' Although that wasn't the primary reason for her offering to drive Jake, she still thought they might as well report the stolen bike in person. It wouldn't hurt.

'The police station?'

'His bike was stolen from right under our noses in the school car park this morning.'

'Seriously?'

'Yes – seriously,' Faye said in a deadpan voice. 'I don't think some of the other teachers are particularly sympathetic, to be honest.'

Marcus didn't have to ask why. 'Well, I guess that's one less souped-up incarnation of his previous gilded life that those teachers don't have to be reminded of every time he goes into work.'

'But he's still got that car.' Faye had seen the rather nice car parked outside his house. She thought that it was little wonder he didn't drive it to school. If the bike worth several thousand pounds was out of place, the flashy car would certainly raise some envious hackles at work.

Marcus leaned forward in his seat and lowered his voice to barely above a whisper. 'I think it's a wake-up call, if you ask me. He doesn't belong there, you know, working in that school, with those kids.'

'What are you saying?' Faye hoped Marcus wasn't implying that Jake's new career was beneath him.

'I'm just preparing you. All this … it's just killing time. He'll wake up and come to his senses.'

'What does that mean?' Was he suggesting that this was some sort of breakdown, and when Jake got over the loss of his wife, he'd leave his teaching position and return to the Ross Corporation?

'Just don't get attached, that's all I'm saying.'

'Attached?'

Marcus made a show of rolling his eyes. 'I see the way you look at him.'

'I don't know what you mean. We're just colleagues.'

Marcus put his elbow on the table and his chin in the palm of his hand. His dark eyes studied her. 'If you say so.'

Faye changed the subject. 'Jake could get into big trouble with his job if they found out the real reason he'd left work this morning.'

Marcus looked nonplussed. 'I see.' He studied his fingernails and glanced at the door, still waiting for his taxi..

'Ah, but I don't think you do.' Faye shook her head. 'You see, Jake had a more important issue to deal with this morning.' Faye stared at Marcus. She should have been angry with him, but she just felt strangely relieved that all Jake had found that morning was a broken pane of glass, and not something much worse.

'I don't understand,' Marcus finally spoke into the silence.

Neither did she; on the one hand, Jake acted like he couldn't stand the sight of Marcus, but that morning he had put his career on the line for him.

Marcus sat back in his chair. 'Me?' he slapped a hand on his chest. 'You're saying he just walked out of work for me?' His surprise was evident.

Faye nodded. She wasn't sure he fully understood the gravity of the situation. Jake could lose his chance to gain his qualification. Something he was putting his heart and soul into. They could both lose their positions. 'After he got the phone call from Lydia, that's all he had on his mind – finding you.'

Marcus got up from his chair and paced. 'But I don't understand. I never stay at his house. How did he know to come here first?'

'He didn't.'

'Huh?'

'He didn't come here looking for you. He wanted to get his car first, so he could go and look for you.'

Marcus stopped pacing. 'That was a stroke of luck, then.' He was standing at the small window next to the front door. He lifted the thick net curtain to one side and peered out. Faye presumed he was looking for the taxi.

Marcus dropped the net curtain and turned to face Faye. 'Did he tell you where he was last night?'

Faye glared at him. Why was he so fixated on where Jake was last night? 'He was just babysitting. He told you.'

Faye looked at the kitchen door; this conversation was beginning to get awkward. She didn't relish the thought of telling Marcus about the previous night. But she had nothing to hide. 'Jake was with me last night.' That didn't come out right. Faye hastily rephrased, 'What I meant to say was …'

Marcus interrupted, 'That it's not what I think?' He threw her a sly grin. 'I knew there was something going on between you two.'

Faye rolled her eyes. 'He slept on the couch.'

'Shame.' Marcus sighed.

'Pardon?'

Marcus walked back to his seat and sat down. He clicked his tongue and shook his head at Faye. 'Who would have thought, eh?'

'What? Who would have thought – what?'

Marcus didn't have to answer that for Faye to know what he was getting at.

She didn't want to talk about Jake's love life behind his back, especially when he was just in the next room, but she did want to put the record straight. 'The fact is, he was seeing someone. There have been others too.'

Since she had known him, Jake had appeared to have no shortage of female admirers. She was in no way prying, but when he'd babysat, on occasion he'd left his mobile phone around, and when she'd come home she'd seen names flash up on his phone, and overheard him from time to time quietly speaking into his mobile.

Who was it last time? She tried to recall her name, 'Melissa, Melanie …?'

'Michaela.'

That was it! 'Lucky guess,' she said to Marcus.

'Not really.' Marcus lowered his eyes. 'There are a lot of girls in the offices of Ross Corporation who used to work with Jake, and they often ask after him – you know how it is.'

Faye narrowed her eyes. 'Actually, I don't. Why don't you enlighten me?'

'He's tried to cut himself off from as much of his old life as possible, but I know where he works, where he lives.' Marcus shrugged. 'It's not like I dish out his phone number. I can't do that because he won't let me have it,' he said simply. 'But I can arrange chance meetings.' He looked pleased with himself. 'I suggest to them when and where they might accidentally bump into him, like the local grocery store around the corner from his house – and the rest is up to them.'

There was something about this scenario that didn't quite add up – like why, for instance, Marcus should be so concerned about Jake 'getting any', as he had so crudely put it. Why would he try to set him up on dates?

'And believe me,' said Marcus, 'there's no shortage of takers. He's tall, good-looking and rich.'

'Rich? On a teacher's salary?' Faye scoffed. 'Now that I'd like to see.'

'Why, you see it every day, Faye.'

This was news to her.

'My father still takes care of Jake, financially speaking; he insists that Jake's salary, including bonuses, are still paid into his bank account – much to Jake's annoyance, I'm sure. Although, for the life of me,' Marcus glanced around the sparse hall of the rented house, 'I can't see what he spends it on, can you?'

Faye thought that it did at least explain why he had an expensive bike, and a rather flashy car, and could afford to insure them.

Marcus focused his attention on Faye. 'You see, my father still expects Jake to come to his senses, to come back to the fold, so to speak. After all, we're the only family he's got.'

'So why do you do it – set him up with those women?' Faye was curious.

'I'm just a good Samaritan.'

Faye had an idea it wasn't that simple. She had an idea that Marcus thought one of these women might just encourage Jake to quit his teacher training and return to the Ross Corporation, come back to the fold, as Marcus put it.

He sighed. 'I didn't think he'd meet anybody in his teaching job.' Marcus stared at Faye. 'Guess I was wrong.'

Faye felt her face grow hot, even though she had nothing to

feel embarrassed about. 'You've taken last night completely the wrong way, you know.'

'Have I?' Marcus leaned towards her. 'He may have slept on your couch, but know this – Jake hasn't spent an entire night with any of those women he was supposedly dating.'

Faye looked towards the kitchen. 'But what about Michaela?' she whispered.

'I reckon she figured it out, just like the others.'

'Figured what out?' Faye said bemused.

'That they weren't in a relationship.'

'What do you mean?'

'He never invites them back to his place. Never involves them in his life.' He lowered his voice to barely a whisper. 'And he never stays over the entire night – ever.'

Faye stared at him, wondering how he knew all this about Jake's personal life – it was downright intrusive. She glanced at the kitchen door and lowered her voice to barely a whisper too, even though they were talking in hushed voices as it was. 'How do you know all this?'

'Office gossip,' Marcus shrugged. 'There's always another willing victim waiting in the wings for their turn, always thinking the same thought: *this time it will different – I will be the one.*' But inevitably, when things don't work out, women gossip,' said Marcus. 'Failing that, I've always got Sherlock to ask.' Marcus flicked a finger in the direction of the front door. 'Oops!' His hand flew to his mouth as though he had just blown a huge secret.

'Who?' Faye got up and walked to the door. She lifted the net curtain at the window by the door and saw a large, shiny black car parked across the street. The man in the car was looking at the house. Faye let the curtain fall back into place and turned away from the window to look at Marcus. She folded her arms. 'Who is that?'

Marcus stole a furtive glance in the direction of the kitchen but said nothing.

Faye had a pretty good idea. But did Jake know that someone from the Ross Corporation was keeping tabs on him?

10

'Is someone watching Jake's house?' she said incredulously. Just how far did the Ross Corporation's tentacles reach into Jake's life?

Marcus was now giving her the silent treatment.

'Do you know there's a law against stalking? I could report you and your mysterious friend out there, which might not turn out to be good news if one of you had an illegal substance on your person.' Faye studied him intently. Was that sweat breaking out on his forehead?

'I need to use the bathroom,' Marcus said suddenly, rising from his chair.

'Oh no you don't.' She wasn't about to let him flush it down the toilet. 'Now, answer the question – is that man in the black car watching Jake's house?'

'Yes … well, only when Jake's in.'

'And when he's not?'

'Then maybe he'll watch him when he's somewhere else.' Marcus was being cagey.

'You mean you're having him followed?'

'It wasn't my idea.'

'Then who?' Faye demanded.

Marcus shot a worried look towards the kitchen door.

Faye didn't care if Jake heard, because he was going to find out one way or another. 'Who?' she demanded again.

'Alright, alright,' said Marcus, waving his hand in the air in a futile attempt to get her to lower her voice. 'It was my father's idea. He's already lost one child, and he said *I'm damn well not losing another.* Those were his exact words.'

Faye got the picture. Jake was no longer living and working in his ivory tower. This was the real world. He was not being chauffeured to work and flown around in private jets. Working in an inner-city neighbourhood wasn't without its risks. That morning was a case in point, when his bike had been stolen. Even so, Mr Ross had no right to go behind his back and do something like this. 'I thought your father was decent, honourable – at least, that's how Jake speaks of him.'

'He is, Faye, but when I found out what he was doing …'

'You didn't know?'

'No.' Marcus got up and walked over to join Faye beside the front door. 'When I found out about it, I confronted my father, and you know what he said?'

Faye shook her head.

'He said, *Marcus, family is everything to me.*'

Faye's thoughts turned to her own father. Where had it all gone so wrong?

'How could I argue with that? God knows, I don't want anything to happen to Jake either.' Marcus brushed the net curtain and glanced out of the window. '*No babysitters.* That's what Jake said.' Marcus turned to face Faye. 'He said, *I don't want anybody on my tail.*'

Marcus sighed. 'Jake knew my father was concerned, and it

was a real possibility that he would hire some … protection. Jake didn't want some company-employed jackass following him around.'

Faye shook her head – she wouldn't want that either, someone following her around, watching her every move. Something altogether more disturbing occurred to her. Occasionally, she'd been on a course lasting all day, so Jake's babysitting duties had extended beyond simply looking after Natty during an evening when Faye was out at a class. When Natty had been with Jake, going to his house, to the park, to the shops, had there been somebody following their every move?

She turned to the front door. 'What's his name?'

Marcus returned to his seat without a word.

Faye stormed over to him. 'What's his name?'

Marcus stood up. 'Whatever you're thinking of doing, a word of advice – don't.'

Faye ignored him. She marched up to the front door, opened it and took a step back, surprised to find a man standing on the front porch with his back to her.

He turned around and lifted his trilby from his head.

She looked past him to the large black car – it was empty. She turned her attention back to the man standing on the porch. 'Is that your car?'

He turned. 'Do you mean the Mercedes-Benz?'

Faye didn't know what make of car it was. 'It's the black car.'

'Why, yes – that's my car,' he said in a clipped accent. He turned to look at her. 'Is there a problem?'

Faye looked at him, confused. If this was the guy following Jake, he wasn't at all what she had imagined when Marcus had mentioned his father hiring some protection.

'Do you want to come in?' She presumed he had been about to ring the doorbell. Faye stepped aside and glanced at Marcus.

He shrugged his shoulders as if to say it was out of his hands, and with a sigh, sat back down.

The man hovered in the doorway. He appeared unsure whether to enter or not.

'Well?' she said impatiently.

The sound of her voice seemed to snap him out of his indecision; he took three quick steps inside.

Faye closed the door behind him and looked him up and down. He was tall, slim, and immaculately turned out – from his polished black leather shoes to the crisply folded kerchief in the left breast pocket of his black suit. Gold cufflinks peeped out from the starched white shirt beneath his suit. And he was older than she'd expected; she guessed he was in his sixties, around her father's age.

He clutched a brown leather briefcase to his chest, and when she spoke, he quickly side-stepped away from her like a frightened hen. Faye had to do her best to keep a straight face. She'd definitely had some preconceptions over whom the Rosses might have employed to follow Jake around. How exactly would this older man protect Jake? Her eyes roved to his briefcase. She wondered what was inside.

He looked more like a door-to-door bible salesman. *You're in the wrong job, mate*, she felt like saying. Instead, Faye pointed at his precious briefcase and blurted, 'Have you got bibles in there?' Of course, she wasn't being serious. She didn't expect him to take her question literally.

He took a step back and hesitated. 'No – not at all. Just some papers. Here …' he stuttered, 'Ta-ta-take a look.' He hastily started to unclip the briefcase, as though she was being serious. He seemed to be having trouble with the clips – his hands were shaking badly.

Faye stared at this so-called *bodyguard* who didn't look as though he could protect himself, let alone someone else. Faye turned to Marcus and said, 'You've got to be kidding me! Are you serious?'

Marcus smiled and replied, 'You have no idea.' He looked past her, and she turned to see something small and black, something that looked like a toy gun, in the old man's hand.

'Deadly serious,' the old man answered. No stutter.

Faye froze. The briefcase in his hand was open and empty.

'You did ask what was in my briefcase. The answer is protection.'

Faye swallowed. 'Is that real?' Apart from visits to museums exhibiting old military items, like guns and rifles, she'd never seen what she assumed was a handgun in real life. Was it even legal?

'Would I carry it around if it wasn't?'

Faye pursed her lips and gave Marcus a sideways glance. The look on his face said, *I told you not to interfere.*

The old man stowed the gun away in his briefcase, closing the lid and flicking the catches. He walked towards Faye, who jumped out of his way, and hung his trilby on a hook by Jake's front door. 'Now,' he said, placing the briefcase on the floor, by the chair that Faye had vacated. 'I don't think we've been properly introduced.' He held out his hand. 'I'm Aubrey Jones.'

Faye reluctantly moved forward to take the proffered hand. She reluctantly told him her name, although she imagined he knew it already. He probably knew everything about her. 'I'm Ms Ames.'

'No hard feelings?' Aubrey said, clasping her hand before taking a seat.

She wasn't so sure – she still hadn't recovered from the shock of seeing the gun. Aubrey hadn't pointed it at her – thank god. He hadn't even been holding the handle. He'd just picked it out of his briefcase. But he was clearly making a point – don't make quick judgements, and *don't* underestimate me.

He had obviously intended to teach her a lesson; appearances can be deceptive. He had known exactly what he was doing from the moment Faye had opened the front door. He had seen her at the window, looking his way. He had anticipated her next move by making his own move first and surprising and confusing her at the front door. It didn't make her feel any better to discover it wasn't some bumbling fool following Jake around; strangely, it made her feel uneasy. She didn't trust the man at all.

'You're a very good actor, Mr Jones.'

'Acutely observed.'

Yeah, but a little late, thought Faye. Her eyes roved to his briefcase. She nodded.

'I used to act,' Aubrey said. 'A long time ago – on the stage.' He was smiling.

Faye believed it. She stared at the man, who had acted so convincingly that she had mistaken him for something as innocent as a door-to-door bible salesman.

Aubrey pointed at Marcus. 'Be a gentleman.' He motioned at Faye to come and join him.

Marcus got out of his seat.

Aubrey rose as Faye came over to take the vacated seat. When she sat down, he took his seat on the other side of the small table.

From the corner of the hall, Marcus gave a snort of derision.

'There's no harm in some manners, Marcus. I'm sure Lydia would appreciate seeing a few more from you.'

Faye drew in a surprised breath – that was not how an employee spoke to his boss's son, especially when that son was running one of the most powerful companies in England.

Faye stared at Marcus, waiting for his reaction, for him to give Aubrey his marching orders and fire him on the spot.

'I know.' Marcus dropped his eyes and scuffed his foot on Jake's rug. 'I'm sorry.'

'I should think so.'

Faye stared at Mr Jones. *Who on earth is this guy?* she wondered. Whoever he was, he was an enigma, holding a gun in one breath, and then waiting for her to take a seat, like an absolute gentleman, in the next. Faye was even more confused than she had been before.

'Now, Ms Ames, where were we?'

'On the stage, I think.' Faye stole a glance at Marcus, who was still looking at the floor like a scolded child.

'Ah, yes. But there's no money on the stage. I tried to get into moving pictures, but I wasn't exactly the Marlon Brando or James Dean of my generation.' Aubrey looked down at his wiry frame.

'More the James Stewart type,' Faye suggested, warming to his obvious charm, but still keeping a wary eye on this deceptive man.

'Why, yes!' Aubrey seemed pleased with the remark. 'I suppose I am. I was born in the wrong era, you see; too mannered. I was never the rebel, more the gentleman.' He sighed. 'My name up in lights was never to be.' He brightened. 'So, I decided to use my talents in a more lucrative line of work.'

'Being a bodyguard?' Faye couldn't imagine there being a whole lot of money in that.

'A bodyguard,' Aubrey repeated, shaking his head. 'I don't think the term does anything for me, do you?'

'No. Not at all,' Faye readily agreed, but not entirely for reasons of his physique. He was too old, certainly, but that wasn't it. He seemed too educated for that line of work; more suited to the boardroom than the streets. But then, as Aubrey had already cleverly demonstrated, appearances could be deceptive.

'I like to keep up with the times,' said Aubrey. 'In fact, I like to think of myself as being in the information business.'

'Information?' Faye couldn't see what that had to do with tailing Jake all day.

'Yes. I rather enjoy using my acting ability to gather information.' He glanced at his briefcase. 'Far more than other methods of persuasion.'

'Persuasion?' Faye didn't like the inference.

'Have you heard the old adage, sticks and stones may break your bones?'

Faye nodded, adding, 'But names will never hurt you.'

'Well, it doesn't work in the playground,' he said cheerfully. He leaned across the table and spoke in a hushed voice. 'And the truth is, in my experience, names hurt very much indeed. They can damage a reputation. And with some – no, most – things, reputation is everything.'

Faye was interested to know just what experience he was referring to. Her mind began to throw up some distinctly unsavoury possibilities – like blackmail.

Aubrey elaborated. 'You don't need guns to protect and defend. If the police were in the information business, then maybe they'd have some real power out there on the streets.'

Faye looked at him, perplexed.

'Sticks and stones,' he said. 'Sticks and stones. What I do know is that by staying ahead of the game, it's surprising what resources you can have at your disposal – if and when the time comes.'

It sounded ominous.

Faye sat back in her chair and regarded the old gentleman sitting opposite her. For a moment, she decided she had him sussed. He was an old, retired family friend with an overactive imagination and nothing to do all day but mope around the house until someone had had a bright idea. Why don't we give him something to do? Make him feel useful. Let him keep an eye on Jake – at a discreet distance of course – taking notes, keeping logs, even carrying a gun. What harm could it do?

But she didn't feel convinced by this more than plausible, if rather stupid, scenario. Aubrey Jones was clearly no fool, and he didn't give the impression he needed somebody else to tell him what to do with his time. In fact, he appeared very much in control. Faye glanced over at Marcus, who was standing by the door, avoiding Aubrey, still waiting for his cab.

'Nice wood.' Aubrey ran his fingers down the smooth dark wood panelling behind his chair. 'I wonder if this was already here when Jake moved in?'

Marcus looked at the wood. 'Who cares?'

Aubrey gave Marcus a disapproving glare and turned his attention on Faye. 'Speaking of which, where is the master of the house?'

Master of the house; it sounded like a phrase straight out of an old black-and-white British movie. Was this another one of his acts?

Marcus rolled his eyes in the direction of the kitchen door. 'Jake's in the kitchen.'

The more she listened to his accent, the more she thought she could detect some inflections that hinted at other origins.

'So, why are we all sitting in the hallway?'

'I'm waiting for a cab.' Marcus looked at his watch.

'What's wrong with the kitchen?'

Marcus bit his lip and stared at the floor.

Aubrey nodded knowingly. 'Was it something you said?' he said sarcastically, 'or was it merely your presence here that precipitated this current predicament?' Aubrey looked at the two outcasts, waiting in the hall. 'Because I must admit, I am a bit surprised to find you here, Marcus.'

Marcus glared at him. 'Don't worry; I wasn't invited, if that's what you mean.'

'Well, isn't it nice to hear that some things in life don't change, is it not, Ms Ames?'

She had absolutely no idea what had just passed between Aubrey and Marcus, but she was going to put the record straight; Jake had good reason to be angry with Marcus.

'Jake cut his hands on some glass.'

Aubrey rose slowly from his chair with a look of concern. 'What happened?' He caught sight of the broken glass on the floor.

Faye turned her attention to Marcus.

So did Aubrey. 'Marcus, what happened here?'

'I screwed up again, that's what happened.' Marcus walked over to the table and snatched up his bag. 'I'm waiting outside.' He started towards the door.

Aubrey unexpectedly jumped up and crossed the hall so quickly that he reached the front door ahead of Marcus, barring his way.

They stood in silence, facing each other.

Faye watched the confrontation uneasily. Her hand brushed the cricket bat in the umbrella stand. She was ready to break up a fight, something she'd unfortunately grown accustomed to in her years in a classroom.

She watched as Aubrey reached out a hand. Faye's body tensed as she anticipated the first blow, then relaxed as Aubrey rested his hand on Marcus's shoulder and started to speak; his voice barely above a whisper. She caught snatches, a word here and there, meaningless out of context. Then Aubrey paused, drew back and finished with, 'You'll see. Just give him time.'

Marcus nodded.

Aubrey patted his arm affectionately and returned to his seat. Marcus turned around and looked straight at Faye, who was trying to look for all the world like she hadn't seen or heard a thing. But she'd witnessed how Marcus listened to this man. She'd seen what influence Mr Jones seemed to hold over his employer's son, and wondered whether the same held true for Jake. Faye wanted to know more. Who was this guy?

11

'Tell me, Mr Jones, have you known Jake long?'

'Aubrey. You can call me Aubrey.'

'Very well.'

Aubrey was still looking at Marcus. 'We go back some,' he said absently.

Marcus coughed into his hand.

'What?' said Aubrey indignantly. 'So I don't like to discuss the passing of time.'

'You mean your age,' Marcus corrected him.

'Alright, I don't like to discuss my age; not when ladies are present.' He glanced at Faye. 'And pretty ones at that.'

Really, thought Faye, *you're old enough to be my father!* Still, it was nice to get a compliment, even if it came from a very good actor. 'So, how long have you known Jake?' Faye repeated her question.

Aubrey mumbled something incoherent.

Marcus cupped his hand to his ear. 'Pardon? I didn't quite catch that.' Marcus was clearly enjoying himself, making Aubrey squirm.

'Thirty years – give or take,' answered Aubrey, throwing his hands in the air in defeat.

'There. That wasn't too difficult, was it?' Marcus said with a smirk.

Faye began, 'But that's …'

'Nearly Jake's whole life,' Marcus confirmed. 'That's how long they go back – Aubrey's known us since he was in his thirties.' Marcus pointed at Aubrey. 'So you don't have to be a maths whizz to guess his age – give or take.'

'Marcus!' Aubrey was clearly mortified.

Marcus put his bag down by the front door. 'You say you like to keep up with the times, Aubrey, but nobody lies about their age anymore.'

'I do,' he said sullenly. 'And I'm not lying; it's simply not a polite topic of conversation.'

Faye felt sorry for him. 'You don't look a day over …' Aubrey looked across at her eagerly. 'Fifty-five.'

'Why thank you Ms Ames. I'm inclined to agree.'

'I bet you are,' Marcus scoffed.

'I'm in better shape than some thirty-somethings I know.' Aubrey inclined his head in Marcus's direction.

Faye wondered how much he knew about Marcus's weekend outings to some insalubrious parts of London.

'I'm thirty-three,' Marcus retorted. 'You never remember my age. How come you always remember Jake's?'

Aubrey shrugged.

'It's not that hard,' Marcus persisted. 'Remember – Jake comes in the middle. I'm a year older than Jake, and Ellie's six years younger.'

'Who's Ellie?' Faye asked.

Marcus and Aubrey both turned to look at Faye. The larking around stopped instantly.

Faye suddenly realised that was a stupid question.

'My sister Eleanor, Jake's wife,' said Marcus.

Should she apologise for bringing that up? It wasn't her fault that Jake didn't talk about her.

'Jake doesn't discuss his personal life with her,' Marcus said to Aubrey.

'Apparently not,' said Aubrey, staring in her direction and making her feel inexplicably uncomfortable.

Faye looked at her watch. Would Jake decide he was up to finishing off the day at work? She didn't know how he could. She was still wondering how she would explain to the head Jake's bandaged hands. Faye was anxious to get back to work. She turned to the kitchen door and noticed the round brass doorknob was already turning slowly.

'Will someone kindly …' the sound of Jake's agitated voice came from the other side of the door, 'open this door?' He was obviously having some difficulty gripping the smooth brass handle with his bandaged hands.

Faye reached for the door.

'Wait!' Marcus startled her. 'Shall we let him stew a moment longer?'

Stew? Perplexed, Faye turned from the door to find Marcus looking in Aubrey's direction.

'I think that's an excellent idea, Marcus,' Aubrey replied, 'considering he led me on a wild goose chase last night. I was stunned when he didn't come home. I exhausted all the possibilities of where he might have gone.'

Faye looked at Aubrey, sheepishly hoping Marcus did not tell him where exactly Jake had been the previous night.

'And don't forget leaving me to sleep on the porch last night;

that upset my apple cart, I can tell you.'

Faye turned on Marcus. 'Upset *your* apple cart?' She motioned at the glass on the floor. 'Look what you did to Jake's home, to Jake.'

Aubrey put his hands on his hips, looking at the glass, and nodded in agreement, his expression turning serious. 'You're right. It's not a joking matter.'

Marcus ignored them both and added. 'It might make him think twice the next time he stays out all night without telling anyone his whereabouts.' Marcus nodded theatrically in Faye's direction.

'Ah.' Aubrey turned his head slowly and settled a knowing gaze on Faye. 'Now, isn't this a turn-up for the books?' He smiled. 'Lucky fellow.'

Faye shot Aubrey a look. Was he being serious? 'Look, it's not what you think.' Faye caught Marcus mouthing the last three words as she was saying them. 'Well, it isn't,' she glared at him. 'Besides, I'm too old for Jake.'

'Says who?' Aubrey.

'Me.'

'How old are you?' Marcus.

Faye hesitated.

'Oh, come on, not another one with a problem divulging their age. Besides I told you mine.' Marcus peered at Faye with a malicious grin.

Yeah, well, it's a bit different when you're closer to forty than thirty, thought Faye. Still in this instance, it might prove a point. 'I am thirty-eight.'

'Why, you're still just a baby!' Aubrey sounded disappointed. 'For a moment there I thought I was in with a chance. Young fellows have all the luck,' he said glumly.

'But don't you see? I'm six years older than Jake.'

'So what?' Aubrey threw up his hands. 'Besides, Jake's always been an old soul.'

That was true. Faye had noticed that. When he had applied for the student teaching position, she hadn't expected to meet such a world-weary thirty-two-year-old. But once she'd found out about his background, and discovered some facts of a more personal nature, she'd put it down to his recent loss. Now Aubrey was about to enlighten her further.

'I often wondered if losing your parents so young does that to a person.' Aubrey shook his head solemnly. 'A kid must get to thinking that the world is not such a friendly place after all.'

'I can hear voices out there, you know.' Jake's tone told Faye he couldn't hear the details of the conversation.

'We know,' said Aubrey and Marcus in unison.

But still, Faye blushed at the thought that Jake might have overheard that snippet about her age, although she had no idea why that should bother her.

'Is that you, Aubrey?'

Aubrey looked up. 'Got me, Jake. How are you doing?'

'Not very—' He halted. 'What are you doing here?'

'I came to pick up Marcus, take him to work.'

Faye looked from Aubrey to Marcus; by the looks on their faces, neither of them seemed at all concerned that Aubrey had just told a barefaced lie.

'Well, isn't somebody going to open this door?'

No one made a move.

Faye stepped forward and put her hand on the doorknob.

'Will you *please* open the damn …'

Faye flung it open.

'... door,' he breathed into her face. 'Oh.'

Faye glanced back at her two hallway companions. 'I think they were having some fun with you.'

Jake looked over her shoulder. Marcus lifted his hand and gave a little wave. Aubrey gave a funny half-salute.

'No kidding,' Jake said flatly. 'And where were you when I wanted out of the kitchen?' Jake was not amused.

Before Faye could explain that Aubrey and Marcus's conversation had caught her off-guard, Aubrey spoke. 'A little bird tells me that Marcus has been causing trouble again.'

Faye shot Aubrey a look. She sincerely hoped that little bird was just a figure of speech and in no way a reference to herself.

'Yeah, tell me about it,' said Jake. 'Have you seen my hallway? I've a good mind to ...'

Marcus barged passed Faye. 'You've a good mind to *what*?' he said squaring up to Jake. 'Punch my lights out?'

'Now *that* is not a bad idea,' said Jake, glaring at Marcus.

'Boys, boys,' Aubrey was on his feet. 'Play nice.' Aubrey placed a hand on Marcus's shoulder and steered him away from Jake. 'After all, we are in the presence of a lady.' He bowed his head in Faye's direction.

Another compliment! Faye thought, suddenly feeling very self-conscious, with three sets of male eyes focused on her.

'And *this lady*,' said Faye glancing at Aubrey, 'has got to get back to work.' She headed for the door. 'Jake?'

Jake was heading for the stairs. 'I need to pee.'

'You need help with that?' Marcus sniggered.

'No, thank you.'

Jake was a considerable time.

Outside, a taxi turned up. 'That'll be my ride.' Marcus grabbed his bag and looked at his watch. 'This cab driver is not getting a tip, I can tell you.' He opened the front door. 'Faye.'

She was still looking up the stairs after Jake. She turned to Marcus.

'It's been a pleasure,' said Marcus.

Faye raised her eyebrows. She couldn't say the same herself; not at all. Not after the trouble he'd caused. Then it occurred to her that perhaps he was just being sarcastic. She didn't know him well enough to tell. Maybe if they'd met under different circumstances, they might hit it off. But not today. She scowled at him.

'Aubrey,' Marcus nodded in his direction.

'Remember what I said, Marcus – just give it time.'

The cab driver honked impatiently.

'Oh, get lost!' Marcus shouted out of the door. 'I spent enough time waiting for you!' Marcus closed the door behind him.

Aubrey stood up with his briefcase in hand. 'Well, it's a mass exodus. I'm off.' He glanced up at the ceiling and whispered, 'But not very far.' He winked at Faye and held out his hand. 'It's been a pleasure, Ms Ames.'

'Call me Faye.'

'I thought you'd never ask. May I?' He took Faye's hand and bent down to plant a soft kiss.

Faye glanced furtively over her shoulder to check Jake was not at this moment walking down the stairs. This old guy was actually coming on to her!

He delicately withdrew a small white business card from his left breast pocket. 'Call me any time.'

Faye took the card.

12

Faye was left alone in the hallway, wondering when would be a good time to tell Jake that he had a permanent chaperone. She turned the small white card over in her hand. There was no name, no address, no job title – just an eight-digit phone number neatly printed in the centre.

'For chrissakes!'

Faye tucked the card in her pocket and glanced up the stairs. 'Do you need a hand with something?'

'No. Yes.'

'Well, which is it?' Faye shouted up the stairwell.

'I'm in the bedroom,' Jake called down.

Faye was familiar with the upstairs layout after settling Natty into what had turned out to be one of many sleepovers at Jake's when Faye had been out on dates and had known she might be home late – or not at all. This arrangement had suited everybody concerned, especially Jake, who hadn't relished the idea of sleeping on Faye's lumpy sofa – although he had ended up doing so the previous night.

Faye couldn't resist poking her head into the spare bedroom. The bed and desk were familiar, but there was now a frieze running around the centre of the room, cutting the pale blue walls in half; Astronauts floated along in a starry blue-black space. Definitely Natty's doing, thought Faye. No pink ponies for her.

She moved into the room and brushed the face of the dinosaur coverlet on the bed, her eyes roving to several multicoloured stacking boxes – also a new addition to the room. She randomly picked up a toy from the overflowing toy box. 'Natty!' she exclaimed, half annoyed and half amused. This girl knew she was onto a good thing; she was milking the guy for all he was worth!

'Did you say something?' Jake's voice came from the next room.

It occurred to Faye that she wasn't standing in the spare room. This was Natty's room now. Her thoughts turned back to the discussion at the breakfast table, to Natty's insistence that Jake was her daddy. Looking around at all this new stuff, it was little wonder that Natty was confused.

'Just a minute,' called Faye, bending down to put a toy back in the box before she left the room. Something caught her attention – a tassel poking through the stacking box below. Curious, she lifted the yellow box off the top to take a closer look. She picked up the material and held it up. It was a small brown suede waistcoat with tassels down the side. 'Cute.' She laid it on the bed. Underneath was a hat squashed out of shape. Faye picked it up, turned it over and put a fist inside to reshape the hat. It was a Stetson, brown suede to match the waistcoat. She put it on the bed beside the waistcoat. She turned back to see what else was in the box, a leather belt. She picked it up. It was stuck. She gave it a yank. It flew out of the box; something else came out of the box with it and flew across the room, clunking loudly against the door before it landed on the floor with a dull thud.

'What was that noise?' Jake emerged from his bedroom wearing a clean shirt, unbuttoned. 'I seem to have a problem doing up buttons,' Jake held up his bandaged hands as if he needed to offer proof of his new-found disability.

Faye stared at the belt that was dangling in her hand; she waved it at Jake. 'What's this?'

'Ah.'

'Ah? Is that all you can say?' Faye paused. 'And what is that?' She pointed at Jake's foot. He was moving something around, trying to hide it from Faye's view. Faye strode over to Jake and held out her hand. 'Give it to me.'

Jake didn't move.

Faye sighed, knelt down and got a grip on the object that he was making a lousy job of hiding beneath his foot. 'Let me have it.'

Jake reluctantly moved his foot.

Faye picked it up. 'Are you that stupid?' She stood for a moment, glaring at Jake, who was avoiding eye contact.

And there was more; the wooden rocking horse in the corner which must have cost a thousand pounds, the widescreen television. No wonder Natty wanted to come here; there was no way Faye could compete with all this on a teaching salary. And why should she? Jake wasn't Natty's father.

This had to stop. And she wasn't just thinking about the toys.

Faye thrust both objects into Jake's chest and stormed out.

Jake fumbled, moved quickly to the bed and dropped the toy gun and holster on top of the Stetson, squashing the hat.

'I'm an idiot!' Jake stared at the offending objects. He turned to the door. 'Let me explain, Faye.'

Faye thundered down the stairs as he emerged from the bedroom. He called out, 'I had this bright idea; rather than Natty bringing her toys with her every time she stayed over, I thought why not buy her some toys that remained here?' He looked over the banister. Faye looked up at him. He continued, 'The only thing is, these little shopping trips with Natty become a bit too regular, and before I know it, she's ordering stuff online too. But hey, I'm a guy. We're weak. What can I say?'

Faye stood, her face tilted upwards, frowning at him.

'So, this one time Natty sees this little cowgirl outfit and she's just like got to have it – you know how it is. So, I buy her the outfit, which comes complete with hat, gun and holster, without thinking. If I had a shred of common sense, I'd have realised I should have consulted you first.'

'Yes – you should have!' Faye turned on her heel and stalked to the front door, slamming it shut behind her.

13

Jake sat at the table in the hall. 'Now what?' He knew Faye was heading back to school. He'd heard a car engine start after she'd stalked out of the house. He'd rushed down the stairs, taking them two at a time, hoping to catch her, but he'd heard the car moving off before he reached the front door. He looked at his hands. He couldn't really drive until they stopped throbbing so much. He'd have to call a taxi.

He spent thirty minutes staring forlornly at the clock in the hall and listening intently to each passing car in the hope that Faye had changed her mind and come back. Then he began to debate whether or not to return to school, but he didn't want to explain to the head why his hands were in bandages. He hoped Faye would explain away why he hadn't returned to work.

Jake resigned himself to the fact that he would not be going to work that day. He went upstairs to get his bloodstained clothes and put them in the wash.

He'd just stepped into his bedroom when his mobile phone rang. He'd left it on the bedside table when he'd changed his clothes.

Jake dived onto the bed, landing on his stomach, and gingerly picked up his phone, careful not to drop it. Racking his brain for a suitable apology, Jake said, 'Yes?' down the phone, expecting to hear Faye's voice. It wasn't Faye. Instead, it was the head, calling about his absence. Faye had told the head that he'd had an emergency at home. The head didn't elaborate, making Jake wonder whether Faye had given any details – Jake hoped not. He didn't want to ask. However, the head was understanding – Jake had proved an exemplary student teacher.

Jake rolled over onto his back. She'd covered for him. Did this mean all was forgiven? Somehow, he doubted it.

'So I heard how it went with your bike.'

'Pardon me?'

'The bike theft?'

Jake looked at his hands, and thought of Marcus. That had been the least of his concerns after he'd got that call from Lydia.

The head added, 'Faye told me she reported it, and the police will be in touch.'

Jake breathed a sigh of relief. So, she *was* covering for him. 'Thanks.'

'Sorry to hear that someone broke into your home.'

Jake raised his eyebrows.

'Faye told me that she'd taken you home to get your car, and that was when you'd discovered you'd had a break-in.'

'Uh, yeah.' Jake winced. So that was what Faye had told him. He hoped she hadn't mentioned Marcus.

'What bad luck to have your bike stolen and your house broken into, both on the same day.'

Jake agreed.

'Bad luck slipping on the glass like that; how're those hands?'

'They're not bad at all – fine, really.' Jake sat up and was having trouble keeping the phone held to his ear.

'Is that a fact? Faye says they're in pretty bad shape.'

He knew what was coming; the head was going to tell him to take some time off. 'I'm sure in a day or so …'

'It sounds to me as though it's going to take time to heal.'

Jake felt relieved they were in agreement. 'Yeah, but in a day or so I'll be …'

'I think it best that you take the week. The summer term is winding down. There's only a week to go, so you're not missing much. Then there's the summer break for your hands to heal properly, and you can recharge your batteries too. Then we will all look forward to seeing you in the autumn term.'

'Pardon?' Jake nearly dropped his phone. He didn't want to be off all week. He'd miss the school, seeing the kids, his colleagues – Faye most especially. And as for the summer – he already had plans, which didn't involve recharging his batteries.

'You're going to be no use in school with an injury.'

Jake sighed. He had a point. 'But what about the summer clubs?'

'I'm aware that you were looking forward to running some of the summer clubs, but unfortunately I think that is out of the question now.'

'What?'

'I know you were keen, and I really appreciate your dedication in volunteering to spend time over the summer break in school, but I think under the circumstances you should just take the time off.'

Jake shook his head furiously. 'I'm sure in a week or so my hands will be fine.'

'That's as may be, Jake. The thing is, it's easy to get burnt out in this job. I appreciate your dedication to the kids, the job, I really do. The school will still be here in September – I can guarantee that. But the question is – will *you*, if those injuries are not taken care of and you don't take a proper break? You can put your name down for the following summer, but my advice to you is to have a holiday.'

Jake was silent. He didn't want a holiday. He knew the long school summer break was looming in a week's time, and he wasn't interested. Work took his mind off everything – and the huge bonus was that he saw Faye every day. He might not see her at school during the summer, but that hadn't stopped him putting his name down for just about every single summer club.

'Look, you've got nothing to prove, Jake.' There was a pause. 'Granted, there were some who were sceptical in the beginning. After all, it's a huge career change from being a corporate lawyer to teaching in an inner-city school, but you've proved you are cut out for the job. Now, go take a holiday, for goodness' sake.'

Do I have a choice? Jake sighed heavily. 'Can I speak to Faye?'

'No, I'm afraid she's in a meeting.'

Jake wondered aloud if Faye would still be his mentor when he returned in September.

The head didn't hesitate. 'I've allocated you a new timetable with a different year group and mentor. It's already been arranged.'

Jake got off the phone feeling like he'd just been kicked in the guts. He'd been away for two hours, and they'd already organised who he would be teaching in the autumn term and had replaced his mentor. Was that Faye's doing? Or was he just being paranoid? The thought of life without Faye, without Natty, was …

The phone rang downstairs. Jake looked at his mobile, perplexed. Nobody rang his home number.

Jake rushed down the stairs. Could it be Faye?

He picked up the phone in the hall, trying to remember the last time he'd used a landline. 'Faye?'

'Is … Mr Campbell-Ross?' The line crackled with heavy interference, dissolving some of the words in static.

'Hello, say again?'

'Is that Mr Campbell-Ross?' The voice came clearer this time, but only just; it was an older guy, possibly late fifties, sixties perhaps. Jake didn't recognise the voice.

'Yes, it is. Who am I speaking to?'

'My name … Arnold Wright.' The line was still bad.

'Where are you calling from?' Jake spoke slowly, enunciating each word, even though when he spoke the line was completely free of any other noise save for his own voice.

'From … Scotland …' A particularly loud crackle followed, forcing Jake to move the phone out of earshot for a couple of seconds.

'You're kidding.' Jake had made many international calls across the pond in the course of business, and some personal ones, and the lines were always crystal clear, as if he was speaking to a neighbour in the next street. 'What's wrong with your connection?'

'Heaven knows, we're always on to them t … ge … fixed.'

Jake empathised; it was the same the world over, trying to get a public utility company to come out and fix something.

'What can I do for you, Mr Wright?' And why, he wondered, was a guy he was positive he didn't know phoning him from Scotland?

'It's Martha … bless her.'

Jake sighed. He'd heard about these old folks making random calls. His wife, bless her, had probably passed away, and with nobody to speak to, the sad old guy had randomly phoned someone up, in the hope of finding a sympathetic ear. *How*, thought Jake, *did he get hold of my name and number?* As soon as Jake moved in, he'd organised his landline to block calls from unknown numbers and list his number as private. He'd also changed his mobile phone number. Unfortunately, that hadn't stopped Marcus finding out where he lived. He'd given Lydia his new mobile phone number in case of emergencies. He'd regretted that.

'Are you still there?' Jake asked, listening to the rise and fall of the static, imagining he could hear voices out there in the ether. He didn't want to put the phone down on a sad old man. 'Where did you get my number?' Jake frowned. He wasn't living in the Ross Corporation's apartment building with its added layers of security, and private unlisted phone numbers.

'… Martha, bless her … not very well.'

Jake looked at his watch. 'I'm sorry to hear that.'

'She has … old letters. I'm try … get hold … people bef …'

Jake understood. Mr Wright's wife was dying, and he was trying to contact old friends and acquaintances who might like to see her before she died. 'Look, I'm so sorry, but you have the wrong number. I don't know you or your—.'

'Martha – her name … Martha.'

'No, sorry, still doesn't ring any bells. Well, I hope you find who you're looking for,' said Jake, trying to wind down the conversation and bow out gracefully before he lost his temper and told the old man to sod off. The sound of the static was really getting on his nerves.

'… name in … letter ... William Ross …'

'William?' Now he had Jake's attention. And now it explained why Mr Wright had made this call, because trying to speak to

William in person would be virtually impossible. Even if he did succeed in negotiating the Ross Corporation's labyrinth of a phone system, he'd only get as far as William's PA, who would not direct just any mere mortal to his office – William's direct business line was for corporate calls only. Although William was spending far more time at home these days, Jake wasn't about to give out his home number. That was strictly off-limits too – even though he couldn't see the harm in a lonely old guy trying to trace friends of his nearly-departed wife.

'I'm really sorry, Mr Wright, but I can't give you that number.'

'That's alright ... already spoken ... Mr Ross says sorry to hear … bout Martha. Can't come see ...'

That surprised Jake. Where had he got William's home phone number from? There was one explanation. If they had been friends who went back many years, then that would explain how he had that number.'

'Still … try … get hold … Ralph.'

'Ralph? Who's Ralph?'

'I … don't know.'

'What's in the letters?' Jake's interest was aroused.

'No … not … phone … diff … cult … talk.'

Jake understood – the line wasn't improving. And besides, these letters were obviously of a personal nature, nothing to do with Jake.

'Will you come … see … letters?'

'You want *me* to see the letter?' He hadn't planned to return to Scotland, but then he hadn't exactly planned on being on holiday for the next week – he was at a complete loose end. Maybe this was just what he needed; perhaps Martha had something she wanted to pass on to William and this person called Ralph, and if they couldn't make it in person, then he was the next best bet. Why not help an old guy carry out a last wish for his wife? Jake was definitely warming to the idea.

Over the phone, Mr Wright was trying desperately to persuade Jake through the static that he'd enjoy a trip to Scotland.

'Never mind that,' Jake said. 'I'll come.'

'You will?' This was followed by a particularly loud burst of static. 'That's … fantas … thank you … Martha … really app … ciate it.'

'Just let me get a pen to write down your address. I'll try and catch the first flight out, and I'll phone you as soon as I arrive, Mr Wright.'

'Call … Arnold.'

Jake wrote down the address that Arnold gave him and was still holding the receiver to his ear after he heard Arnold click off and the line go dead. He sat like that for a full minute before slowly replacing the receiver. He stared at the address. If he had known just where exactly in Scotland Arnold was calling from, he wouldn't have been that eager to agree to the trip; this was most definitely *not* what he'd had in mind for a holiday.

Jake picked up the phone to ring Arnold back and tell him he'd changed his mind before realising Arnold had not given a return number. He was about to dial directory enquiries. Then he thought about how he hadn't been back to Scotland for months; not since the accident. He knew it was about time he made the trip. Perhaps it was fortuitous that he should get this phone call now.

He put the phone down. He had a bag to pack and a flight to book. His conscience was telling him he had to go.

Jake booked his flights online and then sat staring at the laptop, at a loss to explain how a trip home that morning to collect his car had led to enforced time off work and a flight booked for Scotland.

Jake retreated upstairs and found his mobile phone. He knew Faye was at work, but he wanted to speak to her before he left; to let her know he was taking the head's advice and going away for a short break. Failing that, he'd have to leave a message.

It went straight to voicemail. As he left his message, he hoped her failure to answer was because she was teaching and not because she was avoiding his call.

14

Jake made himself a sandwich and picked up his phone to call Faye again. He'd left it all morning, hoping she'd call back during her break. It was now lunchtime. He frowned. She still wasn't picking up. He looked at the sandwich and didn't feel hungry. He glanced at his watch. He'd have to get a move on if he was going to check in to the airport hotel. His flight wasn't until the next afternoon, but he just didn't fancy hanging around his house until the next day. He had made up his mind.

He bounded up the stairs and was just packing some clothes into a small carry-on holdall when the doorbell rang. He looked up. 'Now what?'

It was still ringing when he opened the door.

Marcus was standing there with his finger on the buzzer. He removed his finger when he saw Jake. 'Ah, I was starting to think you'd gone already.'

Jake looked Marcus up and down then looked past him to the street, where Marcus's black Saab was parked. 'What the hell are you doing here? And what do you mean – gone already?' Jake said in surprise. *How on earth did he know I was going away?* he wondered.

'Faye says you're going on holiday.' He sounded worried.

'Faye told you?' Jake stared at him angrily. So she hadn't answered his calls, but she'd spoken to Marcus. 'So, I'm going on holiday. What's the big deal?'

'But you don't go on holiday, not since—'

'Well I'm going now – no thanks to you.'

'What's that supposed to mean?'

Jake held up his bandaged hands. 'I can't do my job with these, can I?' Jake shut the door in his face. Then swiftly opened it again – Marcus was still there. 'And when did you get on a first name basis with Faye?' Jake involuntarily opened the door wide. Marcus took it as an invitation to step inside, which he did. Barring physically throwing him out, Jake knew he wasn't going to get rid of him that easily.

Jake reluctantly shut the front door.

Marcus hovered in the hallway, poking his head into Jake's lounge. 'You've done some decorating,' Marcus said conversationally.

Jake gave him an uninterested look and walked up the stairs.

Marcus followed. 'I didn't notice this morning.'

Yeah, but you noticed Faye, Jake thought. Just how much had Faye noticed Marcus? They had been out in the hall talking for a considerable time. It occurred to Jake that perhaps the two of them had hit it off. After all, didn't women like them tall, dark and handsome? He had money. Apparently he'd even appeared in some high-brow magazine in a list of London's most eligible bachelors – an unwanted accolade he himself had been only too familiar with not that long ago. And things were not going well with Lydia.

Jake tried to brush the thought aside, but it kept coming back.

'What do you want, Marcus?' Jake opened the wardrobe door

in his bedroom and took out four shirts and a couple of pairs of jeans. He didn't plan on being away long.

'Where are you going?'

Jake returned to the wardrobe to dig out some underwear and socks. He didn't forget to pack some jumpers – it could be chilly if he went for a walk down by a loch, even in summer.

He threw them in his hand luggage, along with the shirts, and looked at Marcus. 'What – did you think I was going to spend my time off work moping about the house?' It was, in fact, exactly what Jake had had in mind before Arnold Wright had called.

Jake had one final look in the wardrobe to see if there was anything else he might need.

'You're not going to tell me where you're going, are you?' Marcus said.

'Nope.' Jake turned around to find Marcus standing on the other side of the bed, studying something on his bedside cabinet. Jake knew what he was looking at, but Arnold's address was tucked safely in his wallet, and the time he had written down on the notepad by the phone had no reference to a flight or destination. Marcus had no way of knowing where he was going. Jake realised he had nothing to worry about. Marcus wasn't going anywhere; he had a multi-million-pound corporation to run, and he never took time off – ever.

Jake zipped up his bag. He was done packing.

'When are you leaving?'

'None of your bloody business, but you're leaving right now.' Jake pointed at the door.

Marcus walked around the bed towards Jake. 'Faye told me you were so concerned about me that you dropped everything this morning to look for me.' Marcus spread his arms wide as though he were going to give Jake a hug, or worse, was expecting to receive one. 'And I thought you didn't care. Awww ...'

'I don't.' Jake elbowed past him to pick up the notepad with his flight time. Returning to the wardrobe, he picked out a clean, pressed white shirt and hung it on the wardrobe door. He glanced at Marcus. 'Why are you still here?'

Marcus sat down on the end of the bed.

Jake turned his back to him and managed to undo the top two buttons of his shirt. He gave up with the rest and just pulled the shirt over his head. 'Blast.' Jake's hands were stuck in the sleeves of the shirt.

'You need some help with that?'

'No.' Jake managed to prise his hands out of the sleeves without disturbing his bandages. He tossed the shirt on the floor, and in the corner of his vision saw Marcus's hand reaching for it.

Jake put on the clean shirt. With his back still to Marcus, he attempted to do up the buttons. It wasn't working. He was having difficulty manipulating the buttons into the holes with his fingers so tightly pinned together under the bandages.

'Dammit.' Jake let his arms fall to his sides in defeat.

'Jake?'

Jake turned around.

Marcus was still sitting on the bed. Jake's shirt was neatly folded beside him. 'You need a hand with that?' he said gently.

This time, Jake didn't object.

Marcus stood in front of Jake and tentatively took the second button from the top. Jake rolled his eyes in frustration; he had a feeling he was going to regret packing so many shirts.

'Feel like you're five again?' said Marcus in an amused tone of voice.

'Yes. Thank you.' Jake stared up at the ceiling.

Marcus finished and stood back. 'Need tucking in?' He chuckled.

Jake hadn't thought of that. He looked down at his shirt. It looked okay over jeans; it was the look he had preferred in his student days. Of course, he wasn't exactly twenty anymore, but he thought he looked passable.

Marcus slumped back on the bed and propped himself up on his elbows, watching Jake. 'Can you drive like that?'

Jake was having difficulty lifting the bag off the bed. 'None of your damn business,' said Jake irritably as he slipped the shoulder strap over his left shoulder and hoisted the bag off the bed. Jake walked straight past Marcus and out of the door.

Downstairs, Jake picked up his jacket and car keys and turned around to say a silent goodbye to his house and his new life – for now.

'You're going right now?' Marcus had followed him back down the stairs like an abandoned puppy whining for some attention.

Jake turned on Marcus. 'Look, they've given me the week off, and then it's the school summer holidays. I've got over six weeks of free time.' Jake wasn't about to give him any details of the trip, but perhaps if Marcus thought he wasn't going to be around for six weeks, he'd stop showing up at his house.

'I am going on holiday right now. So why don't you stop beating about the bush and get to the point – what do you want?'

Marcus looked at the floor.

Jake studied him. Here was a smart guy. He was the head of a global business in all but name. The events of a few months earlier had inadvertently propelled them both into success in their professional lives, albeit along vastly different routes. And it had propelled them both into chaos in their personal lives. Jake's was practically non-existent, apart from the women he kept *bumping into* in his local supermarket. He remembered them from the London offices of the Ross Corporation – and he knew who was behind it.

What did Marcus think he was trying to do? Fix him up on a date? Perhaps Marcus thought if he got really involved with one of those women, he might be persuaded to return to his old job with the firm.

But what really annoyed Jake was Marcus's attitude to Lydia. Hadn't Marcus learnt anything from that tragic event almost seven months ago? Jake would have thought that the loss of Ellie would have cemented Marcus's relationship with Lydia – not driven them apart. Jake had expected that in time, Marcus would patch things up and make it work with his fiancée, but if anything, he seemed to be veering more violently off the rails.

And this gave Jake pause for thought.

There was an unexpected upside to his holiday that he had not considered until now. He would not be around to pick up the pieces – and Marcus knew it. That's why Marcus was there, attention-seeking again. Marcus was losing his audience; an audience he was scaring every time he went off the rails in a spectacular fashion during one of his benders. Jake was sick and tired of being that audience, witnessing that crash.

Jake didn't have to ask Marcus what he was doing there because he already knew. 'I am not going to be around to pick up the pieces.' Jake poked a finger in Marcus's chest. 'So you had better get your act together.'

'What's that supposed to mean?'

'You know what I'm talking about.'

Marcus's face looked a picture of dumbfounded innocence.

'Do you think I'm that stupid? I know the signs. It's a part of our teacher training, to be on the lookout for substance abuse in the children in our care.' What Jake didn't know, and what he was sure Marcus wasn't going to tell him, was just what substance he was abusing.

'I'd better go.' Marcus made a sudden move to the front door.

'Oh no you don't.' Jake moved quickly, positioning himself between Marcus and the front door, blocking his escape. He wanted some assurance from Marcus, some sign that he understood.

'I just wanted to apologise. That's all,' Marcus said unexpectedly.

Jake stared at him. Was this it? Was he finally getting that apology after waiting almost seven months? Was Marcus finally giving in and acknowledging what he had done, if not for him, then at least for Eleanor?

Marcus turned and looked down the hallway.

Jake followed his gaze. 'You mean you're apologising for this morning.' Jake couldn't hide his disappointment. 'It's not important.' Jake turned towards the front door.

'There's something else.'

Jake turned back. Expectation hung in the air. He studied Marcus. They had been best friends once – the three of them, Marcus, Jake and Eleanor.

A best friend to Eleanor, a best friend to Marcus; Jake had been the glue that had held the three of them together. But left alone, Marcus and Eleanor had always acted like any normal siblings – like they hated each other.

Jake had been the calming influence – the negotiator. When Jake was there, they had played, when Jake was not, they had fought. And things had never changed; as they had grown older, they had not grown closer. Marcus and Ellie had always been like chalk and cheese. Where Marcus was loud and brash, Eleanor was quiet and shy. Where Marcus excelled in the classroom and on the sports pitch, Eleanor struggled.

Eleanor, as her mother had so often reminded her, had never been destined to be a great success like her brother. She had told her she should forget college, settle down, produce babies, and lead the role of the pampered, rich wife. Jake had come to realise that her mother, the actress who never was, had never been able to bear the thought of Eleanor achieving something – being somebody in her own right.

Thanks to Marcus, she had got that wish. Thanks to Marcus, Eleanor would never have the chance to reach her potential.

Jake decided he didn't care a jot whether Marcus set the record straight now or not. He was past forgiving. The time for apologies had expired.

Jake turned his back on Marcus and opened the front door.

'There's something else,' Marcus said again.

Jake stepped outside and slammed the door shut. Whatever it was, he didn't want to know.

15

Jake marched down to his car, opened the boot, and flung his holdall inside. He slammed it shut, hard. Then he yelped and put his hands under his armpits, trying to dull the pain.

He leaned against the back of his car, waiting for the pain to subside, staring down the long street of terraced houses, identical to his own, some divided into small flats. He lived in a London borough where his neighbours were not much different from himself, with average jobs on average wages. There were some young couples who had just started out on the corporate ladder in the city. Jake knew, on their potential wages, it wouldn't be long before they'd be moving out, onwards and upwards to an upmarket area like Camden, or St. Johns Wood.

But Jake liked it just fine where he was. His neighbours, unaware of his family connections and who he had been in his past life, had befriended him not because they knew who he was, but just because they were friendly, amiable people.

'Why do most people equate a better life with having a bigger house, a better car, more of everything?' he remembered remarking to Faye one day while chatting.

'Human nature, I guess,' Faye had answered. 'Doesn't

everybody want to better themselves? Doesn't everybody look up to people who live somewhere like a posh area of London, in a fancy house, and aspire to be like them?'

'Do you?' he had asked.

Faye had laughed at the question. 'Do you see me in one of those sorts of places on a teacher's pay? No amount of aspiration's going to get me a big, posh house, I can assure you.'

'I'll tell you something that might surprise you,' Jake had replied. 'It works the other way too.' In the past, he had sometimes stood at the window of his beautiful apartment in the building owned by the Rosses and had cast his gaze down at the average man in the street, wondering what it was like to earn an average wage; to work, really work, for the roof over his head. 'Sometimes I used to feel …' He had shaken his head, finding it hard to put into words.

'What – you used to feel what?' Faye had pressed him for an answer.

'I felt like my life …' Jake was thinking about his upbringing in London, with the best schools, a college education, whatever he wanted, regardless of cost – he had chosen America, Yale. 'It all came so easy. It wasn't right, somehow. It was like I was living somebody else's life.' *Marcus's life*, he had thought. If his parents hadn't died, and he'd been brought up by them, instead of by William Ross, his life would have turned out very differently.

'But you're training to teach now. Something must have happened that caused you to change direction?'

'Don't you read the papers?' he remembered barking at her. He knew that was unfair. Of course she had. Everyone who interviewed him for the position must have known about his background. But her question suggested she hadn't just gone on the assumption that the loss of his wife was what had taken him there. However, despite that, she had hit a nerve, and it was a raw one; had he used the circumstances to get out of a life he wasn't sure he wanted? Was he that heartless and that gutless that it had taken a tragedy of such magnitude to propel him into starting over? Why hadn't he made the leap earlier?

Jake had been honest enough to admit the truth to Faye. 'I needed a place to go, away from everything that reminded me of her.'

'Some people would have taken a holiday,' she had remarked.

'I did,' Jake had said.

And he had made it permanent – or so he had thought. Jake looked over at his house, picturing Marcus inside; his old life kept seeping back in, first through the back door and now the front.

Jake got in his car. He was ready for his holiday.

He started the engine and gingerly took the steering wheel, Fortunately, he had power steering, and the car was an automatic, so there was no gear-stick to handle, otherwise he could forget about driving with bandaged hands. It did occur to him that this might be illegal. Would he be pulled over if he was spotted driving with his hands like this? Jake dismissed that idea. He did not want to wait around for a taxi, especially as Marcus was still there. He might insist on accompanying him to the airport. Jake had a scary thought – Marcus joining him on the flight.

Jake relaxed, reminding himself that Marcus wasn't going anywhere – he had a business to run. Jake, on the other hand, had several weeks off to do as he please. 'I'd rather be at work,' he said glumly to himself.

He took one long look back at his house before moving off from the kerb. Jake had left a door key on the hallway table by the phone and hoped that when Marcus left, he would have the presence of mind to lock up. There were no concierge services there to check the doors were secure at night.

At the end of the street, Jake took a left turn into a similar street with nearly identical houses. He approached the T-junction at the end, which led out to the main road and eventually the motorway. The traffic light was red. He slowed to a stop.

He sat there, thinking about Marcus turning up in his newly painted front room. The light turned green. He sat there, thinking some more. Thinking about Marcus overdosing in his newly painted front room. A car horn sounded behind him. He didn't move; stranded in indecision. Cars manoeuvred around Jake's stationary vehicle until the traffic light changed from green to red.

When it was green again, Jake slowly turned left and circled the block, bringing his car to a stop behind the black Saab.

Marcus was sitting on his front step.

Jake got out of the car, walked up the narrow pathway, and stood in front of Marcus.

Marcus looked up, raising his hand to shield the sun from his eyes. 'That was a short holiday.'

Jake had the impulse to hit him for being a smartarse, and for his smug self-assurance that Jake would feel compelled to come back.

Jake sat down on the front step beside Marcus. He stared at the pathway. There were weeds sprouting up through the cracks. He plucked at the one nearest his foot and seriously began to re-consider his plan to go to Scotland. He would be quite happy, more than happy, to hang around the house. He looked at the weeds; he had things to do.

'Where are you going on holiday?'

'Does it really matter?' Jake sighed and pulled on the weed. The tough little thing was staying put.

'Yes, it does. You need to give me some idea of what you've got planned. You see, I'm coming with you.'

The weed was forgotten in an instant. 'Are you nuts?' Jake stood up so fast that he nearly lost his balance. 'You've got a fiancée! Aren't you planning a wedding?' He was conscious of the fact that he was making a scene; somewhere in the street he heard the sound of a window slamming shut. He'd probably interrupted someone working from home.

Jake realised his mistake. He shouldn't have turned the car around and returned. 'And … and you can't just up sticks and leave the company without a word of warning.'

'Why not? You did,' Marcus pointed out.

Jake glared at him. Was this a wind-up? If it was, Marcus was doing a bloody good job of it. He knew the score. Jake's house, phone and physical presence were effectively out of bounds to Marcus. Jake wanted him to stay well away. If it were practicable, Jake would have slapped Marcus with a restraining order to keep him out of his sight. He was not welcome in Jake's life, and he knew it.

Trying desperately to keep his cool, Jake asked once more what Marcus was doing at his house. 'What do you actually want?'

'I knew you'd come back. I need a holiday, and …'

'You *are* serious,' Jake seethed. He'd gone back because he'd thought that maybe, just maybe, Marcus did have something important to tell him. And for another reason – Marcus's behaviour was so erratic that he wondered what he might do if left alone. If he'd known Marcus had just been just kidding around …

'What on earth makes you think I would want to go on holiday with you, of all people? I don't want you anywhere near me.'

Marcus's face was still beaming, as though Jake had just finalised their holiday plans and everything was tickety-boo. Jake stared at him in disbelief. That was it, the drugs had done their work; Marcus had finally flipped.

Jake stormed off in the direction of his car. Then something occurred to him; something almost as objectionable as Marcus's ill-conceived holiday plans. He stormed back.

'Am I being babysat – is that why you're here? Because William told you to come? If that's the case, then you can tell William there is nothing wrong with me. I am perfectly capable of taking a holiday and, if he insists, I'll gladly have Aubrey or anyone else along for the ride. But,' Jake bent double and leaned down into Marcus's beaming face, 'not you.'

Jake stared into the dark eyes of the man he'd thought he knew so well and yet to his cost had discovered otherwise. It had inevitably raised the question: how much could you really know about a person?

Jake lingered a moment longer. Marcus was not going to atone for what he had done, for what he had caused – the loss of Eleanor. Not today, and perhaps, Jake had to acknowledge, not ever.

Jake left him sitting on the step and went up to his front door to double-check everything was locked and secure – it wasn't. He locked the door. This time he was leaving. His mind was made up. He was going on holiday, if for no other reason than to put some distance between himself and Marcus. Either that, or he was about to do something that they'd both seriously regret – Marcus the most, because he was in for a punch in the face.

Jake kept his cool.

'Good. That's settled then.' Marcus got to his feet. 'My bag is already packed and, in the boot. Your car or mine?' He motioned at his shiny black Saab. 'Mine would be better, don't you think?'

Jake ignored him and walked to his car. In the driver's seat, he turned the key and let the engine idly turn over while he watched Marcus open the boot of his Saab, lift out a suitcase, and close it.

He selected reverse gear as Marcus turned and started to walk towards the car.

Jake slowly shook his head. What did Marcus think he was doing? The man was completely insane. Jake started to back up – fast.

Marcus came to a halt, realising the pursuit was futile.

Jake stopped the car and selected *Drive.*

He imagined taking care of one more thing before he left on his holiday. He imagined flooring the accelerator and driving right at Marcus before he had a chance to react, before he had any idea what was about to happen. He was like a sitting duck.

Smack.

Jake slowly shook his head. He couldn't believe the idea of driving his car at Marcus had even crossed his mind. Jake moved away from the kerb, taking it slowly, turning the steering wheel to give Marcus a wide berth in case he was tempted to suddenly give in to his imagination.

Once he had passed Marcus, he accelerated.

He glanced in his rear-view mirror. The boot of Marcus's car was open again. Jake was certain that by the time Marcus got into his car and reached the first junction, he would be long gone.

Jake smiled to himself as he headed in the direction of the motorway once again, heading for the airport. Marcus wasn't aware he was going to the airport. He could be going anywhere; perhaps somewhere in this country that didn't involve a flight.

Even so, Jake didn't want to chance being followed. He had a plan.

He glanced in his rear-view mirror again. His one consolation was that Marcus liked expensive, foreign-made cars. The black Saab would be relatively easy to spot amongst the many SUVs on the motorway. And if, by chance, Marcus made a lucky guess and headed straight for the airport, he had no way of knowing the flight number. And without the correct boarding pass, he had no way of discovering Jake sitting in the departure lounge in London City Airport, which is exactly where he intended to be the next day.

Jake relaxed as the airport sign came into view. He took the exit, just in case Marcus was following him. But he'd already decided he was not staying at the airport hotel after all. He took the slip road to rejoin the motorway. It wasn't long before he exited the motorway, taking a familiar route he'd driven many, many times before to a place where he was going to stay the night before his flight tomorrow. Marcus would never, ever guess where Jake was about to go.

Jake checked his rear-view mirror one last time and grinned. Marcus's black Saab was nowhere to be seen.

16

The doorman was preoccupied, his attention diverted to the street, where he was deep in conversation with an old lady walking a small dog. Jake walked straight past him and opened the glass door.

'Sir! Excuse me. Sir!' The doorman had spotted him.

Jake kept walking.

'Excuse me, sir. You can't go in there.' The doorman followed him inside.

The concierge jumped up from behind his desk in the foyer as Jake strode past, his voice joining in the protest. 'Sir! Can I help you?'

At the lift door, Jake pressed the button. The concierge, who was standing right behind him, was rather unhelpfully telling him where he could find the nearest hotel. If Jake had wanted a hotel, he would have gone to one.

Jake turned around to face his detractors.

There was a moment's stunned silence as the doorman and concierge recognised him.

Harry the doorman spoke first. 'Mr Campbell-Ross! Good to see you.'

Jake knew what he was thinking: *Mr Campbell-Ross – I'm*

surprised to see you. It was written all over his face.

'Sorry,' the concierge said, 'I thought …'

Jake knew what he'd thought; a guy dressed in casual clothes carrying a travel bag had walked into the building, mistaking it for a hotel. It happened all the time.

'If there's anything you need – anything at all,' the concierge said unnecessarily before resuming his post behind the desk.

Harry lingered; he obviously had something on his mind. 'I was so sorry to hear—'

'How's the family, Harry?' Jake cut him off mid-condolence.

'Fine, fine.' He nodded his head. 'Linda's having our fifth – any day now.' A smile lit up his face.

Jake stared at him for a long moment. Anyone casually listening in on that piece of news might have wondered, quite rightly, how a doorman could afford to bring up five children in the capital. But all Ross employees, even if they stood and opened a door all day, were remunerated more than generously, most notably in the form of shares. Anyone fortunate enough to hold stock in the Ross Corporation could afford five kids.

'Congratulations,' Jake managed. He wished he hadn't asked. He envied the lucky few whose lives appeared to flow with uninterrupted ease.

'Our eldest has just started university. She'll be the first person on either side of the family to get a degree,' he said proudly. 'We bought her a car as a going-away present.'

Jake was guessing those shares had come in handy.

'I know what you're thinking – there's quite a gap between the first and the fifth.'

Really, Jake had been thinking no such thing. He was trying his best not to think about Harry's lovely family.

'Let's just say the wife didn't think she could have any more, so our little one is quite the surprise.' Harry beamed.

The lift arrived, and not before time; Jake really didn't want to hear any more details of Harry the doorman's enviable family life.

The lift door opened, revealing a fresh-faced porter who looked him up and down in bewilderment. Jake would be the first to admit he did not look like the typical Ross employee. It wasn't just his casual clothes, but the unkempt look that went with them; the shirt hanging out of his jeans, the two days' worth of stubble. He imagined the bandaged hands weren't exactly helping.

It was no wonder Harry had hung around outside the lift to make the introductions. Who would have believed they were looking at one of the board of directors of the Ross Corporation, even though said director had taken a permanent sabbatical. William Ross had not, and never would, accept Jake's resignation – a fact that Jake had not shared when he'd applied for the Initial Teacher Training position, or at his interview. He did not want anyone thinking he was not committed to his new career and was keeping his options open to return to the Ross Corporation. He might be spending one night in the apartment, but that in no way meant he might come back. He wanted to keep his stay there quiet.

'Derrick, you take Mr Campbell-Ross straight up to the forty-ninth floor,' said Harry by way of introduction.

Derrick turned his attention on Harry with a look on his face that suggested he thought it was a practical joke. In the short time Derrick had been working for the company, he'd never been beyond the forty-eighth floor, and he had never set eyes on any one of the three heads of the corporation – until today.

'Derrick, have you forgotten your training? Offer Mr Campbell-Ross some help with his bag,' Harry prompted.

Derrick tentatively reached for the bag.

Jake did not object. He'd carried the bag three blocks, opting to park the car in a side-street close by and walk, in order to arrive as discreetly as possible and increase his chances of going unnoticed as he passed in and out of the building. If he had been wearing a suit, this might have worked, but that was beside the point, because he had reckoned without the new porter, who most certainly would not have taken him up to his floor without some kind of authority from the front desk.

Jake sighed as he followed the young man into the lift; he'd really thought this was going to be a lot less hassle than booking into a hotel. It was not. Derrick placed his bag on the floor just as five Ross employees returning from work joined them in the lift. None of them recognised Jake; they all took a very long look at him and his bag before facing the front. Jake imagined they were asking themselves the same silent question: *what is this guy doing in this building, in this lift?* And worse still, when each one got out at their floor, each one glanced back with the same silent question: *why is this guy going up to a floor above us?* Jake knew that it would baffle the hell out of them and provide an interesting topic of conversation, especially when they found out exactly who he was. Jake glanced at Derrick and realised he was going to be questioned in the morning.

On the way up, Jake became conscious of an overpowering feeling of rising panic caused by being stuck in the confined space. As the lift emptied, his panic subsided, but only a little; he knew he had to get out. He didn't remember the lift taking this long to reach his floor.

'Derrick,' said Jake, deciding to attempt some conversation in the hope of relieving some of the anxiety as the lift tirelessly stopped at each empty floor. 'Tell me about yourself.'

Now Derrick was the one looking panic-stricken. His eyes darted about the lift as though he were suddenly looking for an escape route; an escape from unexpectedly being put on the spot. Finally, resigned to answering the question, he looked Jake in the eye and in a self-assured tone said, 'I'm seventeen years old and I'm very ambitious. I'm going to night school and intend …'

'No,' Jake said sternly. 'I don't want to hear about that.'

He registered the shock on Derrick's face, but he didn't want to listen to his resumé or some rehearsed spiel about his intended career path of rising through the ranks of the company. He didn't want Derrick to try to impress him. He already knew, anyway. The very fact that Derrick was there said it all; he had beaten the competition at the tender age of seventeen years old to get a coveted job at the Ross Corporation. William always met prospective job applicants, no matter the position they were applying for, so Jake knew William had seen potential in Derrick.

Jake had no doubt that graduates, even postgraduates, would have applied for this position, because everyone knew that once you had your foot in the door – or in Derrick's case, the lift – as long as you had the drive, the ambition, then the job could lead to the top. Everyone was in for a chance to progress. The sky really was the limit.

William often said, *It doesn't matter where you come from; all that matters is where you're going.* Jake wholeheartedly believed in that. He himself was a case in point. It didn't matter that he'd been a corporate lawyer on the board of a multinational company; what mattered was that he'd found his calling teaching kids, some from quite deprived backgrounds, in an inner-city school. Like William, Jake wanted to nurture their potential, so that hopefully one day they might be in Derrick's shoes, or wherever their dreams took them. Jake had found his dream job. He just wished that re-evaluating his life hadn't come about because of what had happened to Eleanor.

Jake really didn't want to dwell on that. He eyed Derrick and thought of William. He might have an old-fashioned approach to running a modern corporation, but William understood his employees. He knew that they wanted security, a job for life, because deep down, all anybody really wanted was to belong. William took great pride in looking after those who belonged to the Ross Corporation family. Furthermore, William believed a university degree alone was a poor relation to a work ethic and dedication to the company, regardless of the role.

It was obvious that Derrick had the determination to succeed, but behind that determination was a reason. Jake wanted to know the reason.

'Derrick, tell me about your family.'

Derrick's was an all-too-common story. His father had bailed when he was twelve years old, leaving his mother to raise three children alone. Childcare costs had made a return to work prohibitive, but she'd had little alternative – they had needed the money. Besides, Derrick's mother had told him she wasn't going to set a bad example to her sons and live on state handouts. So, she had returned to nursing and had left Derrick – the eldest – to look after his two younger siblings – to feed, bathe and put them to bed every night after school, at weekends and on school holidays. For Derrick, adult responsibilities had come early. But this had turned out to have an unforeseen positive side-effect that told a less familiar story – it had kept him off the streets. It had kept him away from the gangs, and it may well have saved his life.

His best friend and just recently his cousin had not been so fortunate. Whether it was a knife or a gun, Derrick wouldn't elaborate; the hurt was still new, still raw. And as always, the gangs had their eyes on new recruits – even those as young as his twelve-year-old brother, Joseph. And therein Jake found the reason behind Derrick's motivation to succeed. He wanted to get his family out of the estate; he wanted to get his brothers away from the gangs. He knew that time was not on Joseph's side, but Matthew, the youngest, was just seven years old. There was still time. But he had to work hard, and he had to work fast.

The lift stopped on the forty-ninth floor. Both passengers stood in a moment's subdued silence.

Jake picked up his bag as the lift door opened.

'Mr Campbell-Ross,' Derrick turned to face him with a look of innocent sincerity. 'I want to thank you for giving me this opportunity.'

Jake stared at this kid, who came from one of the most deprived estates in East London and was starting out with the sort of disadvantages Jake could only imagine – a kid who might one day not make it into work because of a stray bullet, or a random, unprovoked knife attack, or just because he looked at someone the wrong way, or someone held a grudge because he wouldn't join a gang and worked for a living instead. Despite all that, somebody in the company had recognised his potential, and had given him the break he deserved.

'You know what,' said Jake. 'I want to shake your hand.' He felt like the boy deserved a medal.

Derrick looked positively stunned. He tentatively reached for Jake's bandaged hand.

Jake gave him a strong handshake, ignoring his protesting

hand. 'What are you studying at night school?'

Derrick didn't hesitate. 'Law,' he said. 'I want to be a corporate lawyer.'

'That's a good choice, Derrick. The board likes its members to come from a legal background.'

He could tell this was news to Derrick – very good news. The boy was obviously aiming for the top. And Jake wished him every success; he deserved it. If he'd known how many graduates had applied for the position he held, he would not be thanking Jake but congratulating himself, as he should be.

'Derrick, there's something I want you to do for me,' said Jake before vacating the lift. Jake wanted to see Derrick first thing in the morning. He expected Derrick on the forty-ninth floor at nine o'clock prompt. 'I've got something I want to give you before I leave.'

The lift door closed on a bemused seventeen-year-old who would have to wait a full twelve hours to find out what Mr Campbell-Ross, who sat on the board of directors, had to give to a porter.

17

Jake took his bag and vacated the lift, refusing Derrick's offer to carry the bag to his door. But the instant he saw the door to his apartment, the door he had not walked through in almost six months, he regretted his decision to stay there. He turned back to the lift, intending to leave, but the door was already closed, the lift gone.

He realised that he should have stayed overnight at an airport hotel, but Marcus was on his mind, along with the possibility, however remote, that he might have followed him to the airport. It was a ridiculous thought that Marcus might knock on his hotel room door, but Jake just didn't want to risk it.

Booking a hotel in London at the last minute had just seemed too much effort. He was exhausted. This had seemed the easiest option – until now. The only thing keeping his finger from the lift button was the thought of Derrick and what he intended to do in the morning before he left. And besides, he had to get things in perspective; there were certainly worse places he could be spending the night.

An unexpected pang of guilt struck Jake for leaving Marcus behind. It was not helped by the fact that quite inexplicably, and despite everything, a miniscule part of him wished Marcus was there with him. Just then, Jake didn't relish the idea of spending the night in the apartment alone.

Jake opened his wallet to take out the small electronic key card. Why he had kept it all this time, he didn't know. He didn't think he'd use the apartment again.

As Jake slipped the electronic card out of his wallet, another piece of paper came out with it and floated to the floor. Jake bent down and picked it up. He stared at the eight-digit number on the dog-eared, plain white card; a number he knew off by heart. It was Aubrey's phone number. Although Jake had no choice but to spend the night in the apartment alone, the little card had reminded him that at least there was somebody he could talk to. Or could he?

Jake had thought that Aubrey would be sympathetic, would show some understanding for what he was going through and his reasons for leaving the company. But it seemed not. Jake had to accept the fact that Aubrey's loyalty was to William first and foremost. Jake was hugely disappointed to learn that because of his decision to leave the company, he appeared to have lost his mentor and friend. That was an unexpected blow that Jake had not foreseen. Aubrey hadn't been in contact with him these last few months. That wasn't like him. They had always chatted often. The first he'd seen of him was when Aubrey had turned up at his house unexpectedly after he'd cut his hands. But then Jake realised he hadn't exactly gone out of his way to stay in contact either.

He tucked the small white card back into his wallet. Even though he desperately missed Aubrey, he knew it was probably best he didn't phone him, didn't tell him where he was at this very moment – it might just give him completely the wrong idea.

Jake swiped the plastic key card through the lock and the door clicked open. The apartment was spotless, and there were even fresh flowers in the vase on the sideboard. Jake stood motionless in the hall. He had mixed emotions about being there; on the one hand, it felt like he could almost be returning from a day's work at the office, but on the other hand, it felt like he'd just stepped into a stranger's apartment. The life that he had led there, with Eleanor, seemed but a distant memory.

Besides the cleaners, nobody had probably stepped into this apartment since he had closed the door on Christmas Eve. His apartment, like his job at the Ross Corporation, was still vacant, still waiting for his return.

'Well, it's going to be a long wait,' said Jake to the empty hallway.

Jake chose the bedroom furthest from the one he and Eleanor had shared. The room felt as impersonal as a hotel – almost. As he drifted off to sleep, he thought about his journey the next day to see Arnold Wright. He was catching the flight at twenty past one in the afternoon, which gave him plenty of time to get to the airport, have a bite to eat, and wait in the departure lounge. His car was parked outside, ready to roll in the morning. It occurred to him that he could ask Harry to organise a taxi so that he wouldn't even have the hassle of airport parking.

He knew he should be feeling relaxed, he should be feeling calm, he should be looking forward to a trip away.

He slept badly.

At some point in the early hours, Jake had resigned himself to the fact that he would not be sleeping that night, so he had hauled himself out of bed and made his way to the lounge, where he had found a bottle of scotch.

He woke late, on the sofa, a feeling of uneasiness in the pit of his stomach. He didn't remember getting out of bed. There was blood on the sofa. Jake looked at the blood stain, then at his hands. The bandages were pink, and his hands felt raw.

Jake sat up from the sofa and accidentally kicked over the bottle, which was now empty. He watched it roll under the coffee table, wondering what it was doing down there. Then he remembered the previous night. He groaned. This was not a good start to his holiday. He had a motorway drive ahead of him to the airport, and he was probably still over the limit. He realised that driving there himself was out of the question.

He stood up, very slowly this time, and took a good look at the sofa. There were smears of blood all over the place, suggesting he must have been thrashing about in the night. He made a mental note to ask the concierge to dispose of the sofa and replace it with a brand new one. First, though, he had to find the first aid kit.

18

Jake shut the door to the apartment, deciding he'd rather wait outside for Derrick to arrive at nine. When Jake turned around, Derrick was already there, waiting by the lift, a look of expectation etched on his tired features. *Somebody else has had a sleepless night,* thought Jake. Derrick's eyes roved to Jake's bag. He walked over and reached down for it.

'Not just yet.' Jake said. 'Come here.'

Derrick gingerly stepped forward.

'I want you to take this.' Jake handed Derrick the plastic key card. 'Let me show you how this works. Just slip it in there, like so.' Jake watched Derrick. 'That's right – straight down until the little light flashes red to green, see it?'

Derrick nodded.

Jake opened the door to the apartment and walked in.

Derrick stayed where he was, looking down at Jake's bag, obviously wondering what he'd forgotten to pack.

'Come inside, Derrick. I've got something to show you.' Jake led the way.

Derrick, hesitant at first, stepped inside as instructed. Jake took Derrick on a tour of the apartment.

❖

Derrick followed Jake in stunned silence; stunned because every Ross employee in the building wanted to know what it was like up there in *Ross Heaven.* It was what they called the apartments on the top two floors. Derrick – to his utter amazement – was the only employee, apart from the staff of the contracted cleaning company, to see it for himself. Not only that, but he was being shown around by Mr Campbell-Ross himself.

Partway through the tour, when Derrick had stopped to linger in one of the stupendously extravagant marble bathrooms. He wondered if the taps were gold-plated. Then he wondered if the rumours about Jake Campbell-Ross were true; maybe he was having some kind of breakdown. What other reason would there be for leaving all this to teach in an inner-city school like the one Derrick had attended himself? Not to mention what he was doing now – showing a porter around his apartment.

However, Derrick could see that Mr Campbell-Ross knew exactly what he was doing; he was showing him what he had a chance to achieve through hard work and dedication. He'd read about Mr Campbell-Ross. He'd been through his share of hard times as a child, losing both his parents, but he'd fallen on his feet; he'd been taken under the wing of William Ross. However, Derrick also knew that William Ross did not believe in nepotism. Neither Jake nor Marcus would have made it to these two much-coveted apartments on this floor, just below the CEO's, if they hadn't worked incredibly hard to make it. *One day, this is going to be mine*, thought Derrick.

Suddenly aware that he had lingered too long, Derrick called out, 'Mr Campbell-Ross?' and quickly left the bathroom. He found himself in a L-shaped corridor, with Mr Campbell-Ross nowhere to be found. Tentatively, Derrick opened doors. 'Mr Campbell-Ross?' he called into rooms he had not yet seen. There was a library that was like something out of a movie, with three walls stacked floor-to-ceiling with books, and a games room with a full-size snooker table, which made him think of his brother's fold-down toy snooker table, which he'd got for Christmas the previous year. It made him wish his brothers were there too. They'd never believe him when he went home after work and told them what he'd seen.

Derrick failed to find Mr Campbell-Ross behind yet another door, but he did find a second sitting room with a humungous plasma television screen on the wall. Derrick whistled before closing the door.

'Mr Campbell-Ross?' Derrick said to the empty corridor. There were still other doors he had not yet opened, other rooms to explore, but perhaps the tour was over, and Mr Campbell-Ross wanted to leave now. With that thought in mind, Derrick raced to the front door of the apartment, praying he had not made a huge mistake and outstayed his welcome.

Mr Campbell-Ross was standing in the lift, his bag on the floor by his feet.

Shit! Shit! Shit!

Derrick shut the apartment door with a single thought twisting up his insides – he'd blown it. A porter didn't keep one of the directors of the Ross Corporation waiting, even if that director had taken a sabbatical after losing his wife. He'd be back, of that Derrick had no doubt. He cast one last glance back at the apartment. How could he not when he'd be returning to that?

Derrick joined Mr Campbell-Ross in the lift and held out his hand to give him back the plastic key card, praying he was not going to lose his job for outstaying his welcome. He didn't really believe that would happen. If there was one thing he'd learnt while working for the Rosses, it was that despite their immense wealth, they were the kindest, most decent, most loyal people he'd met – besides his own mum. He sincerely hoped he'd be working for them for years and years to come.

Jake did not make an immediate move to take the card.

This is bad, thought Derrick. *This is really bad.* He'd thought the Rosses were nice, compassionate people. Derrick stared at Jake. He didn't want to beg, but he'd have to. *I can't lose this job, I just can't.* The rent on his mum's tiny two-bed flat, in which he shared one of the bedrooms with his brothers, was now extortionate. But they couldn't afford to move somewhere else; they could barely afford where they were. If he lost his job …

❖

Jake could tell by the look on his face that Derrick thought he was in trouble. He wasn't. Jake had started showing Derrick around the apartment, and suddenly it had all become too much; an overpowering sense of grief, of loss, had engulfed Jake. He'd had to get out of there – fast. So, he had walked out of the apartment, leaving Derrick to have a look around for himself.

Derrick made another attempt to hand Jake the plastic key card, but Jake resolutely kept his arms folded. 'I want you to keep it.'

Derrick looked at the card, not expecting to get to keep a souvenir of his tour. Maybe he wasn't in as much trouble as he thought.

'Did you like the apartment?' said Jake, pressing the button to close the lift door because Derrick was too preoccupied with the card in his hand. Derrick had never heard such a stupid question in his life, but of course he wasn't going to say anything of the kind to Mr Campbell-Ross. 'It was … it was …' Derrick was having a problem putting it exactly into words.

Jake understood. He pressed the *G* button, and the lift started down. 'Well, I'm glad you like it – it's yours.'

Derrick looked down at the card in his hand. He had been right all along. By showing him the apartment, Mr Campbell-Ross had been showing him exactly what was possible for Derrick to achieve if he worked his socks off for the Ross Corporation.

'Thank you, Mr Campbell-Ross. I'm going to work very hard and someday I just know I'm going to use this card for real.'

'Not someday, Derrick,' said Jake, watching the floors countdown. 'Today – it's yours today.'

It took a few seconds for Derrick to grasp what Mr Campbell-Ross had just said. When he did, he gaped at Jake and said, 'You're shitting me.'

'I shit you not,' said Jake, amused by Derrick's choice of words.

Derrick shook his head.

'You don't want it?' Jake said, surprised.

Derrick sighed heavily. 'Look, I am so sorry about your wife, I really am. I get it, I do.' His gaze drifted to Jake's hands, wondering what had happened to them. Whatever had gone down, the only conclusion Derrick could draw was that Mr Campbell-Ross was having a breakdown.

Jake followed his gaze, and looked at his bandaged hands. 'I'm not having some sort of crisis, or breakdown, if that's what you're thinking, Derrick.'

Derrick looked anywhere but at Jake.

'The apartment is yours, Derrick. I spoke with a lawyer I know in the company. It's *my* apartment.'

Derrick didn't understand. 'But I thought you have to rise through the ranks of the company, and that's how you move up the floors until you get here, and then …' he raised his eyes, thinking about Mr William Ross's apartment on the very top floor. Rumour had it that he'd never lived there, might not have even stepped foot in the place. That didn't surprise Derrick. He had a beautiful house in London.

'That is very true, Derrick.' Jake had been very pleased the previous night to realise that because William had not accepted his resignation, and effectively he still had his position; he had the power to change just what he needed in order to give his future successor, and his family, a very big break right now. And why not? William had taken him in when he'd needed it. Jake was doing the same for this boy. Of course, he wouldn't be treating him as family, but in effect the Ross Corporation was. This was his home now. This was exactly where he belonged.

'I contacted the person responsible in the company and put the lease in your name. The only caveat for you to remain here is that you continue working for the company, and work your way up to take over my position someday.' Jake put a hand on his shoulder. 'I know you can do it. William knows too. That's why I spoke with him last night, and he agreed to my unusual request.' Jake could tell by the resignation in William's voice that he had finally realised that Jake wasn't coming back.

'I know you don't need this apartment to motivate you to work your way up. You have your family for that. But why can't you have some of those future rewards right now, for you and your family?' Jake continued, 'I know this is most unusual. I apologise for springing it on you like this, but I'm going on holiday today, so I had to arrange it all while I was here.' Jake smiled. 'So, what do you say?'

Derrick didn't say anything. He looked as though he was about to pass out. He didn't. Instead, he began to cry.

It wasn't quite the reaction Jake had expected. But on the other hand, maybe it *was* to be expected. Jake had discovered, during his phone conversations with the lawyer the previous night, that Derrick had attended an interview for a junior position. Derrick didn't know it yet – an official letter was winging its way by post to him, and he'd receive it any day now – but Jake had found out he'd floored the competition at interview. It meant that after just six months, Derrick would be hanging up his porter's uniform and putting on a suit to start as a junior at the city offices of the company.

It would mean a huge change for Derrick in many ways, not least because he would be stepping on to the first rung of the executive ladder. And it was going to have an impact on Derrick's living arrangements.

In one month's time, Derrick would be allocated one of the flats on the ground floor, consisting of a single room with fold-down bed, kitchenette and lounge area, all in one cramped space. They were designed for the juniors such as himself who were single.

It would take several years, and several promotions, for Derrick to work up to a higher floor with a reasonable-sized apartment that could accommodate Derrick *and* his family. Jake had an idea that Derrick was acutely aware that if he was successful an interview, he would be offered starter accommodation in the building. But Derrick would not be looking forward to leaving his family behind.

Jake knew that it was more than likely that in one month's time Derrick would not take up the allocated flat. It wouldn't bother the company; it was his choice. But for Derrick, the work, the studying at night school, the commute from East London, even his safety – walking in and out of his estate wearing a suit – would not bode well for his future. He also guessed that, despite all that, Derrick was about to do the unthinkable.

'I can't accept this,' Derrick said suddenly, thrusting the card back at Jake.

Jake understood. Derrick had his pride. Pride in what he had achieved so far, pride in the fact that he was working hard to provide a good future for himself and his family. Like his mother, Derrick would not accept handouts. 'I don't deserve it. What will people think?'

Jake had anticipated this reaction. 'People will think: *what has Mr Campbell-Ross seen in Derrick that is so special?*'

Derrick stared long and hard at Mr Campbell-Ross.

'Prove me right, Derrick. Think of it as a new kind of incentive scheme; now you've got it – you want to keep it?'

Derrick looked at the card, looked at Jake, and then thrust the key card in his pocket. He looked Jake in the eye. 'You bet I do,' he said with a self-assurance way beyond his years.

Jake smiled. 'I'll be watching with interest to see how long it takes you to make the move upstairs,' said Jake referring to that very top apartment and the position as the head of the Ross Corporation. He wasn't joking.

Jake was well aware that he could have arranged another apartment on a lower floor. It wouldn't be as spacious, but Derrick's family would have managed well enough. At any one time, there were always several vacant apartments as people moved to postings abroad and others returned. Some employees, for personal reasons, did not want to live in the building at all.

Jake knew of one such person, of one such apartment, and he most definitely thought it might be taking it a bit too far to give Derrick that one. William's apartment, the massive sprawling apartment on the very top floor, had been vacant since the building was built. Grace had wanted to remain living in her London home. He'd heard that she'd told William, *an apartment is far too vulgar, darling.*

William, who had never spent a single night of his marriage apart from his wife, had had little choice but to accept that they would not be moving in. William had hoped that in time she would change her mind, but she never had. That left Marcus, who was currently the de-facto head of the corporation.

Jake knew that Marcus could move upstairs, but that wasn't going to happen either. William would not allow it in the current circumstances; not with the rumours swirling around about Marcus and his late-night escapades – rumours that Jake imagined the family, and the company, were hoping they could keep quiet. A company was built on its reputation. As a stock-market listed company, confidence and market sentiment – good or bad – could send share values soaring or plummeting. With William apparently still at the helm, that confidence was still steadfast. If Marcus were to move into the top position and the top floor, there was no telling where things might lead – and everyone on the board knew it.

Jake had no doubt that the apartment on the fiftieth floor would remain empty for many more years to come; perhaps until William and Marcus had both stepped down, and a new successor had been found.

Jake eyed Derrick. It was unthinkable today, the Ross Corporation not being run by a family member, but over time, things would change. Over time, it was possible that the Ross Corporation would go the way of other monolithic companies, where not a single descendant of the original founder worked in the business.

The lift door opened in the foyer on the ground floor.

Before leaving the lift, Jake watched Derrick wiping his eyes dry with his sleeve. If Derrick's two brothers were so inclined, perhaps in the future the three brothers would be occupying those three apartments on the top two floors. Jake smiled at the thought.

19

Jake took Derrick to the front desk.

The concierge stood up and wished Jake a good morning. Then his eyes roved to Derrick, registering his tear-streaked face.

'Derrick – what have you done?' The concierge turned back to Mr Campbell-Ross without even giving Derrick a chance to speak. 'Mr Campbell-Ross, I want to sincerely apologise for anything Derrick—'

Jake held up his hand and produced two envelopes from his jacket pocket, one for the concierge and the other to be handed to Aubrey on his immediate return. They both contained identical letters, which he had written that morning. They were letters of authority giving Derrick, his mother Joyce and his brothers Joseph and Matthew the right to reside in Apartment Two on the forty-ninth floor. The lease was now in Derrick's name. It was imperative that Aubrey was made aware of this.

As the concierge opened his letter, Jake's thoughts drifted back to the night before Christmas Eve, almost seven months earlier, when Aubrey had been helping an ex-employee to vacate his apartment. For some reason, the employee had been fired from his job at the Ross Corporation, which was most unusual. Jake didn't know the circumstances, and didn't ask. All he knew was that part of Aubrey's remit was to escort someone who could no longer reside in an apartment out of the building. In other words, kick them out.

Strangely, Jake remembered his name – Mr Beale. 'This one went quietly,' Jake recalled Aubrey saying. He wondered in passing what had happened to the man. The concierge confirmed that nobody had been 'helped' out of their apartment for some time, which was exactly what Jake would not want to hear had happened to Derrick in his absence. This was what made Aubrey receiving his letter so important.

Given the chance, Jake was sure Derrick would move heaven and earth to earn the right to be in Apartment Two on the forty-ninth floor. Jake would be watching the future of the Ross Corporation with interest, and the future of Derrick in particular, as he had a strong feeling that the future success of Derrick and the company would become inextricably linked.

'Bloody hell!' The concierge had finished reading his letter. His eyes darted to Derrick, a look of disbelief fixed on his craggy features.

Although Jake had left an identical letter for Aubrey, he said, 'Please tell Aubrey Jones the news, the next time you see him.'

'That I will, Mr Campbell-Ross.'

Jake anticipated that when word spread of the new occupant on the forty-ninth floor, there would be a lot more confusion, perhaps envy, certainly anger. Jake expected that Derrick, taking up his new junior post, would not have an easy time of it at the offices of the Ross Corporation; his peers would resent him, his superiors would distrust him, and Derrick's workload would most probably double or triple as a result.

It wasn't going to be a walk in the park, that was for sure. Jake imagined that some of Derrick's peers would be waiting for him to fall flat on his face. But Jake knew that Derrick wasn't afraid of hard work. Derrick wasn't afraid of an unkind word. Experience had taught him there were far scarier things out there in the real world to be afraid of if he failed. In the meantime, there wasn't anything anybody could do about Jake's decision to give Derrick the apartment.

Jake, along with Marcus and William, were majority shareholders in the company. He co-owned the building, and the apartment. That hadn't changed. He could do with it what he wanted – and he liked Derrick. Jake was well aware that he was disrupting the status-quo; he was turning things upside down. But the ship was already dangerously listing; no one was at the helm. Two of the three captains had already effectively jumped ship – Jake to the classroom, William to the golf course – and the third was killing himself slowly. At the rate Marcus was going, Jake doubted there would be any Marcus juniors in the future to take the helm, even if they wanted to.

He thought that it might surprise Ross employees to learn that if anybody could guarantee their futures, and the future of the company, it was a young man who had the greatest reason of all to keep his apartment, to keep the Ross Corporation afloat – his family. That was all that mattered; keeping them safe, keeping them alive. Jake could think of no greater motivator than that.

Over the years, the Ross Corporation had given Jake so much; it had guaranteed his future. He didn't want to just abandon ship without putting something back. But for the past few months, since he'd left, he had racked his brain for what that might be. Now the answer – the future of the company – was standing right beside him. On the spur of the moment, Jake decided to show Derrick one last thing before he left.

'Come with me, Derrick.' Jake returned to the lift, conscious of the fact that the concierge, still standing there open-mouthed, still holding Jake's letter, was watching their every move.

Jake shepherded Derrick towards a lift – not the one they'd taken, but a different lift reserved for the occupant of the fiftieth floor.

Jake imagined that it would surprise Derrick to learn that neither he nor Marcus had ever set foot in that top-floor apartment, or been all that curious to look. Not until now.

Jake glanced at Derrick, who was standing right beside him outside the lift. The look on his face said, *you have got to be shitting me,* except this time he was too surprised to utter a sound.

'I shit you not,' said Jake, a smile creasing his lips, before turning his attention to the keypad. The lift wouldn't open until he entered the keycode. Six empty boxes flashed on the small digital display. Since Jake never had occasion to use the lift, he had no idea what it was, but knowing William, it would have to be relatively easy to remember, and knowing William, it would have to be something connected with the family. He was guessing, but if it consisted of six digits, then a date of birth would be the logical answer.

The most obvious choice was his wife, Grace's, date of birth. Jake knew the day and month, but he wasn't entirely sure of the year. Several wrong attempts later suggested either he was getting the year wrong, or Grace's birthday was not the code. Several more increasingly ridiculous guesses pitching her age anywhere between thirty-five and one hundred and two confirmed the code was not related to Grace.

Jake swallowed hard and keyed the next most obvious choice – Eleanor. She had always been William's favourite. To Jake's surprise, the lift remained stubbornly stationary. The first born, that was probably it; Jake tried Marcus's date of birth next – still no dice. He was running out of options.

Finally, he keyed in William's date of birth; an absurd idea for a security code, and the least obvious choice, but what the hell – Jake keyed it in. Nothing happened. Jake was now stumped. He guessed neither of them would get to see that top-floor apartment.

Derrick, who had been watching Jake's attempts at cracking the code with interest, made a suggestion. 'Why not try your date of birth?'

Jake thought that his own date of birth was not the most obvious choice. But then, on the other hand, maybe as a security measure that was the point. Jake glanced at him and shrugged. 'Worth a try.' Jake keyed it in. To his complete surprise, the six-digit code was accepted and the light above the lift flicked on. Jake turned to Derrick, who was smiling from ear to ear.

'Well done you,' said Jake.

Jake pressed the illuminated button indicating an up arrow. As far as he was aware, the lift had not been used in years, decades even, and he was feeling some trepidation at the thought of getting into it. Perhaps he should have checked with the concierge to find out the last time it had been serviced. For security reasons, the lift remained on the fiftieth floor.

To Jake's amazement, something was happening; he could hear the peculiar ghostly twang and yawn of metal cables straining in the empty lift shaft on the other side of the door as the lift began its descent.

They waited.

Jake began to sweat. The thought of a lift, a confined space, was not good at the best of times, but one that had not been used in years was even worse. Jake suddenly hoped the lift died before it reached the ground floor.

It was not his lucky day; the lift door opened.

Jake and Derrick peered inside. He didn't know what they were expecting; a red carpet perhaps, the walls adorned with beautiful motifs or pictures, a seat even. But there was none of that. It was just an ordinary lift, identical in every way to the one Derrick rode up and down in all day.

Before they stepped inside, Jake felt it necessary to tell Derrick the truth about the apartment on the top floor; Derrick would have to be prepared for an apartment that although on a far grander scale, in all probability would appear quite neglected. They would be the first people to step inside for years – Jake doubted that even the cleaners had access.

'Ready?' said Jake.

The lift whisked them up to the top floor. The lift door opened onto a wide, expansive hallway. Derrick and Jake exchanged glances. The hallway was spotless. Jake shrugged – so he'd been wrong about the cleaners. They stepped out of the lift. At Jake's invitation, Derrick went off to explore.

Jake held back; something didn't feel right.

Based on the layout of his own apartment, Jake took the corridor to the left, down which he assumed, rightly, he'd find the living areas. Jake headed for the kitchen first. It turned out to be a twenty-foot-square monster of a room with monster appliances, solid oak units fronting three walls and a matching island in the centre of the room. Just like the hall, the room was spotless. Jake ran a finger along a section of the worktop to reveal not a speck of dust. He casually sauntered around the room until his attention was drawn to a shelf above the kitchen worktop containing a row of black tins – round and square – delicately patterned in red and gold Japanese designs. He came to a halt in front of them. He knew exactly what they were. He stared at them for some time in mounting disbelief. Finally, he reached out and randomly picked one off the shelf. He opened the lid just as Derrick came racing into the kitchen, skidding to a halt in front of Jake.

'Mr Campbell-Ross,' he gulped, 'I was looking for you everywhere.' He was out of breath. 'You need to come see.' He pointed. 'There are clothes in the bedroom cupboard.' He whispered, 'I think somebody lives here.'

Jake looked down at the open tin in his hands. He brought it to his nose and sniffed – tea.

'Derrick, we need to leave – now.'

The look on Derrick's face said he knew something was up. Derrick got to the lift ahead of Jake.

Jake did not follow him inside. 'Derrick, I want you to do something for me.'

Jake had an idea. He sent Derrick back to the ground floor, back to retrieve the letter from the concierge that he had written to Aubrey to inform him that he'd handed over his apartment to Derrick. 'And for goodness' sake, don't tell him what you'd discovered up here.' As far as everyone knew, nobody had stepped foot in that apartment, let alone lived there.

Jake didn't want anybody else finding out about his discovery – not just yet. He waited by the lift, thinking about the tea leaves he'd found in the tins. Aubrey was a tea connoisseur. It was that fact that had given him away. Jake found the nerve of the man quite simply astounding. This was William's apartment, the head of the company. How had Aubrey got away with it all this time? As far as all the other occupants of the building were concerned, Jake included, Aubrey was located somewhere on one of the forty-eight floors. Jake wouldn't know for sure which floor or which apartment because Jake had never actually seen it – until now. Why had that never struck him as odd?

The apartment being empty did not give Aubrey the right to live there instead. Unless … Jake was thinking about giving Derrick permission to live in the apartment below. Had William given his permission? It was possible – he and Aubrey went way back.

Jake got out his mobile phone. He wanted to speak to William and find out if he had given Aubrey permission to use the apartment in his absence. Jake caught sight of the clock on the wall in the kitchen just above the shelf with the tins of fancy tea. He had a flight to catch. He really didn't have time to get into it all just then. He put his mobile back in his pocket. It would have to wait.

He had the impulse to ring Aubrey's number – Aubrey's mobile phone was always switched on, whatever the hour. But until he knew the truth, that would have to wait too. Jake didn't want to blindly stumble into something he knew nothing about until he got his facts straight.

Jake stood by the lift, his eyes drifting to the adjacent door. Behind that door was a flight of stairs leading down to the forty-ninth floor. Jake knew about those stairs. They were there in case the lift failed. There were similar stairs down to each floor, as with any building, for fire safety reasons.

While he waited for Derrick's return, he thought about Aubrey riding up in Derrick's lift and exiting on the forty-ninth floor, supposedly to see Marcus – who in truth was hardly ever there. He must have then taken the flight of stairs up to this apartment, unbeknown to anybody else in the building.

If he'd taken the lift straight up to the fiftieth floor, the concierge might have noticed. Similarly, anybody using Derrick's lift, or Derrick himself, might have heard the other one moving up and down in the adjacent lift shaft. The fact that Derrick looked just as anxious as Jake felt when they had got into this lift suggested that in the time Derrick had worked there, he hadn't once heard or seen this lift being used.

Thinking about it now, it made perfect sense. In his role as a trouble-shooter for the company, dealing with some of the more unsavoury issues as they arose, Aubrey would undoubtedly have access to all areas of the building with impunity, including the top floor. For this reason, Aubrey could have easily taken it upon himself to live up there with or without William's permission.

Was Aubrey one of those people, full of his own self-importance, who had ideas above his station? Did Aubrey think that his close association with William over the years made him part of the success story of the Ross Corporation, even though William had founded and built the company from scratch and Aubrey was merely along for the ride?

Jake scratched his head. Until he spoke with William or Aubrey, he really had no clue.

The sound of a lift door on the floor below told Jake that Derrick would be back at any moment with the letter. As soon as the lift door opened, he handed it to Jake without setting foot outside the lift. Derrick looked anxious to leave.

Jake took the letter and placed it on the sideboard next to the phone. He hesitated. The idea was that by leaving the letter there,

Aubrey would realise that Jake was on to him – he now knew that Aubrey was living on the top floor. On the one hand, Jake thought what did it matter? He loved the guy dearly, and didn't really care whether he had William's permission or not. He bet William wouldn't really care either. Aubrey worked tirelessly for the Rosses, always had done. On the other hand ... he glanced at Derrick. Aubrey wasn't the head of the corporation, and he never would be. Unlike Derrick. Jake didn't know how long Aubrey had been living up there, but he didn't want Aubrey getting too comfortable ensconced on the top floor. Jake had it earmarked for his prodigy – the young man standing before him, who he had no doubt would make it to the top.

Jake decided to leave the letter there. Aubrey needed a reality check, and Jake had just given him one. This discovery was for the best. Perhaps it was time Aubrey found an apartment that suited his position.

Jake swore Derrick to secrecy. Derrick promised not to breathe a word of what he had seen. Ross employees would have enough to deal with when they found out about the new occupant of Jake's apartment without finding out that Aubrey was already ensconced on the top floor.

They reached the ground floor. Jake picked up his bag and held out his hand to Derrick. 'Good luck, Derrick.'

'When will I see you again?'

Jake smiled at Derrick and left him to finish the longest day at work he would ever experience. It would be seven long hours before he could tell his family the incredible news; they would be moving in as soon as possible.

Jake was just turning to go, when he had a thought. 'Oh, by the way, Derrick. I have some news for you.'

A few minutes later, Jake turned away from the lift, smiling. Derrick was whooping with joy outside the lift at the news that he had secured the new position within the company.

Jake saw the concierge throwing Derrick a look as Jake passed by the desk. Jake walked resolutely past the concierge, aiming to make a quick exit.

Harry the doorman proved more difficult to avoid. He had spotted Jake's approach; he was already holding open the door, and he was looking at Jake's bag.

'Goodbye, Harry,' said Jake walking straight past him out of the door and down the street.

'Goodbye, sir,' said Harry to his departing back, a question hanging in the air: the question of Jake's return.

20

Jake boarded the plane. He felt a twinge of anxiety, and it wasn't about the flight. He had to admit that he was hoping fate would deal him a good hand and he would find they had double-booked his seat, or the plane would break down before take-off. But in Jake's experience, fate never dealt people the hand they wanted. None of these things happened.

Jake settled into his window seat and leaned forward to look out at the runway. At least it was going to be a short flight. He closed his eyes. Maybe fate *was* deliberately dealing him a hand. There he was, on holiday, going to the last place he'd usually consider, all because of a phone call. The weird part was that he had agreed to go at all.

Jake looked at his watch. In around an hour, he would land at Inverness. He needed the bathroom. Checking the seatbelt sign was switched off, he got up and made his way cautiously to the back of the plane, trying to keep his balance and his stomach contents. He was not a good flier.

He made a mental note to take a moment to re-consider next time he jumped in to be a good Samaritan. He knew that William would not venture back to Scotland to meet Martha. And in his experience, Aubrey wouldn't come to Scotland either. He never once accepted William's invitation to Christmas dinner with them at their Highland holiday home, The Lake House, in all the years they'd been spending Christmas there. William and Aubrey went way back, but he'd never heard either of them mention Martha or Arnold Wright. This wasn't too surprising when Jake thought about it. Aubrey was an enigma; he'd known Aubrey all his life, but knew very little about the man. Aubrey kept his past close to his chest. His life was a closed book.

Still, before he caught his flight, Jake decided to phone Aubrey and let him know about his trip. Perhaps he knew this person called Ralph. Maybe he'd decide to come. Aubrey's phone had gone straight to voicemail. He'd silently cursed himself for not trying to contact him sooner. Now he was committed to going. It just seemed like the right thing to do, even though he had never heard of Martha in his life.

Jake walked through the centre aisle, glancing from side to side at the other passengers as he went by. A couple who looked around retirement age were engrossed in reading a road map. He smiled, thinking they were in for a fantastic time, guessing they were going on a road trip around Scotland.

A middle-aged man in a suit diligently typed into a laptop. Glossy-looking executive brochures littered the adjoining empty seat. Behind him, a young couple were having an animated conversation over the backs of their seats with an equally young, equally animated couple behind them. They looked like undergraduate students holidaying together. One of the young men put an arm around the young woman next to him as they chatted amiably, drawing her close.

Jake smiled as he passed by. There was nothing quite like

young love; the kind that brought with it no baggage from past relationships. That was the kind of relationship he and Eleanor had shared. Things had been simple. She had been his first, and he had stayed faithful to her through university, after which time they had married.

There had been no question over the fact that he would have spent the rest of his life with her, and he had always sincerely hoped that, once they eventually came towards the end of their life together, he would go first. But the end of their time together had come upon them with frightening speed. A few short years was all they'd had, and he had no son or daughter to remember her by. That was the absolute worst part – she'd been pregnant when he'd lost her. He'd never forgive Marcus for encouraging her to go skiing on Christmas Day. If only she hadn't gone, she'd still be there. He couldn't change what had happened; couldn't change the past. Since then, he had been drifting through empty relationships, all complicated by his inability to let go and move on.

There was one light at the end of the tunnel, one beacon to guide him back to shore – maybe. The first chance he got, if Faye would just answer her phone, or respond to his messages, Jake intended to attempt an apology. To try and make amends, somehow. He was obviously still in her bad books for spoiling Natty with too many toys.

At the end of the aisle, the toilets were occupied. Jake considered returning to his seat, but he could hear the rattle of the trolley behind the curtain in first class, and guessed that by the time he returned to his seat, the trolley would be making its way down the aisle, blocking his much-needed access to the facilities. He decided to stay put and wait.

The trolley stopped rattling. 'Would you like anything to drink, sir?' came a voice on the other side of the curtain that separated first-class travellers from their poorer counterparts.

'Brandy.'

Jake looked puzzled and took a step closer to the curtain.

'Would there be anything else, sir?'

He listened intently, knowing he must be mistaken.

'No, that will be all, thank you.'

Jake wasn't mistaken. He tore at the curtain and bounded into first class, colliding with the flight attendant. The trolley she had been wheeling up the centre aisle jerked violently, spilling assorted tiny bottles of alcoholic beverages to the floor and toppling a pile of badly-stacked empty foil meal containers right into the lap of a man in the aisle seat.

'I'm so sorry!' said Jake to the flight attendant. In his haste, he had forgotten about the trolley making its inevitable journey towards him behind the curtain. He bent down, attempting to catch the tiny bottles as they rolled around on the floor. He piled them into the crook of his arm while the flight attendant apologised profusely to the aisle seat passenger as she cleared his lap of the leftovers. 'I'm so sorry, all my fault,' said the flight attendant, although it clearly wasn't.

As Jake stood up, she turned to relieve him of the bottles and her perma-smile vanished; she recognised him from standard class. 'Sir, you're not allowed back here; this is for first-class passengers only.'

Jake scanned the passengers behind her. 'I just thought I heard a familiar voice.'

'What – from right down there?' she pointed past Jake's head, presumably meaning his seat.

'Well, no. I was waiting in your little area there and …'

'Sir, that area is for flight attendants only.'

Jake sighed heavily; he could tell this was one argument he wasn't going to win.

The flight attendant continued pulling the trolley. Jake had no option but to back up. 'I just wanted to take a look.'

Forced to re-trace his steps, Jake bobbed his head left and right, trying to get a look at the seated passengers in first class, but the flight attendant, who was tall, was blocking his view.

'You nearly knocked me over,' she commented to Jake, then turned her head to those seated, asking, 'Any more drinks, sir, madam?' The perma-smile back was in place.

'I was a bit over-enthusiastic,' Jake agreed. He flashed a smile, turning on the charm. It might work. Otherwise, he'd just get out his cheque book and pay for a damn seat in first class. There were plenty of free seats 'I was a clumsy oaf,' he added, still smiling. 'Are you alright?' He falsely exuded concern.

It worked. The flight attendant instantly became more amenable.

'Yes,' she said, although some of her hair, which she was wearing up in a neat bun, had fallen to her shoulders. Still, she smiled at Jake, and he smiled back as she wheeled the trolley into the tiny compartment. She did not, Jake noticed, immediately close the curtain on first class.

'May I take a look?' Jake said smoothly, indicating the cabin ahead. He didn't want to create a scene; not just yet, anyway. 'It'll only take a minute.' He gave her a charming smile. 'I promise.'

She looked up at the ceiling and folded her arms as if an old boyfriend had just apologised and told her how beautiful she looked. She rolled her eyes. 'Oh, go on then.'

Jake kept his smile plastered to his face until he got the other side of the curtain. He surveyed the backs of people's heads until he found who he was looking for. On the left, halfway up the aisle, he spied a mop of black hair. Unmistakable. Unbelievable. Jake glided up the aisle, trying to control his temper.

Six rows up, Jake sat down next to Marcus. Jake checked him over just to make sure his eyes weren't deceiving him; that this wasn't just some unfortunate passenger who had a passing resemblance and the voice to match.

It was Marcus all right, his glass of brandy sitting on the little table in front of him. His eyes were closed, his head was tilted back on the leather headrest, and he was wearing a pair of headphones. Jake could hear faint opera music. He looked very pleased with himself.

Before he throttled him to death, Jake wanted to know just how in god's name he had made this flight. Or even knew Jake would be on board.

Jake tore at the headphones.

'Hey!' Marcus sat up in his seat in astonishment.

'Sir!'

Jake turned in his seat to see the flight attendant storming up the aisle.

The few passengers that were in first class were throwing anxious looks in their direction.

Marcus followed Jake's gaze. 'I see the cavalry is coming to rescue me.' Marcus raised his glass to Jake. 'First-class service, Jake. Don't you miss it?'

Jake grabbed his wrist, slopping the brandy down his bandage and Marcus's sleeve. 'What the hell do you think you're doing?'

'Taking a flight – what do you think? How very convenient of you to write your flight time down. I made a call, couldn't have been simpler. I guessed you were flying out of City Airport.'

Jake glared at him. How did he work out which flight he'd be on. How did he even know he was flying somewhere?

'Now, I know what you're thinking,' said Marcus, studying his face. 'How did I even know you were travelling from London City Airport? Well, here's the thing. You can be a bit of a creature of habit, so I'm thinking we've flown from this airport a lot for business, and I remember how much you liked it.'

Jake didn't like it anymore.

Marcus looked exceptionally pleased with himself. He gave a self-satisfied smirk.

Jake grimaced.

Jake wanted to strangle him.

Marcus added, 'I do love this airport. Just one runway meant I knew with certainty which flight you'd be on because I had the flight time. I was sitting in first class before you even boarded the flight. Although I must admit I was a little surprised you'd chosen to go to Scotland on holiday.' Marcus looked at his hand. 'Do you mind letting go of my hand?'

Jake let go roughly, causing Marcus to spill more brandy.

Marcus looked at his glass and shrugged.

Jake watched him finish what was left of his brandy. Marcus smacked his lips and put the glass down. 'So, what's the plan? What are we doing when we arrive?' Marcus caught sight of Jake's sodden bandage. 'I bet that hurts.'

Jake's hand curled into a fist. 'Not as much as this is going to hurt.'

'Sir!' The flight attendant was now standing in the aisle right beside Jake's seat.

Jake sat there with his soggy, sodden bandaged hand curled into a ball, about to knock Marcus's lights out. He looked up at the flight attendant.

'Is everything alright?' she said to Marcus.

'Everything alright?' Marcus barked. 'Alright?' Marcus repeated purely for effect. 'Does it look as though I am alright with some lunatic sitting beside me?'

'Sir, do you know this gentleman?'

Marcus leaned away from Jake and looked him up and down. 'Of course I do. He's my brother-in-law – aren't you?'

The flight attendant looked from one to the other.

'Isn't that right?' Marcus said to Jake.

Jake nodded slowly. Marcus was wearing an expensive business suit, and despite the crumpled shirt and loosened tie, he still looked very smartly dressed in contrast to Jake's old jeans, cheap white supermarket shirt and patchy, threadbare wool jacket. Of course, the bandaged hands weren't helping any.

'There, you see?' Marcus looked back at the flight attendant. 'He says he's my brother-in-law.'

Jake stared at Marcus.

'And I think we should all agree with him, don't you?'

'I think I understand you, sir,' the flight attendant said to Marcus.

Jake turned on Marcus. 'Just what do you think you're playing at?'

'Sir. Return to your seat please.'

Jake ignored her. 'You,' Jake stabbed at Marcus's shoulder, 'are getting the first plane back.'

Marcus shrugged at the flight attendant and held up his hands. 'Whatever you say.'

'Sir!'

Jake got up. 'I'm warning you.' He pointed a finger at Marcus, then turned to go.

Shaking his head, Marcus said with a wan smile, 'Some people! You just want a quiet holiday and you've got lunatics following you around.'

Jake turned slowly back to face Marcus. This was a game Marcus was not going to win.

He felt a hand on his shoulder. 'Sir, do I need to call someone to restrain you?'

Jake looked over his shoulder, expecting to see two burly men about to grapple him to the ground. Instead, he saw the anxious faces of the other passengers in first class, who were probably wishing they were anywhere but there, trapped in a cabin thirty thousand feet in the air with a lunatic. His bandaged hands made him look as though he had already been in one fist-fight too many before he had even boarded the plane, and Marcus's clever little act as the innocent bystander wasn't helping.

Jake felt himself backing down, thinking, *two can play at this game*. Perhaps he could have him arrested at the airport. He didn't know what for. He had an hour to figure that out. But the way things looked right now, Jake had to acknowledge that it was more likely he'd find himself arrested on touch down.

He could see the headline: *A trainee teacher on a flight to Scotland attacked his brother-in-law in first class. Sources* (meaning Marcus) *suggest this mental breakdown was due to the fact that he had never got over the sudden death of his wife in a freak skiing accident.*

Jake backed up between the seats into the aisle. As he turned to leave, a wave of heads returned to whatever they were doing – fast.

Nobody made eye contact. Nobody wanted to antagonise the lunatic.

The relieved flight attendant escorted Jake back to his seat.

'Now, please will you stay in your seat for the remainder of the flight?'

Jake turned to look out of the window. A thought occurred to him. 'Oh, by the way…'

The flight attendant, who was walking up the aisle, slid back and leaned towards him. 'What is it now?' she said testily. 'I do have other passengers to attend to.'

She was getting irritated. Good. 'Can you tell me what the flight regulations are regarding …' he lowered his voice, 'bringing illegal substances on board a flight?'

That got the flight attendant's attention.

He added, 'And I'm not talking about prescription drugs.'

She said slowly, 'What do you mean? Did you bring something in your hand luggage through airport security that you didn't declare?'

'Oh, no. Not me.' Jake unzipped his bag on the seat next to him. 'See for yourself.' He rummaged through his bag, showing her his clothes and the contents of a toiletry bag just to make the point. Then he cast his gaze down the aisle towards the first-class cabin. Marcus wasn't just drinking. Jake didn't know what substance he was abusing, but Marcus was using something. And he could make a very good bet that he had some of it on him, or at least in his luggage.

The flight attendant followed his gaze. She turned to Jake and answered his question. 'You can't bring drugs that are not on prescription through UK airport security.'

'So, what exactly would happen if someone had done that?'

'Are you talking about someone on this flight?'

He slowly nodded his head.

She stared at Jake. 'I need to speak to my colleague.'

Jake felt his foul mood dissipating rapidly. He looked out of the cabin window. The sun had come out.

The flight attendant returned. She sat down in the seat next to him and whispered, 'The person in question would be arrested initially, held for twenty-four to forty-eight hours while investigations were made, and a decision would be made whether charges should be brought. They could end up with a criminal record.'

'Arrested,' Jake mused. 'At the airport on landing?'

'Er, that depends …'

'On when you make the discovery,' Jake clarified.

'Yes.' Her tone was much more congenial, he noticed. 'Do you know of someone who you think has brought illegal drugs on board?'

Jake turned to look out of the window and smiled. 'I do.'

'Was it the man you were having an altercation with in first class?'

'Yes, it was.'

For a moment, it crossed his mind that she wouldn't believe him after that scene with Marcus. He looked at her. 'You do believe me, don't you?'

'We take these matters very seriously.'

He turned back to the window and closed his eyes, feeling the warmth of the sun on his face and smiling to himself. This was going to be one holiday the like of which Marcus had never experienced.

21

After half an hour of fitful catnapping, Jake opened his eyes as the plane began its descent into Inverness airport.

The scheduled flight landed on time at just before three in the afternoon. It taxied to a standstill.

The seatbelt sign remained on. A voice came over the tannoy.

'This is your captain speaking. May I request that all passengers remain in their seats until the seatbelt sign is switched off. May I take this opportunity to thank you for flying with us today. I hope you had a pleasant flight.'

'Very pleasant, thank you,' commented Jake.

The seatbelt sign remained on.

A low murmur developed in the cabin as people waited.

Jake looked around as the cabin door opened. Two uniformed police officers stepped into view. Jake watched them walk up the aisle and disappear into first class. Passengers exchanged nervous glances. Jake smiled to himself.

They reappeared with Marcus leading the way and the flight attendant bringing up the rear.

As they approached, Jake tried to keep a straight face – everything was going according to plan. The look on Marcus's face said he was feeling completely humiliated, being escorted from the plane in front of all these people like he was some kind of criminal. Perhaps the cabin crew had searched his luggage, or they'd just taken Jake at his word. Either way, speaking to the flight attendant had had the desired effect – although Jake had assumed Marcus might be stopped and searched, and arrested in the airport terminal; he hadn't expected the police to actually board the flight on arrival.

Jake was finding it all highly entertaining. The handcuffs only added to his enjoyment.

'Jake, what's going on?' Marcus demanded, attempting to stop in the aisle next to Jake's seat.

Jake shrugged innocently. He noted that the officers carried firearms, which in the pre-terror climate would have been almost unheard of at British airports.

'I know you had something to do with this!'

Marcus was manhandled towards the exit.

'Where are you taking me? Are you arresting me for something?' Marcus moaned at his captors.

Jake turned around in his seat to watch Marcus being escorted out of the plane; there was a hush, as other passengers were doing the same. Jake wanted Marcus to make a scene, but he didn't. Marcus hesitated before he stepped out of the cabin, glancing back at Jake with a bewildered *help me* expression on his shocked face. Jake offered him a wide grin. 'See ya!' he said under his breath, as he waved goodbye.

Ding. The seatbelt sign clicked off and the cabin snapped back into life. The murmur rose as bodies packed the aisle, fighting to retrieve their hand luggage from the overhead compartments.

Jake, still seated, calmly looked out of the window and watched Marcus being escorted to a waiting police van. Jake's smug smile slipped. He couldn't shrug off an uneasy feeling in the pit of his stomach. He tried to put it down to the fact that he was back in Scotland – a place he had vowed he'd never return to after losing Eleanor. But what was really on his mind was that he hadn't considered the repercussions not only for Marcus, but for William's reputation, and that of the Ross Corporation, if Marcus did have something highly illegal in his possession, and word got out.

He followed the queue of passengers waiting in the aisle to exit the plane. Then he found the car rental desk and waited in another queue for what seemed like a long time. While he waited, he made a call. To his relief, she answered.

'Faye?'

'Jake! Where are you?'

He frowned. She knew where he was – he'd left countless messages saying he was going to Scotland, but he'd be back soon.

'Are you still in Inverness?'

Jake sighed and looked at the queue. It was now almost three thirty in the afternoon, and at this rate he wouldn't be heading out of the airport until four. 'Yes, I'm still at the airport, waiting in a queue to pick up a hire car. Look, the reason I …'

'Thank goodness,' the relief in her voice was unmistakable. 'What did you think you were playing at?'

'What?' said Jake, surprised by her cutting tone.

'Marcus just phoned me,' she said stiffly.

'He phoned you?' Jake said in surprise.

'He phoned me from a police station in Inverness!'

Damn. Why had he phoned *her*?

'Is it true – you said something on the flight that got him arrested?'

'Look, he was following me, all right? He thought he could just come on holiday with me when I'd expressly told him he couldn't.'

She didn't respond.

He had it on the tip of his tongue to mention the drugs – even though he wasn't one hundred per cent sure Marcus had brought any on the flight with him. 'I do not want him accompanying me, Faye. He reminds me …'

'So, you had him arrested?' said Faye incredulously.

On the flight, Jake had Googled what might happen to Marcus after his arrest. Assuming he had been found in possession of drugs for personal use, there were various possible outcomes. He was unlikely to receive a prison sentence. He might be cautioned as a first-time offender, or told to attend some sort of drugs-related education programme. Either way, if he was taking recreational drugs – and Jake suspected he was – Jake thought he was doing him a favour. This would be a wake-up call to stop.

Jake felt he had no choice but to explain. 'I think he may have brought something illegal on the flight. I'm just being a good citizen.' He winced, wondering if he should have said that. 'I imagine that if he *is* being charged, he'll just get released on bail.' *By which time, I'll be long gone*, thought Jake. Scotland was a big country. Marcus wouldn't find out where he was going this time.

'You need to go and get him.'

'Once he is released, he can just make his way wherever he …' Although he was still feeling a bit groggy after last night's solo expedition to the land of binge-drinking oblivion, Jake finally caught up with Faye. 'What did you just say?'

'He told me they're keeping him in overnight. Apparently, his luggage has gone missing, and the police want to search that before they decide whether to charge him.'

Jake sighed. So, either they'd found something on him, and wanted to check how much of the stuff he'd brought with him, in case he was dealing too. Or they hadn't found anything, but needed to check his luggage first before they decided whether there was any evidence to charge him. Either way, Jake didn't see what that had to do with him.

'So, in the morning you need to go and pick him up.'

'Are you serious?' Jake said. *I'll do no such thing*, he thought as he took a step closer in the queue to the car rental desk. 'The next thing you'll be asking me to do is apologise,' he added.

The line went quiet.

'Is that what you're asking me to do? Me, apologise, to him? Oh, I don't think so. If you knew …'

'Knew what?' said Faye harshly.

Jake caught his breath. He breathed out calmly, before he said, 'He's going to spend a night in a prison cell – so what? He'll get over it, it's no big deal.'

Silence.

'Faye?'

'Jake, go get him in the morning. Then tell me it's no big deal.'

'Why? Did something happen?'

22

Jake sat in the car, watching the digital clock on the dashboard counting down to Marcus's release. He hadn't pre-booked accommodation for his trip. His intention was just to book in somewhere on arrival. He hadn't envisaged spending his first night at an airport hotel.

A police car drifted slowly passed Jake's hire car and parked in the police station car park; two police officers emerged and escorted an uncooperative youth into the building after he had livened things up by attempting an unsuccessful escape.

Every now and then, Jake glanced at the building, waiting for Marcus to emerge. He was doing this for Faye, he reminded himself, not for Marcus. Jake glanced out of the window yet again.

There was no sign of Marcus.

The clock was ticking. Where was he?

Jake got out of the car.

He went back over the conversation he'd had with Faye the previous day while he was waiting to pick up the hire car. Something she'd said … he couldn't recall, but he had that feeling that something was wrong.

Jake stepped into the police station. He approached the front desk, aware that they could quite conceivably throw him in a cell for twenty-four hours for wasting police time if it turned out Marcus had nothing in his luggage. He knew that he deserved it for pulling such a stunt.

The desk sergeant looked up. 'Can I help you?'

Jake hesitated. He was meant to be on holiday; he did not want to find himself banged up just because he had childishly decided to get his own back on Marcus. Jake was half-inclined to turn around and walk right out of the door. Once again, he had to remind himself he was doing this for Faye. She was right; he'd been a bit heavy-handed with Marcus. Nevertheless, Jake hoped he'd learnt his lesson. Now the least he could do was pick him up and drive him to the airport.

'I've come to collect Marcus Ross. I understand he was due to be released at 9 am.' Jake didn't feel inclined to give his name.

'You need to take the lift to the next floor.' The desk sergeant waved at the lift.

'Can I take the stairs?'

Jake stepped out of the lift on the first floor, wishing he could get over his fear of enclosed spaces. He approached another officer behind a desk in a similar reception room, except that this one had a row of grey plastic seats along one wall and posters carrying phone numbers to Childline and Citizens Advice, and others advising people to lock their valuables in their cars, out of sight. Jake thought of his bag plonked on the back seat in plain view.

'Mr Marcus Ross,' the officer said to himself as he leafed through some paperwork on the top of his desk. 'Is that with a *c* or a *k*?'

'A *c*.' Jake wondered how many Marcus Rosses they had locked up in there. Certainly no others who were stupid enough to take illegal drugs through airport security – if that's what he'd done.

The officer got up from his seat to look for the paperwork. He returned with a release form. 'Yes, here we are. Marcus Ross,' he read from the arrest sheet. 'Arrested for carrying illegal substances through airport security. None were found on his person, or in his luggage, once we received it from the airport.'

Jake frowned. Although he was actually relieved that Marcus wouldn't be charged, it did make him wonder if he'd made a huge mistake. Maybe Marcus wasn't taking drugs at all. Maybe he had not deserved a night in a prison cell.

The police office was still reading the paperwork. 'Interesting. He made two phone calls.'

Jake looked at him. 'I thought he just rang Faye. Um, I mean Ms Ames.'

'Yes, but there was one other person. We hadn't got hold of his luggage at that point, so thought this person might be his dealer, although he was adamant that the person was no such thing. But as a precaution, we ran the name through.'

'What name?' Jake asked, interested to find out who else Marcus had contacted for help.

'Aubrey Jones.'

Of course he'd go to Aubrey, rather than William, if he was in trouble, Jake thought.

'We wouldn't let him make that call to a fictitious name.'

'Fictitious?'

'We ran the name through various channels, social security, DVLA as a matter of routine. Funny, because he swore blind the person was for real.'

Jake stared at the officer in disbelief. If Aubrey Jones didn't exist, then who the hell was living on the top floor of the Ross apartment building?

'Do you know who that guy is that he wanted to call?'

Whatever Aubrey – or whoever the hell he really was – had done that warranted him hiding behind a fictitious name, Jake didn't want to get involved or be implicated.

Jake shook his head, feeling uncomfortable under the officer's searching gaze. 'Right, well, er … where is Marcus Ross?'

The officer consulted his paperwork again. 'I think he's just getting a once-over from the doctor.'

'Is he ill?'

The officer put the paperwork down, and leaned forward in his chair. 'If you're any kind of friend, you'll get him some help.' he said, as though he was giving Jake a piece of fatherly advice. 'One of those clinics, you know …'

Jake was on the verge of asking what he meant by that when the double doors swung open at the end of the hall. 'Ah, I think this will be your man now.'

One of the officers who had escorted Marcus from the plane strode through the door and approached the desk, glancing at Jake.

Jake watched him sign the release papers. He couldn't wait for this to be over. He was beginning to think Faye was right; he had caused a lot more trouble than it was worth.

Jake looked back at the double doors. Marcus was standing just the other side, his suit jacket in his right hand, draped on the floor, his white shirt crumpled, with one side hanging out of his trousers. His bloodshot eyes were staring fixedly at Jake.

Guess I'm going to find out just how much trouble, thought Jake as he walked over to the lift and pressed the *Down* button, giving the officer at the desk a weak smile.

He glanced back at Marcus, who was making slow progress to the lift. He didn't seem well. He was still staring fixedly at Jake.

The lift door opened. Jake jumped in and pressed *G* for the ground floor. When he turned around, Marcus hadn't joined him in the lift. Jake sighed and pressed the hold button. He'd forgotten that Marcus would have to collect his things.

He waited.

At the desk, the officer passed Marcus a plastic bag; Jake guessed it was the contents of his pockets. Then a suitcase appeared.

'There's only three days' worth there, so you want to get yourself checked in somewhere pretty soon, OK?'

Marcus nodded. He turned around with the bag to hand. He was almost losing his balance. He made his way cautiously towards the lift.

'Remember what I said!' The officer directed that comment at Jake.

Jake recalled that piece of advice: *If you're any kind of friend you'll get him some help, one of those clinics ...*'

The lift door closed with Marcus inside.

A sudden jerk as the lift started down threw Marcus off balance. Jake grabbed at him.

'Get off me.' Marcus weakly struggled out of Jake's grip and held onto the metal handrail that ran the circumference of the lift.

'What's this?' Jake picked up the plastic bag that had fallen to the floor and held it up. Marcus turned and glared at Jake without speaking.

Jake drew a sharp breath at the sight of him; thick black rings encircled his eyes. It was as if someone had punched him in the face, except they weren't bruises. Were those tears in his eyes?

Marcus slowly held out a shaky hand, palm up.

Jake handed him the bag, wondering what was inside.

Marcus took it and turned to face the front of the lift in stony silence.

'If you want an apology,' Jake said finally, 'I'll give you one.' He stole a glance at Marcus. He was still facing the front of the lift. He continued holding onto the rail.

'I admit it was a stupid thing for me to do,' Jake conceded. One look at Marcus had convinced him of that.

Marcus said nothing.

The lift door opened onto the ground floor; they stepped out together, Jake trundling Marcus's suitcase along behind him. He was forced to stop halfway to the front door to let Marcus catch up. Together, they walked slowly past the reception desk, Jake throwing Marcus sideways glances and debating whether he should take him to a hospital. If he'd realised his actions were going to trigger some sort of breakdown …

Of course, in his naivety he'd forgotten that most people never had cause to enter a police station, let alone a police cell. He realised that it must have been a huge shock. And Marcus wasn't like most people anyway; he was used to, well, an altogether different style of life.

Jake couldn't believe he had been so stupid as to think Marcus would be in any fit state to just hop on the next plane home after that experience. Besides, the man could barely walk.

Jake opened the door for Marcus. They stepped out into the street. He looked at Marcus again. Why hadn't he phoned his fiancée or William? Aubrey would have been on the first flight out, if he had managed to contact him, but Jake couldn't figure out why he had called Faye, someone he barely knew.

Jake got to the car ahead of Marcus and put the suitcase into the boot before opening the passenger door. He waited with the car door open, expecting Marcus to get in beside him. He watched Marcus open the rear door and get in the back instead.

'I see,' Jake mumbled under his breath as he slammed the car door shut, circled the car and got in the driver's side. Jake felt his temper rising. He'd said he was sorry; what more did the man want?

Jake started the engine, mulling over Plan A – going straight to the airport to deposit Marcus on the next available flight home. Since that obviously wasn't going to happen, it was on to Plan B; except there was no Plan B.

Jake sat in the car, wondering what to do. He felt like a chauffeur, what with Marcus sitting in the back. 'Where to, sir?' Jake said, kidding around. He looked in his rear-view mirror. Marcus wasn't visible.

'Marcus?' Jake twisted round in his seat.

Marcus was lying down on the back seat, his knees drawn up to his chest, his suit jacket on the floor. His eyes fluttered open. 'What did you say?'

Jake leaned over and squeezed his shoulder. 'Marcus,' he said gently, 'where do you want to go?'

'Sleep,' said Marcus wearily, closing his eyes.

Jake turned in his seat and looked at his watch; it was only nine-thirty in the morning. Plan B was already forming in his mind.

He manoeuvred the car into the mid-morning flow of traffic. Heading out of the city, Jake made his way north, following the signs for the A9 in the direction of Perth, which would take him all the way to his destination. It was a route he knew well. He would let Marcus catch up on his beauty sleep during the forty-minute journey to Aviemore.

It didn't take long to join the main road. It was a popular tourist route for people visiting the shores of Loch Ness or to visit Urquhart Castle; the castle ruins were a must-see on the banks of the loch. Jake knew this area well. He had often taken detours off this road to see the lochs and visit the castle with Marcus and Eleanor when they were younger. But Jake had not returned to Scotland for sightseeing – he would not have returned there if it had not been for that strange phone call from Mr Wright.

The plan now was to drop Marcus off at a hotel where he could rest. Perhaps after a few hours of much-needed sleep, he'd feel better. Then he could order some room service and have a bite to eat. The plan would leave Jake free to visit Mr Wright.

Martha clearly knew an Aubrey Jones, but did she know the man behind the fictitious name? After what Jake had discovered about Aubrey at the police station, he wanted nothing more than to find out just who he really was.

Jake glanced over his shoulder. Marcus was still semi-comatose on the back seat. He started the car. 'Plan B it is, then.'

23

Jake was making good time. He could hear Marcus snoring in the back of the car. They were travelling into the Highlands, and the landscape on either side of the road had given way to the beauty and magnificence of heather-covered moors, rolling hills and the distant peaks of the Cairngorms as he drove towards Aviemore.

Jake stopped at a small service station to stretch his legs and admire the views. Marcus didn't stir as Jake parked the car and made his way to the shop. He ordered coffee and bought one for Marcus too – he had a feeling he would need one when he woke.

When Jake returned to the car, Marcus was still asleep. He considered waking him but thought it best to let him rest.

Jake turned back on to the main road. He passed a road sign stating how many miles it was to Aviemore. He was home. Scotland. He had been born there, he had been orphaned there as a child, and although he had only spent a few short years of his early life living there, it still felt like a homecoming, every time. Jake kept a casual eye on the road signs; he had been down this route many times. Those had been good times, returning to The Lake House for Christmas. A sudden wave of nostalgia for his old life hit him, along with the thought that returning was a mistake.

The exit approached.

Jake was having serious doubts about Plan B, about this whole business. It was meant to be a holiday, and there he was, driving towards his past. He wanted to drive right on by the exit, perhaps find a hotel further on, but exactly how much further would that be? There were hotels and B&Bs in Aviemore. He hadn't planned to stop anywhere else.

Jake quickly glanced over his left shoulder at Marcus and sensed that it would be a bad idea to prolong the journey. Reluctantly, Jake changed lanes and descended onto the slip road, taking the first exit at the roundabout to make the gradual ascent through the rugged, mountainous and utterly captivating landscape, heading for home.

As he followed a black four-wheel drive, its rear window obscured by suitcases, its roof loaded with skis, memories surfaced of his own trips in a similar car loaded with much the same equipment. It seemed like another life. It *was* another life.

The car in front turned off, leaving just the open road snaking through the empty landscape to the Cairngorms. The last time he'd done this drive, he'd come alone because stupidly he'd worked until late and had missed accompanying Eleanor on the train from London. At Christmas, the landscape had looked so different. It had been a wintry scene, straight from a Christmas card, with snow-capped mountains and snow-frosted plains. He'd forgotten how green the Cairngorms could be in the summer. Jake couldn't remember the last time he'd visited Scotland in a different season. He smiled. It was just possible he might salvage this holiday after all. He would never have consciously chosen to return to this place. It was too full of memories of her. But now he was back, he couldn't help but admire the magnificent scenery. He slowed the car a little to take in the views.

How could he think he would not one day be drawn back to this place that he loved and yet loathed for taking her from him? Had it really been only seven months ago? It seemed like forever since he had driven down this road alone on that fateful Christmas that had altered the course of his life forever.

Although the sun was still shining, Jake could no longer feel the hot sun on his neck. Aware that his speed had dropped below forty, Jake glanced in his rear-view mirror, expecting to see a four-wheel drive on his tail. Instead, what he saw was Marcus's glazed brown eyes burning into the back of his neck. 'Where do you think you're going?'

Jake looked back at the road ahead. It was no longer an empty space; another four-wheel drive much like the last had overtaken him and swallowed up the road. 'Don't you recognise it?'

Marcus had known when he'd boarded the flight that the destination was Scotland, but he would never have guessed they were returning to Aviemore.

'Of course I do!' he said indignantly. 'But what the hell are we doing here?'

Touchy, thought Jake. 'You wanted to sleep, so I'm taking you to a hotel,' said Jake matter-of-factly.

'You're telling me you couldn't find a single hotel in Inverness, so you had to drive all the way to Aviemore?'

Jake ignored the sarcastic remark. Instead, he handed Marcus his takeaway cup of coffee. 'Here, drink this – I think it will help you wake up.' *And hopefully improve your mood*, he thought.

Marcus leaned forward, clutching the back of Jake's seat as he took the cup. 'Urrgh. This coffee is luke-warm.'

Jake wasn't surprised. 'You were out like a light. I didn't want to wake you when I stopped at a service station a while back.'

'What are we doing here?' Marcus reiterated.

'What do you think I'm doing here?' Jake threw the sarcasm back. 'Do I need to remind you that this is *my* holiday? It was your choice to follow me. Well, here we are. This is where I have chosen to spend it.'

While not a strictly accurate account of how he'd come to be in the area, Jake declined to reveal how he had impulsively agreed to meet somebody he didn't know before he had even found out where exactly they were calling from. And what was worse, how he had been stupid enough to go anyway.

'I'm not turning back now. I've got an appointment.' Jake could picture it; Marcus would want out of this place so badly that he'd be pleading for Jake to take him to the nearest airport.

'What do you mean you've got an appointment? I thought you were on holiday?'

Jake smiled to himself. He was going to re-kindle the embers of his nearly-destroyed holiday once he'd fulfilled his commitment to Mr Wright and had got rid of Marcus on the next available flight back to London.

'Who the hell have you got an appointment with?'

Jake looked in the rear-view mirror and felt an *I told you so* coming on. He couldn't resist. 'Didn't I tell you not to come on holiday with me?'

Marcus slumped back in his seat. All Jake could see was the mop of black, greasy hair plastered to the top of his head. 'This is the last place I'd expect you to have come for a holiday,' he said quietly, 'or for any reason.'

You and me both, Jake thought sadly as he drove into Aviemore. The town was busy whatever the season. Aviemore attracted a lot of tourists. The traffic crawled along the main shopping street, passing the train station, and Wilbur's Bookstore on the other side of the road. It had been some time since he'd stepped inside that shop. As he passed by, he wondered when Wilbur would retire. He had popped in there from time to time, over the years, and Wilbur had talked about his grandson, an aspiring writer, whom he hoped would take over his store.

Further along, he spotted the community centre and a couple of modern supermarkets that were open all hours. The town was dominated by thriving shops selling walking and skiing apparel, catering for tourists. Jake came to halt in traffic outside one of the few shops that wasn't aimed at tourists. It always surprised him that the place was still there – Gillespie's General Store.

He raised his eyebrows at the double-fronted shop as he passed by. Something had changed. He'd been in there once or twice, in the past, and had met Mr Gillespie. The shop, like its owner, was functional, practical, no-nonsense. Mr Gillespie wasn't the sort of guy to cater to the whims of the tourist and do fancy window displays to entice people in. But something had definitely changed. There had once been a jumble of goods in the front window, and more of the same spilling out onto the street in a haphazard display. It was a relic from the past, a dying breed still serving what was left of the local, elderly community who, he imagined, shopped there out of loyalty or habit. It was a place they could go where someone would ring up their purchases on an old-fashioned till and even pack your shopping himself – so unlike modern, impersonal supermarkets with self-service checkouts.

The items on the pavement outside of the shop were gone. The window displays had changed quite radically. One side still had groceries displayed in the windows, but these were no longer thrown together haphazardly; they were organised on shelves in baskets.

It was the other window display that had really caught his eye, though, and made him wonder if the place had changed hands. Either that, or Mr Gillespie had had the foresight and business acumen to realise that if his shop was going to survive the competition of the influx of modern supermarket chains, he would have to change with the times and sublet half of his shop to another retailer.

He smiled. If Eleanor had been there, she would have loved the other window display. It was full of curtains, cushions and fabrics, which were draped over a small, upholstered chair and illuminated by a standard lamp in the background. He could just imagine her popping in there to buy some materials to make something. How she had loved being creative with interior design, he thought sadly. It was what she had wanted to do with her life.

Jake read the name above the shop window aloud: '*Robyn's Interior Design*.'

'What was that?' Marcus asked from the back seat.

Jake sighed. For a moment, he'd forgotten his back seat passenger. 'Nothing.'

Jake followed a line of cars as he headed out the other side of the town, where large imposing houses nestled down quieter, more secluded lanes surrounding the village. Jake noted the stream of traffic behind thinning out along the main road as people turned off to their homes or holiday homes at the edge of town.

Jake was heading for just such a place.

There was a rustle of movement at the back. Jake glanced in his rear-view mirror as Marcus slid by to his left and looked out of the car window. 'You missed the turn-off!'

'No, I didn't.'

'But it's back there.' Marcus added sarcastically, 'I think I can remember.'

Jake stayed silent.

Marcus said, 'We're not staying at The Lake House.' It wasn't a question.

'No.' Jake had been planning to book into a fancy hotel in Aviemore, but with his bandaged hands, and Marcus's unkempt appearance, he'd had a change of heart. Instead, he remembered a little wooden single-storey lodge. It had a bar that served food. Apparently, there were rooms for rent there too, although the place was not well advertised. It was located so far off the beaten track that the three of them had joked that it would be the perfect place to hide out from the law if they were in trouble. He hoped the place was still there; he didn't want to stay in town, and he didn't want to stay for long.

Jake took a left turn at the town limits. If he remembered rightly, it was at the end of a dirt track. Not many people besides the townsfolk themselves, and a few people from neighbouring communities, knew of its existence. Jake often wondered why the owners had never erected a billboard on the road advertising the place to drum up more business. But driving through town, Jake thought he could guess why: the remote location was idyllic, and they'd probably find themselves overrun with tourists. From what he remembered, it was one of the few establishments that remained exclusively for the locals, and they wanted to keep it that way. Jake was anticipating a frosty reception when he arrived.

He remembered the first time the three of them had stumbled onto the place, years earlier. They had been teenagers looking for a pub that was so out of the way that they could pretty much guarantee they would not run into the senior Rosses, who they were sure had believed – bless their trusting hearts – that they were at *the pond*, the frozen-over lake, ice-skating.

Their surprise had therefore been immense when they'd stepped foot inside the place and had seen Aubrey Jones – the same Aubrey Jones who always declined their invitation to spend Christmas with them in the Cairngorms – sitting just across the room, surrounded by half a dozen townsfolk. Jake remembered that the three of them had frozen just inside the door. They couldn't think of anyone worse they could have bumped into, save Eleanor and Marcus's parents themselves. Aubrey was William's right-hand man. He sorted things out. And he would sort them out good and proper if he caught them attempting to buy alcohol.

Looking back, Jake didn't know how they'd done it, but they'd retreated backwards out of the bar, three sets of eyes staring fixedly at Aubrey. All he'd needed to do was look up; he couldn't have missed three teenagers in brightly coloured ski wear backing out of the door. But he hadn't looked up, and to their relief he hadn't caught them. That was the first and last time Jake had visited the place. He remembered the question on all their lips – what had Aubrey been doing there? Of course, that incident had long been forgotten – until now.

The question on Jake's mind now was: had the place survived? Was it still there?

Jake drove slowly along the rutted track through the forest of tall pines, which were densely packed on either side.

Half a mile down the track, Jake reduced his speed. He must be getting near. The car crawled into a large clearing. He let it slow to a halt.

Nothing.

'Good.' Marcus sounded smug. 'I've had enough bad experiences for one day, without staying at the Norman Bates Motel.'

Jake looked over his shoulder as Marcus lay down on the back seat, resting his head in the crook of his arm. So, Marcus remembered the place too. He was right: their overriding memory of the place was how creepy it had been, right in the middle of nowhere.

'What is wrong with you, anyway?' said Jake, glancing over his shoulder. He'd had plenty of sleep. Why wasn't he bucking up?

Marcus shut his eyes.

Was the current physical state of Marcus just down to the shock of spending all those hours deprived of his liberty, or was it because he had been deprived of something else? Jake was beginning to wonder whether Marcus's casual drug-use had extended beyond the weekend into something a lot less casual and a lot more serious.

Jake looked back at the clearing. He opened the car door, swung it wide and got out. He needed to stretch his legs. He walked over to where the lodge had once stood. He scuffed the earth with his foot and hit something. Another scuff with his shoe unearthed a piece of wood. Jake squatted and picked up the wood, turning it over to reveal green, peeling paint. At least that confirmed he was in the right place. He tossed it away and stood up.

'Now what?' Hands on his hips, Jake closed his eyes and breathed in the pine-scented forest air.

24

'Are you lost?'

Startled, Jake turned in the direction of the stranger's voice. He couldn't see anyone through the dense pine trees bordering the clearing. He looked back at the car. He felt exposed.

'I said are you lost? Do you need directions?' A smart-suited, clean-shaven young man wearing a bright yellow hard hat and carrying a clipboard emerged from the forest. His paperwork flapped in the breeze.

Jake relaxed. 'Er, no.'

The young man walked briskly towards Jake. He held out his hand as if he was in a business meeting. 'I'm Mr Addison, and I'm afraid you are on private land.'

'I am?' Jake didn't remember seeing a *No Trespassing* sign. 'What happened to the lodge?' Jake pointed at the mound of earth where it had once stood.

'Oh, that old place. It was bulldozed.' The young man nodded his head, and Jake watched his plastic hard hat bob back and forth. 'It was practically falling down anyway. It's a wonder they didn't do it years ago.'

Jake nodded his head in agreement. It had been over fifteen

years since he had seen the place, but even back then it had been in a dilapidated state. 'Who tore it down?' Jake asked with a tinge of regret that the old place hadn't survived.

'The company,' said Mr Addison, as if that explained it all.

Jake looked at him blankly.

'Only local people used that place,' he said. 'It's unusual that somebody from out of town should remember it.' Mr Addison let the remark hang in the air, as though he was waiting for an explanation.

Jake shrugged his shoulders. 'I used to holiday in this area. I thought this would be a nice place to stay.' Which didn't fully explain how he had known about the lodge in the first place, but he wasn't feeling very conversational. He'd just driven from the airport hotel, visited a police station to collect a recalcitrant passenger, and since then, all he'd had was a quick stop to get a coffee at a service station. And now his plan to stay in this most tranquil of settings had been stymied by some land-grabbing company with a total disregard for the local community.

Mr Addison tapped his clipboard impatiently. 'Well, I'd better get back to work.'

'Somebody bought the land?' said Jake.

'Yes, I'm the site manager.

'What have they got planned here?' Jake asked offhand, not really that interested in hearing about the next phase of super-deluxe lodges or whatever they were planning to build in their quest to deface the landscape in the pursuit of money.

The young man appeared to be caught off-guard by the question. He looked down at his clipboard, and then looked up at Jake. He shook his shoulders. 'To be perfectly honest with you, I don't really know. I mainly work on the new development just out of town, which is nearing completion. I was asked to come here and prepare the site. I'm looking at where a temporary site office will go, that sort of thing.' He turned full circle. 'It's an amazing location – isn't it?'

Jake didn't comment.

After an awkward silence, he said, 'Do you need directions back to the main road?'

Jake gave him a bemused look. 'No, I think I can figure it out.' He only had to follow the dirt track back the way he came. It wasn't difficult.

Jake ambled back to the car and turned to take one last look. Mr Addison was on the edge of the clearing, about to disappear back into the trees. 'By the way,' Jake shouted at him.

Mr Addison stopped and turned around.

'When was the last time you took a holiday?'

'Why?' Mr Addison shouted back.

'Take one, trust me.' Mr Addison needed to put work in perspective; nobody should be that enthusiastic about a work project they seemed to know next to nothing about – it was weird.

Jake realised belatedly that he was the last person who should be advising people to take a holiday. He had been so dead against taking one himself. But in the two days Jake had been away from the job, he had discovered something – not going to work wasn't going to kill him.

The fact that his holiday had not gone to plan from the very outset was probably a good thing. If he had stuck to his original idea, and stayed home, he knew that things would be very different. He'd have had too much time on his hands to think about things, to dwell, and he knew that would be a bad thing. Nobody could change the past, but what Jake had discovered in the intervening months since losing Eleanor was that at least he could change the future.

Jake opened the car door.

'Hey!' a voice shouted.

Jake turned around to see the young man still standing at the edge of the clearing. 'Yes?' he threw back.

'If you're looking for somewhere to stay, may I suggest Lark Lodge? It's a great place. I should know. I'm staying there myself. Just follow the lark.' He disappeared into the trees. His yellow hat glowed before it, too, vanished.

Jake sat in the driver's seat in silence, listening to the rustle of dead leaves on the forest floor as the wind picked up. After a restless night at the airport hotel, worried about the following morning and collecting Marcus, not to mention his impending return to Aviemore, Jake was just about exhausted, and he still had to visit Mr Wright before he could really call it a day.

'What was all that about?'

Jake nearly jumped out of his skin at the unexpected sound of Marcus's voice right behind him.

'The place is gone,' said Jake wearily, pulling the car door shut. And now he had to find somewhere else to stay.

'Now can we go and stay at The Lake House?' said Marcus.

Ignoring him, Jake started the engine, put the car into reverse gear and reversed in a wide arc to face the direction he had come; he did it fast.

'Oh, god,' came from the back seat.

'Don't spew in the hire car,' Jake said over his shoulder as he put the car into gear and sped back down the track, kicking up a cloud of dust in his wake.

25

'Follow the lark,' Jake mumbled to himself, frowning as he drove slowly back through Aviemore without a clue as to what exactly he was meant to be looking for. What had Mr Addison meant when he'd said *follow the lark?* The holiday was getting weirder by the hour. He felt like he'd stepped into the Land of Oz. It brought to mind Eleanor's favourite childhood movie, the one she had watched over and over, especially her favourite scene: Dorothy closing her eyes, tapping her shoes together, and saying, *one, two, three – there's no place like home.*

Jake sighed heavily. This place brought back too many memories. That was why there was no way he would stay at The Lake House. Instead, he'd chosen to take Mr Addison's advice and find Lark Lodge; he just hoped there were vacancies.

He concentrated on the road ahead, conscious of the fact that the end of the town was in sight, still with no sign of Lark Lodge. He was beginning to think the search was futile when he spotted a small, bird-shaped sign stuck to a tree. Another sign further along had the lark sitting in a nest, presumably indicating a bed. Jake began to smile. 'Somebody's got a sense of humour,' he murmured as they headed away from the centre, where the larger properties nestled on the fringe of the town near the lakeshore. *This looks promising*, thought Jake. Next up, the bird had a stockpile of nuts and seeds, representing, Jake assumed, that it offered bed *and* breakfast.

The beak pointed left.

'Shit!' Jake stopped the car. He sat at the crossroads, looking left down the familiar street.

'What's the matter?' said Marcus, rising from the back seat.

Jake glanced over his shoulder. Marcus looked very pale, and he was shivering. Jake thought that it wasn't a hotel he needed but a doctor. He said as much.

'I just need to rest, that's all.'

Jake eyed him; he wasn't convinced. 'You've been resting all day.'

'Oh, shut up!'

A car horn sounded behind them. Jake turned further in his seat to look out of the back window. A middle-aged woman sitting in a muddy Land Rover was gesturing for Jake to get a move on.

Jake turned left.

The beak now pointed straight on.

He no longer found it amusing.

Jake kept his eyes peeled for further signs. The houses backed on to the grounds of a house he was all too familiar with. There was a cut-through that led to a locked gate into the grounds of the Rosses' Scottish holiday home. He hadn't anticipated that Lark Lodge would be so close.

He hoped to goodness it wasn't one of the houses towards the end of the road that might have glimpses of The Lake House from its bedroom windows at the back.

Jake followed the signs, taking in the properties as he slowly passed them by. The were all large, all detached, some brick, others rendered, and all with their own substantial secluded gardens up long drives, hidden away from the bustle of tourists and day-trippers in Aviemore, and yet not too far from the amenities the town had to offer. It was the sort of street with the sort of houses where tourists, overcome by the beauty of the place, came to wander and to dream of owning that holiday retreat, that something very special, that something very Scottish.

Jake kept an eye out for the sign.

He was running out of street.

'I really hope this is not what I think it is.' He remembered the last house along this road, with its broken porch, peeling paint and rotting windows. When they were kids, up from London for the holidays, he and Marcus had sometimes sneaked into the cellar, daring each other to stay the night in a 'haunted' house. It had seemed like a big adventure then; now it just seemed like two rich kids trespassing on some poorer neighbours' property.

The couple who had owned the rambling wreck had forever been running local kids off their property who had come to do the exact same thing as Jake and Marcus. But they were good people, and in time they'd done the place up a bit, although Jake wondered whether it had fallen back into a bit of a state.

Mr Belafonte had been a well-respected GP in the community. He'd come over with the Windrush Generation and had then adopted Scotland as his home. He'd served the community with such dedication that he'd worked well into retirement. William had been treated by him one Christmas – he'd thought it was a heart attack, but it had turned out it was indigestion; he always overdid it at Christmas dinner.

It hadn't been Dr or Mrs Belafonte who had sent Jake and

Marcus racing for home on the night of that dare. It had been a girl sitting at the top of the cellar steps saying, 'I see you.' If anybody had asked them at the time, they would have all sworn blind they had seen a ghost.

What they had found out later was that they had been looking at the couple's youngest child, a sixteen-year-old girl who, as it turned out, took great delight in scaring little boys hiding fearlessly, or so they thought, in her parents' cellar.

As the car edged ever-closer to what Jake guessed would be Lark Lodge, his feelings of foreboding grew. He didn't know what Mr Addison was prepared to put up with in the name of 'the company' as he called it, but Jake was on holiday, and he really did not want to spend it in some dive. Yes, the place was old and imposing, in one of the loveliest streets in Aviemore, which should on paper be a good omen, but unlike many of the other properties in this patch that had changed hands over the years, this one, as far as Jake was aware, had remained in the same family. He vaguely recalled that William might have mentioned that the elderly couple had recently passed away, and the property had been left to one of their daughters.

Jake sighed heavily, anticipating a wasted trip. Unless a miracle had happened in the intervening months since he last set foot in this part of the world, Jake expected he would be making a trip back into town to find something halfway decent.

Before he turned the car around, Jake decided to satisfy his curiosity and drive up to the house, for old times' sake. Maybe it wasn't as bad as he remembered, and if not, he intended for them to stay. Marcus was in bad shape; he needed to get out of the car and sleep in a proper bed.

Jake reduced his speed to a crawl and kept an eye out for the house. He spotted the last lark stuck on the last remaining tree, pointing up the drive of the last house in the cul de sac.

'Oh boy, I'm just loving every minute,' said Jake to the bird.

He approached the drive to the house with trepidation. He had the impulse to turn the car around and stop wasting his time. What stopped him was the level of traffic he had encountered on the way through the town. It was July, and judging by the school-age kids around on a Wednesday afternoon, Jake was guessing they had already broken up for the summer break and parents were putting the week to good use, holidaying in Scotland. Holiday accommodation would be sparse.

Jake made a sharp right turn and nearly collided with a pair of seven-foot-high wrought iron gates that were obscured from the road by the tall hedging that bordered the property. He slammed on the brakes. On the left was a wooden sign announcing Lark Lodge, with a silhouette of a lark and an artistic sketch of the outline of a house. Jake liked the sign. Next, his attention was drawn to the arched gates in front of him. At the top of the gates were the words *Lark Lodge*, carved out in wrought iron. He didn't remember this, but then he only had a vague recollection of the grounds.

Jake was about to open the car door and get out when the gates let out a metal clang and slowly edged open – outwards.

Jake swiftly put the car into reverse and backed up.

'What's going on?' Marcus was now sitting up, surveying his surroundings.

Jake ignored him, his attention diverted by the thought of another car swinging into the drive, straight into his reversing behind. When he thought the gates had opened sufficiently to get the car through, Jake drove in. The gates slowly closed behind him.

Taking the winding drive really slowly in case he came across anything else unexpected, Jake noted the well-tended lawn on either side. It was a good sign. He hoped. There were neat flower borders, and a cream table and chair set outside some French doors. Things had certainly changed. He might not remember the grounds too well, but he'd have remembered this.

Jake's eyes grew wide as Lark Lodge came into view. The house was impressive; the broken shutters and peeling paint were gone, replaced by bright green shutters which beautifully complemented soft cream wooden windows, and re-pointed and sandblasted grey brickwork. From the cellar windows up to the small turrets at the top of the house, it was obvious that the place had been completely restored to its former glory – it looked stunning.

It looked exactly how Jake imagined a building of this age would have looked when it had first been built. The work carried out on the old house must have been extensive. There was only one possible explanation; Dr and Mrs Belafonte, and their old green Bentley, must indeed be gone. Their daughter, who had inherited the place, must have sold it on. He wondered in passing if it was the same teenage girl who had once scared him and Marcus witless.

The drive ended in a large, oval-shaped gravel car parking area in front of the house. Jake drew up alongside the only other car parked outside. He got out and eyed the green Bentley. He looked up at the house and back at the car. Maybe the new owners had bought the car too – it was a beautiful car.

Jake slammed his car door shut and went to open the rear door for Marcus. Jake peered in at him. 'An amazing transformation, isn't it?'

Marcus nodded slowly at the house.

Jake remained where he was for a moment, looking at Marcus looking at the house. He wondered what was going through his mind. Jake had a feeling this was going to be a sobering experience for both of them being back in Aviemore.

'Come on,' said Jake trying to sound casual, as though it was no big deal to be back. He circled the car to get his bag and Marcus's suitcase out of the boot.

Jake shut the boot; his hands smarting. He picked up the shoulder straps, put his bag over his shoulder, and grabbed the handle of Marcus's case. When he looked up, the door was still open. Marcus was still inside the car. Jake sighed. He moved forward and stopped by the open car door to tell Marcus that he didn't give a toss how ill he was feeling – if didn't get out of the car straight away, he would be forced to carry his own case up to the house. There were steps. He'd have to lift it.

Marcus got out of the car.

'Ready?' said Jake.

Marcus turned his attention to Jake. 'Wasn't there somewhere else to stay – in the town centre, perhaps?'

Jake glared at Marcus. He'd driven all the way there, and now Marcus had the audacity to complain about the choice. 'Why don't *you* suggest somewhere then?'

'I did!' Marcus threw up his arms.

'I am *not* staying at The Lake House.' Jake was adamant. 'Besides, we're here now and …' Jake turned towards Lark Lodge, 'it looks quite nice.' It was quite the understatement. It looked amazing. But would they have vacancies? And if they did, would the proprietor be happy for two guys, one with bandages, the other looking the worse for wear, to stay at their establishment?

Jake heaved a sigh. *What do I have to lose?* he thought. *I'm here now.* On the porch, Jake put his bag down and rang the doorbell. Noticing Marcus wasn't beside him, he turned round to find Marcus still standing by the car. Jake waved his arm in a *will-you-come-on* gesture of annoyance.

Behind him, Jake heard the front door open.

An old lady in a stained pinafore greeted him with a slightly bemused expression on her craggy face. 'May I help you?' her voice wavered.

'Mrs Belafonte?' It couldn't be. Mrs Belafonte must be ninety by now; how could she run a guesthouse? He thought she'd passed on. But perhaps William had his facts wrong.

'Yes?'

'This is Lark Lodge?'

'Lark Lodge,' she repeated vaguely.

'The guesthouse,' Jake confirmed.

'Guesthouse?' She opened the door wide and looked left then right as though she had misplaced something. Then she turned back to Jake, smiled, and shut the door.

'What the …?' Jake shook his head. He knew for a fact this was Lark Lodge; it said so on the gates. But this was obviously no guesthouse. Mr Addison had got it wrong. Jake had no option but to pick up his bag, take the suitcase, and return to the car.

'What, no room at the inn?' Marcus said with a wide grin.

Jake scowled as he walked past Marcus, depositing the bag and suitcase on the gravel beside the car. He opened the boot and had just lifted the first bag back into the car when he heard footsteps on the gravel. He was just about to tell Marcus to stop larking about and help him out, when a woman's voice called out. 'Excuse me … hello …'

Jake moved from behind the open boot to see a middle-aged woman trying to run but instead taking large steps across the gravel towards them. The first thing Jake noticed, and the most striking thing about her, was her hair which was beaded with an assortment of different-coloured plastic beads that flew around her head like a swarm of multicoloured bees as she strode.

'Excuse me, don't go,' she said breathlessly, not slowing down even though she had caught his attention. Jake thought she was going to run straight into Marcus.

'Whoa!' Jake held up his hands.

She skidded to a stop as Marcus gingerly took a step back.

The woman was wearing skinny black jeans and a snug-fitting purple cotton shirt with a flower print, which accentuated her figure. The outfit was not complemented, though, by her old-fashioned apron, which was dusty with flour. A streak of flour dusted her left cheek.

She wiped her hand down her apron and held it out to Marcus. 'I'm Gayle,' she said cheerfully.

Marcus did not make a move to take her hand.

Jake quickly stepped forward and took her hand instead. 'I'm Jake.'

She smiled at Jake, her smile fading as she glanced at Marcus.

'Oh, this is Marcus.' Jake felt like prodding him in the back, but to Jake's relief, he reluctantly offered a shaky hand.

She took it, shook once and then turned her attention back to Jake, her smile back on full beam. 'Would you like a room?'

'This is Lark Lodge, the guesthouse?' said Jake. He was confused.

'Yes. I nearly missed you. I was in the pantry, and you can't hear a thing in there, not a car turning up or even the doorbell, though god knows, it's loud enough – the doorbell, that is. Anyway, I was carrying the pot of flour into the kitchen when I thought I heard someone outside on the gravel.' She beamed. 'And here you are.'

'You have rooms available?' Jake inquired.

Marcus scoffed at the question; by the looks of the deserted driveway, it was obvious they had plenty.

Jake wondered how many other potential guests had been turned away by Mrs Belafonte answering the door.

'She's a beauty, isn't she?'

Jake looked back at Gayle, puzzled by the question.

'The car.' She nodded at the green Bentley.

'Oh, yes,' Jake readily agreed, although he probably wouldn't enjoy driving it with no power steering and its old suspension. It was just nostalgia. Jake still preferred the smooth sleek lines of modern cars, the comfy interiors, the easy handling. He looked lovingly at his shiny blue rental and knew he was going to have a hard time handing it back.

'Do you need a hand with that?' Gayle offered as Jake heaved his bag back out of the boot for the second time.

She was standing with her hands on her hips, eyeing Marcus disapprovingly.

'Please.' Jake's hands stung, but he was ever the gentleman and handed over Marcus's suitcase – it was lighter.

They walked side by side to the wooden porch steps. Jake stole a glance over his shoulder – Marcus was following a little way behind, grudgingly.

26

Jake stood in the hallway, admiring the mahogany panelling and polished wood floors. Despite the plethora of wood, the hall was bright, with natural sunlight streaming through the open doorways of the downstairs rooms and through the large landing window at the top of the stairs.

'There are several rooms free, although you won't have the complete pick of the rooms, as I already have other guests staying with us at the moment.'

Jake already knew about Mr Addison. He wondered who the other guests were. Probably tourists. Jake stared at the guesthouse owner. It was her, he was sure of it – the teenage girl he'd once met who'd given him and Marcus the fright of their lives.

'I'm Gayle, by the way. Gayle Belafonte.' She held out her hand.

Jake was about to take her hand. He looked at his bandaged hand. 'Oh, um … I had a little mishap. Slipped on some broken glass.'

Gayle surprised him by gently taking his hand in hers. 'The bandages need changing. I can look at that for you. I used to be a nurse.'

'Really? Thank you. I'd appreciate it.' His gaze shifted to

Marcus as he stepped into the house, looking dishevelled and quite unwell. *Can you look at him too, and sort him out?* Jake kept his thoughts to himself.

Marcus caught Jake staring at him. 'What?'

Jake shook his head at Marcus and turned his attention back to Gayle. He caught Gayle peering at him. She said, 'Do I know you?'

He very much doubted that she'd recognise them as the two little boys who'd sneaked into her parents' cellar. Rather, he imagined she'd seen their photos in the papers, or on the news. He saw her eyes flicker to Marcus too. He'd have to give their names. Then she'd ask why they were staying in her guesthouse and not at The Lake House.

Jake sighed. He did not want to go into his reasons for choosing to stay at her guesthouse rather than the Rosses' holiday home around the corner. 'I'm Jake Campbell-Ross, and this is Marcus Ross.'

Jake saw her eyebrows rise in surprise. Everyone knew the Ross name around the area. It crossed Jake's mind that apart from William's visit to see Gayle's father, the local GP, one Christmas, they didn't ever meet or have anything to do with the local community. They just stayed in their little wealthy family bubble. It was what Jake now loved about his new life – it didn't consist of private jets and business board meetings; his world no longer revolved around the Rosses' global corporation and the people working in it. He didn't begrudge the time he'd spent in the company, or the family. If Eleanor was still there, that would still be his life. And it had been a good life. He'd just realised when he'd left it all behind that it wasn't meant to be *his* life – it was Marcus's, through and through.

Despite the state he was in, Marcus surprised Jake by holding out his hand to shake Gayle's. 'Very pleased to meet you, Gayle. You know, you scared the crap out of us when we were kids.'

Jake's eyes went wide. He slowly turned to Marcus, glaring at him. Why had he brought that up?

Gayle slapped her knee and laughed. 'Oh, my goodness. I knew it! It *is* you two! The little boys I had such fun scaring in the cellar all those years ago.'

Jake smiled. 'Yes, that was us. Sorry about trespassing on your parents' property. It was very wrong of us.'

Marcus chimed in. 'Yeah – ditto. I think it was my idea, actually. I was an entitled little rich kid who thought I could do whatever I wanted.'

Gayle shook her head. 'Hey, you don't have to apologise. I remember the house was a bit of a magnet for local kids – some rumour I'd heard in town that it was haunted. Because of how rundown it was, I guess it did look like some scary old house from an American horror movie, didn't it?'

Jake exchanged a smile with Marcus. It was true.

When my parents moved in, they'd taken out a large mortgage to afford this place, so it took many years for them to do the place up.'

Jake was still admiring the hallway. 'Well, they did an amazing job. The place couldn't be more different.'

Gayle nodded and smiled. 'It wasn't my parents who did all this. They had the place renovated to a degree, years ago, but it became rundown again as they got older. Even so, what they did to the place was nothing like it is now.'

'Well, whoever did all this has quite a talent.'

Gayle smiled. 'I know. Perhaps you'll get to meet her during your stay. She's quite the interior designer, and she's my friend.'

Jake raised his eyebrows. 'Interior design? Her name isn't Robyn, by any chance?'

Gayle looked at him in surprise. 'Yes. Do you know her?'

'No, not at all. It was a lucky guess. I did see a new shop, I mean outlet, in Mr Gillespie's general store with the name, *Robyn's Interior Design*. I passed it by as I drove through Aviemore, and the rather lovely window display caught my eye.' Jake continued, 'My wife would love … would have loved—' he stopped short. Gayle and Marcus were staring at him.

Gayle stepped into the awkward silence. 'Come, let me show you around.'

'Yes, I'd like that,' Jake said, relieved Gayle hadn't taken what he'd just said, bringing Eleanor into the conversation without thinking, as an opening to start talking about her, and what a tragedy everyone in the local community had thought it was when they'd found out about the skiing accident on Christmas Day. Jake didn't want to hear it. He imagined it had been the talk of Aviemore.

It hadn't occurred to Jake that unless he checked into a hotel or guesthouse under a false identity, which he would not, everyone would know who he was the moment he told them his name, and inevitably the topic of what had happened on that ski slope last December would raise its head – for most people. But it turned out that Gayle was not most people. Somehow, she understood that although well meaning, Jake did not want to hear words of sympathy from strangers.

Jake smiled at her back as she led the way down the hallway, opening doors and showing them the lounge, the dining room, the kitchen where breakfast was served between eight and ten, and the study – which had been her father's study but was now a safe space for relaxation, meditation and reading. 'Whatever floats your boat,' said Gayle, cheerfully.

Jake frowned at Marcus when he whispered, 'Right now, some booze.'

'There's a drinks cabinet in the lounge, if you fancy a tipple.'

Jake turned and grinned at Marcus. Gayle had heard him.

Marcus frowned and shut his mouth.

Jake looked at Gayle, who was glancing at Marcus over her shoulder with an expression of wry amusement.

'Now, which rooms would you both like?' They started up the stairs. Depending on your budget, I've got large, with a super king-sized bed, mid-range – a standard double or twin. And a small – that's a single bedded room, although I'm afraid I only have one of those left. I already have a guest in the other one.

Jake found this all rather amusing, considering that they were Rosses; they could have bought a whole house on a whim just to stay a couple of nights if they'd wanted to. It had not slipped Jake's notice that the Ross Corporation – meaning William Ross – was still depositing money into his bank account each month, unbelievably including bonuses, as though he was still an active employee of the company. And he was still one of the three majority shareholders of the company.

Despite numerous phone calls to make the payments stop, his requests had fallen on deaf ears, despite William's longstanding belief that even if they were family, they had to work hard for their positions. The worst part was that Jake was living on some of that money. He knew he was on a low starting salary as a student teacher, but he'd seen the pay scales. Even when he progressed, he didn't know how he was going to support himself, living in

London on a teaching salary. He honestly didn't know how classrooms teachers did it. That was why he imagined Faye had worked her way up to being a deputy head, and was not only working full-time but doing an additional qualification so she could apply for a headship.

Thinking of the money, Jake knew that neither he nor Marcus would dream of doing something as extravagant as buying a property on a whim. The Ross family were not the kinds of people to flaunt their wealth, or spend it frivolously.

Jake said, 'We're happy to share. A mid-range twin room would be just fine.' Jake wasn't thinking about the money, though. He wanted to keep an eye on Marcus that night; he was still undecided about whether he should call out a doctor. Marcus did not look well.

27

'I have two interconnecting rooms – if you prefer.'

'Oh really?' Jake much preferred that idea. He could keep the interconnecting door open. And there was always the option to slam it shut in Marcus's face if he was getting on his nerves, which was definitely a possibility.

Marcus had already spoiled his trip. It was hard enough that he was back in Aviemore without Marcus having followed him. The night's stay in the airport hotel hadn't helped. He'd debated whether to get a flight home in the morning, back to London, leaving Marcus in Scotland. The only thing that had stopped him was that phone call. The tone of Faye's voice said he had better do as she asked and collect Marcus from the police station. So there he was, babysitting Marcus, who wasn't looking any better despite resting in the back of the car for the whole trip.

'Right, let's head on up to the two rooms in the attic.'

'The attic?' Marcus halted on the second stair.

'Yes, there are lovely views of the Cairngorms.' She added, 'And you'll get a glimpse of the Rosses' holiday home … too.' Gayle stopped, and slowly turned around, her eyes wide. She looked down at them both and winced. 'Sorry, I said that.'

Jake guessed she mentioned The Lake House to all her prospective guests, in case they wanted to catch a glimpse of one of the wealthiest families in the country, whom they'd only ever normally see if they popped up in the news.

Marcus looked as though he hadn't heard her. His attention was on navigating the stairs.

Jake thought that one staircase was enough for Marcus to negotiate just then. He frowned at Marcus. If the stairs up to the attic were anything like those at The Lake House, Marcus didn't have a hope of making it up to the top of house and the two interconnecting rooms that Jake rather fancied. Jake sighed and took Marcus's arm to give him a helping hand, wondering why he was sweating. He'd barely taken two stairs.

Jake resigned himself to the fact that they'd have to take whatever room was available on the next floor. 'Actually, we'll take the mid-range twin room, after all.' He added, 'I'm sure there will be other guests who will appreciate the view more.'

Gayle looked at him for a long moment. They both knew he wasn't talking about the views of the Cairngorms. She said, 'I understand.'

Jake nodded, wondering if she thought the mention of the views towards The Lake House might have put him off those rooms. After all, he reckoned she must be wondering why on earth the two of them were not staying there. Thankfully, she didn't ask, but he did notice her smile slip a little. He imagined she would have charged much more for two rooms, and the views.

Jake added, 'But we'll still pay the same room rate as if we were staying in two rooms on the top floor.' *It's not like we don't have the money.* Jake didn't say that out loud.

'I do not accept charity, Mr Campbell-Ross. You will pay the room rate for your chosen room, and nothing more.'

'Of course, of course.' Jake felt embarrassed for even suggesting it. *But what about the whole house*, Jake suddenly thought. They could, if they wanted, just rent the entire house, and compensate Gayle, her mother, and her guests handsomely to stay in a rather swanky hotel while Jake and Marcus had the run of the guest house.

He looked at Marcus, and was wondering if he should suggest something that outrageous when a huge dog came belting towards them.

'What the hell is that?' yelped Marcus.

'Ah, there you are,' said Gayle smiling. 'I wondered where you were hiding. Say hello to Olive.'

'Olive?' exclaimed Marcus, holding on to the banister for dear life. 'I'd rather not.'

Jake, on the other hand, rather fancied petting the exuberant Old English Sheepdog that was belting towards them, her tongue hanging out of her mouth, her long fur rising and falling as she ran down the hall.

Gayle rushed back down the stairs towards them. 'Sorry. I'll take her into the kitchen and shut the door.'

Jake said, 'Ignore Marcus. This is not one of his better days.' He stepped from the stairs and crouched down to say hello to the large dog.

Olive ran into his arms, tail wagging furiously, giving Jake lots of doggie kisses as though he was a dear, dear friend whom she hadn't seen in an age.

Gayle stood there with her hands on her hips, tutting. 'Really, Olive, anyone would think you don't get any fusses in this household.'

'You have a lovely dog, Gayle,' commented Jake.

'Ah, she's not mine. She belongs to Mr Addison.'

'The guy from the housing development?'

'You've met Nick?'

'Only in passing, when we bumped into him.' Jake decided not to get into where that had been. 'I mentioned that I was looking for somewhere to stay the night, and he said *follow the lark*.'

Gayle grinned. 'That was Robyn's idea. Did you like the little signs guiding you here?'

'No.'

Jake turned around and glared at Marcus. 'We did – yes. I'd like to meet Robyn.'

'I'm sure you will. As I said, she does pop to see me, so you might be lucky. Now, if you ever need any interior design work on the—' Gayle halted.

Marcus sat down on the stair, holding on to the banister spindle, and looked at Gayle. 'On the …?'

Jake rolled his eyes at Marcus's rudeness. They both knew what Gayle had been about to say. 'We'll be sure to pop into her shop and ask. Won't we, Marcus?'

Marcus frowned at them both. He said, 'You accept pets here?'

Gayle turned around and looked at him. 'Well, we accept Olive. I hope that's not a problem.'

Jake stepped in before Marcus got them both thrown out. 'That is not a problem at all. I think she's so cute.'

Gayle smiled. 'Yep, she seems to have that effect on most people.' Jake caught her giving Marcus a sideways glance.

He gave Olive a scratch behind the ears, which she seemed to enjoy. He smiled. He'd never had time for pets, although unbeknown to Faye, he had been looking for a puppy for Natty.

But he had told Natty that the puppy would have to live at his house because Natty had told him Mummy didn't have time to look after a pet, even though Natty had promised she'd do it herself.

As with everything else Natty had asked for when he'd been babysitting her, he'd had no hesitation putting his hand in his pocket and spoiling her rotten. But after Faye's reaction when she discovered all the toys, all the things Faye could not afford, he realised he'd made a huge mistake. He imagined she was probably thinking, *how do I compete with that?* What sort of expectations was he giving her daughter? Expectations that she could have whatever she wanted, he realised. It was little wonder that Faye had stormed out and was barely talking to him.

Olive attempted to get past Jake and say hello to Marcus too.

Gayle noticed. She quickly stepped past Marcus on the stairs, and joined Jake at the bottom of the stairs, taking Olive by the collar. 'Right, back to your bed in the kitchen, Olive. We can't have you monopolising my guests. I'm sure they would like to see their room now, and have some time to unpack before dinner.'

'Dinner?' repeated Jake. You do evening meals here too?' He'd assumed that it was bed and breakfast only.

'Oh, yes. We do now. We used to be just a bed and breakfast, but since I stopped hairdressing, I'm now devoting all my time to running Lark Lodge. I thought, why not offer my guests an evening meal too? It's optional, but I do a nice selection.'

Gayle walked down the hallway, pulling a reluctant Olive along with her. Gayle called out from the kitchen, 'This evening, there's a pot roast or a cottage pie. If you're vegetarian I do a vegetable curry, or vegetable lasagne with lashings of cheese sauce.'

Marcus whispered, 'I think I'm going to throw up.'

'You'd better not!' Jake exclaimed. He threw Marcus a black look. 'For god's sake, get up.'

Marcus held on to the banister and pulled himself up.

'What was that?' Gayle asked, emerging from the kitchen and closing the door.

Jake turned around as Gayle rejoined him at the bottom of the stairs. He was thankful she hadn't heard Marcus's comment. Jake glanced at his bandaged hands. 'Um, you mentioned that you used to be a hairdresser. Sorry, but I thought you said you'd been a nurse?'

Gayle chuckled. 'Yes, I took early retirement when I returned home to look after my parents. Then I fell back on hairdressing, something I used to do before I went into nursing. My father passed away and left me this house. It was my friend's idea to turn it into a guesthouse.'

'Your friend, Robyn?' Jake asked.

'Yes, that's right.' Gayle smiled. 'Now the guest house has really taken off, I gave the hairdressing up too – although if my guests need a haircut or colour, I will certainly oblige.'

Jake furrowed his brow.

Gayle must have caught his expression. 'Ah, you're thinking that if my little guesthouse is doing so well, why have I got so many rooms free?'

Jake nodded. 'Yes, the thought had crossed my mind.'

Gayle chuckled again. 'Ah, you've been lucky. Apart from my two longer-term guests, my last holidaymakers, who were on five-night breaks starting Friday, left today. There are just two nights, tonight and Thursday, when I have no one booked in. Then it's busy again from Friday onwards, apart from the odd single-room vacancy. You see, I do special offers on three, five, and seven-night breaks, and that does attract a lot of guests.'

Jake thought it was his lucky day. Two nights fitted in with his plans perfectly. He was away in Scotland for seven nights – his return flight booked for a week's time. Once he'd seen Arnold Wright, and Martha – whoever they were – he hadn't planned on sticking around Aviemore any longer than he had to. Scotland was a big place. There were plenty of other areas to explore that wouldn't come with painful memories of the previous Christmas.

Gayle said, 'Sorry, I didn't mention that I'm fully booked from Friday. I hope you weren't planning on staying longer.'

'Not at all. Two nights fits in perfectly with my plans.' Jake glanced at Marcus, hoping that he had bucked up by the time they checked out of Lark Lodge on Friday, when Jake intended to take him back to the airport. Marcus was not accompanying him on his onward journey for the remaining five nights of his stay in Scotland. Besides, Marcus had a business to run. Thinking of which, he raised his eyebrows, wondering whether he'd told Lydia, or anyone else, where he was.

'Shall we head up to the room?'

Jake looked at the suitcase. He could manage it, but not his bag as well. 'I'll nip back down for the bag.'

'I'll take it.' Gayle picked up the bag.

Marcus started up the stairs first, holding tightly to the banister, taking it slowly.

Jake frowned at his back, wishing he'd just get a move on.

A little way along the landing, Marcus came to an abrupt halt outside a bedroom door. He was still sweating, Jake noticed.

Marcus turned to him. 'I need to lie down.'

Gayle continued past them. 'The room is along here, at the end of the hallway.'

Jake glanced at Marcus. He sighed and called out to Gayle, 'Is this room free?'

Gayle turned around. 'Yes, but—'

'Great, we'll take it,' Jake replied.

'Um … alright,' she said slowly.

As he watched her walk back down the hallway towards them, it occurred to Jake that she'd just had two men walk into her house. One looked ill, and the other as though he's been in a fist-fight. They were lucky – if it wasn't for that fact that Gayle knew who they were, it would not have surprised him in the least if, like her mother, she'd just shut the door in their faces.

Gayle paused at the door. 'I'm afraid this room just has a double bed.'

'Ah.' Jake hadn't thought to ask. He looked at Marcus's pleading eyes. He'd just have to take a separate room. Unless … 'Is there a couch?'

'Yes.'

'Great.'

Gayle looked at them both. 'Well, if you're sure …'

'Yes, absolutely.'

'This room is the most expensive one, I'm afraid.'

'Of course it is,' Marcus commented under his breath.

Jake turned around and glared at Marcus. 'Ignore him. Marcus is a little out of sorts,' he began, biting his tongue to prevent himself from saying, *Marcus is an idiot.* If he carried on, he was going to get them thrown out of this nice lady's establishment. 'He's feeling a bit under the weather, so I wanted to keep an eye on him tonight.' He added as an afterthought, 'You know how it is.' He wasn't sure what he meant by that last comment, but Gayle's mother's strange behaviour came to mind.

Gayle's gaze drifted to Marcus. She leaned in, peering at him.

Marcus took a step back. 'What are you looking at?'

'Marcus!' Jake berated him. 'For god's sake, don't be so rude.' Jake swiftly turned to Gayle. 'Sorry. He had a rough night last night.' Jake would rather not get into where Marcus had been.

'Yeah – and whose fault was that?'

Jake ignored him. He looked at Gayle. She was an ex-nurse. He wondered what she made of Marcus. Whatever she was thinking, she didn't say. Jake wondered whether he should ask her to check Marcus over. He decided to hang on until the morning – maybe Marcus would be feeling better by then.

Gayle put her hand on the doorknob, but she didn't open the door immediately.

'I want you to know that I don't normally make this room available to paying guests. It's usually reserved for friends only, but I'm going to make an exception just this once.'

'Thank you,' said Jake sincerely. 'That's most kind.' He glanced at Marcus, hoping he kept his big mouth shut and didn't come out with some sarcastic comment.

'This room was re-decorated as a surprise gift from a special friend,' Gayle continued, 'so I would ask that you to treat it respectfully, please.'

'Yes, of course.' Jake said earnestly.

Gayle looked at Marcus. So did Jake.

Marcus, who had been staring off in another direction, realised that everything had suddenly gone quiet. He looked first at Gayle, then at Jake.

There was a moment's uncomfortable silence in which Jake, who a moment earlier had wanted Marcus just to keep his trap shut, was now wishing for exactly the opposite.

Gayle stood there, one hand on her hip, the other resting on the doorknob, keeping the door to the room firmly shut.

Jake rolled his eyes. Marcus hadn't heard a single word she had said.

'Be assured we'll treat the place as if it were our own,' mumbled Marcus.

Jake stared at Marcus, dumbfounded that he had even been listening.

Satisfied with Marcus's response, Gayel unlocked the door and walked in, depositing Jake's bag on the floor by the couch. She turned around a full three hundred and sixty degrees, taking in the room as if for the first time, smiling approvingly at the old-fashioned deep red and gold wallpaper and the large oak fireplace with its cast iron grate, its brick hearth, and its basket of wood and kindling.

Marcus shuffled into the room.

Jake stood in the doorway, eyeing the double bed. He decided the situation was ridiculous. He needed another room.

'You're sure you don't want another room?' Gayle read his mind.

But instead of saying yes, Jake found himself saying no. 'The couch will be fine.' He trundled Marcus's suitcase over to the bed before picking up his own bag and slinging it on the couch opposite the bed.

Catching Gayle's disapproving glare, he lifted his bag gingerly off the couch and placed it carefully on the floor. 'As long as that's still fine with you,' he smiled tightly.

'I'll fetch you a spare duvet, and some pillows.'

'Thank you, Gayle.' Jake closed the door and sighed in relief. He looked at Marcus and thought, *this is going to be a long two nights.*

28

'What was that all about – saying that she doesn't normally rent this room?' Marcus said loudly, about two seconds after Gayle had shut the bedroom door. Marcus shook his head. 'The most expensive room in the house – my arse.'

Jake wanted to tell him to shut the hell up, but he just didn't have the energy. Instead, he sat down on the couch under the window, feeling the soft brown leather beneath his fingertips. The couch was longer than an average bed, if a little narrow, but the leather cushions looked comfortable enough, even though there were enough creases and crevices to make Jake wonder if it was as old as the house.

'Ah, if couches could talk, what stories they would tell.'

'What did you say?' Marcus was trying out the bed.

Jake sighed. 'Never mind.' He was thinking of an incident that seemed like a lifetime ago, but was in fact just before the previous Christmas, when he'd got home from work late and had slept on the couch. He and Eleanor had had a disagreement. Eleanor had just found out she was pregnant. For the first time ever, she'd wanted to spend Christmas in London, just the two of them, absorbing the news. Jake had obstinately refused, thinking of

William first and foremost, and the family tradition of all spending Christmas Day together at The Lake House.

When they had arrived at The Lake House, separately, he'd fallen asleep on the couch and had spent a second night alone – it had been Christmas Eve. They'd never spent another night together. The next day, she was gone.

Jake did not want to think about all the what-ifs and what-might-have-beens. If only he'd listened to Eleanor's wish not to spend Christmas in Scotland.

'Are you sleeping there?' Marcus asked as he got into the double bed and crawled under the covers fully clothed.

'Do you see another bed?'

Marcus drew the covers up to his chin.

Jake rolled his eyes. 'Can you at least take off your shoes?'

Marcus shut his eyes.

Jake got up from the couch and stood at the end of the bed. He lifted the duvet, revealing Marcus's black leather shoes, and removed them one by one. Jake glanced at the small gold-coloured lettering on the inside labels. 'Gucci,' he remarked as he placed them on the floor beside the bed.

Jake pulled the heavy velvet curtains closed. A shaft of light danced around the walls until the curtains hung still. He looked at his watch. 'Marcus.' Jake walked back to the bed. 'Marcus, I'm going out.'

Marcus turned over on his left side, taking most of the covers with him. Jake walked around to the other side of the bed. 'Marcus, I'm …'

'I heard you the first time.' Marcus muffled voice spoke into the pillow. 'Will you go, now? Please.'

Jake had the sudden urge to drag Marcus out of the bed and

get him on the first plane possible, out of his sight. He controlled the urge. But he did not move from the bed.

He was thinking.

He thought of the saying *be careful what you wish for*. Jake had wished hard that Marcus had shown some remorse, some sign that what had happened on Christmas Day had affected him as traumatically as it had Jake. And therein was the rub; Marcus had not only returned to his life quickly, but with Jake gone, he'd taken the company from strength to strength. It seemed that nearly having a breakdown and then totally restructuring his life was not for him; no, it had seemed like business as usual. Until now.

Now it looked to Jake as though he was getting his wish; almost seven months on, Marcus was finally facing up to his demons. What had happened was coming back to haunt Marcus like it had, in the beginning, haunted Jake's every waking hour, and still haunted his dreams.

Jake had seen it coming for months – the crash was inevitable. But Jake didn't want it on his holiday. Besides, Jake wasn't so sure he wanted his wish to come true now. He had grown accustomed to this dance between them; Jake's blaming of Marcus for the tragedy, and Marcus's denial of responsibility – he wouldn't accept that it was his fault Eleanor had given in after he had goaded her to join them on their traditional Christmas Day ski, when she had clearly stated she did not want to go.

If Marcus was finally going to accept responsibility for what he had done, then where would that leave Jake? Where would he be without Marcus as the focus of his anger, his hurt, his blame? Jake knew exactly where – reflecting on the fact that his marriage had been over long before the tragedy, and facing the possibility that she might have been seeing somebody else that Christmas Eve.

Where had she been that evening, when he'd fallen asleep on the sofa before she'd returned?

Jake left Marcus to sleep.

Glancing at the sofa on his way out, Jake was having second thoughts about his sleeping arrangements. He looked at his watch; it was already midday. There was no time to sort it out. He wanted to see Arnold Wright that day; to get that over with as soon as possible so he could leave this place of memories.

Jake put his coat on and stepped out into the hallway. He realised it was better this way. He didn't want Marcus tagging along, being his usual awkward self. Jake closed the door quietly behind him.

'That's Robyn's room, you know.'

Jake jumped at the sound of a voice right behind him. Someone must have crept up on him as he was closing the door. Who had spoken? The voice sounded familiar. Looking up and down the hallway, he couldn't see a soul.

A stair creaked. Gayle's mother, who had answered the door to him and had swiftly shut it without explanation, appeared at the top of the stairs and came towards him. She must have spotted him through hallway banisters as she walked up.

'Ah, Mrs Belafonte.' Jake had been surprised when she'd answered the door to him and had realised she was Gayle's mother. William had clearly got his facts wrong. Both her parents hadn't passed away after all.

'She's coming back, you know,' she said to Jake.

'I'm sure she is,' said Jake casually. He remembered Gayle mentioning that the room was special. She'd said, *this room was re-decorated as a surprise and a gift from a special friend.* That made sense. Gayle had mentioned that her interior designer, Robyn, was also her friend. Jake smiled reassuringly. 'We are not going to be here long. Just two nights, and then we'll be gone.'

She stared at him for a long moment. 'Gone? Why are you leaving?'

'Er … because there will be other guests arriving.'

'Other guests? I don't know what you mean.'

Jake heard Marcus snoring. He glanced at the bedroom door.

She followed his gaze. 'Is Robyn in there?'

Jake stared at her and scratched his head. 'No, that's Marcus. The guy who arrived with me.'

'You're not David! What are you doing in Robyn's room?'

'David?' He looked at Gayle's mother. *Who the hell is David?* he thought. *Something isn't right here.*

'Why don't we both go downstairs and find your daughter.'

'Gayle?'

'Yes, that's right – Gayle.' Jake led the way, hoping she followed. Thankfully, she did. However, when he started down the stairs, Jake didn't hear her walking down behind him. He turned to find her standing at the top of the stairs, looking uneasy.

Jake raced back up. 'Here, let me help you.' Jake offered her his hand.

Tentatively she took the first stair. Taking one step at a time, they made it to the bottom.

He let go of her hand just as Gayle rushed out from the lounge, carrying a book and wearing large round reading glasses. 'Mother!' she exclaimed, 'have you been upstairs again?' Her face registered alarm.

Her mother gave her a look of indignation. 'Maybe,' she said, shrugging, 'or maybe not.' She gave Jake a mischievous grin and walked off towards the kitchen.

Gayle glared after her before turning to Jake for an explanation.

'She was walking up the stairs when I came out of my room. I think she got a bit confused. She asked me what I was doing in Robyn's room, and mentioned some guy called David?'

Gayle took off her reading glasses. 'She spotted you coming out of the bedroom. You're right, that must have confused her. My friend Robyn lived here for a bit. You're in her old room – it was hers and David's – her fiancé. He moved in here too for a bit.'

'Oh, I see.'

Gayle lowered her voice. 'Do you know how many times I tell my mother not to go upstairs? Maybe she's forgotten, but her bedroom is downstairs now.' Gayle looked towards the stairs. 'I thought that if I didn't shift her downstairs, she's going to have an accident one of these days. I know what will happen – she'll get tired coming down one day.' She looked back at Jake. 'Like today, for instance.'

'I'm glad I could be of help,' Jake said. He didn't have time for this. Jake turned to go.

'Sometimes ...' Gayle mused.

Jake rolled his eyes and adopted a sincere expression before turning back to face Gayle.

She continued, 'Sometimes I think my mother does it on purpose.' She looked sheepishly at Jake. 'That wasn't a very nice thing to say, was it?'

'I wouldn't say that …' Jake began, maintaining his thoughtful pose.

'I would. Of course, she doesn't do things just to annoy me,' Gayle tapped her temple. 'It's not her fault she's got dementia.'

'Ah.' Jake nodded. It explained a lot.

'Even so, how does she manage to do the exact opposite of what I tell her, every time?'

'I really can't help you with that one.' He noticed the library book in her hand had a word abbreviated on the spine – *Psych.* Perhaps Gayle was trying to find out from a book.

'I'm sorry,' said Gayle, noticing Jake's coat slung over his arm and the car keys dangling from his hand. 'I'm keeping you.'

'No, not at all,' Jake lied.

Gayle glanced up the stairs. 'Marcus not going with you?'

Jake followed her gaze, thinking up a plausible excuse. 'He's resting for the afternoon.' He made a hasty retreat to the front door.

'Okay,' she said simply. Jake turned to look at her for a moment. She hadn't even asked him what they were doing in Aviemore. How refreshing that Gayle wasn't trying to pry into their lives. If the local press got wind that they were here, he could just imagine the headline: *Mr Campbell-Ross revisits the scene of the tragedy seven months on.*

Jake was not revisiting anything. He was there for entirely different reasons. But that was beside the point. He knew Gayle would not be telling any local reporter, or even probably her friends, just who was staying at Lark Lodge. Jake wanted to kiss her for that. Of course, he didn't. But he had decided that Gayle was all right – more than all right. And if he had reason to return to Aviemore again, he'd be sure to stay at her exceptionally beautiful house.

Jake stepped outside and turned around to face Gayle. 'I'm sorry to hear your mother has dementia.' It explained why, when she'd opened the front door to them when they'd arrived, she'd promptly shut it again.

'She does remember whose room that is.' Jake pointed upstairs, indicating the room he and Marcus were presently occupying.

'Yes, she does, some of the time.' Gayle added. There are days she even remembers who restored her home to its former glory.'

'Your friend, Robyn.' It wasn't a question, but Gayle nodded her head all the same, smiling.

'Well, I guess today was one of those days.' Jake smiled ruefully.

Jake didn't add that he wondered how many other people had been turned away by a charming old lady who had no idea that these strangers had arrived to stay in her beautifully renovated house. Jake wondered if Gayle was aware her mother was unintentionally sabotaging her plans to run Lark Lodge as a guesthouse – although it still sounded as though she had no shortage of bookings.

'As I said before, Robyn didn't just do up the room you're staying in,' said Gayle. 'That was just the beginning … I was sceptical at first, but look at how the place turned out.'

'It used to be the worst house in the street. Now it's the best.' Jake winced, realising he'd spoken his mind. That didn't seem to bother Gayle. She grinned. 'Never a truer word was spoken. I agree completely.'

Jake looked past Gayle at the bright hallway with its gorgeous oak panelling that had given such a fantastic impression of the house as soon as he'd walked through the door.

'You've got some pretty special friends, you know that?'

'I know. And so does Mother.' Gayle started to close the door. 'Oh, by the way, if you ever need any interior design work done on the … um … a property.'

Gayle had already asked him this, but Jake noticed she stayed clear of mentioning The Lake House, or his loss. He wondered if she'd read something in a book on psychology that may have touched on dealing with grief. He had noticed a lot of self-help books lining the bookshelves in the study as they passed by on the tour of the ground floor earlier.

'If I do, I'll be sure to look her up,' said Jake, although he had no plans for making any alterations to The Lake House, let alone returning there.

It might have surprised Gayle to know that it was he who owned The Lake House. It had been his parents' home. It was where they'd raised him as a child before he was orphaned.

This was not common knowledge. As far as most people were aware, The Lake House had simply been used as a cherished holiday home for many, many years. But back then, soon after Jake had lost his parents, The Rosses had moved in, spending a time living in The Lake House to try to give Jake some normality; allowing him to remain in his childhood home after losing his parents.

However it wasn't long before the demands of the Ross Corporation encroached on the family's Scottish idyll. Although William had wanted to remain living in the house with his family, it had not been possible. Inevitably, a short time later, they had relocated to London permanently, vowing to spend each Christmas there in Aviemore, recapturing the time they'd spent there as a family when Marcus, Jake and Eleanor were children.

Jake wondered what would happen the next Christmas. As far as he was aware, nobody had visited The Lake House for the last seven months. The house had lain forlorn and forgotten. He couldn't see that changing any time soon. But Gayle had given him pause for thought. Who hadn't seen photos of mansions snapped up by the rich and famous, only to be left uninhabited and forgotten, falling in a state of disrepair?

As he turned to go, he smiled and said, 'Perhaps I will look up Robyn and enlist her services to spruce up The Lake House.' Jake was thinking that perhaps it was time to let The Lake House go. Maybe if he did that soon, then another family would move in by Christmas, and the rooms would echo once more with laughter, and the house would be filled with joy and happiness. It was never going to happen again there for the Rosses, he thought sadly.

His smile faltered. He knew it was a mistake going back there. Everything reminded him of losing Eleanor.

His thoughts turned to Faye. He didn't want to lose her too. He'd give it all away – the money William kept depositing in his bank account, The Lake House, if Faye would just forgive him. After that conversation at the airport yesterday, he knew he still had some way to go to earn her forgiveness. How would he do that if he was hundreds of miles away in Scotland?

He was walking to the car with that thought going through his mind, when Gayle called after him, 'Will you both be joining us for dinner over the next two evenings? I just like to know so that I can plan the meals accordingly.'

Jake wished she hadn't put him on the spot. He regretted booking two nights. It had nothing to do with the accommodation, staying in this beautiful house. The fact was that he regretted booking an entire week away. *New plan*, thought Jake. Tomorrow they were both heading home.

29

Jake sat in the driver's seat with the engine ticking over and unravelled the dog-eared piece of paper on which he had written down the address that Arnold Wright had given him. The place was called Cedar Grove. It wasn't familiar, but then Jake hadn't lived in this part of the world since he was a child. The centre of Aviemore, the ski slopes in the Cairngorms, and the part of town where The Lake House was situated were the only places he had frequented during their annual winter holidays there.

He looked back at the house when it occurred to him that he could have asked Gayle if she was familiar with a place called Cedar Grove. Jake put the address in the SatNav instead, and was pleasantly surprised when directions popped up.

A few miles outside town, along a winding country road with glimpses of a loch through the trees bordering the route, he spied a small billboard advertising Cedar Grove. Soon after, the line of trees suddenly vanished, replaced by a high brick wall obviously bordering the property. The SatNav indicated that the destination was up ahead on the left.

Jake slowed the car as he came upon a driveway. Two pillars marked the entrance with the word *Cedar* engraved into cement on the left, and the word *Grove* on the right.

Jake swung the car slowly between the pillars and drove up the gently sloping drive. There were no houses packed close together as he had anticipated; just a carpet of neat green lawn either side of the drive. It reminded Jake of exclusive developments with homes so expensive the developer could afford not to build on every inch of the land, leaving an enormous amount of communal space for the residents to enjoy, like this.

Jake backed the car into a parking space alongside a single row of parked cars. He switched the engine off.

He'd expected some sort of housing estate with new-build properties. In reality, a glass structure resembling a domed conservatory separated two dark red gothic buildings. Jake looked at the crumpled address. There was no house number. When he'd seen the sign advertising the place, he'd assumed it was a new housing development. Jake looked up at the houses again. Could he be mistaken, or was this in fact one house?

Jake got out of the car. He walked along the smooth tarmac, up ten wide stone steps onto a veranda spanning the length of the substantial property. Jake approached the front door, which appeared to be propped open. Out of courtesy, Jake rapped on the open door before poking his head inside. A smartly dressed middle-aged couple – deep in conversation – approached. Jake stepped forward and held out his hand. 'Mr Wright, I'm Jake. Jake Campbell-Ross.'

They stopped in front of Jake and exchanged bemused glances.

'From London,' Jake put in, extending his hand further. No one took it. 'Oh, this?' He glanced at his bandaged hand. 'I'm perfectly fine. It was just a little accident, that's all.'

'I'm sorry, but you've got the wrong …' the man began.

'We spoke.' Jake interjected, 'on the phone.'

The woman brushed past. 'Excuse us,' she said to Jake, eyeing him warily as she pulled her husband's arm, encouraging him to quicken his pace.

Jake stepped aside with his hand still outstretched to let them pass. He watched them walk down the stone steps towards a parked car. 'My mistake.' Jake shrugged and walked inside.

A plethora of doors skirted the hallway interior and two staircases rolled up to greet each other under a massive arched window. Tilting his head back, Jake slowly turned full circle, taking in the assortment of tapestries and old oil paintings adorning the walls; in this respect it was not dissimilar to William's large four-storey London home. It was just on a much grander scale.

'Can I help you?' a businesslike voice ventured.

Jake turned abruptly in the direction of the voice. He thought an explanation was in order as to why he'd just walked in off the street uninvited. 'The door was open,' Jake pointed out to the smart middle-aged woman who had appeared out of nowhere.

She leaned slightly to one side, taking in the open door behind Jake. 'It always is,' she said simply.

'I've come to see Martha.'

'Come with me.' She turned on her heel, her pencil pleat grey woollen skirt flapping around her ankles as she clicked down the hallway in razor-thin heels.

'Mr Wright phoned me,' Jake explained to her back as he followed her down the hall. 'We made arrangements to meet.'

'Oh, I think you're mistaken.'

Jake opened his mouth to protest just as she disappeared through a door. Catching up, Jake hovered in the doorway. The woman was standing behind a large desk flicking through a notepad open in front of her. She had a biro in her hand.

'Come through.' She didn't look up.

Jake glanced at the door, noticing a small, gold-coloured rectangular plaque with the word *Reception* in black lettering. He stepped into the room.

'I thought this was a private house?' said Jake.

'Used to be,' she said. 'Now, what is your name please?'

'My name?'

We keep a log of visitors to Cedar Grove.'

Jake hesitated. He did not want to get into a conversation about what happened last Christmas when she found out who he was.

The receptionist looked up, pen hovering over her note pad.

'I'm Jake Campbell-Ross.'

Their eyes locked for a moment. Jake anticipated that she'd say something, but to his relief she did not. Jake watched her write his name in the book.

She closed the notepad and walked around the desk, extending her arm towards the door. 'This way, if you please.'

Jake walked out of the room ahead of her, bemused by the old-fashioned turn of phrase.

'So, what exactly is Cedar Grove?' said Jake, pausing while she closed the reception door. 'I assumed that it was a new housing development.'

'Yes, I suppose people would think that with the billboard advertising the place.'

She led the way back along the corridor towards the main entrance, her high heels clicking on the polished parquet floor. They mounted the left-hand staircase and headed towards the majestic landing window.

'This is a hospice,' she said, glancing back at Jake as she passed the window.

'A hospice?' Jake stopped halfway up the stairs and looked through the impressive landing window onto the beautiful grounds below – grounds that, according to a billboard, would soon be littered with houses and apartments. He wondered if the owner was in the process of selling. Jake intended to take a closer look at one of those billboards on his way out.

Jake turned away from the window and walked up the remaining flight of stairs. The receptionist was already at the top, arms folded, waiting for Jake. She led Jake along the galleried landing, passing numbered doors. 'We cater for a variety of different …' she paused, 'circumstances.' They stopped at the last door.

'Circumstances?' repeated Jake.

She nodded. 'All terminal, I'm afraid.' She knocked on the door softly.

'It must cost a fortune.' Jake muttered to himself.

'Yes, I expect the running costs are quite high.'

'No, I meant looking after the … sick people.'

'Residents; we like to call them residents. And it doesn't cost them a bean.'

'They don't pay?'

She put her hand on the doorknob. 'Cedar Grove is a charity, Mr Campbell-Ross.' She opened the door and ushered Jake inside. 'I'll leave you now,' she said, 'but remember that this resident tires easily, so don't be too long.' She closed the door.

30

Jake stood just the other side of the door, uncertain about what to expect or what he was doing there.

At first glance, the room appeared empty. It was not how Jake would have imagined such a room would be – clinical, like a hospital. In fact, the room was just how Jake had imagined it would be before the receptionist had said the word *hospice*; it was totally in keeping with what Jake had seen so far of the house. The delicate rose print wallpaper, large oak furniture and soft-cushioned, old-fashioned sofas and high-backed chairs harked back to another era and suggested that the benefactor had donated the property lock, stock and barrel. The charity on the receiving end had had the sense not to change a thing, which strangely pleased Jake. He didn't see a bed, so he guessed this was more like an apartment than the single bedroom he'd been anticipating.

He didn't know why he felt so relieved that they'd clearly kept so much of the original interior; after all, the property had nothing whatsoever to do with him, although he felt he had been there before. Not in this room, but he had walked up the staircase; he was sure of it. He'd had the strongest feeling of déjà vu.

He vividly remembered looking out of that same picture

window overlooking the grounds. There was something else; Jake was almost certain he had been there with his mother. Beyond that, he drew a blank. With many childhood memories, it was difficult to distinguish the real from the imagined, but Jake felt certain about his memory of the beautiful arched window.

He wondered how long Cedar Grove had been a hospice. If it had not been a hospice all those years earlier when he was a child, then whom had his mother taken him to visit there? Jake was very interested to find out what connection his mother might have had to the fine old house and its generous benefactor.

Jake's eyes roved to the far end of the room, where two high-backed red leather chairs were positioned in front of a latticed, leaded window overlooking the grounds. One of the chairs was occupied.

'Mr Wright?' Jake ventured, moving into the room, his eyes fixed on the back of Mr Wright's head. 'I'm Mr Campbell-Ross. Mr Jake Campbell-Ross; we spoke yesterday on the phone.'

The last word had barely passed his lips when the old man leapt from his chair and whirled towards Jake at such a velocity that for a minute Jake thought he was hallucinating. Jake took a step back in surprise as the old man approached; he could feel his back up against the door.

'Good heavens, did I give you a fright?'

Something in his tone made Jake wary, as if giving him a fright was exactly the man's intention. Nevertheless, Jake took a step forward and, feeling just a little foolish at being afraid of an old man, extended his hand. 'Are you Mr Wright?'

'None other – call me Arnold.' Mr Wright looked down at Jake's bandaged hand. 'Nothing serious, I hope?'

Jake stared at Mr Wright, wondering whether he saw the irony in that observation. For someone nearing the end of his life – which Jake presumed was the case, if he lived in a hospice – he looked quite the picture of health; a rotund little man whose bright blue eyes twinkled mischievously under a full head of wiry white hair. He sported a ruddy, red face, as though he'd just feasted on a hearty meal and had been relaxing in his chair with an after-dinner brandy. Jake eyed him, and suddenly realised he'd jumped to conclusions. If he was living here with his wife in this apartment, that didn't mean he was ill too. He clearly wasn't.

'Do you want a fresh dressing? I could call a nurse.' Mr Wright pointed at the door.

'No,' Jake said quickly. 'Thank you.' He didn't want to hang around this place any longer than he had to.

Mr Wright looked as pleased as punch to see him. The feeling wasn't mutual. Jake wished he hadn't agreed to travel to Scotland to see him, and Martha. At first he'd been curious, after Arnold had mentioned she knew William. Now he wished that his curiosity hadn't got the better of him.

They stood in awkward silence; Mr Wright positively beaming, Jake offering an uncomfortable smile. 'Sorry I couldn't make it yesterday; my plane was delayed on arrival.' Jake brushed aside the mental image of Marcus being escorted across the tarmac to a waiting police van.

Mr Wright waved it away. 'Arnold – please,' he insisted. 'Besides, I'm not going anywhere,' he said brightly.

Arnold returned to the window but did not resume his seat in the high-backed chair; instead, he motioned to the chair next to his.

Jake walked over, intending to sit in the other chair. He froze. Jake looked across at Arnold in surprise.

'Before we talk about Martha's letters,' he said in a whisper, 'I'd like you to meet her.'

Jake looked down at Martha. She was asleep, her head tilted on one side, resting on the wing of the chair. Her features were barely discernible through a fountain of long blonde hair that cascaded over her face in a silky, pale flow.

'A hairdresser comes once a week. They even colour it, you know,' said Arnold. 'It's the first thing people notice about her. She was very proud of her locks; said they were her best feature.' Arnold turned away from her to look out of the window.

Jake continued to stare at the woman with the beautiful hair. Jake thought that she looked so still, she could almost have died.

'She has.'

Jake shot Arnold a look. 'Pardon me?'

'I guessed what you were thinking,' said Arnold. 'That she looks as though she could have passed.'

Jake was surprised that Arnold had guessed his thoughts.

'She has, in a way,' he said softly, turning from the window to look at Jake. 'You understand what I'm saying, don't you, Jake?'

Jake stared at him long and hard. Shaking his head, he said, 'No, I do not.'

Arnold sighed heavily. Then he crossed the room to take a seat beside the bed.

Jake left the sleeping woman and followed Arnold. There were two low sofas positioned opposite each other in front of a fireplace. They both sat opposite one another.

'Alzheimer's.' Arnold shifted his gaze to Jake. 'It's not that uncommon, apparently, for someone in their sixties. People just assume it only afflicts those of advancing years. But it doesn't,' he said sadly.

'I'm sorry.'

'So am I,' he paused. 'I don't want her to suffer. And this is suffering, being locked inside like that, knowing things, wanting things, but just not being able to … to …'

'At least she has you,' Jake offered.

An uncomfortable silence followed in which Jake sensed he had said something wrong. Jake stared at the man, who looked a picture of health, and suddenly had a thought. 'You're not a resident here, are you?'

'Resident, here?' a twinkle of understanding flickered across his face. 'Oh, you thought …' he chuckled, surprising Jake by his light-hearted demeanour under the circumstances. 'Dear me, no.'

'Ah, I see now how I've confused you. I didn't give you my home address because …' He trailed off.

Jake followed his gaze to the window. He understood; Arnold would be right there, spending every waking moment that he could with his wife, while there was time.

'I lost my wife,' Jake said suddenly, impulsively, surprising himself by sharing such an intimate, painful detail with a stranger. He had never shared his thoughts, not even with Faye, refusing to open the door to a topic he did not want to discuss; refusing to open the door to feelings he wanted to keep buried.

Jake silently cursed himself for opening that door. He knew what was coming; he waited for the inevitable battery of concerned questions that masked people's morbid curiosity. Instead, Arnold simply said two words. 'Did you?'

Jake stared at him. What did he mean – *did you?* Jake didn't understand the question. Was he referring to whether she actually died up there, on the mountain? As far as Jake was concerned, that was beyond question. Or was it simply the case that Arnold, quite bizarrely, had not heard about the accident that had claimed her. That made no sense. He couldn't fail to have heard about it on the news, or read about it in the paper – unless he was from another planet. It had been the top news story in town at Christmas.

'Anyway,' Arnold slapped his knee with the palm of his hand as though he had been listening in on Jake's rambling thoughts and had heard enough; it was time to move on. He pointed at a lady's black leather handbag perched on the bedside table and asked Jake to fetch it. Jake passed Arnold the bag.

Arnold did not make a move to take the bag. 'You open it.'

Jake sat down on the bed and undid the clasp. He glanced at Arnold's wife and hesitated; despite Arnold's presence, Jake still felt uncomfortable opening her handbag. What if someone walked into the room and saw what he was doing?

'Go ahead – it's all right.'

Jake gingerly put his hand in the bag and brought out a crumpled brown envelope.

Jake turned the envelopes over and noted the names written on the fronts – William Ross and Ralph – but there were no addresses.

'She has moments of lucidity when she knows who I am. Lately, when I thought she was having one of her more lucid moments, she talked to me as though I was somebody else.' He lowered his voice. 'Sometimes she calls me Ralph.'

'Ralph. Is it a name from her past, her first husband, perhaps, if she was married before?'

Arnold slowly shook his head. 'It could all be irrelevant. I just don't know anymore.' He sighed. 'The only thing of which I am certain is that when she sees the letters,' he dropped his eyes to the envelopes in Jake's hand, 'she gets very agitated.' He sighed heavily.

'I want to help, I really do. But I don't know what she's trying to tell me. All I know is that it had something to do with those, and the two people's names on the envelopes – William Ross and Ralph.'

'No surname?' Jake asked.

Arnold shook his head. 'Afraid not.'

Jake imagined that now Martha's condition had advanced, there would be few lucid moments in which to organise her affairs herself before she died. Arnold clearly had no choice but to step up and sort out her private affairs now.

All the same, Jake thought that it was all rather strange, being married to someone and having secrets from them. Jake glanced at the letters. That was how this felt; almost as though there was something Martha wanted to hide.

He wasn't quite sure what Arnold expected him to do for Martha now that he was there, although he understood why Arnold had contacted him. He imagined Arnold didn't just want to send the letters on to their intended recipients, in case the letters didn't reach them, and went astray.

'The worst thing is she pleads with me, with her eyes …'

Jake stared at the envelopes.

'… as though she knows her faculties are going.'

He no longer wanted to read the letters. Perhaps it was best if he just gave them to William or, better still, Aubrey to sort out. Aubrey would know what to do. He always knew what to do. But this wasn't business, Jake reminded himself. This seemed personal. Perhaps, in hindsight, it was better that he had not got through to Aubrey on the phone about this. What if Martha was someone from William's past that he'd rather Aubrey knew nothing about?

'… but there's a part of her still trying to reach me.'

He suddenly felt as though he couldn't breathe.

'Are you alright, Mr Campbell-Ross? You look a little pale.'

Jake stood up. 'I've got to go,' he said abruptly. He didn't even make a show of looking at his watch or offering an excuse.

Arnold looked up at Jake in surprise. 'Oh, of course. Sorry, I do tend to chat,' he said apologetically as Jake strode to the door. 'I'm always here. Come back – anytime.'

Jake paused in the doorway on his way out and took one last look at the two high-backed chairs by the window before closing the door.

He walked along the galleried landing – fast. He took the stairs two at a time and was relieved to find the reception hall deserted. He headed full pelt for his car.

Jake hadn't bothered to lock the car, so he got straight in. He struggled to get his bandaged right hand into his coat pocket to retrieve his car keys. 'Oh, for heaven's sake!' When he finally got them clear of his pocket, they slipped out of his hand and onto the floor. 'Dammit!'

Jake was about to reach down when he noticed it; he was still holding the crumpled manila envelopes in his left hand. How had that happened? He tried to recall handing them back to Arnold before he left. He could not. He must have walked out without realising it. Jake closed his fingers around the envelopes and turned his attention on the hospice.

Staring through the windscreen at the building's entrance, Jake toyed with the idea of just handing the envelopes in to reception, but that seemed callous; after all, the letters seemed to hold a great significance for Martha. He doubted that Arnold would have let him leave with them if he hadn't thought Jake would return, hopefully with some answers. Well, he was wrong. Jake stuffed the envelopes into his coat pocket. He'd send them back by recorded delivery with his apologies for wasting his time. Cowardly – yes. But it wasn't until he'd arrived, and seen Martha, that he realised he'd bitten off more than he could chew. All this just brought back painful memories of Eleanor.

Jake leaned forward to retrieve his car keys from where he'd dropped them. They weren't visible, so Jake reached under the seat until his fingers brushed the key fob. He grabbed the car key and felt something else under the seat.

'What's this?' Holding up the bag he'd found under the seat, Jake had a mental image of Marcus shuffling into the lift at the police station that morning, carrying his belongings along with this small plastic bag. He realised that when Marcus had fallen asleep in the back of the car, his grip must have loosened on the bag, and it must have fallen to the floor and slid forward under the seat.

Jake examined the contents – there were phials of greenish coloured liquid.

What were they? And more to the point, Jake wondered with a pang of concern, when did he need to take them?

Jake opened the plastic bag and took out one of the phials, handling it carefully in case he dropped the small bottle. Jake held it close in an attempt to read the label. The writing on the label was poor, barely legible, but even so, Jake immediately recognised the generic term for methadone.

This was bad. This just confirmed Jake's suspicions. This wasn't just Marcus using drugs for recreation – he was in deeper than Jake had thought. Marcus would be climbing up the walls if he woke up and found there was no heroin and no methadone. Jake threw the bag on the passenger seat and started the engine. Forcing himself to manoeuvre slowly past the parked cars, Jake sped down the drive. With a brief glance left, he threw the car in the direction of Aviemore. By the time Jake passed the first Cedar Grove billboard, he had forgotten his intention to stop and take a closer look.

31

Parking next to Gayle's car, Jake got out of the hire car, plastic bag in hand. He raced to the front door. Gayle opened the door as he approached. Jake swiftly put the plastic bag behind his back.

'Jake. Welcome back.'

He glanced furtively at her as he entered the hallway, hoping she hadn't been watching him from the kitchen window as he approached, looking like a drug addict who had just scored.

She closed the door behind him.

Jake kept his hand behind his back. He knew it looked odd. 'Is Marcus up and about yet?'

'Oh, he went out soon after you left,' said Gayle over her shoulder as she walked into the kitchen.

'He did?' Jake looked down the hallway, confused; Marcus hadn't so much as fallen asleep as fallen into a coma before he left. 'Are you sure?'

'Uh-huh. I gave him a key to the front door before he left, so he can return when he wants. Sorry, I forgot to give you a key too. I've been watching out for your return to unlock the front door.'

Jake glanced up the stairs and decided to go and see for himself.

In the bedroom, he discovered that the curtains were still drawn but the bed was empty, and Marcus's Gucci shoes were gone. Jake shut the bedroom door. Where the hell had he gone without a car?

Jake returned to the kitchen and stood in the doorway, watching Gayle. She stood by the oven, wearing a large pair of oven gloves. She opened the oven door and lifted something out.

Jake's mouth watered at the thought of home baking.

She turned around. Her massive oven gloves were wrapped around a small, deep, rectangular foil tray. She stopped when she saw Jake standing in the doorway. 'Come in and join me for dinner.' She set the foil tray down on the large wooden table in the centre of the room.

Jake eyed the tray. 'What is it?'

'Haggis hotpot, and I've got plenty more.'

Jake spied several empty rectangular cardboard boxes on the worktop near the oven, bearing pictures of hotpot.

'Come, sit.' Gayle pulled out a chair for Jake to join her.

Jake hesitated. He was not a great fan of fast food, and that included pre-packaged frozen meals. But he was hungry, his stomach was complaining, and he had to admit that it did smell surprisingly good for a ready meal.

'I was waiting for you to return.'

'You didn't have to do that, Gayle.'

'I tend to eat my evening meal later anyway,' Gayle replied.

Jake eyed the food tray and hesitated.

'Ah – you were expecting home-cooking,' said Gayle, tipping the foil tray and dishing it out onto a dinner plate. 'I'm sorry to disappoint, but cooking is not quite my forté, although on occasion I do cook a roast, and my cooked breakfasts are very nice indeed, if I do say so my—'

'Gayle,' Jake interrupted, looking past her out of the kitchen window. The eerie stillness of dusk was quickly descending on the garden. Jake had lost track of time. It was later than he'd thought. It would be dark soon, and there was still no sign of Marcus.

'Did Marcus mention where he was going?'

Gayle shook her head. 'Not a word. I was here in the kitchen when I glanced out of the window and saw him walking down the driveway. I didn't hear the front door go. When I went out to have a look, the front door was wide open.'

Jake sighed. 'Sorry about that.'

Gayle picked up the knife and fork beside her plate. 'He seems preoccupied.'

Jake knew exactly what Marcus was preoccupied with. He could feel the bulge in his pocket where he'd stuffed the plastic bag containing the methadone. He'd also seen the state of their room when he'd nipped upstairs. Both his bag and Marcus's suitcase had been emptied completely; their contents had been strewn around the room in a frenzied search for the methadone that Jake had in his possession. Marcus, by that time, would have been frantic, desperate to find Jake, desperate to get something into his system.

Jake turned on his heel and headed for the front door, then did a quick about-turn. He poked his head around the kitchen door. 'Gayle.'

She looked up.

'Thanks for the offer.' He pointed at the hotpot. 'Sorry, but I'm not stopping to eat dinner. I'm going to look for Marcus.'

'Maybe next time, I'll cook something myself.' She pointed at the food on her plate. 'Tastes good, though.'

Jake didn't have time to hang around and tell her she'd got it wrong; that his reason for declining the offer had nothing whatsoever to do with the food. He really did need to find Marcus.

Jake shut the front door behind him and headed for his car. He patted his pockets for his car keys and felt the phials. He walked faster.

He sped down the driveway, flicking on his headlights. Suddenly, he slowed. It occurred to him that it might not be wise to speed down the driveway if Marcus was walking back at that very moment.

He reached the end of the driveway. There was still no sign of him.

'Now where?' Jake pondered as he sat in the receding light at the end of the driveway. There was only one place he could go, and that was into town. Aviemore was the only place that had a chemist, and in Marcus's irrational state of mind, he was probably thinking he could just waltz in there and pick something up over the counter.

Jake drove down the street.

After a short distance, he stopped the car. What if he was way off beam and Marcus had in fact gone out for something else? Jake had an idea what that might be. He backed up the car and stopped a little way up the street from Lark Lodge. He remembered the lane between the houses that led to a gate – a hidden entrance that he doubted people knew about. The lane was overgrown, the gate probably rusted with age. Would the gate be locked? Jake had no clue whether he'd need a key to get into the grounds of The Lake House. He presumed so. Jake didn't have one. Nobody had used that cut-through for years. He decided not to bother walking up the lane to find out if the gate was open.

Jake put the car into gear and drove down the street, taking an immediate right turn. A very short distance along the main road was a familiar turn-off which led to one single property set back from the road that fronted a loch – The Lake House. The extensive walled garden backed on to Gayle's property.

Jake turned into the lane, driving several hundred yards before he slowed the car to a stop at the entrance to a driveway. He sat listening to the hum of the engine. A streetlamp cast a hazy yellow glow a short distance up the drive. Beyond that, all Jake could make out were grey shapes in the gloom. It was getting dark fast. Jake pumped the gas and steered the car into the driveway. He took it slowly. He followed the drive around the back of the house, barely giving it a second glance as he passed by. If Marcus was there, he knew exactly where to find him.

Jake brought the car to a stop. He left the headlights on and got out; the two beams of light illuminated the empty shingle parking area at the back of the house and the old stone steps leading down to the garden beyond. Jake took the steps two at a time, entering the gardens.

He cut diagonally across the lawn, heading for the six-foot hedging that to anyone not familiar with the house would assume marked the boundary of the grounds. It did not. Jake walked through a narrow gap in the hedge to reveal a smaller, secluded area of garden. He stood there, letting his eyes adjust to the deepening gloom; Jake could make out the grey shapes of bushes and trees and the hedge on the other side – but there was no sign of Marcus.

Jake's eyes focused on the centre of the garden. He couldn't see much at all, and within a matter of minutes it would be pitch dark. It didn't matter, though; he didn't need to see what was there to know why Marcus might have gone there.

Jake backed out of the garden.

'I couldn't go in.'

Jake whirled around in fright and kicked something with his shoe.

'Ow. Jake!'

Looking down, Jake discovered Marcus sitting on the damp grass to one side of the gap, his back against the hedge, knees drawn up to his chin. Jake rolled his eyes. 'For goodness' sake – why didn't you say something so that I knew you were there!' Jake kicked him again, intentionally this time.

'I just did!'

'No, I meant when I first walked into the garden. I thought I was alone. This isn't one of those places that you … well, you know.' He crouched down opposite Marcus.

'Thought I was a ghost, did you?' Marcus said through chattering teeth.

Jake reached out and put a hand on Marcus's shoulder. 'Are you intending to sit here all night?' It was cold, and Marcus had no coat. Jake got up. 'Come on let's get out of here.'

'Jake, I …' Whatever Marcus was going to say was lost in the attempt to stand up.

Jake watched him take a few faltering steps before grabbing Marcus's right arm and swinging it around his shoulder. With the other arm wrapped around Marcus's waist, Jake guided him back up the garden into the beams of light from the waiting car. He was thinking about Marcus's arrest. In hindsight, Jake had realised that Marcus would not have taken anything with him on the flight or in his luggage – he wasn't that stupid. So, he must have made arrangements to get hold of something when he landed. Then he had found himself incarcerated overnight in the police station at Inverness with no chance of meeting up with the contact and spending an inordinate amount of money on illegal drugs. And now he was going cold turkey. Jake knew this had not come about through choice.

The police officer was right; if he was any sort of friend, he would get him some help. But they weren't brothers, and they weren't friends – not anymore. And yet for all Jake's desire to see Marcus suffer for his role in Eleanor's death, the reality of seeing Marcus in such a state was having an unexpected side-effect – Jake was hurting too.

Jake helped Marcus into the front seat of the car and toyed with the idea of asking Gayle to take a look at him when they got back. He got in the car next to Marcus and reversed in an arc away from the gardens.

'What was that?' said Marcus.

Jake stopped the car.

'Did you hear it?' Marcus turned to Jake.

Jake sat very still and listened intently; there were noises coming from the house.

He put the gear shift in neutral, handbrake on, switched to main beam and opened the car door.

Marcus grabbed his arm. 'Where are you going?'

'To take a look. Do you mind?' said Jake, glancing his way. With the car door open and the interior light on, Jake got a good look at Marcus; he didn't look well. He was deathly pale, and beads of sweat lined his forehead above black sunken eyes.

Marcus released his grip on Jake's arm.

Jake got out and stood for a moment, staring at the house. The sight that confronted him was fast approaching the state of Gayle's house before Robyn had worked her miracle. Jake was amazed at the state of the house. From what he could see, a couple of exterior window shutters had come loose and were swinging in the wind. The paint on the windows was peeling, and a large crack had spread across one of the window panes in the lounge. The glass would need replacing And that was just the downstairs. The upstairs, not illuminated by the headlights, disappeared in a sea of black.

How could a house go downhill like this in such a short space of time? He couldn't recall the last time the exterior of the house had been painted. As a family, the Rosses had all led busy lives. Hiring a decorator for a holiday home was perhaps not up there on their list of top priorities. At Christmas, he doubted anyone had really been paying attention to the exterior of the house when they'd all arrived; thoughts of redecorating would have been far from their minds.

Jake heard a loud bang coming from the direction of the house. He ducked his head instinctively and moved out of the glare of the headlight around the side of the car. He looked into the passenger window at Marcus, who had heard it too; he was hunkered down in his seat.

Something banged again.

Jake moved towards the house, but the headlights suddenly went dim. Jake glanced back at the car. Marcus had dipped the headlights and was watching him intently, shaking his head from side to side and motioning for him to get back in the car. Jake ignored him and moved stealthily across the shingle drive, wincing at every crunching step.

At the back of the house, Jake relaxed and stood up straight, grabbing the kitchen door before it swung shut again in the wind.

Stepping into the kitchen, he scuffed a pile of dead leaves that had blown in through the open door. He flicked a light switch, but the electricity was out. Jake knew where to find the fuse box, but he didn't fancy breaking his neck on the steep cellar steps.

He stepped outside and shut the door.

'What did you find?' said Marcus as Jake got back in the car.

'It was just the kitchen door banging in the wind.' Jake threw the gearshift into first and headed back around the side of the house.

Marcus turned to look out of the back window as they drove down the driveway. Then he faced the front again and turned to Jake. 'We should have had the place decorated or something. I'm surprised how it's deteriorated in the last few months.'

Jake nodded.

'What did it look like inside?'

'I don't know.'

'What do you mean you don't know? You were in there, weren't you?'

'No electricity,' he said, glancing at Marcus, who was shaking. 'You cold?' Jake switched the heating on.

'We should call someone.' Marcus's teeth chattered.

'It can wait until morning; the house isn't going anywhere.'

Clear of the driveway, Jake drove the short distance back to Lark Lodge and discovered that they no longer had the place to themselves. Another car was already parked in their spot next to the Bentley. Jake helped Marcus out of the car, and together they made their way across the gravel drive, passing the other guest's car. Jake spotted a yellow hard hat perched on the rear parcel shelf.

Marcus unlocked the front door. There was no sign of Gayle, or any of the other guests. They went up to their room. Marcus lay down on the bed as Jake quietly shut the bedroom door.

'Where were you? You were gone ages.'

Jake stood by the bed. 'I just had something to do. I thought you'd be asleep for hours. I didn't think you'd wake up while I was gone.'

'When you didn't come back, I went to look for you.'

Jake raised his eyebrows. 'You thought I'd gone to The Lake House?'

'Yeah.'

Jake slipped off Marcus's Gucci shoes again, placing them by the couch this time, as if that would somehow stop him from wandering off.

Jake sat on the edge of the bed, looking down at Marcus; he was shivering and sweating profusely. Jake reached out and touched his forehead. His skin felt clammy to the touch. 'Have you got a fever?'

'No.' Marcus grabbed Jake's hand.

Jake winced.

'Where's the plastic bag I was given in the police station?' Marcus held onto Jake's bandaged hand tight.

'Let go of my hand, Marcus,' Jake said calmly.

'Have you got it?' he demanded. He squeezed.

A sliver of pain ran up Jake's hand like a knife. Slowly, Jake produced the plastic bag from his coat pocket and tossed it on the bed next to Marcus.

He let go of Jake's hand.

Jake cradled his sore hand. 'It was in the car where you dropped it.'

Marcus snatched the bag off the bed.

Jake watched him get up and head for the bathroom. 'Marcus,

I know you're using. Just how serious is—'

Marcus slammed the bathroom door.

32

Jake could feel something tugging at his hand. He opened his eyes. The room was bright; he must have left the light on. He turned his head to see Marcus sitting on the edge of the bed, looking at him. 'Have you finished with the bathroom yet?' Jake mumbled sleepily. He realised that he must have dozed off while he was waiting. 'And turn that light off.'

'The light's not on.'

Jake shook his head, trying to shake off the heavy tiredness he felt. He glanced at the ceiling light. Marcus was right – it wasn't on. He rubbed his face with his other hand and pulled himself up into a sitting position.

'Hey!' Marcus protested as Jake left a trail of bandages down the bed.

'Sit still.' He shifted position and finished wrapping Jake's hand in fresh bandages.

'What time is it?' Jake noticed a shaft of sunlight coming through a chink in the curtains.

'Early. And will you hold still.'

Jake watched Marcus put the finishing touches to the bandage. Marcus still looked tired, but he was shaved and dressed, no longer in a suit but in clean, sand-coloured chinos and a blue cotton shirt. What was more, he seemed to have made a miraculous recovery from the previous night. Either the methadone had worked better than Jake had anticipated, considering the state Marcus had been in, or Marcus had a local source of drugs, which begged the question: how long had this been going on?

'You're turning into a regular little medical dispensary,' said Jake sarcastically.

'I got them from Gayle,' Marcus said coolly, referring, Jake hoped, to the bandages.

'You sleep well?' Jake glanced over at the sofa, where he could see bedclothes in disarray. Jake looked back at Marcus for a response.

'There, that's all done,' he said, letting go of Jake's hand.

'Is that an apology, then?' said Jake, inspecting his newly bandaged right hand; the hand that Marcus had grabbed the previous night, intending to hurt in his desperate bid to get hold of the methadone in Jake's possession.

'An apology for what?' Marcus took his other bandaged hand. 'I think *you* should apologise to *me*!'

'What the hell have I got to apologise for?' Jake promptly snatched his hand away. 'It was only the one hand that needed re-bandaging, or don't you remember?'

'Suit yourself.' Marcus shrugged and tossed the roll of fresh bandages onto Jake's lap. 'You do it.'

Jake reached for the roll of bandages and noticed that the bandage covering his other hand had mysteriously acquired a pink hue. 'How did that happen?' Barring a run-in with a drug-crazed lunatic of a brother-in-law, he'd thought his hands were healing. Jake sighed and started unwinding the bandage to his left hand.

Marcus seated himself on the sofa opposite Jake. 'Earlier on, you asked me whether I slept well.'

'Well, did you?' Jake continued unwinding the sodden bandage.

'No, I did not.'

Jake wasn't surprised. He glanced at Marcus. 'I was going to take the couch, but I obviously fell asleep on the bed while you were in the bathroom – sorry.' In truth, Jake wasn't feeling sorry in the slightest; not after Marcus's behaviour.

Jake unwound the last of the bandage and did his best to keep his face expressionless as he pulled away the last strip, which was painfully stuck to the wound. His hand still looked a mess. He reached for the fresh roll of bandages.

'The sofa was surprisingly comfortable,' said Marcus.

Jake looked up in surprise. In his experience, the sofa was never fine, although that usually had less to do with the comfort factor and more to do with the reason you found yourself relegated to the sofa in the first place. Jake unfurled a length of fresh bandage. 'I thought you said you did not sleep well.'

Marcus nodded.

'Maybe your meds didn't kick in …'

'That wasn't it!'

Jake stopped what he was doing and looked at Marcus. 'I give up. Was I snoring or something?'

'No.'

Jake was getting irritated by the game of twenty questions. 'You know what – whatever it is, will you just …' Jake's hand hurt and now his head hurt too, 'shut up!'

'What – like you did last night?'

Jake didn't know whether it was because he was tired or perhaps not fully awake yet, but Marcus wasn't making any sense.

Look, whatever you want to say, will you just say it? I am not in the bloody mood for word games.' Jake held Marcus's gaze a moment longer, waiting for his response, but he just sat there staring at Jake, making him feel uncomfortable; it was obvious there was something on his mind. Finally, Jake decided that whatever it was couldn't be that important, so he turned his attention to his injured hand. The wounds had been healing; there were scabs covering them, but somehow, he had managed to open them up afresh.

'You were thrashing about in the night.' Marcus broke the silence.

Jake looked up. At least that explained why he needed to re-bandage this hand too. 'So, I had a restless night. So what?' He hadn't slept well at his apartment in London either, but he felt he was acclimatising to his first holiday in almost a year.

'You spoke.'

Jake finished the bandage and tied it securely.

'In your sleep,' Marcus continued.

Jake got out of bed and looked down at the crumpled clothes he had slept in. He reached for his shoes and then glanced about the room for his bag; he needed a fresh set of clothes. He noticed that Marcus must have cleared up the room that morning while he slept, repacking their cases with the clothes and items he'd thrown all over the place in his frantic search for the plastic bag he'd left with from the police station.

'Where's my bag?' Jake glared at Marcus as if he was hiding it intentionally to keep him stranded in the room.

Marcus crossed the room to the wardrobe. He got out Jake's bag and closed he wardrobe door. 'Don't you want to know what you said?' he asked.

'In my sleep?' said Jake as Marcus dropped the bag on the bed. Jake unzipped it. He put his hands straight on a pair of clean jeans, but finding a sweatshirt was proving trickier. He gingerly lifted some clothes out of the bag and glanced at Marcus. He had a feeling that Marcus had something he was itching to get off his chest. 'What the hell does it matter what I said?' Jake added.

'It matters, Jake,' Marcus said softly, as he took a seat on the sofa, watching Jake.

Something in Marcus's tone made him stop, his hand still in his bag. He had a good idea what he had said in his sleep, and most probably shouted out every single night. At home, alone, there was no one to hear him. There was no one to remind him each morning what had gone on while he was sleeping – he made sure of it. That's why he wasn't in a relationship. It was why he didn't stay in the same house as anyone else if he could help it.

He thought back to the previous Friday night, when he had babysat Natty. Marcus had reminded him of his bad dreams, his fitful sleep, and how he shouted out in his sleep. The question he was now asking himself was whether he had woken Natty. Was that why she had come down in the middle of the night for a glass of water and some reassurance about the strange noises she'd heard?

Jake had reassured her she had just a bad dream – but had she? It made him think of the times she'd stayed over at his house. He hadn't woken her there. Perhaps she'd been out like a light, and hadn't heard him. Or maybe it was the case that for some reason, on those occasions, he had not had a nightmarish, fitful night's sleep. He certainly didn't recall having nightmares when she'd stayed over.

Marcus continued. 'I was woken by the sound of heavy

breathing, but it wasn't just heavy breathing – you were gasping for air like someone, or something, was sitting on your chest and squeezing the life out of you.'

Jake slowly pulled out a shirt from the holdall, the search for a sweatshirt forgotten.

'You were calling my name, *Marcus, Marcus,* over and over.'

Jake slowly zipped the holdall back up.

'*Marcus. Not me! Leave me!* you said.' He paused. 'Then you just said her name, *Eleanor*, over and over.'

Jake closed his eyes.

'That's how I managed to find you, you know, after the avalanche.'

Jake's eyes shot open. Not this again. How many times had Marcus told him this story? He still didn't believe him. Jake dumped the bag on the floor.

'Remember, I told you in the aftermath, I could hear your voice – like you were talking to someone, telling them to leave you buried in the snow, and find her, find Eleanor.'

'What the hell are you talking about?' Jake turned on Marcus. He was furious. He pointed angrily at him. Then he suddenly felt tired; tired of having the same argument, tired of hearing the same lies. He hoped that one day, Marcus would just be honest. Or, at the very least, be honest with himself about what had really taken place on the mountain on Christmas Day.

'I don't want to hear it,' Jake said flatly. He stood up, took his clothes and opened the bathroom door.

'What is it you don't want to hear, Jake?' Marcus said defiantly, 'The truth?'

'And just what is that, Marcus?' Jake said from the bathroom door. 'That you found me because you heard me calling out?'

Marcus nodded.

'Well, that's bullshit, and you know it. How could I call out when I was buried in the snow, for god's sake? *Completely buried.* That's how I wake up every morning, like I can't breathe, like I'm buried on that mountain again, like …' Jake stopped abruptly.

'Eleanor,' Marcus finished.

Silence.

'You know what your problem is?' said Jake bitterly. 'You can't accept the fact that you made a choice up there.' He stabbed a finger in the direction of the mountain beyond the house. 'And you can't live with it!'

'No, you're the one with the problem.' Marcus got up from the sofa. 'You can't live without someone to blame.' He marched to the bedroom door, flung it open and walked out, slamming it shut behind him.

Jake stepped into the bathroom and slammed the door shut too.

33

Jake opened the bedroom door and poked his head out into the hall. There was no sign of Marcus. That was good. He shut the door behind him, feeling fresh and revived after taking a shower and putting on a clean set of clothes. Showering had taken longer than he had envisaged. He'd had to wrap his hands in disposable plastic shower hats, which Gayle had thoughtfully provided. It had looked ridiculous but at least it had meant he could shower without getting his bandages wet. He hastily tucked in his shirt. He'd still had trouble buttoning up his shirt with his bandaged hands, but he'd managed. He put on his jacket and walked down the stairs with the car key to hand.

The kitchen door down the hall was ajar. Jake could hear voices as he stepped off the bottom stair. He identified Gayle, then Marcus. Another man's voice punctuated the conversation. Jake guessed it was Mr Addison, the man with the clipboard from the forest, and the owner of the yellow hard hat that was perched on the rear parcel shelf of the grey Ford parked outside.

Jake didn't feel hungry, and he didn't feel like company. He walked straight past the kitchen without glancing in, hoping his presence would go unnoticed.

It didn't.

'Jake, is that you?' Gayle called from the kitchen.

He'd made it to the front door – just. 'Yes.'

'Aren't you having any breakfast?'

'Not right now.' Jake opened the door. 'There's something I need to do first.' He stepped out and hesitated. Did he really want to do this? He wasn't sure. Maybe if he walked? He shook his head as he glanced at his watch; he would rather get a move on so he could get rid of Marcus on the next available flight to London. Jake had no qualms about depositing him back at the airport that day.

He had originally intended that they spend two nights at Lark Lodge, thinking that Marcus would need that time to recover. But the methadone had worked wonders. Marcus looked bright and breezy, and the picture of health; almost like his old self – the Marcus Jake remembered from before Christmas.

Perhaps I should take some too, thought Jake, rubbing his forehead. He had a headache and felt groggy with tiredness. He dismissed the idea instantly. The last thing he wanted was to end up in hospital because he'd taken something he shouldn't. Jake didn't have a drug problem – thank god.

He started towards his car. It was then that he noticed his rental car was wedged in between the Ford and the Bentley. He was positive he hadn't parked like that the previous night; he would have remembered climbing over the passenger seat to get out. Mr Addison must have shifted his car. Jake looked back at the house. He had the impulse to march in and interrupt their cosy little breakfast by hauling Mr Addison out of the kitchen to shift his car. Jake sighed. He could simply climb over the passenger seat to get in.

He did neither; slipping his keys back in his coat pocket, he decided to walk after all.

Strolling out of the gates and down the road, he stopped briefly under a streetlamp. The lamp was still lit, but the sharp morning light had faded its fierceness to a soft yellow glow. He turned down a narrow lane between Gayle's house and the next. He knew where it led. The previous evening, he had been tempted to leave the car and take this cut-through to the grounds of The Lake House behind Lark Lodge. Luckily, he hadn't. When he'd found Marcus, he'd been in no state to walk back.

Marcus could have walked it now with no problem, but Jake didn't want his company on this visit. He strolled towards the gate, hoping it was unlocked. The lane was overgrown. He couldn't imagine that anybody used the lane, or even knew where it led, although he did notice that the grass underfoot was trodden down as though someone had indeed used it – and in the recent past. Jake frowned, wondering who that someone was.

Jake stopped at the old gate, as tall as the wall. He took the round iron handle and turned it clockwise. The door creaked open. Jake breathed a sigh of relief. That meant he didn't have to return to Lark Lodge to collect the car and face the possibility of Marcus asking him where he was going.

Jake stepped into the grounds of The Lake House and stood for a moment in the warm sunshine.

Whoever had said that things always looked better in the morning was right; daylight had chased away the dark shadows that had been feeding Jake's imagination. All that remained were neatly pruned privet hedges, a lush green lawn shimmering with morning dew, and beautiful flowered borders.

Jake scratched his head. The beautifully maintained garden

was totally at odds with what he had seen of the house last night; it didn't make sense. Jake kept walking.

Perhaps last night in the dark they had got things a little out of proportion; perhaps the house was going to look better in the morning. Jake slowed his pace when the house, in all its dilapidated glory, came into view. Like the gardens, it was stunning, but for all the wrong reasons.

It looked smaller than Jake remembered, which would have been understandable if he had last seen it as a kid, rather than a few months earlier. The grey brickwork seemed greyer, the row of windows – long, elegant Georgian sash windows sitting proudly either side of the front door, matched by equally spaced, equally grand windows on the first floor – were all in need of re-painting. The row of small dormer windows in the roof – servants' quarters in years gone by – had fared little better. One of the shutters that had become dislodged from the wall swung in the breeze, a strong gust threatening to rip it off its hinges or worse, send it crashing through the window it was designed to protect.

As he stood staring at the house, an image came to mind; an image that this house reminded him of. It was the strangest thing; this house, with its grey hue and shrunken appearance, reminded Jake of Eleanor's father William. Since the accident, that once vibrant businessman had physically shrivelled into a grey shadow of his former self. His child, his only daughter, was gone. And the house's reason for being – the family, and the Christmas get-togethers – had vanished. Marcus had asked the previous night if a house could deteriorate like that in under a year. Jake could answer that now. They had neglected the house; it was no longer a part of anyone's life. It was unwanted, discarded, overlooked. William had cast off his connection to the house along with his old life. That was why he now spent so much time on the golf course instead of in the boardroom.

Jake shook himself, trying to shake off his irrational thoughts. It was just a goddamn building – it didn't think, feel, love and pine. And it had deteriorated because they had abandoned it, refusing to get involved in sending in cleaners and decorators to look after the place in their absence, which was foolish, because it was going to cost more to put it right. But it was also understandable – Eleanor had loved the place and without her, nobody had had the heart to return.

Lost in thought, Jake drifted towards the house, arriving at the gap in the hedge, finding himself standing in the same spot as the previous night. Reluctant to enter at first, Jake hovered in the gap, looking in on the hidden garden. Unlike the house and grounds, nothing there had changed. Except that Jake knew this wasn't true at all. If nothing had changed, if no one had come, then the outer ring of lawn would be overgrown and the carpet of flowers would be riddled with weeds – choking, dying, dead. Jake decided it had changed after all – the lawn was lusher, the flowers were more vibrant, the garden was more alive than he remembered.

He entered. Staying on the grass close to the hedging, he circled the small garden, arriving back where he had started without finding what he was looking for – six stepping-stones leading to the centre. He retraced his steps. At the edge of the grass, he knelt and parted a spray of flowers, revealing a stepping-stone. Not wanting to trample the flowers, but desperate to reach the centre of the garden, Jake attempted to part the flowers a little with his foot as he tentatively took one step at a time, feeling the hard stone beneath his shoe and scattering brightly coloured petals in his wake.

Jake had just found the last stepping-stone when a sound startled him. He opened his eyes and stepped sideways, flattening more flowers. It sounded like a knife being sharpened on stone – a scraping that made the hairs on the back of his neck stand up and his nerves bristle. Jake looked around the garden, but he was completely alone.

A piece of hedge fell to the ground. Jake looked up and saw a young man standing with his head and shoulders visible above the seven-foot hedge. Jake watched as he made short quick clippings on the top of the hedge with a pair of shears, his light orange hair waved in front of his eyes as he cut, a freckled nose screwed up in earnest concentration. Now things made sense; someone had hired a gardener to take care of the place. Aubrey came straight to mind. He always took care of things. But if that were true, then why stop at the gardens? Why not employ people to look after the house? At this point, Jake really didn't care. He closed his eyes and made another wish: that the young man would go away and leave him in peace.

A moment later, the scraping sound stopped. Jake opened his eyes. The young man was gone. But the peace Jake wished for did not last long. It was interrupted by a young man's surprised voice, 'Hey, you scared me! I didn't think anybody was here.'

Jake turned to see the young man with the wavy orange hair standing in the gap between the hedges, the shears dangling from his right hand and a pair of step ladders awkwardly balanced on his right shoulder. He was staring at Jake wide-eyed.

Then his gaze shifted, and the look of surprise turned to one of dismay.

Jake followed his gaze and looked down at the patch of trampled flowers underfoot. He looked up, unrepentant. 'I came to visit my wife,' he said.

Jake watched the young man slowly turn around, the ladders balanced awkwardly on his shoulder, and walk back through the gap in the hedging. Jake followed him and stood like a sentry, guarding the entrance for several minutes, ensuring he would not return, ensuring he would be left alone. Satisfied that the young man was not coming back, Jake returned to the centre and cast his eyes down to the small white oval memorial stone that was engraved simply with the words: *Eleanor, Chosen, 25th December.*

They were Jake's words and Jake's comfort.

Chosen; a single word, yet the full meaning, a true understanding, eluded Jake. He had felt that this simple word spelled a deeply cherished hope that she had to have been chosen for a reason, because it just hadn't been her time. How could it be anyone's time at the age of twenty-six?

Jake held out his hands and touched the two other memorial stones – those for his parents – weathered with age, standing solemnly side by side. It hadn't been their time either.

Jake retraced his steps through the gap in the hedge, back into the main gardens. He stopped just beyond the hedge and looked around the garden; there was no sign of the lad with the stepladders and shears. Jake breathed a sigh of relief and walked back across the gardens towards the gate. He was in no mood to apologise, no matter how much trouble the gardener had gone to over the flowers. He felt that his lost family were there, and no pretty flower display was going to change that fact.

Jake paused and closed his eyes, remembering the house with its brilliant white windows and blazing green shutters sitting majestically in the centre of the grounds. All was as it always had been – in his memory. This was still his house, and this had briefly been his childhood home until fate had dealt the cruellest of hands.

He had come to them late in life – a son – when they had all but resigned themselves to remaining childless. His father, an army officer, had intended to spend his retirement with his wife and young son in the peace and tranquillity of his beloved Scotland. But, a month before his early retirement, their plans had been cruelly cut short by a road accident. Fortunately, Jake had not been with his parents at the time, otherwise he would have perished too.

They had left behind a confused and lonely little boy with no relatives and an uncertain future – until William had stepped in.

They had bumped into each other, literally – Jake's father and William – on the ski slopes beyond the house when Jake's father had been on leave, not long after Jake was born. They had both become fathers for the first time late in life, and something had clicked; they had become firm friends. It was during one of Jake's parents' Christmas parties at The Lake House, when he'd invited William and his family, that Jake's father had confided in William, out of earshot of his wife of course, his fears for his newborn son. What if something should happen on his final commission?

How prophetic.

Of course, William had reassured him that he would always be there to advise Jake if need be, little realising how great those needs would become. But William was stoical; he had barely known the man for four years, yet he had taken care of his son without a second thought and had welcomed him into the family fold. Further, he had ensured that Jake never lost touch with his roots by making it a tradition that all the family spent each Christmas at his house, The Lake House, so that Jake could 'visit' his parents. It was an arrangement that had worked surprisingly well. So well, in fact, that even as adults, wherever they might be, they had descended without fail on the house at Christmas.

The house was cursed.

Jake opened his eyes. Of course, that wasn't true. There had been many, many good times and an abundance of fond memories, but Jake recognised that it was all it held for him now – memories. There was no future there for him. The question he was now asking himself was what to do with the house. It was such a waste, this beautiful old house standing alone, forlorn, forgotten. It needed people; children running around its lawns, laughter in its corridors.

Jake looked in the direction of the hidden garden. It had been William's idea to have Jake's parents buried in the grounds of their beloved house. But William could not have foreseen the events that would lead Jake to contemplate the future of the house – the future without Eleanor.

34

Jake was about to head back, but he turned on his heel and crossed the lawn to the house before he could change his mind. He was not all that eager to go inside, but finding the kitchen door open the previous night had given him cause for concern; had the house been broken into while he'd been away? A big house standing empty was easy prey for opportunists. Jake had heard of instances where thieves had been blasé enough to turn up in vans and empty a house of its entire contents while the owners were away.

There were no valuable antiques, cash or jewellery there. In fact, there was nothing of great value in the house; only the sentimental value it held for Jake. If somebody had been in the house, Jake thought it more likely that it was just local kids daring each other to stay the night in an empty house, complete with memorial garden and possibly ghosts. Of course, Jake didn't believe in any of that mumbo-jumbo; the place wasn't haunted, and there was no such thing as ghosts. But it was the sort of thing kids would do – he should know.

There was another reason for Jake to linger; it was time to say his final goodbyes. He was seriously thinking of selling the place, letting it go.

Jake tried the front door first. It was locked. No sign of forced entry. He still had the keys somewhere, but he had left them back home in London, not intending to stick around long enough to see the house.

Jake returned to the back garden, stopping at the back door. He knelt down and lifted the mat by the French doors, expecting to find the old spare door key under the mat.

There was no key.

Jake stood. That key had been under the mat, unused for years. If it had still been there, it would probably have been full of rust. It was just as well the door was already unlocked. He wasn't surprised after what had happened at Christmas that they'd probably overlooked locking up a door when they'd left. There were no broken panes of glass, and the door didn't look as though someone had forced entry to the house. His only concern was whether anyone else had discovered the unlocked door, which would allow them to gain entry to the house quite easily.

Leaves crunched underfoot as Jake stepped through the door into the kitchen. Shafts of sunlight filtered through the leaded windowpanes, throwing small squares of white light onto the cream linoleum and lime green kitchen units.

Jake walked straight through the kitchen, skirting the large wooden table in the centre of the room, and opened the door to the hall. He stopped abruptly; something had caught his attention. He slowly turned back, his eyes settling on the kitchen table. Jake let go of the door. He walked back to the table and picked up a china mug. A dried black substance lined the bottom. Jake held it up to his nose and sniffed – coffee. The red-headed lad with the shears and ladders came to mind. Jake had nothing against him stopping in the house to make a cup of coffee. Jake put the dirty mug back on the table. But what if it wasn't the gardener discovering the back door was open and making himself a cuppa?

This was not good news. He had thought it could be kids larking about, but he hadn't bargained for squatters. The state of the house had advertised its emptiness, advertised a vacancy. Jake cursed at the thought.

He went over to the kitchen cupboards and opened doors and drawers at random to see if there were any tell-tale signs of people living there, but all the cupboards were empty, apart from some condiments that were always left in the kitchen. Jake opened the pantry door and poked his head inside; it was cold and dark. He breathed in the pungent, yet not unpleasant, odour of food. Jake moved his hand around in the air until he felt the plastic flex of the light switch. He pulled. Nothing – the electricity was still out. Either someone had turned the electricity off before they all left after Christmas or there had been a power cut. Either way, it probably meant a trip down to the fuse box in the cellar to turn it back on. Jake didn't bother. There was light enough from the kitchen to see that most of the shelves were empty, apart from a large jar of instant coffee, along with some sugar, teabags, and long-life milk. Like the condiments in the kitchen cupboards, they were the basics always left for when they arrived there on holiday before the supermarket delivery arrived.

Jake closed the door to the pantry and looked at his watch. It was a little after eight in the morning. If anyone was still there, they were about to get a rude awakening. With that thought in mind, Jake decided to start his search in the bedrooms at the top of the house and work his way down.

A few minutes later, Jake was back where he had started in the back passage outside the kitchen – alone.

There was nothing but dustsheets covering every object in the house. Room after room, Jake had flung open each door, not stopping to enter, not stopping to reflect. There were memories in the house; memories no amount of dustsheets could contain.

Jake opened the door to the last room in the house – the cellar. He couldn't imagine anyone would be down there with the other comfortably furnished floors on offer. Still, he liked to be thorough.

He took the steep wooden steps slowly. The only light came from a small window on the far side of the cellar, which left the top half of the staircase in complete darkness. A third of the way down Jake knocked his forehead on the ceiling. He stopped and rubbed his head with one hand while running his fingertips along a piece of cold metal plate fixed to the wall where he had just hit his head. Jake didn't need a light to know what it was.

In metal class at school one year, they'd had to make something useful. Jake couldn't remember what he had made, but Marcus's little creation had been much more memorable. Jake was in his mid-teens and had grown several inches that year, so Marcus had used his metal class to make a sign that hung in that exact spot to remind Jake to watch his head. Marcus's teacher was not too enamoured with his choice of words, but they'd had the desired effect: *Duck, dipshit.* Jake smiled at the memory.

At the bottom of the stairs, nursing his forehead, Jake's smile vanished. In the centre of the room was another dustsheet, filthy with years of accumulated dust.

Jake stood motionless; his hand stuck to his forehead. There was no one down there. He knew he should go. But he was riveted to the spot, his eyes fixed on that dustsheet.

Jake dropped his hand from his forehead and moved towards

the workbench. He circled it slowly without touching it, just simply taking in the peaks and troughs, the flow of the material.

Jake fought the memory – unsuccessfully …

❖

'I got a letter from Santa!' Eleanor shouted excitedly, her pigtails bouncing in wide arcs as she jumped up and down, waving her letter from Santa in front of two uninterested little boys.

Jake glanced at Marcus. They had both been interrupted from their frantic snatch and tear at the presents under the tree by Eleanor waving her stupid letter at them. They exchanged a glance, knowing exactly what the other was thinking.

'I got a letter from Santa and he said he used my drawing I sent him!' Eleanor repeated excitedly.

'Oh yeah? How do you know? Maybe it's a lie …' Marcus said, drawing out the last word; his intention was to hurt.

Jake looked at Eleanor. She stopped jumping excitedly. Her face fell. Jake saw her top lip covering her bottom lip, the way it always did when she was thinking.

'Santa doesn't lie, does he, Jake?'

Jake turned to Marcus, who was looking at him with his eyes crossed, which made Jake laugh. They both knew something this Christmas that she didn't know. It was their secret. Well, it was theirs and everyone else's who wasn't a baby like she was. Neither of them knew what she was on about when she'd said that Santa had used her drawing, but what they did know was that Santa was a lie. Jake knew that Marcus couldn't wait to tell her, and he didn't care if he got into heaps of trouble because it would be worth it for Marcus just to see his sister cry.

'Let me see,' said Marcus reaching for the letter in her hand.

Jake shook his head, *no*.

'It's *my* letter,' she said. 'See – it says *Dear Ellie*. That's me,' she said proudly, holding it in front of Marcus's face.

He snatched it.

The letter tore.

Eleanor stood very still with her hand still outstretched, holding her piece of the torn letter. Then her bottom lip started to quiver, but she did not cry. She pointed at the torn piece of paper in Marcus's hand. 'Give me that.'

Marcus shook his head and grinned.

Then Eleanor bit her bottom lip and launched herself at her brother.

Marcus's hand shot up in the air, holding the letter out of reach, frustrating his little sister's attempts to make a grab for it. On the fourth try, amid Marcus's hysterical whoops of laughter, Eleanor lost her balance and fell hard. There was an almighty crunch.

Marcus stopped laughing instantly.

Jake helped Eleanor to her feet and they both looked down at the crumpled box. She had fallen on a large Christmas present that was still unwrapped.

'Hey, that's my present!' Marcus rushed forward and fell to his knees, tearing off the wrapping to reveal a broken toy. He looked up. 'Look what you've done to my present, you stupid …' He got off his knees and started to move towards his sister, his plump fingers curling into fists.

Eleanor backed away, clutching her torn letter, her eyes wide.

Jake stepped in front of Marcus, blocking his way to his sister.

Grace must have heard the commotion from the lounge across the hall. She appeared in the doorway of the children's den.

'Look what she's done to my present,' Marcus wailed at his mother as she came into the room behind Eleanor, halting her retreat.

'What have you done?' Grace grasped Eleanor's shoulders and turned her around to look at her. 'Just because you haven't got a big present like your brother,' she shook her shoulders, 'you think you can go and ruin it for everybody else?'

Now Eleanor did start to cry.

Jake turned around at the sound of Grace's voice and saw Eleanor's tear-streaked face. He was just about to turn on Marcus and thrash him for getting Eleanor into trouble and making her cry when he saw William approaching from the hall, carrying a tray with three tall glasses of squash. His round, red face made him look like Father Christmas without the beard. His big smiling face said he had no idea what he was about to walk in on.

As he entered the room, everyone fell silent.

Eleanor rushed forward and wrapped her arms around William's legs. Suddenly, everybody was talking at once. All except Jake.

Depositing the tray on the sideboard, William knelt in front of Eleanor.

'I didn't do it on purpose, Daddy. I fell.' Eleanor wiped her runny nose with her forearm.

'What's this?' said her father, lifting her hand with the torn letter.

The words tumbled out. 'Marcus said Santa lied about using my drawing!' She sniffed. 'Then he tore it.'

'Did not!' Marcus shouted across the room.

'Did too.'

'Did not.'

William sighed. 'Alright, alright.' He held up both hands and glanced in Jake's direction. 'Jake.'

'Yes sir.'

'Can you tell me what happened?'

Jake knew what he was being asked to do; take sides. He looked from Eleanor to Marcus. One of them was going to get into big trouble. Jake opened his mouth, aware that he could no more choose between them than he could choose to cut off his left hand or his right hand. The result would be the same; the loss would be the same. But the choice was made easy because Jake realised that he didn't have to choose after all if he simply told the truth: Marcus had torn the letter and wouldn't give it back. So, he did. They had been warned not to spoil it for Eleanor just because she was the youngest and still believed. Marcus had hurt Eleanor, and Jake wasn't going to let him get away with that.

William turned to Marcus. 'Well, young man, do you think an apology is in order?'

'But she broke my present. She's the one who should be sorry.'

'No, I shouldn't,' Eleanor threw back, 'you tore my letter!'

William scooped Eleanor up in his arms. 'You're coming with me, young lady.' He walked to the door and turned around. 'And you …' he playfully pointed Eleanor's left leg at Marcus, 'you are going to think up a very good apology to give to your sister when she comes back. As for you,' he then pointed her leg at Jake. Eleanor giggled. 'You are coming with us.'

Jake jumped up and left Marcus sitting on the floor, staring at the piece of paper in his hand with a very cross look on his face.

Grace left the room too, retreating to the lounge, where no toys were allowed. Jake could hear the television in the lounge as he followed William out of the room.

'Where are we going?' Jake said to William's back as he followed him down the hallway, being careful not to get too close to one of Eleanor's feet, which was swinging back and forth.

'Patience, Jake.'

In the back passage by the kitchen door, William unexpectedly opened the door to the cellar. Over William's shoulder, Eleanor stared at Jake with huge saucer eyes. They were never allowed down there in case they had an accident on the stairs, so this was the biggest adventure ever.

William switched the cellar light on. The stairs were wooden, dusty and very steep. William turned to Jake. 'Hold on to the banister, and take one stair at a time.'

Jake watched from the top step as William carried Eleanor down the stairs, placing his hand protectively on the top of her head as he ducked under the ceiling. They both disappeared deep into the bowels of the house.

Jake shivered. He felt scared; scared he might fall down the steep stairs and scared of what might be lurking down there.

Eleanor reappeared, putting one foot on the bottom stair and resting both hands on her knee. She peered up at him. 'Aren't you coming down, Jake?'

William appeared next to Eleanor. 'Shall I come and get you?'

'No.' Jake said quickly taking a step forward, feeling mortified at the thought of being carried down the stairs like a baby. He wanted to be brave in front of Eleanor.

Jake hesitated on the second step and looked back at the open door into the hallway.

'What is it?' William called up.

'It's just …' Jake looked back at William. 'Can I go and get Marcus?'

'No,' William said firmly.

Jake took one step at a time, holding tightly onto the banister rail, never taking his eyes off Eleanor. She stayed where she was at the bottom of the stairs, swaying her leg and cocking her head from left to right, watching his slow descent. When he got to the last step, she lifted her hand from her knee and held it out. Jake took it and stepped off the stairs. She smiled at him sweetly. They walked hand in hand to the workbench where William was standing with both hands holding the bottom of a brilliant white sheet that covered some strange object.

35

Jake stood holding both ends of the dustsheet, which was now almost black, thick with years of accumulated dust. He remembered William throwing off the dustsheet with a flurry, in the same way he recalled his mother throwing a clean sheet in the air and letting it gently settle like a feather onto the bed.

Jake tensed his arms, then threw them both up high in the air. Almost immediately he was hit by a fit of coughing and sneezing as the thick black dust whipped off the sheet and surrounded him.

He dropped the sheet instantly and furiously waved the air with his hands, trying to dissipate the dust. His eyes watered. He backed away until his shins hit the bottom stair. Fumbling for a tissue in his jacket pocket, he sat on the stairs, blew his nose and wiped his eyes.

Stuffing the tissue back in his pocket, Jake leaned forward, resting his elbows on his knees and his chin in the palm of his hands. He sat motionless, staring straight ahead at the object now uncovered on the workbench. From this vantage point, his eyes travelled along a bright hallway, through rooms busy with furniture, up the wide curved stairwell, in and out of strikingly decorated rooms – all this in miniature.

He sat for some considerable time, taking in the intricate detail of the custom-made doll's house on the workbench. It still gleamed and sparkled and looked as wondrous as the day he had first set eyes on it.

'Exactly how long has it been?' he murmured. He remembered that Christmas in particular because it was the first year he hadn't believed in Santa. He reckoned that maybe it was something everyone remembered if they'd been fortunate enough to have kind-hearted parents who had allowed them to believe in the first place.

'How old was I?' he got up from the step and walked over to the doll's house. 'Nine?' He bent down and peered into the second-floor bedrooms. 'Ten?' He bent down further, peering into the rooms. He picked up a tiny chair. 'I was almost eleven, so Eleanor must have been five.' He turned it over in his hand, careful not to snap the matchstick-thin legs. Then he carefully put it back it in the dining room.

He felt it was important somehow to place the events in time. He remembered now. She'd spent hours drawing a doll's house of her own design – how could he have forgotten?

Jake's vision blurred. He blinked and felt a faint tickle as tears ran delicately onto his cheeks. 'Damn dust,' he said as he wiped his face dry with the sleeve of his jacket.

Jake picked up the dustsheet from the floor and carefully draped it back over the doll's house, tucking it under the base as best he could as the memory of that day re-surfaced once more …

❖

'You know, I heard Santa's elves down here, night after night, hammering and sawing. They certainly had their work cut out for them this year, Eleanor.' William smiled at his daughter.

Eleanor tentatively held out a podgy finger and touched the doll's house as if she couldn't quite believe her eyes.

Jake watched in awe. 'Santa's elves worked in this house?' A part of him still wanted to believe, still wanted to stay in that magical place for just a bit longer.

'That's right, son.'

It made him feel good when William called him *son*, even though he knew he wasn't really William's son. They were fostering him after his parents died, which William explained meant that he could live with them as part of the family.

'It was too big for Santa to bring on his sleigh, otherwise he would have had to leave everyone else's presents behind at the North Pole,' explained William. 'We wouldn't want that – would we?'

Jake shook his head vehemently, looking at Eleanor, who was doing the same. He suddenly realised why Marcus had been left out. It was because he would just spoil things. And besides, he wasn't really sure that he believed Marcus about there being no Santa. Just because he was a year older than Jake, it didn't mean he was right all the time, did it?

'What say us fellas,' he patted Jake on the back, 'carry it upstairs to Eleanor's bedroom?'

'Yes sir,' Jake said excitedly.

Marcus was standing at the living room door, watching, as Eleanor appeared in the hallway. His eyes went wide as William and Jake emerged from the cellar with the doll's house. 'See! I told you that Santa used my drawing – he said so in my letter,' Eleanor said triumphantly. She stuck her tongue out at Marcus before racing down the hallway to the stairs.

❖

Jake smiled at the memory. Before Santa, with the help of his elves, had made her that huge doll's house right there in the cellar of The Lake House, she'd always asked for furniture or little figurines for her old doll's house. She loved delicately arranging furniture and playing families. There was a time that she decided she wanted to do a bit more than just play with her doll's house. She'd put on her dungarees – the ones she didn't mind getting paint and glue on when she used her arts and crafts materials to draw and paint. She'd tied up her mass of brown hair as best her little chubby fingers could and then she had set to work.

Jake recalled hearing raised voices in Eleanor's bedroom one day. Her mother was standing over her, demanding to know what she thought she was doing. Even Jake got a shock when he saw the inside of her doll's house, walls and all, lying discarded in a heap, leaving nothing but an empty shell.

Jake remembered Eleanor's mother turning away from the bedroom door, mumbling something to herself about why her daughter was such a disappointment; why she wouldn't wear pretty dresses and play like a normal daughter? Jake had remained in the doorway, watching, fascinated, as she erected new walls and pasted little bits of wallpaper.

She'd let him join in and together they'd chosen colours and made little pieces of furniture. Jake smiled when he remembered Marcus crossly calling him a sissy when he'd discovered Jake playing with Eleanor and not him. Marcus had hovered at the door, watching, and then had grudgingly edged closer until he too was sitting on the floor beside them, totally absorbed in refurbishing Eleanor's old doll's house.

Then, a few weeks before Christmas one year, when she'd

turned five, Eleanor's father had crept in late one night from work to give his sleeping daughter a kiss goodnight – so the story went – and stubbed his toe on her part-refurbished old doll's house. When he'd moved it out of the way, he'd spied some drawings of a doll's house underneath. The next day after school, Eleanor set to work on her doll's house, but the drawings were nowhere to be found. Jake remembered searching for them. Even Marcus joined in the search, helping his sister, which was a first.

'You can draw them again, can't you?' Jake had suggested, seeing her distress when they couldn't find them. She'd said that she couldn't. The drawings were special. It was a plan for how she wanted her doll's house to look the next time. She had made drawings and chosen colours, and on her drawings for each room she had stuck little material swatches – all the things she could think of for a new design were on that drawing – but it was gone. Her mother told her that the cleaner had probably thrown it out as rubbish; what did she expect if she was going to be so careless and leave things lying around on the floor?

Eleanor had been inconsolable until the letter from Santa had arrived. Jake knew that so many kids posted their Christmas list to the North Pole, but how many got a reply from Santa? The reply said that he'd magically found her drawing. It was Eleanor's fondest childhood memory. William had told her that on Christmas night, while doing his rounds delivering presents, Santa must have found her lost drawings and had an idea: why not use her designs to have a very special doll's house made for a very special girl?

Jake remembered with fondness how William had told Eleanor that Santa must have drafted in his elves, sending the reindeer with the sleigh back to the North Pole to collect them, along with all the materials and tools they'd need to build the doll's house right there in The Lake House. Then he had finished his rounds, delivering presents all around the world, before returning to collect the elves.

Of course, Eleanor had believed every word, and for one more magical Christmas, Jake had ignored Marcus and had chosen to believe too.

Jake stood for a moment, astounded by the miniature house, the miniature rooms that had been created by a specialist bespoke company, they had found out later, all from a five-year-old's clever design.

He hadn't really appreciated what talent she'd had, what talent she'd been born with – until now. He felt responsible for taking away her opportunities because of the life they'd led. If they'd never married, moving back and forth between London and America as the Ross Corporation dictated, perhaps she'd have had the opportunity to create the life *she'd* wanted. If they'd never married, maybe she would have settled down somewhere and started a business making bespoke doll's houses for other children to enjoy. For *her* children to enjoy, though Jake sadly.

Perhaps he wouldn't be standing there in an empty house, staring at a discarded doll's house.

Jake climbed the cellar steps and shut the door on those memories, sad memories, and thoughts of a future that would never be.

36

'Where the hell have you been?'

Jake eyed Marcus as he walked up the drive towards Lark Lodge and veered into the front garden. Marcus had been sitting in the garden, reading a newspaper. He closed it and folded it in two as Jake approached. Jake slumped next to him on the wooden swing for two that was positioned on the lawn under the study window.

Jake leaned his head back on the high-backed cushion and closed his eyes.

He felt the swing gently begin to rock back and forward.

'Are you alright?' Marcus's hand brushed his shoulder.

Jake opened his eyes and stared at the ocean-blue sky. 'Is your suitcase packed?' Jake turned to look at Marcus. 'I really need to get out of this place.'

The swing became still. Marcus looked at Jake with a questioning expression.

Jake didn't feel like offering an explanation. Instead, he rolled his head back to look at the sky. A solitary grey cloud drifted into his frame of vision, which he thought seemed quite apt. In fact, a massive great black cloud with thunderstorms, lightning and torrential rain would just about suit his mood – not this blue sky, that pitiful cloud.

Marcus spoke. 'What are you going to do about the envelopes?'

'Huh?' Jake willed the cloud to grow to immense proportions.

'These.' Marcus thrust his hand in front of Jake's face, obscuring his view of the cloud.

Jake slowly focused on the two crumpled envelopes Marcus was holding up in front of his face. He sat up abruptly and checked his coat pockets – empty. 'Where did you find them?' said Jake, reaching for them.

'On the floor in the bedroom – where else?' He sounded defensive, as though Jake was accusing him of rifling through his pockets.

Jake sighed. The two letters he'd inadvertently walked out of Cedar Grove with the previous night, after he'd visited Martha, must have fallen out of his pocket when he'd pulled out the plastic bag for Marcus. Maybe he should take them back to Arnold straight away, before he *really* lost them. Jake turned to Marcus as he stuffed them back in his pocket. 'What are you looking at me like that for?'

'What's going on?' Marcus said flatly.

Jake got up. 'I don't know. You read the letters. Why don't you tell me, Sherlock?' Jake turned to go but Marcus caught his arm, pulling it hard.

'Tell me.'

'What is with you?' Jake tried to shake his grip free, but he couldn't. He stood still and held his arm up with Marcus's hand still attached to his sleeve. 'Is this going to be another episode like last night? Because I'm running out of bandages,' he said sarcastically.

Marcus's grip slackened. He let go.

'Thank you.' Jake lowered his voice. 'Now suppose you tell me exactly what drugs you're on.' Marcus's behaviour appeared to be getting more erratic and paranoid. Jake knew methadone was a treatment for heroin dependence. Even so, he wanted Marcus to just admit it. Jake was thinking of the saying: *you have to admit it, to quit it.* If only Marcus would just acknowledge he had a serious drug problem.

Marcus's face hardened. 'Suppose you tell me about those.' Marcus indicated the letters in Jake's pocket.

'Ok.' Jake shrugged, realising Marcus wasn't ready to tell him about his drug habit just yet. 'Have it your way.' Jake headed across the lawn to the front door. He heard Marcus's quick footsteps on the gravel drive behind him as he approached the door too. Reaching for the doorknob, Marcus's hand closed around it first. He did not open the door.

'Well, aren't you going to open it?' Jake said impatiently. He turned to Marcus in exasperation. 'What?'

'I'll tell you about the drugs.' He held Jake's gaze. 'But first you have to tell me about the envelopes.'

'All right,' Jake interrupted, not sure why Marcus was making a big deal about the letters; they had nothing to do with him. 'Now can we go in?'

Marcus twisted the doorknob and flung the door wide, letting Jake enter first.

As they approached the bedroom door, he glanced at Marcus and thought, *your suitcase had better be packed, because I've just about had it with you.* Jake kept that thought to himself as he walked into the room. He noted Marcus; suitcase on the floor by the door, jacket hanging from the handle. The wardrobe door was wide open and empty. There were no clothes strewn about the bed. He was packed and ready to go.

Good.

Jake zipped up his own bag, which he'd barely unpacked. He glanced at Marcus, who was moving towards the sofa.

Marcus sat.

Not good.

Jake lifted his bag off the bed.

'The contents of those envelopes first,' Marcus said coolly, leaning forward and tossing a cushion behind his back, making himself comfortable.

'We'll discuss it on the way,' Jake said firmly, walking to the door. He felt his anger brewing like a pressure cooker about to blow. The letters had nothing to do with Marcus. He shouldn't even be there. The time had come to leave, but Marcus was going to do his best to ruin his day.

Jake dropped his bag and retrieved the envelopes from his coat pocket. 'These damn letters,' he waved them at Marcus. 'If it wasn't for these …' Jake crossed the room. 'Do you think I'd come here for a holiday?' He stared down at Marcus.

'Have you even looked inside the envelopes?'

Jake's temper exploded and he didn't care if Gayle and her mother, along with the whole bloody neighbourhood heard. 'I'm not reading the damn letters!' He threw them on the bed; he missed, and they dropped to the floor.

Jake walked to the window and looked out. He calmed down. 'I guess it serves me right.' He wished he'd never taken that call from Arnold Wright.

'Why do you keep calling them letters?'

'What do you mean?' Jake snarled as he turned from the

window and slunk to the end of the bed.

Marcus knitted his brow. 'Give them to me and I'll show you …'

'No!' Jake flopped down on the end of the bed. 'I need to return them to Arnold.' He bent down and picked the envelopes off the floor.

'Who's Arnold?'

'Oh, for heaven's sake!' Jake got up from the bed in frustration and paced the floor as he recounted the whole business, from the phone call back in London from a stranger about Martha and the letters she had for William.. He explained that he'd been prompted to make the trip because he'd suddenly had time on his hands and had felt sorry for an old man and for an old lady who was at death's door. 'There, are you satisfied? I'm an idiot. I wish I'd never agreed to come.' Jake stood in front of Marcus. 'Can we go now?'

'I think you need to look at the contents of those envelopes.' The sound of Marcus's calm voice was irritating beyond belief.

'And I think you need to shut up!' Jake stuffed the letters in his pocket again, and walked to the door. 'I'm going to give them back.' He lunged at his bag and missed, banging his hand on the doorframe.

'Ouch,' said Marcus. 'I bet that hurt.'

Jake glared at Marcus as he grabbed the bag and stormed out of the room, slamming the door behind him.

Jake leaned back against the closed door. His hand was throbbing. He stood like that for several seconds, breathing deeply and trying to get a grip. It was working – sort of. Marcus had always had the capacity to wind him up. Since he had lost Eleanor, there had been times he had seriously wanted Marcus to disappear out of his life permanently, but he was afraid of what might happen if he just walked out on Marcus. Just then was a case in point. Would he spiral again, and go on a bender? Jake did not want another phone call from Faye about Marcus, even though if Marcus landed himself in jail again, it would not be Jake's fault.

Jake sighed and opened the bedroom door; he swung it wide and stood in the open doorway, eyeing Marcus. He was still seated on the sofa. 'Are you coming or not?'

'I don't know – you tell me,' Marcus quipped. 'You seem to be doing your best to ditch me.'

'And why do you suppose that is?' Jake watched the smirk disappear from Marcus's face.

Marcus got up and walked towards the door.

Jake moved into the room, holding the door in readiness to close it behind them.

Marcus collected his jacket and suitcase from by the door. He paused in front of Jake, and leaned in close, whispering, 'Why don't you say it to my face? Say it out loud, then see how bloody fantastical, how bloody absurd it sounds.' Marcus stood his ground, staring at Jake intently.

Jake stared back, taking in those dark eyes and the faint two-inch scar just above the eyebrow – one of the battle-scars of childhood that people all seemed to collect.

'Yeah, just as I thought,' Marcus brushed past Jake. 'You can't say it to my face, so you write it down for posterity – cruel, Jake.'

'What are you talking about now?' Jake was confused. He shut the bedroom door and followed Marcus down the stairs.

'That's why I can't visit the memorial garden, and see that stone.'

Jake caught up with him at the front door.

'You know what?' Marcus scoffed. 'You're the one with

problem, not me. Don't you see?'

Of course Jake did. He was the problem because he had made the mistake of telling a truth which Marcus could not and would not accept. If it had been the other way round, on that mountain on Christmas Day, could Jake have done the same as Marcus – made that choice, leaving Eleanor to her fate? More to the point, could he live with himself afterwards?

He didn't know the answer to that question but what he did know was how he loathed Marcus for just carrying on as though nothing had happened, for thinking everything could stay the same.

Jake searched his face; was it possible that Marcus had convinced himself of the lie? Convinced himself that what he had said happened at Christmas was true? It was understandable; it could be a way out, a way for Marcus to live with what he had done.

'I can't visit the garden without your little inscription staring back at me, accusing me.' Marcus's words cut into Jake's thoughts.

'My what?'

'Perhaps you shouldn't keep it to yourself. Why not tell the family?'

'I don't understand.'

'You can't tell them, can you? Who would believe your absurd little concoction?'

Jake sighed. How could he tell the family? Didn't they have enough to cope with, with the loss of Eleanor, without knowing what had really happened on that mountain when the three of them had got caught in that avalanche? It wouldn't change anything; it wouldn't bring her back. This disagreement over the facts; it was just between the two of them. And Jake wondered if it was ever going to end.

He had suggested counselling in the past. He could suggest

hypnosis. Wasn't that all the rage, to find and face up to all those repressed memories? What good would that do? This was so obviously Marcus's coping mechanism, to believe the lie, to believe he wasn't the one who had chosen to dig Jake out of the snow first instead of his sister.

'So, you have your little lie engraved, so it makes you feel good, and me feel bad,' continued Marcus started shaking his head. 'Was it worth it?'

Jake opened his mouth to speak.

'Was it worth our friendship?' Marcus turned abruptly, opened the front door and walked out.

Jake stared after him, trying to piece together what had just happened. One comment, just one comment, would set off the whole damn argument again. Jake realised in that moment, watching Marcus walk down the front steps, that this was never going to go away. This heartache and their friendship was never going to mend.

37

'I thought I heard voices.'

Jake was in the hall, watching Marcus through the open doorway. He was standing by the hire car, looking cheesed off, waiting for Jake to join him.

Jake turned at the sound of Gayle's voice. She marched down the hall towards him, wearing green wellies and leaving a trail of muddy footprints in her wake.

Olive was right behind her, muddy paw prints and all.

She stopped in front of Jake and pointed at his bag. 'You're leaving?'

'I'm afraid so.'

Olive sniffed his bag and whined.

Jake took out his wallet and handed Gayle the cash for a two-night stay.

Gayle took the money. 'Oh, you've given me too much.' She attempted to hand half of it back.

Jake shook his head and refused to take it. 'I booked two nights, so I'm honouring that booking.'

'But you've only stayed one night.'

'I know, but you might have had another booking.'

'I still might,' said Gayle holding out some of the money.

Jake wouldn't budge on the issue.

'Are you leaving because you had a rough night on the couch? You should have taken two rooms.'

Jake reassured her. 'The sofa was fine.' He decided not to mention that it was Marcus who had ended up sleeping on the sofa, nor the reason he'd felt compelled to share a room in the first place.

Gayle rolled the notes and tucked them in the pocket of her jeans.

Jake looked down at Gayle's wellies.

She followed his gaze. 'Oh Lord!' She looked down the hallway and saw the muddy trail. 'Gardening's not my thing.' She turned back to Jake. 'Marty usually does the garden, but it's such a lovely day that I got a sudden urge to get outside. I only nipped in for a glass of water. I was about to take off my wellies at the back door when I spotted you with your bag.'

Gayle tutted at the mud on the floor. 'Now I'm wishing I hadn't bothered doing any gardening.'

'Marty?'

'Yes, the gardener. The house I can manage, but the garden …' Gayle held onto Jake's arm as she struggled out of her left Wellington boot. 'He comes once a week.'

'The red-headed lad?' Jake remembered the young man. 'I saw him at The Lake House.'

Gayle put the boot on the mat by the front door. 'Is that where you went this morning?'

Jake nodded.

She leaned on Jake's arm once more as she struggled out of her other boot. She set the boot down on the mat with the other one.

'Look, the reason I didn't mention where I'd been—'

'It's okay, you don't have to explain.' Gayle rested her hand on his forearm and gave it an affectionate squeeze. 'You haven't been back since …' She trailed off, knowing Jake would understand.

'No.'

'Eleanor's brother?' She glanced outside.

'Same. Not until last night.'

Gayle nodded. 'Did you like the room?'

'Sure.'

Jake picked up his bag, thankful that Gayle still hadn't asked why they hadn't stayed at The Lake House. He guessed it was obvious; how could they, after that terrible Christmas?

'If you pass this way again, be sure to stop by.'

'I will,' said Jake, although he thought it highly unlikely that he would ever return.

He stepped outside. He could see Marcus still waiting by the car, his arms folded. Jake turned back to Gayle. 'Thanks again for the room.'

'No, I should be thanking you.'

Jake frowned. 'I'm sorry – what?'

'For your wonderful gardener. I know your family are his biggest employer. I'm just glad that he had the time to do my garden.'

'Your garden looks fantastic,' Jake said, and he meant it.

'As does yours, I'm sure.'

Jake nodded. 'Yeah, it makes quite a contrast to the house. When I first saw it I couldn't get over how it's started to deteriorate in a little under a year.'

'That is sad.'

Jake realised that Gayle hadn't seen the house up close recently

– if ever. Jake admitted, 'I shouldn't have been all that surprised. I've neglected that house. I was more taken aback by the grounds.' The gardener must have remained on the payroll, and not only that, had continued to do his job despite the fact that nobody ever came to the house. 'The peculiar thing is that I thought the gardener was some old guy.'

'Marty took over from his father when he retired.'

It had always seemed normal to Jake that he didn't know what went on at his own house. The company always took care of everything. He'd assumed that this would stop when he stopped working at the Ross Corporation, although he was still a company director.

'I remember now. He occasionally brought a kid along.' Jake remembered the freckle-faced, ginger-haired little lad who couldn't have been more than twelve when he'd last seen him. 'When did his father retire – do you know?'

'I think around about the time …' she trailed off, aware of the delicate nature of mentioning the name Eleanor Ross. 'He loves that old house; said it was so sad the way everyone had deserted the place.'

Jake was thoughtful. 'I wish I'd known that he'd retired after all those years.' Jake imagined that the company had probably done something for the gardener when he retired – hopefully given him a bonus. Even so, Jake would have liked to do something for him too.

Jake glanced over his shoulder at the car. Marcus was mouthing something and making a point of looking at his watch. Jake sighed and turned back to Gayle. 'I'd better go.'

Jake stepped onto the gravel drive, realising that it was probably the beautifully manicured lawn and flower borders that had kept squatters away from The Lake House. How could the house appear abandoned if the gardens looked so well cared for?

He did an about-turn and asked Gayle, 'Will you tell Marty, next time you see him, that I'd like to do something special for his dad, in recognition of all the hard work he's put into the garden over the years?'

Gayle folded her arms. 'No.'

Jake stopped. It wasn't the response he was expecting from Gayle when he'd asked her to pass on a message to Marty. He looked quizzically at Gayle. She was normally so accommodating.

'Do you want to know why I won't do it?'

Jake nodded. 'Yes, I do.'

She unfolded her arms and took a step towards Jake. 'You should speak to Marty yourself and let him hear some praise for his father from one of the Rosses themselves.'

Jake eyed Gayle. She was right: an apology was in order for not even realising Marty's father had retired, and he should also welcome Marty to The Lake House and thank him for continuing his father's excellent work. 'You're absolutely right,' said Jake. 'Thank you, Gayle.'

'You're welcome.'

Jake turned to go, hoping Marty was still at The Lake House. Jake knew he hadn't long returned to Lark Lodge, so hopefully the young gardener would still be there.

'Jake.'

He turned back.

'Perhaps in another life we could have been neighbours.' Her eyes drifted in the direction of The Lake House over the garden wall.

Jake vividly remembered that as a small child, not long before his life had been turned upside down and he'd gone to live with the Rosses, he had told his mother that he would never leave the place. He sighed. 'Gayle, I'm afraid life has an awful habit of getting in the way of the best-laid plans.' Those plans had been spectacularly derailed when his parents had died.

'Who said they were the best-laid plans?'

Jake frowned. 'I don't understand.'

'Perhaps there's a reason that fate, or whatever higher power you believe in, stepped in to change the course of your life. Maybe that wasn't meant to be the plan for your life.'

Jake stared at her. Was she seriously suggesting that losing his parents, losing Eleanor, was for the best? Jake knew what she was doing. He'd seen the shelves full of books in the study; self-help psychobabble purporting to help people see a way through their grief, their loss, their troubles, to arrive at the other side; she was just trying to make him feel better by saying that things happened for a reason.

Jake could never accept that. He could not see what possible reason would there be for losing his wife and unborn child.

A sudden thought crossed his mind; if he hadn't lost them, he would never have met Faye or Natty.

Jake just offered Gayle a tentative smile. Perhaps that's what she meant; every cloud has a silver lining – even if it's the darkest cloud of them all, something good had to come out of a tragedy.

He knew she meant well, but the conversation wasn't helping – especially when he stepped out of the door and saw Marcus. Jake frowned at him as he approached the car. He opened the car door and slung his bag onto the back seat.

'Have a safe journey,' Gayle called out, waving goodbye.

Jake waved back before getting in the car. He sat in the front seat and watched Gayle walk inside the house and shut the door.

'God, I bet you couldn't wait to get out of there. What on earth was she prattling on about?'

Jake switched on the engine and turned to face Marcus.

'What are you looking at me like that for?'

'You're such a …' Jake searched for something appropriate; a word came to mind, 'dipshit sometimes.' He put the car into gear and moved off.

'What's that supposed to mean?'

Jake rubbed his forehead; it still felt tender where he had banged his head on Marcus's sign in the cellar of his house.

Jake cleared the drive and started down the street. Marcus turned his attention to the car radio, switching it on and tuning in the radio stations. After a short distance, Jake took an abrupt turn.

'Hey!' Marcus reached for the dashboard in surprise, but it was too late. He slammed into the car door. 'I thought we were going straight to the airport?' Marcus took his hand off the dash and rubbed his sore arm.

'I need to see someone before we leave.' Jake drove along the road leading to The Lake House. He turned up the driveway.

'Not again,' Marcus groaned, 'didn't you see enough this morning?'

Jake stopped outside the house. 'I need to see the gardener.'

'I don't think it's the gardener you need to see. Unless,' Marcus was staring at the house, 'he's responsible for that.'

Jake had forgotten that Marcus had not seen the house in daylight, in all its dilapidated glory. Jake opened the car door. 'Are you coming?'

'What for?'

Jake shrugged and got out of the car. There was no point

dragging Marcus along to find Marty. He slammed the door shut. Then he hesitated. Instead of heading into the garden, he walked around the car, crouched down and tapped on Marcus's window.

Marcus pressed the button and released the electric window. 'What now?' He was still staring at the house.

'Marcus,' said Jake, waiting for his full attention.

Marcus lowered his eyes to look at him.

'I'll come with you, if you want to see …'

Marcus's face hardened. 'Didn't you hear a word I said to you this morning?'

Jake threw up his hands – he didn't have time for this. He stood up, casting about for any sign of Marty. The lad was nowhere to be seen. Jake entered the gardens as he tried to go over the conversation with Marcus before they left Lark Lodge, but that morning just seemed to be a jumble of Eleanor and Marty and Arnold, and the two envelopes in his pocket, and questions; so many questions. Jake rubbed his forehead and felt a raised lump and a headache coming on.

He stopped and listened for the scraping sound of rusty shears. All was quiet apart from the twittering of birds and the irritating high-pitched cackle of radio frequencies as Marcus tuned in the car radio. Jake continued to wander the grounds until he found himself standing at the gap in the hedge leading to the hidden garden for the second time that morning. He wandered inside.

There was no sign of Marty.

Jake walked over to a narrow stone bench set back in a recess cut out of the hedging. Anyone unfamiliar with the garden would not immediately see the bench. Jake brushed away some hedge clippings that had fallen on the seat and sat down.

His head was now throbbing. He hoped that if he sat still for a few moments, the headache would subside. He stared at the garden; the flowers seemed even brighter and more vibrant the second time round. The memorial stone seemed smaller. The inscription seemed clearer.

The inscription.

That single word.

'Oh, god.' A dawning realisation washed over Jake as he recalled what Marcus had said to him that morning: *I can't visit the garden without your little inscription staring back at me, accusing me.*

Now he understood. Jake read the inscription out loud. '*Chosen*.' He closed his eyes and shook his head. Why hadn't he seen it before?

He opened his eyes. It explained why Marcus found it difficult to visit the garden. Jake had had his reasons for using that word, and they had been nothing to do with Marcus – but evidently that was not how Marcus saw it. To Marcus, it meant something different entirely. It was an accusation, it was blame, and to Marcus, it was a lie. And it was there for all to see – family, friends – but only for the two of them to understand.

Jake rubbed his temples with his balled hands. His headache was not improving, but he couldn't sit there all day; Marcus had a flight to catch.

Jake left the garden and headed back to the car, this time hoping he didn't bump into Marty; he had something else a lot more pressing to sort out first.

He tried to go over what he was going to say to Marcus, how he was going to explain. Would Marcus believe how blind he had been? How unintentional it had been to use that word? He could scarcely believe it himself. He wouldn't have been that callous.

As Jake walked back to the car, he kept telling himself he didn't care what Marcus thought. Jake was the one who had severed their friendship, had cut Marcus off at every turn since the accident. So why did Jake feel the need to explain, to atone, to ask for Marcus's forgiveness? It didn't add up.

Jake had thought he had it all figured out – his new job and new home back in London; discounting the small matter of Marcus interrupting the flow, and the nightmares he still suffered from. Although he knew things weren't perfect, at least Jake had felt that he was getting his life back on track. So why was this happening? Why did he feel increasingly like he was losing it?

He had known that the holiday was a bad idea. Nothing had made sense, and he needed things to make sense. Like the inscription. That single word summed up the truth that Marcus could not face; that had driven them apart. And yet Jake was looking to apologise for it; to tell Marcus he had made a mistake, when he so clearly had not.

'I am so screwed up!' said Jake, unable to shake the feeling that in some way he had been wrong about Marcus. But how was that possible? That crazy thought had been nagging at him for months – a *what if* scenario; what if Marcus had been telling him the truth all along? What if he had not been lying about what had really happened to Eleanor?

38

Jake made his way back across the gardens. He walked up the stone steps and approached the car to find that Marcus was no longer sitting in the passenger seat. The car radio was still on.

The music coming from the car radio stopped and a DJ's irritatingly manic voice blared out some unintelligible slang. Jake leaned through the open window and pressed the radio knob with his finger; it clicked off. Blessed silence.

Jake extracted himself with some difficulty, lifting his head too soon and knocking the back of his head on the car door. He yelped. He stood beside the car, rubbing the back of his head. His headache got even worse.

'Where the hell did he go?' Jake's eyes settled on the house.

Jake set off in that direction. He was just making his way past the front door when he noticed the small flowerpot to the left of the door had been shifted. A circle of green moss marked the spot where it once stood. Jake tried the front door. It opened. He walked in and turned around to close the door, glancing at the flowerpot; Marcus must have found another spare key.

Jake shut the door and stood for a moment staring at the framed photograph on the wall to the left of the door. It was a school photograph of the three of them. They were sitting sideways on, their faces turned to the camera. Eleanor, the youngest, was in front, leaning into Jake's chest and smiling sweetly for the camera. Jake was sitting up straight, his expression an almost-smile as though he had been caught unawares by the camera. Marcus was sitting behind him, sporting a wide, toothy grin with two new adult front teeth in otherwise bare gums.

Jake hadn't seen this picture in a long while. He took a step back for a clearer look and noticed the row of coat hooks on a long wooden rack screwed to the wall directly above the picture. The picture had obviously been hidden for some years beneath a jumble of assorted coats, bags and skiwear. Now void of these things, the picture had reappeared.

Jake plucked the picture off the wall and ran two fingers gently down the portrait over the smiling Eleanor. He sighed and hung it back carefully. 'Marcus!' he shouted, staring at Marcus's toothy grin.

There was no response.

Jake carefully hung the picture back on the wall and walked to the stairs, glancing into the lounge on the left and the den on the right. There was no sign of him. He bounded halfway up the stairs, calling out his name several times.

There was still no answer.

Jake walked slowly up the rest of the stairs and peered around the thick spindle at the top of the stairs. All the bedroom doors were closed, just as he had left them that morning during his search for the non-existent squatters. Jake didn't bother walking up the next flight of stairs; he saw no reason why Marcus would have gone up to the bedrooms on the second floor.

Jake scratched his head and meandered down the stairs. At the bottom, he turned left and headed to the kitchen. He flung open the door, expecting Marcus to be there. Jake stood in the doorway, perplexed. He had searched everywhere else; if Marcus was in the house, there was nowhere left to …

That was when he noticed that the door to the cellar was slightly ajar. Jake hadn't bothered to open the fuse box and switch the electricity back on when he had gone down there. He suddenly had a nasty vision of Marcus lying at the bottom of the cellar steps in a crumpled heap.

Jake grabbed for the door and was momentarily blinded by the bright bare bulb dangling a couple of inches from his face. Several rapid blinks later, he was able to see clearly down the cellar steps, all the way to the bottom. Marcus had not taken a tumble.

'Marcus – you down there?' Of course he had to be. Who else would have switched the electricity on?

'Jake, Jake – you've got to come down here and take a look at this.'

Jake was relieved to hear his voice. Because of the events back in London – because of Marcus's unpredictability, his penchant for disappearing at a moment's notice and turning up in a bad state, in places he really should not be frequenting – Jake was getting used to Marcus scaring the crap out of him.

'I've seen it already.' Jake knew what Marcus had found down there. 'I came down here this morning.' He didn't feel that inclined to take another look. Jake waited at the top of the stairs.

'Oh shit!' Marcus voice again.

'What is it?' Jake walked down the stairs and stopped halfway. With one hand resting on Marcus's metal sign, he leaned down so his head cleared the ceiling. The dust sheet was off the doll's house again. Marcus stood beside it, concentrating on something in his hand. There was a look of dismay on his face.

Jake took his hand off the sign and walked down the remaining steps, pretty sure what was up. Marcus turned to Jake, holding out a miniature chair upright in the palm of his hand, like the one Jake had picked up earlier. Except that this one had a broken leg. And that, Jake remembered, was exactly the reason as kids Marcus was hardly ever allowed to go near Eleanor's doll's house – he was always so clumsy.

Marcus said, 'I nearly fell down those stairs. I banged my head on the way down and almost lost my balance.' He carefully placed the chair back in the doll's house. 'Why didn't you turn the damn electricity on while you were down here?' He tried to stand the chair upright on three legs. 'Did you want me to break my neck?'

Now that, thought Jake wickedly, *might not have been a bad idea.* 'What are you doing down here anyway?' Jake retorted.

Marcus shrugged and absently reached inside the doll's house for another piece of furniture.

'I wouldn't do that if I were you,' warned Jake.

Marcus withdrew his hand, empty.

'A bull in a china shop,' Jake commented.

Marcus gave Jake a sideways glance before bending down and resting his forearms on the dusty workbench. He peered into the tiny rooms.

Jake walked around to the other side and crouched down. He peered through the miniature living room at Marcus. 'We need to talk.'

Marcus looked across the miniature room at Jake. 'About what?'

Jake hesitated.

Marcus shifted. Now all Jake could see was Marcus's blue cotton shirt as a backdrop to the living room.

'It's pretty impressive, don't you think?' said Marcus. 'My little sister was quite the designer,' he said with a hint of sadness and regret. 'I wish I'd appreciated that more when she was—' he stopped abruptly.

Jake raised himself up and peered at Marcus through a miniature bedroom. 'What I wanted to tell you …'

Marcus shifted again. 'Bloody hell! How weird is that?'

Jake darted his head to the next bedroom, taking a cursory glance inside. He looked at Marcus and shrugged. 'What?'

'You don't see it?' Marcus said incredulously.

Jake continued to look at Marcus, wondering how he was going to take what he was about to say next. 'Look, about that word, the choice of inscription. I didn't mean …'

'Maybe if you come and look at it from this direction.' In the tiny room, Marcus's finger was gesturing for Jake to come over. Marcus hadn't taken his eyes off the room, and Jake hadn't taken his eyes off Marcus. He obviously hadn't heard a word he had just said.

Jake rolled his eyes. 'I told you.' He stood up, 'I've seen it today already.' Grudgingly, Jake walked around the workbench and stood beside Marcus. 'Besides, I thought you were anxious to get to the airport?' Jake reminded him.

Marcus grabbed Jake's arm and tugged in an effort to force Jake to bend down.

'What is it?' Jake crouched down next to Marcus.

Marcus pointed at the room again. 'Look.' Marcus stared at Jake until he gave in and looked into the room, craning his neck in a mock show. 'There, I'm looking – so what?' Jake didn't get it.

'I mean *really* look,' Marcus insisted.

Jake took in the detail of the miniature bedroom. And then he saw it. Without saying a word, Jake slowly stood up, followed by Marcus. He looked at Marcus a long moment, and then crouched down once more to take a second look to make sure his eyes weren't deceiving him.

'You see it, don't you?' said Marcus.

Jake stood and faced Marcus. 'Bloody hell,' he said, 'it's one of the rooms …'

Marcus nodded.

'… at Lark Lodge.'

Marcus nodded again.

They bent down together, and Jake reached into the room to pick up the sofa that was an exact replica, in all but size, of the one in the sitting room. He held it up. They both peered at it.

'How do you suppose that happened?' said Marcus.

Jake looked up from the miniature sofa in his hand. There was only one possible explanation. 'I guess Gayle's friend Robyn, the interior designer, has been here in The Lake House and seen this.' He imagined she'd caught glimpses of the house from upper floors of Lark Lodge, and her curiosity had got the better of her.

Jake thought of the used mug in the kitchen. Marty must have taken her to see the house. They clearly knew each other because Marty was Gayle's gardener too. But there was just one small snag; the dust sheet was filthy, and it hadn't looked like it had been removed in years. Perhaps she'd lifted a corner and taken a peek?

'But she's got no right to … to … use, to copy,' Marcus's voice was growing louder, 'to plagiarise Eleanor's work!' Marcus was furious.

Jake slowly shook his head. 'Will you listen to yourself?' He bent down and carefully placed the sofa back in the room. 'It's only a child's doll's house.' Jake touched the wallpaper, which he was sure exactly matched the pattern in Gayle's house. 'And besides, I think Eleanor would have been quite chuffed that an interior designer had seen fit to use her designs as a template for her own work – don't you?'

'Yes, ok. Maybe you're right,' Marcus conceded. 'But what the hell was some complete stranger,' his voice was rising again, 'doing nosing around your house and prying into Eleanor's things for anyway?' Marcus was shouting now. 'And more to the point, how did she get in here in the first place?'

Jake stood up and shifted his gaze from the doll's house to Marcus. He wasn't about to tell Marcus that the gardener had been stopping in the house for a drink, and at some point had probably given Robyn a guided tour. The last thing Jake wanted was for Marcus to fly off the handle and let rip at the one person who was keeping the gardens pristine. The grounds were immaculate, and thanks to Marty, did not send out a signal for unwanted guests – squatters. Jake wanted it to stay that way. Which reminded him that he'd gone there again to see Marty, not to revisit the past.

Jake knelt and picked up the dust sheet from the floor. When he got up, Marcus was still standing there, staring at him intently. 'What?' Jake eyed Marcus. 'What would you have me do, Marcus? Get her arrested?'

'Now we're getting somewhere,' said Marcus cheerfully.

Jake looked at him a long moment and shook his head. He threw the dust sheet in the air and watched it gently glide down to cover the house. He caught one last glimpse of the inside, the kitchen this time, and it too looked distinctly familiar. It made Jake wonder how many other rooms in Gayle's house had been lifted from Eleanor's design. He looked over at Marcus and was relieved to see he hadn't noticed. He was too wrapped up in the unfairness of life – that Eleanor was not there to use her talents and somebody else had.

'For trespassing, then.' Marcus said sulkily.

Jake shook his head again. Marcus was talking nonsense. Of course she couldn't be arrested for trespassing. That wasn't a police matter – and he knew it. Jake ignored him as he tucked the sheet under the base of the doll's house, having some difficulty lifting the base with his sore hands.

'She runs her interior design business from Gillespie's General Store. We could go into Aviemore and make a citizen's arrest.' Marcus followed Jake around the doll's house, not offering to help tuck in the sheet.

'Look, she probably knows Marty.' Jake hadn't intended to bring the gardener into it, but Marcus's constant badgering was getting on his nerves. He wanted him to shut up or go away – preferably both.

'Marty?'

'The gardener. He looks after Gayle's garden too, so my guess is that it's how he knows Robyn and how she came to be here in this house.'

'Are you saying the gardener wanders around the house too?'

Jake pursed his lips. Marcus was not calming down.

'Next you'll be telling me pretty much the whole damn town has occasion to come to this house.'

Jake sighed. 'Look, all I'm saying is that the gardener probably comes in here from time to time for a drink. So he goes down in the cellar to switch the electricity on and takes a peek under the dustsheet. He happens to mention it to Robyn, and one thing leads to another … Wouldn't you be just a little bit intrigued about what sat under that dust sheet? Wouldn't you take a look?'

'Yeah,' Marcus said sourly, knowing Jake was right. He changed tack. 'So why doesn't the gardener bring his own coffee – hasn't he heard of a thermos flask?'

'Oh, boy.' Jake sighed heavily. After all that hard graft in the garden, he should not begrudge him the use of the electric, a kettle or a coffee mug.

'I still think it's not on,' Marcus said sulkily. He caught the change in Jake's expression. 'What are you grinning at?'

Jake stood across from Marcus, smiling at the dirty dustsheet. A thought had just occurred to him. 'I think it's kind of fitting.'

'What are you talking about?'

'That we stayed in Eleanor's room.'

Marcus looked down at the dustsheet. 'I guess so,' he murmured. He looked up at Jake. 'I wonder if she used any of the other rooms' designs.' He reached for the dust sheet and started to lift one of the corners.

Jake darted around the doll's house and came up beside Marcus, putting a hand over his to prevent him from taking another look. 'Let it go,' Jake whispered.

Marcus's eyes narrowed. 'Will *you*?'

They stood facing each other and Jake realised they were talking about something far more significant than the doll's house. Jake sighed wearily. 'Look, whatever happened after the avalanche, when Eleanor and I were buried in the snow up there, you need to just let it go.' Jake tried to make his voice sound as reasonable as possible for both their sakes because this was liable to turn into a shouting match – or worse.

'What do *you* think happened?' Marcus spat. 'No wait. How stupid of me,' Marcus tapped his temple, 'I don't need to ask you that question because you've already written it down for posterity, haven't you Jake?'

The word on that memorial stone was coming back to haunt Jake. 'Look, about that, I …'

'Yeah, what about that? According to you I made a choice up there and now I can't live with it. Is that it, Jake?'

Yes, that is it, thought Jake. They had been buried in the snow, and Marcus had chosen to leave his sister to dig Jake out first, with catastrophic results. To cope with what he'd done, making that choice, Marcus had built a fence, a wall, a subconscious lie to screen himself from the awful truth – the awful realisation in those vital seconds after the accident that he could not save them both. He had been forced to choose between them – a choice which would condemn the other. Marcus had needed to believe, for his own sanity, that someone else was there, someone else had made that choice, not him. That was the lie.

A miniscule part of Jake felt that perhaps if it had been the other way round, if he had been in Marcus's shoes on that fateful day, he would have wanted to do the same.

'And now you're telling me to let it go,' Marcus said in an accusing tone. 'Well, I'm not the one having nightmares – am I?'

Jake stared at the doll's house. He wanted to tell Marcus that he finally understood. For the first time since the accident, Jake felt that he might just be able to forgive Marcus. He looked up, but Marcus was already heading back up the stairs.

The moment was lost.

Jake tucked in the corner of the dustsheet and followed Marcus back up the steps. At the top, he switched off the cellar light and stood for a moment in the gloomy darkness. He'd never known this house to be so still, so silent. It almost felt that with Eleanor gone, the house, like Jake, was still mourning her loss.

Jake swung the cellar door open, expecting to find Marcus waiting for him in the hall. He wasn't. Jake shut the door, glanced in the kitchen and then strode up the hallway towards the front door, guessing Marcus had gone back to the car.

He guessed wrong.

Jake walked down the grassy bank and entered the gap between the hedges. He stopped at the entrance and looked in; Marcus wasn't standing there as he had expected. Jake walked in, his attention focused on the memorial stone. He kept being drawn back to this place – he was making up for lost time, for all those visits he knew he should have made over the past few months but had not. Jake stood in front of the flowers, staring at the memorial stone, relieved that Marcus hadn't come. He didn't want to talk to Marcus there, in front of this.

'The flowers are nice.'

Startled, Jake whirled around to see Marcus sitting on the bench set into the hedge.

'Didn't expect to see me here, did you?' Marcus gestured with his hand for Jake to step aside. 'You're blocking my view.'

'I'm what?'

'You heard.' Marcus waved his hand again. 'Step aside.'

Jake stepped aside and stared at Marcus, unsure whether to leave so he could have some time alone. He decided that it was a good idea, so he turned to go. Outside in the main gardens, just beyond the hedge, Jake stopped abruptly. 'You're a bloody fool,' he admonished himself. He took a deep breath and retraced his steps.

39

Jake approached the garden bench. 'May I sit?'

'You can do what you like,' Marcus replied without looking up.

'Would you rather be alone?'

Marcus slowly turned his head to look up at Jake. 'I am alone.' He looked across at the memorial stone in the centre of the garden.

Jake hovered, unsure what that response was meant to mean.

He sat. Jake didn't know whether Marcus wanted silence while he sat there, but Jake desperately wanted to say something. He turned to look at Marcus's profile. 'Back in the house, in the cellar, I wanted tell you something,' Jake began.

'Don't talk, Jake – please.'

Jake had known it was a bad idea. He got up to leave.

Marcus reached for his arm. 'Don't go.'

Surprised, Jake sat again.

Marcus turned to him. 'Will you do something for me?'

Jake looked over at the stone, feeling absurdly guilty all of a sudden. 'Sure, anything you want – just name it.'

'Will you look at the contents of the envelopes?'

'But …' Jake stopped short. Marcus was probably right – this wasn't the time or place to talk about what had happened on that mountain. He was surprised by Marcus's question though. 'Why are you so bothered about those?' He imagined it was because his father's name was on one of the envelopes.

'For starters, I know you,' said Marcus. 'You'll just feel as guilty as hell if you don't at least look at them for a dying woman. Oh, and I think you'll find them quite interesting.'

Jake raised an eyebrow. Marcus had piqued his interest. 'All right. The envelopes are in my coat pocket. I left them in the car.'

Marcus nodded. After a time, Jake left Marcus alone in the garden and made his way back to the car. He sat motionless in the car, staring at the house for a while before gathering up his coat from the back seat and taking out the crumpled envelopes from his pocket. He looked at them. He did not feel in the mood to get involved in other people's issues. He had enough of his own. But for some reason, Marcus thought it was important for him to see them.

Jake opened an envelope, fishing inside with his fingertips for the letter. Strangely, he couldn't feel a sheet of paper inside. He turned the envelope over. A single photograph fell into his lap. He picked it up. A child, a boy of not more than five years old, stared back at him with a remarkable likeness to himself. He was holding a ball in a playful pose, suggesting he was about to throw it at the photographer as soon as the picture was taken. With the other hand, he was brushing a mop of blond hair out of his blue eyes.

It must have been this that had got Marcus's attention; it was unmistakably Jake in the photo. Jake wondered how this picture had come to be in the hands of a complete stranger. He examined the photo carefully, trying to ascertain whether he was looking at a childhood photo of himself or not. He didn't recall the photo being taken, or indeed ever having seen it.

He turned the photo over. '*Ralph*,' he said, reading the single word scribbled in the upper left-hand corner. 'Then this can't be me in the photo.'

He recalled that during his visit to see Arnold and Martha, Arnold had mentioned that Martha had said the name *Ralph*. Jake had suggested that perhaps it was someone from her past, maybe a previous husband, even though Arnold was adamant that this wasn't the case.

A tap on the car window startled Jake. The red-headed young gardener was peering in at the window. Jake hastily put the photo back in the envelope. When he looked back, the lad had stepped from the car and was standing a few feet away, the rake he had been carrying now lying on the shingle drive.

Jake reached for the car door handle. He got out of the car. 'Marty, isn't it?' Jake extended his hand and discovered that the lad, on closer inspection, was a little older than he'd first thought; perhaps twenty.

'Mr Campbell-Ross.' Marty leaned forward to take his hand. He had a mobile phone in the other hand. 'Gayle texted me, said you might be popping round.'

Jake nodded, not surprised. Gayle probably knew he nipped in the house for a drink and a break, and didn't want him getting into trouble if Jake caught him. She didn't realise that Marty wouldn't be in trouble – far from it.

'I'm sorry for growling at you this morning.' Jake glanced in the direction of the hidden garden.

'You gave me quite a start, I can tell you.' He laughed light-heartedly, which made Jake relax. Both their moods seemed to have improved since they'd first met.

'Yes, I suppose it was a shock to find some stranger wandering around the garden.'

'Oh, I recognised you straight off,' said Marty.

Jake thought back to the red-headed lad he'd occasionally seen with his father, helping him on his gardening round.

'I'm glad I caught you before you left,' said Marty, 'the reason I wanted to speak to you—'

Jake held up his hand. 'I've spoken to Gayle.'

Marty looked at him quizzically, 'Gayle?'

'From Lark Lodge,' Jake added unnecessarily.

'Yes, I know where she's from.' Marty held up his phone. Jake wouldn't have been at all surprised if Marty added, *Duh!* He didn't, but he did add, 'What's this about?'

Was it his imagination, or had Marty's tone changed? 'She mentioned,' Jake tried to sound casual so that it didn't appear that they had been talking about him behind his back, 'that I had neglected to thank your father for all his hard work over the years, so I want to wish him a very happy retirement.'

'Okay,' Marty said slowly. 'Do you want me to pass that on to my dad?'

Jake smiled. 'Yes, of course.' He had one other request. 'Can you tell me, was your father paid a bonus?'

'A bonus? I don't think he got anything when he retired.'

Jake's face dropped. The Rosses were known for their generosity. Marty's father should have received some recognition, hopefully in the form of a generous bonus, when he'd retired. William always saw to those sorts of things personally. Jake had an idea that Mr Henshaw's retirement had probably been around the same time as the family tragedy. Now he understood why William had neglected to give Marty's father a nice send-off, and instead he had received nothing.

Jake was going to rectify the situation. 'I want to give your dad that bonus. It's overdue.'

'You do?'

'Yes, absolutely. Call it a retirement present. And for you too, a nice little bonus for all the hard work. I'm not sure how much you're being paid, but I wanted to check you're being reimbursed fully for *all* the work you've been doing since you took over from your dad.' He paused. 'And from now on, of course.'

Marty regarded Jake thoughtfully. 'I already get paid.'

Jake was aware of that.

'Do you think I'd do all this work for nothing?'

'Well, no, of course not.' Jake said slowly, although despite what Gayle had said, it had crossed his mind. Perhaps Marty had been just too polite, or embarrassed, to raise the topic when he'd agreed to take over from his father – maybe Marty had continued the business, but someone had neglected to put him on the payroll.

Jake was still confused. 'I don't understand.' And he didn't have time for riddles. 'Do you get paid – or not?'

'I do, just not by you.'

Jake stared at him. 'Well, of course you don't get paid by me personally.' The Ross Corporation always took care of things.

Marty shook his head. 'That's not what I meant. The company hasn't been paying me either. You see, when my father first retired, the job was being transferred into my name. He had informed the company, written to the corporation, explaining I would be taking over. He would have written to Mr William Ross here at The Lake House. This was the only address he knew, but he couldn't imagine someone would be back here any time soon …' Marty trailed off. 'Sorry.'

Jake breathed a sigh. 'Don't be. I think it's me who should be apologising.' The Ross Corporation was gargantuan; Jake could just imagine that letter bouncing around the company, from one department to another, nobody taking any responsibility for the payment to a gardener working on the Rosses' holiday home far away in Scotland.

Jake got out his cheque book to write two cheques. He always carried a cheque book around with him. Marcus used to find it peculiar, and rather funny. But today was one of those days when it was useful.

Marty said, 'What are you doing?'

Jake was busy writing out that generous bonus to Marty's father. It was a nice round number. He wouldn't need to fill in the cheque stub to remember.

Jake ripped out the cheque with a flurry. One down, one to go. 'Now, how many months to do I owe you since they stopped paying your father?'

'You don't owe me a thing. I told you that I've been paid.'

Jake scratched his head. 'Am I missing something?' This conversation felt as though it was going around is circles. 'Look, if I'm not paying you, and the Ross Corporation isn't, then please tell me how it is that you've been paid for your work?'

'Someone else has been paying me instead.'

Jake looked up in surprise. 'Who?'

Marty said, 'I doubt you'd know her.'

Jake looked over Marty's shoulder to the house beyond. 'Robyn,' he said having a good idea not just the *whom*, but the *why*. 'Robyn pays you.'

'Yeah, she does now. You know Robyn?'

'Nope.' Jake looked back at Marty.

'Gayle,' they both said in unison.

'But how do you know she's the one who pays me to do this?'

'Let's just say it was a lucky guess.' Jake thought of the doll's house and the room they had stayed in at Lark Lodge. Marcus was right: she had stolen the ideas, she had plagiarised them, but by paying for the upkeep of the gardens, when she'd found out that Marty wasn't being paid after all, she'd had the decency to give something back in return. Jake was sure that if he got the opportunity to meet Robyn, he would like her.

'Aren't you going to ask me why she does it?' said Marty.

'No.'

'That's just as well,' said Marty, 'because I wouldn't know.'

Jake looked at the second blank cheque and thought of the money that William was still paying into his bank account. He didn't want money from the Ross Corporation, but he knew William would not take the money back. He eyed Marty, wondering when he'd ever afford a place of his own. 'Are you still living with your parents?'

Marty shook his head, surprising Jake.

'You've got your own place?'

'Oh, no.' His eyes momentarily shifted to The Lake House. He looked at Jake sheepishly. 'My parents retired to Edinburgh. I was going to rent with a friend, but they let me down. Luckily I've got a room at Lark Lodge.'

'I see.' Jake hadn't seen him there, but then he'd only been there one night, and he had skipped breakfast. 'Here. This is for your father. It's the bonus he should have had.'

Marty took the cheque. He looked up the moment he saw what that bonus was. He attempted to hand it back. 'I think you've made a mistake. There are too many noughts on this.'

Jake waved that comment away. He signed another cheque.

'Now, this is yours.'

'I said that I'm being paid.'

'Not by me, so consider this back pay, and a bonus too, all your Christmas bonuses for the next … oh, I don't know … few decades.'

Marty stared at Jake, speechless.

For a moment, Jake thought he might not take the cheque. 'I insist.'

Marty looked at the cheque in Jake's hands. 'The thing is, I wanted to get in touch with someone and explain that I have struggled to keep on top of the gardening job here. My father hired other gardeners to work in the grounds …'

Jake nodded. 'You could hire some more gardeners to help. Of course I will pay for them. What about the gardeners who worked in your father's business before he retired and passed the business on you?'

Marty shook his head. 'They retired too. I'm doing a horticultural course. There might be some students interested in a part-time job.'

'That's a good idea. They could get some experience while they are doing their course.' Jake held out the cheque. 'I think considering you have been managing all this on your own …'

'Trying to …' Marty corrected.

'Well even so, you've done an amazing job. This is well deserved.'

When Marty took the cheque, he said, 'You've only signed it. You've forgotten to fill it in.'

'I haven't.' He glanced around the garden while Marty attempted to hand back the blank cheque. 'I bet you'd like one of your own – a garden.'

'Yeah. I was hoping to move in with my mate in his two-bed rental. It had a little garden. But then his girlfriend said she didn't want me there.'

Jake nodded. 'That's not what I meant. I'm talking about your own garden. Your *own* house.'

'Are you talking about me buying a house?' Marty laughed. 'Yeah – like that's going to happen. Have you seen the cost of houses around here?' His eyes flickered to Jake's handsome house. 'There's a two-bedroomed house on that new development outside of town,' added Marty. 'They're nice houses. Really nice. I do some gardening work for people who've moved into their new homes.'

'Why don't you buy one, then?'

Marty shook his head, his eyes roving to Jake's grand old house, which had so many bedrooms that Marty had lost count. 'Look, I don't mean to be rude, but I don't think you get it.'

'I do get it, Marty. That's what the signed blank cheque is for. Go buy one tomorrow.'

Marty stared at him intently. 'Are you saying I can buy one of those houses?'

'Yes. One with a nice garden.'

'Are you insane?'

Jake wasn't surprised by his reaction.

'Oh, this is some kind of joke, isn't it?' said Marty.

'No, and no.'

Marty shook his head. 'I … I can't just go handing them a cheque for that money.'

'Why not?' Jake opened his wallet, and gave Marty one of his old business cards. God knew why he still kept them. 'If the sales people have got a problem, they just phone me. I'll wire them the money, if they want.'

'I … I can't accept this.'

'You can. Another opportunity like this won't come along.'

Marty stared at the blank cheque with tears in his eyes. 'Why would you do this for me?'

Jake looked around the stunning gardens of The Lake House. 'Because I know you love what you do, and you're good at it, and you bring so much pleasure for people through your gardening and landscaping. The thing is, it's undervalued, like a lot of jobs. You'll end up, down the line, doing something you despise to earn enough money to find a place to live.'

Marty stared at him.

Jake continued, 'I'm doing something I love – teaching. But it would never afford me a house if it wasn't for the money from the Ross Corporation.' Marty would never be like Derrick, studying law, aiming for the boardroom, but his skills were no less important. Why shouldn't Marty have a little bit of what he had given Derrick?

'If it makes you happy, tell me how much a house would cost, and I'll write the cheque out.'

'I … I don't know. The sales person offered me a brochure when I came to mow the lawn of the show home, but I didn't see the point. I think it's because I said how amazing the show home is. The show home has got a lovely garden, the best on the development. That's not exactly a surprise, though, seeing as it is on the biggest plot.'

'The show home,' mused Jake. 'Are you in any rush to move?'

'I do want my own place, but I love it at Lark Lodge. Gayle, her mum, Nick, and Robyn and David who used to live there, they're all like family. And of course, there's Olive.'

'Yes, indeed.' Jake smiled. 'I'm sure they'll all remain like family when you move out.' 'Now, this show home. Presumably you can buy it?'

'Oh, yeah. You can't move into it until the estate is completely finished. Won't be long now. It's next door to the loveliest couple – Rose and George.'

Jake grinned. He got out his mobile phone.

'What are you doing?'

'Phoning the sales office on the development. Have you got their number?'

Marty got out his phone and reeled off their number.

Jake made the call. Five minutes later, after checking Marty's full name, and agreeing an appointment for him to go in with his identity, and proof of funds, the show home, which hadn't even hit the market, was officially off the market – for good.

40

Marty stood there, gaping at him.

'Now, where was I?' Jake looked at the blank cheque. Now he had a figure from the sales person less the deposit money he'd just put down over the phone via his bank card. Jake wrote the cheque and handed it to Marty. 'There. Take that in, along with some proof of identity. I took the liberty of passing on the details of a solicitor friend of mine who can deal with your purchase.'

Although Jake's intention had been to sever all ties with the Ross Corporation when he had started teacher training, and he had not been pleased to discover he was still on the company payroll, the money had given him the opportunity to give Marty and Derrick a much-needed leg-up. He was starting to rethink his position. He wasn't about to chuck in the towel with the new teaching job he loved, but he was still on the Board of the Ross Corporation. Perhaps it was wrong to sever all ties with the company. After all, the Rosses had always been a big part of his life.

Marty finally found his voice. 'My parents are going to freak out. They'll think I've been drug dealing, or something.'

Jake's smile faltered. He wished Marty hadn't said that. 'Just tell your father that you're a Ross employee now, part of the Ross family. You've got a job for life, Marty. Your job might involve a bit of foreign travel, here and there.'

'Foreign travel?'

'There are other properties around the world belonging to the Rosses, and the people who work for them. Obviously you wouldn't be expected to fly off somewhere just to mow a lawn, but if there was a big landscaping project, say of a new Ross building project, that sort of thing, I take it you'd be interested? You'd be well remunerated, of course, with flights and hotels paid for.' Marty was going to be on the company payroll now, with all the benefits that came with it.

'I … I really, really don't know what to say.'

Jake just smiled. 'You don't have to say anything. But I do expect an invite to your housewarming party.'

'Oh … oh, of course.'

Jake shook his head. 'I am kidding. You do not have to feel obligated to invite me over to your house when you move in, honestly.'

'But I want you to come. You and William Ross, and Marcus Ross, and whoever they want to bring too.'

Jake sighed. It was a nice thought, the Rosses dropping in on Marty in his little show home on a new development outside of Aviemore. But unfortunately, that was just never going to happen. This saddened Jake. It was always the same at Christmas; they all met up at The Lake House, but they had never once made friends in the area, or invited anyone else from the local community over to the house at Christmas or New Year in Aviemore. It was about time things changed.

He looked at Marty. 'You know what? I'm going to take you

up on your offer, and I'm going to bring along as many family members as I can.'

'Really?'

'Oh, yes.' Jake tried to sound confident, although he wasn't sure, with their busy schedules, and William's withdrawal from everything, save the golf course, whether that was just a pipe dream.

Marty bent down and picked up his rake. 'I'd love to meet—'

'Jake!' Marcus's breathless voice came up behind them, cutting straight across Marty. Jake turned to see Marcus taking great gasps of air as he struggled up the small grassy slope to the house.

Ignoring him, Jake turned back to Marty. 'You were saying?'

'Yeah, I was just saying I'd love to meet them.'

'Jake!' Marcus called out again.

Marty leaned to the left, looking past Jake. 'Your friend there looks like he could use a helping hand.'

'He is not my friend,' said Jake, cheesed off with Marcus for interrupting the conversation. He rolled his eyes. Marty was about to meet one of the family straight away. 'Do you remember Marcus?' he said to Marty as they both watched Marcus reach the top of the slope and bend over, hands on his sides, trying to catch his breath.

'Yes I do,' he sounded uncertain. 'He looks … different.'

Jake stared at the hunched-over figure and wondered what had happened to that muscular, athletic frame, that guy who used to sprint up these slopes like it was a walk in the park.

Finally, Marcus caught his breath and stood up straight. He looked past Jake.

Jake followed his gaze to Marty. 'You remember Marty?' he said to Marcus.

The look on Marcus's face said he didn't.

Jake said, 'Remember the gardener? He retired a while back.'

'Yeah, sure. Sometimes he used to bring along a fat kid.'

Jake groaned. Looking wide-eyed at Marty, he said, 'Please excuse Marcus. I don't know if he behaves like this on purpose or if it comes naturally.'

Marty sniggered.

Marcus shot Jake a black look. 'What did you just say?'

Jake rolled his eyes at Marcus. 'That fat kid is standing right in front of you.'

'Oh.' Marcus looked him over. 'Well, you've certainly changed. Last time I saw you, you were, like, this tall.' Marcus's shaky hand hovered in thin air around chest height. 'How old were you back then – nine, ten?'

'Fourteen.' Marty's cheeks coloured. 'I was small for my age.'

'Well, you've certainly made up for it now,' said Marcus, sounding way too cheerful.

Jake gave him a sideways glance.

'So, how long has it been?' inquired Marcus. 'You must have finished school – right?'

Marty nodded. 'I'm in college now, studying horticulture. My parents retired to Edinburgh.'

Marcus nodded. 'Lovely city.'

Jake was surprised at the genuine interest Marcus was taking in Marty, because lately Marcus seemed to have his head lodged so far up his own backside that he didn't seem at all concerned by the effect he was having on those around him. Lydia came to mind.

Jake wondered in passing whether he had even told his fiancée that he was in Scotland. Jake imagined he had, otherwise he would have got a call from Lydia. He guessed that Marcus would not have told Lydia the specifics of his trip, notably regarding his recent sojourn in a prison cell. Jake did wonder how long Lydia would put up with Marcus's behaviour before she chucked in the towel and left him.

'Well, we'd better get going.'

In the car, Jake wound his window down. 'Marty, if there's anything you need, just let me know.'

'I will.'

'Oh, and I'll be waiting for that housewarming party invite.'

Marty grinned.

Jake started to wind his window up when Marty tapped on it. 'I wanted to ask you something.'

'Go ahead.' Jake prompted.

He seemed uncomfortable and shifted nervously from one foot to the other. Jake could see his hand tensing around the rake. 'It's about the garden.' He lifted his eyes in the direction of the hidden garden.

'Go on.'

'You like the flowers I planted?'

'Sure, they're …' Jake glanced at Marcus who just shrugged his shoulders, 'very colourful.'

'Good,' he said, although his face didn't register that he was pleased with Jake's response. 'I was worried you wouldn't like how I changed the garden.'

'Why was that?' Jake imagined that most people would have liked the change, but Jake had a feeling that what Marty was really asking was whether Eleanor would have approved. And there was the rub; Eleanor never had been one for flowers, and if Marty had really known Eleanor, he would have been aware of that. Still, it was a nice gesture, and Jake wasn't about to rubbish such thought and hard work, which had transformed a dull, lifeless patch of grass.

'It was just something Robyn said ...' Marty scuffed the earth with his shoe.

Marcus leaned across Jake, peering at Marty through the car window. 'What's she got to do with anything?'

Jake shoved Marcus back into his seat. 'Never mind him,' he said to Marty. 'Now why don't you tell me exactly what she said?'

'Robyn liked everything I did to the garden – everything, that is, except that part of the garden through the hedge.' He hesitated. 'She said it was wrong.'

'Wrong?'

Marty crouched down beside the car and nodded at Jake. 'She said the hidden garden was all wrong.' His eyes were distant.

Jake thought perhaps Robyn had met Eleanor and she knew that she wasn't particularly into flowers.

'Those were her exact words. I tried to get her to be more specific, to tell me exactly what was wrong so I could do something about it, but I couldn't get anything more out of her.'

Jake chose his words carefully. 'Maybe Robyn was right,' Jake said softly, 'perhaps it would be better to have asked first.'

'I know that.' Marty looked from Marcus then back to Jake and lowered his voice. 'But no one was around to ask.'

Jake felt a sudden pang of guilt – how could he have let all these months go by without visiting just once?

'What's it all got to do with that damn Robyn?' Marcus said gruffly.

Jake sat in the car, staring past Marcus out of the side window and watching Marty disappearing down the grassy slope. 'She knew her.'

'Who knew who?' Marcus snapped his fingers in front of Jake's face to get his attention.

Jake recounted the conversation with Marty while he drove.

'So why do you think she pays to have the garden maintained like that?'

Jake cast an exasperated glance in Marcus's direction.

'What?' Marcus said.

'You figure it out, Einstein.' Jake looked back at the road ahead.

Marcus fell silent. Finally, he muttered, 'Guilt money.'

'Pardon?'

'She stole Eleanor's designs and then she starts feeling guilty, so she pays for a gardener – big deal.'

'Actually, I'll tell you what it is.' Jake took his eyes off the road for a second taking in Marcus's sour expression. 'It's a kind gesture.'

'Perhaps she was an old friend from school,' Marcus offered grudgingly.

'Perhaps,' said Jake, but he knew that was not true. He'd never heard of her.

41

On the outskirts of Aviemore, they passed the turn-off that headed to Inverness and eventually the airport. 'I think you missed the exit.' Marcus turned in his seat as the road sign receded.

'I've got one more stop before we leave.' Jake motioned to the glove compartment.

Marcus opened it and pulled out the two crumpled envelopes and dog-eared photograph that Jake had bizarrely stuffed in there when Marty had appeared, unsure why he had wanted to keep them from uninvited eyes.

'I'm pretty sure that's not me.' Jake glanced at Marcus, who was studying the photo. 'Look on the back.'

'I know what's written on the back,' Marcus didn't sound convinced. 'Did you open this one?' Marcus held up the second envelope.

'No – what's inside?' said Jake, fully expecting Marcus to tell him.

'I don't know,' said Marcus, but he must have caught the expression on Jake's face because he added, 'For your information, I do not go around opening other people's letters. They were on the floor. When I picked them up, this photo had slipped out ...'

He held up the photo of the little boy as he glared at Jake.

'Sorry,' Jake said sheepishly, giving him a quick glance.

There was a moment's silence.

'So, do you want me to open this – or what?' Marcus held up the unopened envelope.

Jake sighed heavily. He knew Marcus wasn't going to let it drop, especially if he thought somebody they didn't know might have photos of Jake – however unlikely that was. The likeness was uncanny, but Jake was convinced it wasn't a photo of himself.

He glanced at Marcus. 'Open it.' It didn't interest him in the least. What he was interested in was returning the envelopes and heading straight home. He listened to the rip of paper and the rustle of Marcus's hand in the envelope.

'What have we here?' said Marcus in a peculiar tone of voice.

Jake briefly took his eyes off the road. Marcus was leafing through several black-and-white photographs. 'What is it?' said Jake, trying to catch a glimpse of the photographs.

'Are we going to see this Arnold fellow who gave you these?' Marcus said slowly.

'Well now,' Jake paused while he made a right turn, 'I am taking them back.'

'Taking them back?' Marcus repeated. 'What do you mean taking them back? They're *our* photographs.'

It took a moment for what Marcus had said to sink in. 'What do you mean they're *our* photographs? Show me them.' Jake took a hand off the steering wheel as Marcus passed him a photograph.

'Arnold Wright had better explain how he came by these,' said Marcus, rifling through the remainder.

'Mr Wright can't tell us anything,' said Jake, holding up the photo so he could take a closer look while keeping an eye on the road ahead. Jake recalled that Arnold kept referring to *the letters,* so obviously he had no idea that the envelopes contained old family photos of no consequence; he was going to be hugely disappointed.

'Maybe Martha can explain,' said Marcus.

'No, she cannot,' Jake said emphatically.

'Why – is she dead?'

'Not quite yet, but she's not well enough to talk,' Jake replied, his concentration wandering from the road for a moment.

'Watch it!' Marcus yelped, making a grab at the steering wheel. They were careering across the road into the path of an oncoming car.

Jake slapped Marcus's hand away from the steering wheel and corrected the drift. When he thought he had sufficient control of himself, and the car, he held up the photo again to take a quick look. 'It's my house!' said Jake in surprise. He looked at Marcus.

'For god's sake, keep your eyes on the road, man; I want to get there in one piece!' Marcus snatched the photo out of Jake's hand, spoiling for a fist in the face. 'Look, why don't you just pull over, and then I'll give you the photos.'

Jake didn't want to stop. He now had urgent questions he wanted to ask Arnold about how the photographs, taken at his house, had come to be in Martha's possession. 'Describe them.'

There were four photos, all taken at The Lake House – some in the house and some in the grounds. Without actually seeing them for himself, it was impossible for Jake to tell whether they were taken before or after he was born – but the photos were old. In all, Marcus counted five people present in the photographs – Jake's parents, William, Aubrey and a woman Marcus didn't recognise.

'What does she look like?'

'She's got long hair, almost to her waist, looks kinda thick and silky and …'

'Blonde?'

'Yeah – do you know her?'

'Martha.' Jake remembered Arnold's words: *that's the first thing people notice about her.*

Jake turned up the driveway and stopped outside Cedar Grove.

'When do you suppose these were taken?' said Marcus, passing the photographs to Jake once he'd turned off the car engine.

'Hard to say, precisely,' Jake said, peering at a photo of the group. They were all linking arms, their right feet swinging in the air as if they were in the middle of some sort of synchronised line-dancing routine. And they all looked as though they were finding it incredibly funny. Jake put the photo down without comment.

'Don't you think it's odd that Grace isn't in any of these?' Marcus commented.

Jake could see Marcus's point. William had to be well into his thirties in these photos, and he would have been married to Marcus's mother Grace for a good ten years before they were taken. Jake shrugged. 'There are only a handful of photos here,' Jake pointed out. 'She's probably in some of the others on that roll of film. Perhaps she was the one taking the photos.'

Or maybe it was simply the case that his parents, and Martha, were William and Aubrey's friends and not hers. Jake didn't say out loud what he was thinking, especially as his next thought was that Grace could be a bit of a snob, whereas Jake remembered his parents were like William – just down-to-earth, hardworking people.

Marcus looked at him doubtfully as he handed Jake the next

photo. In it were Jake's father and William, both standing in a relaxed pose, William with a hand on Jake's father's shoulder, who was laughing as though somebody had just told an extraordinarily good joke.

The next photo could have been a carbon copy, except that Aubrey had joined them and was standing beside Jake's father, sharing the joke.

The next photo was different to the others. The two women had been photographed unawares; at least, that was how it appeared to Jake. He recognised the hallway in his house where Martha, her back to the camera but her silky locks giving her away, was pointing in the direction of the stairs for the benefit of the second woman, whose profile Jake recognised – it was his mother. He traced the line of Martha's outstretched hand to the stairs. About two-thirds of the way up, deep in shadows, a small, round face was looking down on them through two wooden spindles.

'Do you see that?' Jake passed the picture to Marcus, pointing at his find. 'I think I can date these photos. That's definitely me, probably spying on my parents' friends. I must have been around four. It would have been shortly before they died.'

They both fell silent.

Marcus turned the picture over and showed Jake the back, on which was scribbled a name and a date. The date was about right, but the name was wrong.

'Ralph,' Jake said. 'I could have sworn that was me in the photo.' He pointed at the face peering through the banister.

'Martha's son?' Marcus asked.

'Must be.'

'So, where were *you*?'

Jake shrugged. 'Probably hiding from all the visitors again.'

Marcus turned in his seat. 'What do you mean – *again*?'

'I was kind of a shy, introspective kid.'

'Yeah – right.'

'No, it's true. Obviously all that changed when I came to live with you, Eleanor, and your parents. But when I lived with my parents at The Lake House, and with my father away on tours with the army, there would just be me and my mother. She'd have lots of friends to stay. She was always throwing open the doors to The Lake House. I'd often retreat to my room with all the adults about.'

'Well, it sounds as though that one time, Martha must have brought her son with her. You would have had someone to play with.'

'I don't remember that.'

Marcus said, 'Why are you surprised? It was a long time ago, and you were only very young.'

Jake nodded. 'I suppose you're right.' He looked at the photos, convinced he now knew what all this was about. Arnold had handed him the envelopes in the hope that he could discern what Martha so desperately wanted, because whatever purpose Martha had for these photos was now lost to the condition she was suffering from. And Jake had it figured. 'That's it!' he said. Martha was looking for a son she had lost touch with. That was what the photos were all about – people who knew her and her son, and might be able to locate him for her.

He told Marcus his thoughts. 'I'm now guessing,' he added, 'that Martha was a friend of my parents and just happened to be there that day when William and Aubrey paid a visit.'

'Hmmm,' said Marcus, not sounding convinced.

'What do you mean – hmmm?' Jake though it was obvious.

Marcus held up the photo with them all linking arms. 'Don't

you think they look altogether a bit too chummy for people who have just met?'

Jake stared at Martha, comfortably ensconced between Aubrey and William in the lineup. He really didn't care which of them had known each other all those years ago. What mattered to Jake was that these photos explained something. On his visit to see Arnold and Martha, he'd had a distinct sensation of déjà vu; he'd been to Cedar Grove before as a child. The fact that his parents had known Martha explained why he'd visited there as a child. She must have been living there for many years. It was a question he felt like putting to Arnold – how long had she been here?

Marcus said, 'I don't get it – where's this kid, Ralph's, father?'

'Perhaps he was taking the photos?' suggested Jake.

Marcus shook his head. 'No, I don't think so. I think *he* was taking the photos!' Marcus handed over another photo, surprising Jake that he had held one of them back until now.

On the back was the name *Ralph*.

Jake scratched his head. 'Okay, I'm really confused now.'

'Take a look.' Marcus said nonchalantly.

Jake flipped the photo over. He looked up at Marcus.

Marcus shrugged and said, 'He was always full of surprises.'

It was a photo of Aubrey, standing on the lawn in the sunshine, one hand tucked neatly in the front pocket of his suit jacket. The other held a cigarette with which he was pointing at something or someone out of camera frame and smiling broadly.

Jake put the photo of Aubrey back in the envelope with the others. Aubrey had always been vague when it came to his past, his background before meeting William, so this piece of news didn't surprise Jake in the least. Especially since he had already found out, courtesy of the British police, that Aubrey Jones did not exist. So,

Jake finally knew his real name – Ralph.

Jake opened the car door.

'Where are you going?'

'I'm still giving these back.' Jake put one foot on the gravel drive.

'But isn't it odd? There's a photo of some kid called Ralph, and he's called Ralph too?' Marcus snatched the envelopes out of Jake's hand.

'Just what do you think you're doing?' Jake turned to see Marcus opening the passenger side door.

'I want to find out more about these, and I wouldn't mind knowing just who Aubrey Jones is – for real.' Marcus got out.

'Look, I feel the same. Give them here. I'm going back in.' He glared at Marcus. 'On my own.'

42

Jake hesitated before entering. He wasn't exactly relishing seeing Martha or telling Arnold that he couldn't really be of help. But at least he could hand the photos back. With that thought, Jake walked in and immediately stopped, stunned.

'I take it you've been here before.' A deep throaty male voice came from a heavily-built guy in a blue uniform, who was sitting behind a long, low desk spanning the width of the hallway. 'It always takes people by surprise,' his smooth deep baritone voice continued. 'But like I said, they wouldn't listen – board of trustees always get their way.' He made a clucking sound with his tongue, noting disapproval.

'You mean the …?' Jake twirled his finger in the air, still getting over the shock of seeing all that beautiful mahogany wood he had been admiring only the previous day now whitewashed along with the walls. He blinked hard, wondering if it was all in his head and Marcus was right – that he did need to check himself in.

'Scandalous, isn't it? You're not the first to walk in here and get a shock, I can tell you. And you won't be the last.'

Jake was relieved to hear it. 'It looks so – clinical.'

'You know, I said the exact same thing.' He leaned forward and pointed a finger at Jake. 'And that's not the only thing that's changed around here. The trustees have gone ahead and sold off some of the land, ostensibly to keep funding this place.'

'The billboard?' said Jake.

'That's right – sacrilege, isn't it? Anyway, enough about that. Who are you here to see?' He made a quick entry on the computer on his desk and then looked up expectantly at Jake.

Jake cautiously approached the desk, discreetly tucking the brown envelopes in his coat pocket. He decided he'd be better off speaking to the woman who had been there the previous day – she'd understand. 'I've come to see a woman – she works here.' Jake craned his neck to see down the hallway. He looked for the door with the word *Reception,* expecting her to be in there and expecting the man sitting in front of him to go and fetch her.

'We've got lots of women here. Are you talking about a nurse?'

'No, she's not a nurse. She's a receptionist.' An assumption of course, thought Jake, but hey if you work out of a room called *Reception* … Jake took another look down the hallway to see if he could see the familiar room, but the big man in front of him was blocking his view, and the long, low desk prevented access to the passage where Jake had walked only the day before.

Jake said, 'You make changes quickly around here.'

He raised an eyebrow. 'You think so?' He leaned over the counter towards Jake. 'You know, I used to be on my feet all day, for thirty-five years, and the last five years I kept telling them I needed to get off my feet, do something a bit more sedentary. Five years it took to get me this position. Five *years.* And that's only because Margaret quit. You'd think they'd have made more effort to keep their longest-serving employee, but once all this changed, she just didn't want to stick around.'

'Margaret – the receptionist – she's gone?' Jake turned to look at the front door as though she had just that moment strode past him on her way out.

'Yep, just up and left. She was close to retirement, mind. Between you and me,' he glanced around the room and motioned Jake to come closer, 'I think she couldn't get the hang of these newfangled things.' He surreptitiously cocked his head at the computer. 'Mind you, I'm no expert myself,' he chuckled, 'two years and I still haven't quite …'

'Two years?' Jake said in surprise. He found it necessary to repeat the question. 'You've been doing this for two years?'

The big guy nodded.

'Does the old receptionist, er …' Jake pointed at the big man.

'Margaret.'

'Yes, Margaret – does she ever get called in to cover for you when you go on holiday?'

'Holiday?' He slowly shook his head. 'I haven't got the money for a holiday.' He rubbed his chin. 'Besides, they'd have a difficult time calling her in, even if they wanted to.'

Jake furrowed his brow. 'How's that?'

The big man leaned forward, elbows on counter. 'Because she's dead.' He drew back and nodded solemnly. 'Yep, she died over a year ago.'

'How could that be?'

The big man thought the question was directed at him. 'I think the job was her life – know what I mean – and once she left, well,' he clicked his fingers, 'that was it – poof, end of story!'

It obviously hadn't been Margaret he had spoken to the day before. The conversation was wasting his time.

'How long?' Jake swirled his hand around the hall.

'The wonderful re-decoration job?' he said in a deadpan voice. 'Not long after she left – that's when they installed this, too.' He patted the desk. 'Say, what happened?' He was looking at Jake's hands.

'I fell on glass, cut my hands pretty bad.' Jake said absently, his mind still racing with questions.

'Nasty – you want me to take a look?'

Jake looked at him doubtfully.

'I'm a healthcare assistant. Well, I was until I started this job.'

'I see.'

He held up his lanyard with an identity card that detailed his name and position. 'I'm Lawrence. And I can tell straight off you haven't had those looked at by a medical professional. If they'd added any more bandages, your hands would be wrapped up like you're wearing a pair of boxing gloves.' He chuckled.

Jake looked at them. He was pretty sure driving was illegal like this as it was. Gayle, a former nurse, had offered to take a look, but he just hadn't had time for her to redress the wounds with fresh bandages. It was Marcus and himself that had done it instead, and clearly not done a good job of it.

'Come through here.' He beckoned for Jake to step the other side of the counter.

Jake stepped through and found himself still puzzling over what he'd been told. How could the place look so different from the previous day?

'Are you okay?'

When Jake looked up, the man was standing next to him, holding gauze and bandages.

'Yes, but I've got to be honest with you, and I swear I am not losing my mind. This place looks completely different.' Jake cast his gaze up the unfamiliar flight of stairs in front of him.

Lawrence nodded and said, 'Meet the founder of this place.' He was pointing up the stairs. A grey-haired, dignified gentleman, who looked quite stern, stared down at them from a very large portrait painting.

'The last of his family to live here, before he formed a charitable trust and it became what it is today.'

'Can you explain it?' He studied Lawrence intensely, hoping for any sign, any reasonable explanation, that he wasn't losing his mind.

'Yes,' said Lawrence, 'of course I can explain it. Oh damn! I've forgotten the antiseptic cream! 'Hold that thought. I'll be back in a jiffy.'

Jake sighed and turned his attention back to the painting. A small gold plate fixed to the bottom of the picture frame appeared to have a name and date engraved. Jake walked partway up the stairs to take a closer look. He read the inscription – *Mr Angus Delaney and Master Ralph Delaney, circa 1963.*

'Ralph?' Jake nearly lost his footing when he suddenly realised who he was looking at.

43

Jake stood there for some minutes, staring at the painting – staring at the little boy, convinced it was Aubrey. His features resembled that of his father, and there was no denying the similarity between Aubrey, now a similar age, and the older man in the painting.

Jake turned from the painting, realising that for the first time in his life, he actually knew something real about Aubrey Jones – Aubrey, or rather Ralph, had a connection with this house. Perhaps he had grown up there. It didn't appear that he'd inherited the house from his father, from what Lawrence had said. Angus Delaney, the last of the family to live there, had left the property in a charitable trust.

Jake had always wondered why Aubrey refused to return with them for the family get-togethers in Scotland. Perhaps it was because of this house, and his father. Jake could only surmise that they'd had a falling-out of some sort, and that was why the house hadn't been left to him.

Perhaps Lawrence knew more about the benefactor of this hospice. He'd noticed that Lawrence had walked down a corridor. He decided to follow.

He made his way cautiously along the hallway, conscious of

the fact that he should probably not be wandering around back there. There could be patients in their rooms or having treatment. Jake didn't want the big guy to chuck him out, because he really should get his hands looked at by a professional – and besides, he had questions about the painting.

Jake could hear sounds coming from a room a little further down the hall. The door was ajar. Jake looked in. The room was immediately familiar; two filing cabinets stood against the back wall, and there was the old desk where the woman in the pencil skirt and razor-thin heels had been sitting the day before. 'Oh, my god. This is the room, and it's exactly the same!' Jake blurted before he could stop himself.

Lawrence turned around with a tube of antiseptic cream. Jake expected him to say, *what are you doing? You shouldn't be here.*

What he did say surprised Jake. 'I shouldn't be here,' he grumbled.

'This is the reception room,' Jake said slowly, looking around the familiar room.

'And don't I know it,' said Lawrence ruefully. 'I'm forever forgetting myself and walking down to the old supply room only to remember when I get here that it's now the other reception.'

'The *other* reception?'

'Lucky there's a first aid kit in here.' He walked past Jake, hovering in the doorway. 'Have to do this at the reception desk, I'm afraid.' He held up the antiseptic cream. 'I can't leave my post for too long.'

Jake hovered by the door a moment longer, staring into the room, before heading back to the front desk. All this was freaking him out. 'What do you mean *the old supply room*?'

'Yes, like I said, that used to be the old supply room, way back when, where they kept spare sheets and blankets, and medical supplies locked in a cabinet. But then someone, don't ask me who, had the bright idea to turn a wing of the house over to self-contained apartments, obviously for people who could afford them. I think the trust had to find ways to bring in some money to do some repairs to the building, and this is what they came up with. They've got their own entrance to the building, and even a receptionist who doesn't dress like this …'

He indicated the starched white, clinical uniform he wore. 'So their relatives, when they visit, aren't reminded that it's really a hospice, and their apartments are really very sheltered accommodation. That entrance just a short way down the road. It takes them around the side of the house, which, with the main entrance door, and Georgian bay windows, looks remarkably similar to the front of the house. That's where they'll find the receptionist in her own little office. That's what I was going to explain to you when I realised I hadn't got this cream.'

'Grey pencil skirt, high heels, hair in a bun?' Jake asked, wanting to be absolutely sure.

'Yes, that's her.'

'Oh, thank god!' Jake exhaled in relief as he followed Lawrence back down the hallway. 'I'm not losing my mind.'

'I should hope not, at your age. Mind you, things have been known to happen to people – it's not uncommon to suffer stress, anxiety, depression – stuff that plays with your mind.'

Jake nodded, staring at Lawrence. He got the feeling that the man was talking from experience. 'I walked in that entrance last time I was here.' Jake frowned at the thought of Marcus with the envelope full of photos. If he hadn't been constantly distracted as he drove, chances are he wouldn't have missed the first entrance, which would have taken him around the side of the house to where the apartments were – where Martha was.

That reminded Jake of something. 'I really haven't got time to get my hands looked at. I've got to see someone here.'

Lawrence grabbed his arm. 'They can wait. These can't. You don't want to get septic shock, do you?'

Jake shook his head, even though he had no idea what that was, apart from the fact that it sounded bad.

'Take a seat.'

It sounded like an order.

Jake sat silently on a padded office chair, his right hand resting on the counter, his eyes fixed on the painting on the wall, on the boy in the painting. 'So, you know Martha?'

'Not at all. Although the nurses do their rounds, including the private wing, as a receptionist on this desk, I'm not meant to cross over to the other side.'

Jake raised his eyebrows, wondering what he meant.

Lawrence chuckled. 'I meant not crossing to the other side of the house – obviously unless something in particular warranted it, or in emergencies.'

Jake looked at his old bandages as Lawrence unfurled them. 'Am I an emergency?'

Lawrence whistled. Jake glanced at him, then down at his hand as the last of the bandages gave way to a pretty ugly sight. 'Do I need stitches?' Jake was not in the mood for a visit to a hospital.

'No – they're clotting nicely. It looks worse than it is.' He cleaned the wounds. 'Looks like you went a few rounds with a pit bull, though.' He chuckled.

Jake offered a weak smile, his attention drawn back to the painting. 'What can you tell me about the child?' Jake's gaze was riveted on those fierce blue eyes.

'Swap seats.' Lawrence got up, and they exchanged seats. Jake placed his left hand on the counter. He held his newly bandaged hand up for inspection. A light bandage neatly covered his hand, extending around his wrist. His fingers were completely free.

'The kid in the painting?' His eyes roved to the painting on the wall behind Jake. 'Ralph Delaney – the son.' He returned his attention to Jake's hand. 'That's a sad story.'

'What happened to him?'

'Apparently, his mother wasn't well – it was her nerves.'

'Her nerves?' Jake didn't understand.

'People with what we now recognise as mental health conditions like severe anxiety, depression, post-natal depression, were little understood. They would be diagnosed with a nervous disorder. Some were sent to psychiatric hospitals for a considerable time. They were institutionalised. Sent away.'

'His mother was sent away?'

Lawrence nodded. 'I'm afraid so. Soon after she went, when the boy was still very young, his father sent him away to boarding school. It was not long after that portrait was taken, I believe. And that's the last anyone heard of him.'

'But he was so young to be sent away from his home.'

'Yes, he was just a wee little thing.'

'What happened to him?' What Jake was wondering, which he knew Lawrence couldn't answer, was why he had changed his name.

'We can only presume that he couldn't forgive his father for sending his mother away, sending them both away, and that was why he never returned to this place. That was how all this came about. With no son and heir to claim his inheritance, the hall was left to a charitable trust as a hospice to accommodate elderly people with certain mental health conditions. There was a caveat. The daughter could remain living in part of the property if she so wished.' He paused, the bandaging not quite complete, and looked at Jake. 'Rumour has it,' he said in a hushed voice, 'that his younger sister, who inherited a substantial sum herself, used the money to bribe the doctors to deem her mother fit to return home.'

'Is that true?' Jake said.

'I don't know about that.' He resumed dressing Jake's hand. 'But I do know that after Mr Delaney died, when his son was in his teens, the newly appointed executors of the will went to see Ralph Delaney at school, before they made any decisions with respect to the will, only to find he was no longer there. They say he was afraid of his father.'

'Why?'

'One can only speculate. He'd seen his mother sent away to a psychiatric hospital. Perhaps he was afraid his father would send him away, like he did his mother.'

Jake looked at him, shocked. 'Why would he do that to his son? Are you saying he has … had … mental health issues?'

'Not at all. Perhaps he was a shy, introspective child, and his father couldn't understand him. Rumour has it the boy was very close to his mother and he was afraid his father might look for traits in him that his mother had. But we were never sure where those rumours came from.'

Jake stared at Lawrence as he continued telling the story. 'When the executors discovered that the son had disappeared, they waited, with the assurance that no rational person would not turn up to claim what was rightfully theirs. But he didn't reappear, and they got on with the job of redirecting some of the assets, namely the house, to a new charitable foundation which they set up as per Angus Delaney's wishes. That's when the executors took on their new role as trustees looking after the place.'

'How do you know all this?'

'My father was a local history enthusiast. When my late mother came here with late-stage dementia, my father saw that painting and wanted to know more. Of course, some of it is fact, about the house, and a little of what happened to Mr Delaney's wife, but we can only surmise why Ralph Delaney disappeared from his school and never returned. Perhaps he met with some unfortunate accident, and died when he was at school, and the school covered it up.'

'Your father thought otherwise?' Jake asked.

'Yes, until his dying day he was convinced that the boy was out there somewhere.'

They both paused to look at the portrait – Jake turning in his chair to look at that innocent, blond-haired child. It dawned on him that this child had his existing life cruelly stripped from him when his mother had been committed. He would have faced a monumental dilemma: if he returned to his home to claim what was rightfully his, he might have faced the possibility that it would happen to him. Perhaps because his father had told the trustees he was just like his mother – who knew? But what Jake did know was the day Ralph Delaney disappeared, Aubrey Jones was born.

'My father speculated that he may have travelled abroad to make his fortune.' He cut off the bandage on Jake's left hand. 'I often wonder what became of him.'

The bandaging was finished off in silence.

Jake's lightly bandaged hands felt a lot less restricted than before and looked a lot less eye-catching.

'Where's his sister now?' Jake asked. Aubrey had never mentioned another living relative, let alone that he had a sister.

'In the other wing, in one of those apartments,' Lawrence replied nonchalantly.

'What!?' said Jake with a start. Jake slapped his forehead. Of course she was Aubrey's sister. The trouble was that Jake had had so much on his mind, he'd missed the obvious.

'I'm surprised you didn't guess,' said Lawrence.

'Jake – are you ok?'

Jake turned at the sound of Marcus's voice, surprised to see his silhouette in the doorway. 'Come over here,' he said. He had something to show him.

'You with him?' Lawrence pointed at Marcus. I told him I didn't know Mr and Mrs Wright. I looked it up on my computer screen, just to be sure, and I can tell you that they most definitely are not patients here.' A businesslike tone had replaced the friendly banter.

'Never mind that,' Jake waved that comment away. 'Can I see Aub … Ralph's sister?'

Marcus arrived at the counter. 'What's up?'

He eyed Jake warily. 'You're not from the press, are you?'

Jake shook his head vehemently.

'It's just we have had some instances of the local press snooping around for a story on the poor woman.'

Lawrence looked at Marcus.

'Me? From the press?' said Marcus, adopting an air of superiority that made Jake inwardly groan.

'Do I look like a hack to you?' He put his arm on the counter, flashing his Cartier watch. 'For your information, I head a multi-million dollar …'

'Shut it, will you.' Jake had heard enough. 'Nobody wants to hear you blowing your own trumpet – least of all me.'

Marcus – his mouth wide open – to Jake's surprise, actually shut up without protest.

'No – you carry on.' Lawrence pointed at Marcus. 'I want to hear this.' He rested an elbow on the countertop and his chin in the cup of his hand in an attentive, thoughtful pose.

Marcus looked at Jake.

Jake sighed. 'Well go on then, you've got your audience. What are you waiting for?'

Marcus, who had been on a self-congratulatory roll before, seemed to run out of steam. He turned to Jake. 'Where was I?'

Jake said in a deadpan tone of voice, 'I head a multi-million dollar …'

'Construction company,' Marcus nodded, taking over the story, 'and we build business premises and private homes for some of the most powerful individuals and business players in …'

Jake zoned out as Marcus trumpeted on … and on …

'This company was started by my father – William Ross. Perhaps you've heard of us.' Marcus gave a sardonic grin. 'The Ross Corporation?'

Jake rolled his eyes. The Ross Corporation may be on everybody's lips from London to Chicago, but here, in Scotland?

'Of course I've heard of you,' Lawrence said nonchalantly, making Marcus's chest puff out in pride, Jake noticed. Well, he had a lot to be proud of. William certainly was an amazing businessman; he was to construction what Soros was to the stock-market or Gates was to computers.

'You're building something on that land, where the old diner used to be.'

This was news to Jake. He recalled meeting Mr Addison in the clearing where it had stood before being pulled down, but he hadn't mentioned the Ross Corporation. Although Jake recalled that he hadn't asked the name of the company that the young man worked for.

Lawrence leaned forward and lowered his voice. 'Can you tell an old man what it is? It's the talk of the town, you know, but nobody can find out a thing – it's all very hush-hush, isn't it?'

Jake also recalled that Mr Addison hadn't appeared to know what exactly was going to be built on that land either.

Jake looked at Marcus. He could tell by the look on his face that it was news to him too. He looked positively stunned. Nobody did anything without Marcus's seal of approval. Although there were many projects simultaneously on the go all over the world, and Marcus couldn't be in direct control of each one, he would certainly have been involved at the planning stage.

This meant only one thing; Marcus was losing his grip, and worse, somebody on the board of directors was aware of it. They had gone over his head on this one, and Jake wasn't surprised in the least. The way Marcus had been behaving in his personal life of late had been bound to spill over into his work sooner or later. Something needed to give, and it just had.

Jake watched Marcus fish in his jacket pocket and take out his mobile phone. He flicked the lid, and a look of consternation crossed his face. He held the mobile high in the air and turned full circle. 'I'll be outside.' Holding the mobile out in front, he walked out of the door.

Jake resisted the urge to tell him it would be a long walk to get a phone signal. Jake wasn't interested in the company's present ventures, and he certainly wasn't interested in hearing Marcus's inevitable rant about this unwelcome piece of news. Jake hoped he was some considerable time in his quest for that elusive mobile reception.

All Jake wanted to do was see Aubrey's sister. He had an idea. He took the envelopes out of his pocket and leafed through the photos until he had the one he was looking for. He put it on the counter and slid it face down towards Lawrence. 'You said you always wondered what became of him.' Jake lifted his hand to reveal the name, *Ralph*.

He looked at Jake. 'What's this?'

'Take a look.' Jake watched as he picked up the photo and turned it over.

'Is it him?'

'I think so,' said Jake. 'It's in the eyes.'

They both agreed. There was no mistake.

'Where is he now?'

'I don't know,' Jake lied. This was as far he was going to go with this in order to get access to Aubrey's sister. Aubrey's reasons for keeping his identity a secret all these years were his and his alone, and were not for Jake to blow wide open just out of curiosity. But Jake could only marvel at his own short-sightedness. It hadn't occurred to Jake, when he'd shown Lawrence that photograph, that Aubrey had just lost his anonymity. Jake tried not to think about that.

Lawrence stood up. 'You'd better come with me.'

Jake eyed him. 'Where are we going?' Jake could hear the waver in his voice. He didn't fancy a tour of this place.

Lawrence turned to Jake, passing back the photo. 'To see Ralph's sister – Martha.'

Jake raised his eyebrows. He remembered what Lawrence had

said about avoiding that part of the house unless it was an emergency, or a situation arose that warranted it. Jake guessed this was one of those situations.

Jake was about to follow Lawrence when he heard Marcus calling his name. He turned around to see Marcus rushing towards him, his face like thunder, and his mobile phone held high in the air. 'I can't get …'

'I know,' Jake cut in. 'Look, I'm busy right now, so go wait in the car.'

'Don't you …' Marcus pointed a finger at Jake, 'order me around like I'm some kind of kid,' he said petulantly. Then his eyes shifted to Lawrence, his interest aroused. 'Where are you going?'

Jake sighed heavily and turned to Lawrence. 'Can he come too?' This wasn't going the way he had planned it.

Lawrence seemed to be giving Marcus the once-over. Perhaps he was wondering whether there might be something in it for him – namely some information on that hush-hush project in the woods. He acquiesced.

'Come on,' said Jake, barely concealing his exasperation.

Jake followed Lawrence back down the hallway, past the other reception. Heavy footfalls behind signalled Marcus bringing up the rear. Jake stopped and turned, putting his finger to his lips for Marcus to tread quietly.

'If I remember rightly,' said Marcus, not making any effort to keep his voice down, 'I'm not the one making the racket.' He bounded along the hallway, past Jake and Lawrence, and up the other staircase that Jake remembered from the previous day.

Jake frowned at him. Where did he think he was going? He could see Marcus still had his phone to hand. He was still looking for a mobile phone signal.

44

At the top of the first flight of stairs, Marcus stopped at the large oval picture window. On his way up, Jake stopped momentarily beside Marcus to admire the view. But Marcus wasn't admiring the view. His phone bleeped.

Jake threw up his hands. 'Is that all you can think about?' Someone had better be prepared, because Marcus was on the warpath and heads were going to roll, even if they were the heads of people who sat on the board of directors.

'Meet me back at the car,' said Jake. They left Marcus by the window, making his call, Lawrence telling him that it was on the proviso he left the building straight afterwards, and didn't go just wandering off.

Jake caught up with Lawrence, who appeared in a hurry. Jake recalled that Lawrence couldn't be away from his post for too long. He did not want to get him into trouble. 'I have visited before.'

'Yes, so you told me.'

'I can find my way from here.'

Lawrence nodded. 'I'm sure, but even so I must ask Martha if she's okay to accept visitors.'

Jake frowned. The other receptionist hadn't said that.

'Or you could ask Arnold.'

'Who?'

Jake shook his head. 'Never mind.' He imagined that as Lawrence didn't normally venture over to this side of the building, he probably wasn't aware that Arnold visited Martha every day. 'I recognise all this – the carpeted staircase and the hallway.'

Lawrence explained how the property had been kept as two separate wings. Apparently, Martha's family had stipulated that one wing should be kept in its original condition; renovated, of course, but retaining all the original features, so that it appeared almost as it was when she used to live there as a child.

'It helps with the memory loss to be in familiar surroundings,' said Lawrence.

Jake nodded. He was aware of Martha's condition. This wing was very different to the other, more clinical, wing of the house. Lawrence told him that those residents had a bedroom, and common areas, but not entire apartments like this wing.

This part of the house felt much more like a home, albeit a large country manner type of home.

Where Martha resided had the added bonus that visitors could come and go pretty much as they pleased, and take their relatives outside, in their own gardens, in the grounds, or even into Aviemore for a morning or afternoon, and a day trip further afield if they wished.

'Is something the matter?' said Lawrence, noticing that Jake was dragging his feet as they approached the bedroom door.

'No.' Jake pointed at the door. 'Shall we?' Suddenly he wanted to get the visit over with. He was feeling uneasy, guilty even, like somebody about to take a peek at a personal diary; a peek into a private part of someone's life – Aubrey's life – that they knew was strictly off-limits.

Jake moved forward, his curiosity leading the way, and stopped in the open doorway, watching Lawrence. Lawrence walked over to the two chairs by the bay window, but Martha was not in the same spot.

Lawrence turned around and looked at his watch. 'I think she might still be in bed.'

Jake wasn't surprised. They'd left Lark Lodge relatively early, and the journey there hadn't been long, even though they'd got a bit waylaid by the conversations with Lawrence. Jake glanced at his hands. He did appreciate the fresh bandages.

He followed Lawrence down a hallway in the surprisingly large apartment and watched him knock softly on the door before entering. Jake had expected Lawrence to tell him to come back later. Instead he beckoned Jake inside the room, and whispered, 'I wouldn't normally do this, let people visit before one of our guests has been got up and out of bed, but I get the feeling time is of the essence, and you need to see her now.'

Jake nodded. 'Thank you, Lawrence.'

Lawrence walked over to a large double bed, and spoke softly to a woman lying flat on her back, covers pulled up to her chin, eyes closed, long dyed blonde hair swept to one side, almost covering that side of the pillow.

Lawrence waved at Jake to come over.

Jake gingerly stepped into the room, expecting Arnold to be waiting for him, but there was no sign of him. Jake stopped at the end of the bed, hands resting on the top of the ornate reproduction iron bedstead.

'I told her she's got a visitor. Sometimes they wake, sometimes not.' Lawrence spoke softly.

Jake opened his mouth, about to ask what was wrong with her – then he remembered. Alzheimer's. Something was puzzling him. He thought those residents with advanced conditions were moved to the hospice. He voiced his thoughts to Lawrence.

'Martha gets preferential treatment, at the discretion of the trustees, because her father owned this house. So she stays here, in her own place, until the end.'

Jake nodded. It made sense. She certainly wasn't dying of old age, but she was dying. Jake noticed her eyelids start to flutter open. This was the first time Jake had actually seen her face. The previous afternoon when he'd visited, she had been asleep, her head tilted on one side, resting on the wing of the chair, which meant that Jake had been unable to see her face through the fountain of long blonde hair that partially covered her face.

He turned to Lawrence. 'I've seen her somewhere before. Before my last visit.' Jake searched her face, trying to track down the memory. He knew he'd seen photos of her, but it was more than that; he knew he'd seen her in person before. He watched as her eyes opened. First, she looked up at the ceiling, and then she turned her head left and right. Finally, her bright blue eyes, not dulled by time, travelled down the bed to settle on Jake.

'There you are,' said Lawrence, offering words of encouragement. 'I've brought you a visitor, Martha.'

'Martha.' Jake's hand tensed around the cold iron metal. 'I'm afraid you were sleeping when I visited before.'

She was trying to lift her head off the pillow. Lawrence slipped another pillow under her head.

Jake heard the old lady's tremoring voice say, 'Ralph – is that really you?'

Lawrence shook his head, and replied, 'No, Martha, this is—'

Lawrence let out a chuckle and looked up. 'Say, what is your name, son?'

'Jake. It's Jake.'

'No, you're Ralph,' Martha said, starting to get agitated.

Lawrence said, 'I think it might be best if you return another time. It wasn't a good idea visiting when she's barely woken up.'

But she was asleep in her chair the last time, Jake felt like saying.

Jake had no choice but to follow Lawrence out of the bedroom. He took a backward glance, and caught Martha, eyes wide, holding out a trembling hand. He felt terribly sorry for her. She wasn't that old – in her late sixties, if that.

Back in the lounge, Jake caught sight of the two chairs by the window. He walked over to the window again, expecting to see Arnold sitting in a chair.

He sat in a chair, closed his eyes and rubbed his temples with his fingertips. All he'd wanted to do was hand the two envelopes back, but their contents, the photos, had just raised more questions. He heard Lawrence's voice in the room next door.

'That's right, Martha, you rest a while. You've had quite enough excitement for one morning, haven't you? One of the nurses will be along soon to get you up and give you breakfast.'

This was followed by some low, incoherent mumbling, and calm reassurances from Lawrence. 'I'm sure he'll come back soon.'

Jake felt a hand on his shoulder. He stopped applying pressure to his temples and opened his eyes to find Lawrence hovering behind his chair. He looked concerned. 'Are you alright, son?'

No, I'm not, thought Jake.

Lawrence sat in the chair next to him.

'When I visited before,' Jake whispered urgently, 'her husband gave me these,' he thrust the envelopes towards Lawrence. 'She was sitting in this very chair. Her husband was already here, and he must have got her out of bed to see … me.' Jake caught Lawrence shaking his head.

Lawrence frowned. A rarity with his easy-going, good-natured personality.

Jake noticed. 'What is it?'

'You met her husband?'

'That's what I just said.'

'Well, that's just not possible.'

'How come?'

'I'll have you know that I do not snoop on our guests' personal lives, but obviously everyone knows Martha – the daughter of the owner and benefactor of Cedar Grove. And I know for a fact that she never married.'

Lawrence said, 'Whoever visited couldn't have been her husband.'

Had he said they were married, or was it just something Jake had inferred? Jake realised, now he thought about it, that during the conversation with Arnold over the phone, and when he'd met him, he couldn't actually remember Arnold saying Martha was his wife – not once. Jake rubbed his temple again, still as confused as ever. 'So, who was the guy visiting Martha?'

'Ah, I remember now. Old Arnold,' said Lawrence. 'He visited often.'

'Yes, Arnold Wright.' Jake looked at him hopefully.

'Now I'm with you.'

Thank you, god, thought Jake. Things were finally making some sense.

'Little guy with white hair. Used to be one of her neighbours, I believe, before she moved here. The nurses chat. He had a bit of a thing for her, apparently.'

'Yes.' Jake couldn't hide his relief. Out of interest, Jake asked, 'Did she have any other visitors?'

'I don't know, as I'm on the other reception. But I can tell you this; I'm going to be pricking my ears up if I hear of any tall, slim well-dressed older gentleman visiting Martha.' He winked at Jake knowingly.

Jake could only marvel at his own short-sightedness. It hadn't occurred to Jake, when he'd showed Lawrence the photograph, that Aubrey had just lost his anonymity. Jake tried not to think about that. If and when Aubrey next visited his sister, he could bet Lawrence would be watching very closely, and that after more than forty years of carefully guarding his secret, the truth would be out.

Jake tried not to think about that right now. 'About Arnold – I need to see him,' Jake persisted. 'Can you give me an address, or do you know when he plans to make his next visit? You see I need to talk to him about …' Jake decided not to mention the photos again. 'About something.'

'Look, I'm really sorry but …'

Jake anticipated what he was going to say about confidentiality. 'I know, I know, you can't give me that information, but it's really important that I—'

'No, I can tell you – that's the thing.'

Jake looked at him perplexed.

Lawrence seemed to be choosing his words carefully. 'Arnold passed away.'

'He died?' Jake thought of that vibrant man who had been sitting in Lawrence's seat just yesterday. Jake shook his head in wonder at how precarious life was; one moment you're here, the next you're gone. Eleanor brushed past him in his memory. 'He was a picture of health yesterday – what happened? Was it an accident?

'Yesterday?' Lawrence repeated. 'Hold on, I think we're talking at cross purposes. I assumed you were talking about a visit you made here a while back.'

'What do you mean?'

'He took sick and died suddenly within a short time of being admitted here,' said Lawrence. 'The name escaped me because he was only here a short while, and it was some time ago now.'

'Some time ago?' Jake said with a start. 'How long, exactly?'

'I'd have to check on my computer – my memory is definitely not what it used to be. A year – give or take; it was around the time I started my new position on reception. Unfortunately, that's when Martha started to go downhill. Ironic, isn't it? He was the healthy one visiting her, and then he goes just like that,' Lawrence clicked his fingers, 'and she's still here.'

Jake felt sick to his stomach.

Lawrence looked at him. 'Hey son,' he put a hand on Jake's arm, 'you've gone awful pale all of a sudden.'

Jake got up from his chair on unsteady legs. 'I want you to go look on your computer – I want to see …'

'Now look,' Lawrence got out of his chair. 'I can't be showing you confidential records.'

'Please, Lawrence, this is really important – matter of life and death because …' Jake really didn't know how to say this without sounding completely insane. 'I think I had a conversation yesterday, right here in this room, with a dead man.'

Lawrence stared at him a long moment. Finally, he said, 'I'll go and call up the record.'

Jake, who had been holding his breath without even realising it, breathed out and took in a couple of rapid gulps of air before following Lawrence to the door.

Lawrence opened the door and then abruptly halted, sending Jake careering into his back. For an instant, Jake thought he had changed his mind.

Lawrence turned around. 'Come with me.'

'Where are we going?' Jake asked as he followed Lawrence down the hallway in the apartment.

'Back to her bedroom.'

'Oh, I thought you said we should return another time, and not visit when she's barely woken up?'

'I've changed my mind.' Lawrence looked at his watch. 'The nurses normally do their rounds now. I'm sure I heard someone else walk into the apartment.'

Jake hadn't. He'd been too busy getting over the shock that Arnold had passed away.

They returned to her bedroom, pausing by the open door. 'Ah, good. There's a nurse in the room giving Martha her daily meds. Let me check that you can stay and see her. I'll come and get you when I've found the record. It's just she doesn't get a whole lot of visitors now, not since Arnold …' he trailed off.

Jake nodded and watched from the doorway as he had a word with the nurse. She beckoned him inside room as Lawrence stepped out. Jake glanced at Lawrence as he walked along the hall and disappeared down the stairs. Jake turned into the room and shut the door. Visions of Arnold leaping out of the chair the previous day and scaring him half to death, with an unrepentant expression on his face that said he knew exactly what he was doing, nearly sent Jake flying out of the room in the belief that with Lawrence gone, Arnold would reappear. Jake decided against closing the door to the apartment. Instead he left it wide open in case he needed to make a quick exit in fright. He was relieved to leave the sitting room and walk down the hallway to Martha's bedroom.

45

Jake hovered by the door.

From the bed, propped up on pillows, Martha caught sight of him. 'Ralph.'

Jake walked over to the bed. There was a single chair positioned on the other side of the bed. Jake decided to remain on the side nearest the door, in case he needed to bolt. Besides, the nurse was sitting in that chair filling in some paperwork on a clipboard.

He crouched down beside her. 'Martha, I'm not Ralph.'

He doubted she would understand what he was saying to her. According to the man he had spoken to in the apartment the previous day, who Jake believed was very much alive but had for some reason chosen not to reveal his true identity, Martha only had small windows of clarity opening briefly through the fog of her condition. The way she kept calling him Ralph suggested this was most definitely not one of her better days.

She opened her mouth to speak. Jake leaned closer. 'Good heavens,' she said, 'you're Scottish.'

Jake drew back, a wide grin on his face. Somebody just opened a window. Although her speech was slow, and at times slurred, he could understand her perfectly. 'Do you know,' he said to her, 'you're the first person to say that since I arrived in Scotland?'

'Am I?' she said. 'Well people are stupid, I must say.'

Jake laughed at that. 'How right you are,' he said.

She studied his face. 'You're not Ralph, are you?'

'No. I'm Jake.' He took one of her frail hands. 'Jake Campbell-Ross.' He thought he saw a flicker of recognition cross her features. He didn't know how much of this she was taking in or how much she understood.

Jake swiftly got out the envelopes. He didn't want her to tire and fall asleep again before he showed her the photos; he really wanted to help her find whoever she was looking for, see her loved ones before she went. Jake really did understand the importance of this. 'Martha,' he said holding up a photo. 'Martha, look at the photos, your photographs.' He picked up her limp hand and put a photo between her fingers.

Her fingers tensed. She looked down at the photo.

'Who is that, Martha?' said Jake, pointing at the photograph in her hand, the one of Aubrey.

'Ralph.' She was smiling now.

'That's really good, Martha.' Jake quickly put another photo in her hand.

'Are you Ralph?' she said, looking at Jake.

'No, Martha – I'm Jake, remember? Now look at the photo.' Jake stroked her hand.

She touched the next photograph with a frail bony finger. 'That's Ralph and Rosemary, and …'

She'd lost her train of thought.

Jake realised it wasn't the one he wanted to show her. He was about to put the group photo of the four of them doing the line-dance jig back in the envelope and show her a different photo when he realised this was his opportunity to find out more about Aubrey.

'Martha, tell me about Aubrey—' Jake hastily rephrased. 'I mean your brother, Ralph.' Jake glanced at the nurse. He didn't want to bring up her brother in front of one of the staff, but this was his chance to speak to Martha and find out about Aubrey. 'Where did he go to school? Why did he disappear and not return to claim his inheritance?' Although Lawrence had speculated about what had happened to him, as had his father, who had been interested in the family history of the house, that was all it was – speculation. Martha could give him all the answers first hand. 'Where did he go when he disappeared?'

Martha shifted her gaze from the photo to Jake. She said, 'Ralph.'

'Yes, that's right, I'm talking about Ralph. Your brother, Ralph. You both grew up here, right? Until your brother was sent away to school. You must have been just a toddler. I bet you missed your big brother terribly. Has he been here to see you?' Jake looked towards the door as though he'd walk in right this second.

When he looked back at Martha she had dropped the photo in her hand. Jake shook his head and picked up the photo, holding it up. 'Martha, can you tell me about Ralph?' He noticed her eyes were glazing over.

The nurse looked up from her paperwork. 'I'm afraid she tires easily.'

Jake sighed. He wasn't going to get any information from her that day about her brother. He changed tack and showed her the photo of a small boy taken at The Lake House. The name on the back of the photo was also Ralph, but this wasn't Aubrey. This photo was more recent, of a boy around his own age. Jake suspected someone had written that name on the back of the photo by mistake. 'Look at the photo, Martha.'

Frustratingly, she continued to gaze at Jake. She said, 'He should have married me, not that other girl. Then we would have been a family.'

'Who should have married you, Martha?' Out of the corner of his eye, he noticed the nurse leaning forward in her chair, clearly also interested to hear what she might say.

'You came, Ralph. I knew you would.'

'Martha – I am not Aub, I mean Ralph. Now look at the photograph, please. I'm trying to help you.'

Her eyelids were now half-closed.

At that moment, the nurse's mobile phone rang.

Jake swivelled round to look at the nurse.

'Sorry,' she apologised. 'I have to answer this.' She stood up, and headed for the door. 'I'm just going to step outside.'

Jake saw her stood in the doorway, with her back to them quietly talking.

Jake held up the photo. 'Martha, can you tell me who this is – the small boy in the photo?' Jake put it directly in front of her face so she could see. He held the photo like that for several seconds, hoping beyond hope that when he put it down, she wouldn't be asleep.

She wasn't asleep, but she couldn't answer Jake's questions because he had made her cry.

Oh god! thought Jake. What was Lawrence going to say when he came back and found her in this state? What would the nurse say when she got off the phone? Jake frantically patted her hand, plucked a tissue from the box on the small table beside the bed and wiped away the tears – but they just kept on coming.

'There, there.' Jake said stroking her hand, casting furtive glances at the door. 'Everything's going to be alright.'

The nurse did glance over her shoulder, but didn't seem to clock that anything was amiss.

He had no idea what to say or how to make her stop. But just sitting there holding her hand seemed to do the trick. After a time, she calmed down. Jake threw the last used tissue in the wastepaper bin.

Jake repeated his question. 'Who should have married you, Martha?'

'Ralph's father, of course.'

Jake looked at her. 'You mean the boy in the photo, Ralph, is your son?' So the name on the back of the photo wasn't a mistake, he realised. 'Is that who you are trying to find?'

Martha focused on Jake. 'I want to see my son.'

For a moment, Jake thought she was going to start with the crying again. But she must have cried herself out.

She looked at Jake, her eyes searching. 'Will you find my son, bring him to me?'

'Yes.' Jake closed his eyes. He had just made a promise to a dying woman that he had no way of knowing he could keep. Her son could be anywhere in the world. For that matter, her son could be dead. He knew his approximate age – he'd be in his thirties now. But Jake knew he needed more information. He opened his eyes. 'Martha,' he said, 'I need to know …' He stopped. She was asleep. 'No, Martha, don't do this to me.'

At that moment, Lawrence walked into the room. 'Hey, she's smiling,' Lawrence observed. 'She must have enjoyed your company.'

He didn't notice the half-empty box of Kleenex or the half-full wastepaper basket.

Jake followed Lawrence out of the apartment and down the stairs, feeling pretty lousy. Martha probably wouldn't remember a word of the conversation when she woke up. But Jake would.

Jake joined Lawrence at the computer. Jake suddenly had a brainwave. If Martha was Aubrey's sister, then Aubrey must know about her son, surely.

'There – see for yourself.' Lawrence stepped aside, allowing Jake full access to the computer. He glanced furtively around the reception hall. 'Can you make this quick? I shouldn't be showing you records of previous residents, even if they were here a very short time and are not deceased.'

'May I?' Jake pointed at the stool.

'Go right ahead!' Lawrence threw up his hands. 'You know I could get in trouble for this.'

'I know.' Jake sat. 'But thanks.' He turned his attention to the screen. All the details Lawrence had told him about Arnold tallied with the computer record. Jake stared at the screen.

'You know what I think?' Lawrence pulled up another stool beside Jake. 'I think you saw a re-enactment.'

Jake turned to look at Lawrence.

'My wife and I watched this programme on telly that reckons buildings take images, like photographs, that it then replays from time to time. So, when you think you are seeing a ghost, what you are witnessing is a re-enactment of an event from the past that has already happened. Know what I mean? Like a photo.'

Jake could see where he was coming from – but it was complete rubbish. You don't hold a conversation with a re-enactment. 'I know what I saw,' said Jake, turning away from the computer to face Lawrence. 'What I saw was somebody pretending to be Arnold Wright.'

Lawrence shrugged. 'If you say so.'

46

Jake walked out into the bright sunshine.

Marcus had been waiting just outside the door. He fell in step, walking alongside Jake back to the car. 'I got through on my phone eventually, and everyone I've spoken to so far swears blind they have no idea we are developing something on land outside Aviemore,' said Marcus, under the false impression that Jake was at all interested in what he had to say. 'I need to get to London as soon as possible. I swear to god someone's head's going to roll when I find out who gave the go-ahead to buy that land.'

Jake scuffed his shoe on the kerb and glanced back at the house.

'Are you listening to me?'

Jake didn't answer.

'You were a long time. I thought they'd gone ahead and admitted you.' He laughed. 'I had the impulse to leave you here, do us both a bit of good.'

Jake glanced at Marcus, not really hearing what he was blabbering on about. He fished in his pocket and brought out the envelopes.

'No luck, then?'

Jake glanced at Marcus and shook his head. He fished again and found the post-it on which Lawrence had written down Arnold's last known address. He put the photographs back in his coat pocket.

Reaching the car, Jake looked back at the house.

'You're very quiet.'

Jake was.

'Do you want me to drive?'

Jake turned slowly from the house to face Marcus. 'Please,' was all he could summon.

Marcus switched on the engine, put the car into gear and took the handbrake off. He turned to Jake. 'I'm not insured to drive this.'

'Just drive,' Jake said impatiently without looking up.

They reached the end of the driveway. 'Where to?'

Jake looked up from the post-it in his hand. He tried to keep his voice level. 'Head back to town.'

'Back to Aviemore? I want to go to the airport.'

'We will. I've just got one more stop before we leave.'

'You said that last time,' mumbled Marcus.

Lawrence had helpfully given Jake directions to a row of terraced stone cottages a few miles from the village, down in the valley, not easily located if you weren't familiar with the area.

Jake checked the address on the post-it again. 'It's the next right.' Jake looked out of the window as they turned down a steep, narrow track. It levelled off, cutting a winding path through the valley floor.

The cottages could be around the next bend. Jake didn't want to risk sailing straight past them; the narrow road would make it difficult to turn around, and who knew how many miles they would have to travel further on until they could double back.

'Slow down. It's not far.'

Marcus glanced at him. 'What's not far? Where are we going, Jake?'

Jake didn't reply. He kept his eyes peeled for any sign of the cottages while Marcus kept his eyes on the road. Jake, his attention momentarily diverted by the beauty and serenity of the heather-covered mountains rearing up on either side, happened to look Marcus's way and catch him grinning insanely into his rear-view mirror.

Jake flipped the sun visor down and looked in the vanity mirror to see a young couple, looking decidedly irate, swinging a tatty red Ford Fiesta left and right on their tail, trying to get past and escape Marcus's twenty-miles-per-hour crawl. Jake looked again at Marcus, who was clearly enjoying himself.

How was it possible that Marcus, who had just found out that he was not fully in control of his father's business affairs, could be so cheerful? Jake was guessing that Marcus was relishing the thought of that surprise visit he was going to spring on the London office of the Ross Corporation. As Marcus had said, heads were going to roll. Jake thought of Aubrey ensconced on the top floor of the company apartment building in London and considered wiping the smile off Marcus's face by telling him the business side of things was not the only thing he was losing control of. He decided it could wait.

Jake turned in his seat to look out of the back window. 'Oh, for pity's sake, will you just pull over and let them pass?'

Marcus frowned and swung the car abruptly towards the kerb. Jake looked past Marcus out of the driver's side window as the young couple passed by. The young woman in the passenger seat was mouthing something that Jake guessed was probably quite obscene. He wondered what Marcus was mouthing back.

'Marcus!' Jake said to the back of his head.

Marcus turned in his seat to look at Jake.

'Now I've got your full attention, can you stop faffing about and help me find this address?' Jake held up the post-it.

Marcus's eyes shifted to look past Jake out of the passenger window. 'Well, blow me – isn't that the house?' Marcus pointed.

Jake turned and looked out of the window to find they were parked directly outside.

'I'm guessing this is the home address of one Mr Wright. Am I right?' Marcus laughed at his own play on words.

Jake grimaced and got out of the car.

'I'll just sit and wait then.' Marcus got the message.

Jake shut the car door and looked up at the house. Like Lawrence had said, the terraced cottage was one of a small row of six standing alone, deep in the valley. There wasn't another house in sight, even though the village was just a few miles up the road.

The stone cottages had dark wooden windows that just added to the dreariness, and they had a distinctly neglected, forgotten feel, not helped by the fact that one of the row, the one next door, had all four windows boarded up. Somehow, he couldn't quite connect this drab house to the bright, cheerful, Arnold Wright.

Jake walked up the overgrown pathway. He stood in the small, pitch-roofed porch and knocked on the door. He waited. The strong smell of damp wood coming from the firewood stacked high on one side of the porch made Jake want to step back outside for some fresh air.

An old man answered the door. 'Yes?'

Jake hesitated, unsure what to say, unsure exactly what he was doing here.

'Can I help you?'

'Did ... does Arnold Wright live here?' Jake still could not believe what was on that computer screen. He had to check it out for himself. There just had to be a logical explanation.

'What is it you want?'

'Do you know Arnold Wright?' Something in the old guy's tone made Jake think he did.

'Are you going to continue answering my questions with a question?' The old man blinked at him.

'No, of course not. Pardon me. My name is Jake Campbell-Ross, and I'm looking for an Arnold Wright who knew a woman called Martha.' The uninterested look on the old man's face said that Jake was wasting his time. 'I'm sorry to disturb you. I've obviously got the wrong house.' Jake stepped out of the porch, glad to be free of that damp woody odour. 'Sorry,' he repeated to the old chap, who was still standing in the doorway. Jake started back down the path.

'My son.'

Jake was halfway down the overgrown pathway when he heard the old man's voice. He turned back to see the man standing in the porch, leaning heavily on a wooden walking stick. He looked well in his nineties.

'Come in, why don't you?'

Jake walked back up the pathway as the man opened the front door wide.

Jake walked into a gloomy entrance hall.

'Through there.' The old man lifted his walking stick off the carpeted floor and pointed at a door.

'In here?' Jake tentatively opened a door.

'Isn't that what I just said?' Standing in the hallway, the man regarded him for a moment before walking off.

Jake walked into a neat, cosy sitting room.

The wall opposite the window contained floor-to-ceiling bookshelves lined with books. 'A little light reading, anyone?' said Jake, randomly picking Dostoevsky's *War and Peace* off the shelf. It weighed a ton and hurt his hand. Jake put it back, scanning the other bookshelves, which were crammed with literary classics.

The old man walked into the room, carrying a tall glass of clear liquid. 'I like to read.'

Jake turned away from the bookshelves. 'Really?' he said sarcastically, biting his tongue to stop any more verbal damage. He hadn't meant to be rude, but the events back at the hospice had wound him up like a tight coil and he needed answers. His son must be dead, so why was someone pretending to be him? It wasn't exactly a question he could just ask outright.

'Yes, really.' The old man eyed him warily as he placed his glass on a small circular table set under the window. He left the room.

Jake walked over to the wooden mantle shelf set over an open fire blazing in the hearth. The long narrow shelf was jam-packed with framed family pictures, some colour, and some black-and-white. Jake picked up a framed picture of a woman in bright sunshine, kneeling on grass holding a toddler, her face next to his, smiling for the camera.

'My grandson.'

Jake glanced over his shoulder as the old man entered the room carrying another tall glass.

'Cute.' Jake replaced the picture on the mantle shelf.

'Not anymore.' He offered Jake the glass. 'All grown up now, moved to Edinburgh.'

Jake took the glass and gave a little sniff – he could smell lemons. Jake took a gulp of the white liquid; it stung the back of his throat. 'It's good,' said Jake in a croaky voice.

'It should be. It's homemade lemonade, none of that supermarket rubbish.' The old chap seated himself in a worn leather chair to one side of the hearth. He put on a pair of pince-nez and picked up a book that was balanced on the thick arm of the chair.

He started to read.

Jake stared at him. He had just let a perfect stranger in off the street and made him a glass of homemade lemonade, like it was the most natural thing in the world.

And it was.

Sometimes Jake longed to return to this part of Scotland; he often imagined what it must be like to live in a community where you could welcome somebody into your home without fear, know your neighbours as friends. It was another world. And it could be his, if he chose it.

'Is this Arnold?' said Jake, holding out a photograph he had found on the mantle. It was just a guess, going by the age of the photo, but unfortunately it wasn't a close-up, and the photo was slightly out of focus, so he couldn't make out the man's features.

'Let me see.' The old chap put down his book and held out his hand. He studied it. 'I haven't seen this in a long while.'

'It was tucked behind some other photos – there.' Jake pointed.

The chap thrust the photo back at Jake. 'Put it back where you found it, please.'

Jake put it back, but not so out of sight this time.

'Arnold – his wife died, sudden-like.'

Jake turned back to find the old man taking off his pince-nez. He put them beside the book on the table.

'May I?' Jake sat in the vacant leather chair opposite and leaned forward to place his empty glass on the brick hearth.

'At first he came to live here awhile because he couldn't bear to return to his empty house in the village.' The old man continued, 'I knew how that felt when my wife died – god rest her soul.' There was a moment's contemplative silence. 'But after some time, I suspected he was staying on for other reasons – not that I was complaining, mind,' he added quickly, 'I like company.' He picked up his glass of lemonade from the oval table beside his chair and took a sip.

'Other reasons?' said Jake.

'I had a neighbour – Martha.'

Jake nodded.

'She lived next door until she took ill. Very nice lady, kept herself to herself mind, but I could always call on her to run me an errand, and she always had time for a friendly natter over the garden fence.'

Jake smiled.

'Arnold – he rather took a fancy to her, see.'

Jake did.

'But we think she had a man friend already.'

'Man friend?' Jake didn't understand the turn of phrase.

'Yes, used to visit her, regular-like. He was a smart looking fella, always turned up in a fancy car – different one each time. Poor Arnold didn't think he'd be in with a chance. Especially after I heard them talking in the garden; said he was building them a house.

'Building them a house?'

'Yeah, but she didn't sound that pleased about it, said she liked where she was just fine. I must say I was pleased to hear that because she was such a nice neighbour. Not soon after that she nearly burnt the place down and mine with it. That's why it's boarded up next door. She had a lucky escape; left a pan boiling on the stove and clear forgot about it. Took her to hospital and that was the last I saw of her or her man friend.'

Jake nodded. So, that was when she'd returned to Cedar Grove to live out her days under supervision. Jake instinctively knew who that man friend was who visited – it wasn't what the old man thought. It was her brother. It was Aubrey.

'Did she have any other visitors?'

'Only Arnold. He'd find any excuse to pop next door; would she like her lawn mowed? Would she like this, would she like that? I kept telling him to leave the poor woman alone. But he wouldn't give up, and before long they were going to the pictures and having quiet little dinners at hers. Honestly, the women of today!' He downed the remainder of his lemonade and put the empty glass on the table beside the book. 'I'm sure it was all quite innocent, but oh how Arnold loved the excitement, the thrill of being the *other man*.'

Jake didn't want to bring up who the man was who'd been visiting Martha. Instead, he asked, 'Did she mention her son – Ralph?'

'She had a son?' The old man looked surprised. He raised his eyebrows.

'But Arnold's not in any kind of trouble, if that's what you're thinking.' Jake wasn't sure why he'd said that. Of course he wasn't. He was dead and gone. Jake still had it on the tip of his tongue to ask, *do you know why someone is impersonating your son?*

The old man rose from his chair. 'I think it's time you left.'

'I'm sorry for your loss,' Jake said quickly.

'Look here, I don't know what you're after or who sent you, but I want you to leave.' The old man moved surprisingly quickly to the front door and opened it.

Jake walked past him and out the door. He turned around in the porch. 'There was some misunderstanding. I came here to, um … to check he is dead. Jake winced. He shouldn't have said that, but it was obviously in the back of his mind.

The old man eyed Jake: his face softened.

'If you don't believe me, about my son,' he said before closing the door, 'visit the old oak.'

'The what?'

47

Jake walked down the path towards the car. Marcus had his eyes closed and was moving his head back and forth in rhythm to music blaring out. Jake got in the car and switched the radio off.

Marcus opened his eyes. 'I was enjoying that,' he said glumly.

'That was weird,' said Jake, looking back at the house.

'Classical music is not weird. I know you're a jazz man yourself, but you really need to broaden … you're not talking about the music, are you?'

Marcus started the car and moved off as Jake recounted the conversation with the old man, including the mysterious mention of *the old oak*. 'Wasn't exactly helpful, was he?' muttered Jake.

'Then why did he invite you inside?'

'I don't know,' Jake said wearily. 'Let's head for the airport.'

Marcus unexpectedly turned off onto a stretch of road unfamiliar to Jake. 'Where are we going?'

'You'll see.'

What Jake wanted to see was the back of this place and the back of Marcus. 'I thought you were anxious to get back to London?'

'I am,' said Marcus, 'but I've been driving around all morning not knowing what the hell is going on. So,' he grinned, 'it's my turn.'

Jake wondered what he had let himself in for, but he was too tired to argue. He slumped down in his seat and watched the world go by.

'Here we are.' Marcus pulled into a carpark, put the handbrake on and switched the engine off.

Jake turned in his seat to look at Marcus. 'You've got to be kidding!'

'Uh-uh.' He shook his head and got out of the car.

Jake sat for a moment, staring at the row upon row of gravestones. Marcus tapped on his window, making Jake jump. Marcus waved his hand for Jake to get out.

Jake opened the car door. 'How did you even know where this place was?'

'When things looked bad, we discussed it, remember? The family did, for Eleanor, as her final resting place.'

Jake remembered now.

'So, one day I came to have a look.' Marcus stared off in the distance. 'It's bigger than I remember,' he said, striding off.

'Ok, so what are we doing here?' Jake called after him.

Jake followed Marcus in the direction of the most recently departed. By the time Jake reached them, Marcus had already walked off in another direction.

Jake peered at the sticks. They were numbered, with no names – the graves so fresh that memorial stones had yet to be erected. Jake glanced at the row of brand new memorial stones behind these, which were dated the previous year. Jake looked up and spotted Marcus a little way off to his right, talking with what looked like the gardener or caretaker. He was shaking his head, no.

Marcus walked back towards Jake, rubbing the side of his head. 'Gardener wasn't much help.'

'So what?' The surroundings were not conducive to Jake's mood, or to his holiday, come to that.

'I think I was hit by a damn acorn or something.' Marcus nursed his head.

'An old oak.' Jake suddenly recalled the old man's parting words. He started walking towards the massive tree that Marcus had just been standing under.

Marcus said, 'Yeah, tell me about it. This isn't called Old Oak Cemetery for nothing. Damn tree!' he added. 'The gardener will only say the same thing to you that he said to me,' Marcus said, mistaking Jake's intention.

Jake ignored him and walked over to the tree. He stared up at the massive branches overhead, hiding a dozen gravestones from the bright sunshine.

Marcus hung back out of the range of the falling acorns. 'I'd be careful under that thing if I were you.'

Jake looked about him at the gravestones under the big oak tree. They looked old. Some of them had not fared well, and most of the inscriptions gone, worn away by time.

'What are we looking for?' Marcus

Jake worked his way along the gravestones, glancing at the inscriptions and reading where they could be read. He had no idea why he was doing this. It occurred to Jake that the old chap could have been referring to something different entirely when he'd said, *visit the old oak*. He passed one gravestone after another.

Marcus gingerly stepped under the tree and started to examine gravestones, every now and then glancing at the tree as though it were going to sprout legs and make a beeline for him.

'I've found something,' said Marcus.

'What is it?' Jake weaved his way through the memorial stones to where Marcus was standing.

'I think I've found your man,' said Marcus, tapping the top of a decaying memorial stone with the palm of his hand.

Jake stopped in front of the memorial stone. He looked at the name carved on it and then back at Marcus. This was not Arnold Wright's gravestone.

'Read further down – there's a newer inscription. Must be a family plot,' Marcus said.

Jake squatted down in front of it, pulling out a fistful of dead flowers and weeds at the base of the stone. He was just about to toss them away when he caught the disapproving eye of the caretaker. Jake placed them carefully to one side and read the inscription, then the date. Jake stared at it; there was the proof, if he needed it, that Lawrence and his damn computer had been right all along, which meant … someone had to be impersonating a dead man. Unless …

'I need to get back to the hospice right now.' Jake couldn't get up fast enough and couldn't get moving soon enough; he'd just had an epiphany.

'Why – what's going on?' Marcus was blocking Jake's way through.

'Don't you see?' Jake's eyes were wide. 'Arnold can tell me about Eleanor. No,' he stopped, turning wildly back to the memorial stone, 'he can go get her, bring her back with him. I could see her, talk to her. She might be dead, but it doesn't mean we can't—'

Jake turned back just as Marcus's fist connected with his right temple, sending him keeling sideways, his feet slipping on the wet dewy grass. He lay clutching the side of his face in shock.

'That's for putting up that memorial stone at The Lake House, you son-of-a-bitch,' Marcus seethed. 'I should have done that a long time ago. I don't care about the word you put on it. I don't care if you believe what I say happened when we were skiing last Christmas or not. What I do care about is my sister,' he paused, 'and you.' Marcus stared down at Jake. 'We've all had our ways of coping after the accident, but yours – yours beggars belief. How could you! How could you do it? Why did you erect a memorial stone in her name, and have the word *Chosen* inscribed on it – why, dammit, when she isn't dead! Answer me!'

Jake lay very still on his side. He had a clear, stark revelation. Marcus was right: they'd each had their ways of coping with what had happened up there on the mountain. Marcus's coping mechanism had been to turn to drink and drugs; his had been to convince himself that she was dead; to put up that stone in the grounds of The Lake House.

After what they'd discovered had happened to her, once they'd pulled her out of the snow, she might as well be dead. And the family had kept the outcome of the accident from the press, the public. That had further enabled him in his delusion.

He opened his eyes to see Arnold Wright's memorial stone, at a ninety-degree angle, rearing over him. He didn't attempt to get up. He didn't attempt to move. And he was scaring Marcus. 'Jake.' he could feel Marcus's hand on his shoulder. 'Jake.' A hand brushed his temple where he'd been hit. 'Jake – can you get up?' Marcus's voice was becoming more insistent. But it wasn't a case of whether he could get up; Jake was quite sure he could get up. The question was, did he want to get up – ever? If he could just lie there quietly for a while, perhaps all the hurt would go away.

'Jake?'

Jake suddenly became aware of his shoulders shaking – heaving, almost. For the first time since Eleanor's accident, he was actually crying. There had been no time to grieve – he'd made sure of that, and this was the end result, lying on the cold, damp ground in front of a stranger's grave, sobbing his heart out.

'Oh god, Jake – I'm so sorry.'

After a while, when the sobbing had subsided, he thought he heard some stranger's voice – the cemetery gardener's, perhaps – telling Marcus that he had better call an ambulance, and Marcus telling him to get lost, which, for Marcus, was quite restrained. Jake would have expected a few choice swear words the old gardener had probably never heard of.

Bizarrely, the thought of Marcus attempting to be polite made him smile. He could still feel Marcus's hand on his shoulder and his knees pressing in the small of his back. He guessed Marcus was kneeling beside him; he was going to ruin those beige chinos. A chill ran through him. He suddenly felt cold – so cold. He began to shiver.

'Come on.' Marcus said gently. 'Let's get up before you catch pneumonia.' He squeezed Jake's shoulder. 'I've got something for you in the car.'

Marcus helped him up. To his own and Marcus's surprise, Jake pulled Marcus close and hugged him fiercely, then let go and walked back to the car. He got in. He could see Marcus still standing where he had left him, rooted to the spot, momentarily stunned.

48

Marcus got in the car in silence.

He turned to Jake and placed a hand on his shoulder. 'Come with me to London. Let's go and see her together.'

'No. I have to find Martha's son.'

Marcus's hand dropped from Jake's shoulder.

'I made a promise. He is the boy in the photo.'

'Oh, for heaven's sake, not those photos again. I thought you gave them back?'

'Not exactly.'

'You know, you really should get your priorities straight.'

'Oh, you're a fine one to talk; you're only going to London to sort out your business affairs.'

'Life goes on, Jake; life, work – you know that.' There was no malice in Marcus's voice.

'How many times have you been to see her?' Jake wasn't a betting man, but he expected he would be able to count off the number of times on one hand.

Marcus went very quiet.

'You haven't been?' Jake said, astonished.

Marcus shook his head.

'Not once?'

Again, Marcus shook his head. 'Not once,' he whispered. 'I thought you …'

Jake shook his head, staring at Marcus. 'Me neither.' His voice was small.

Their eyes locked in mutual understanding; they had both assumed the other had been to see her. And they had both been wrong. And what of William? They knew he had flown out to America not long after the accident and hadn't been back since. The golf courses were much nicer over there, apparently. And what of Grace, Eleanor's mother? Would she have visited her daughter?

'Christ – what must she think of us?' Marcus's expression was pained.

'Well, that's the point, isn't it? She won't think. She probably won't even know. Let's face it, she's not really with us in any real …'

'Oh stop, Jake! For god's sake will you just … stop.'

They sat in deafening silence. Deafened by the sound of their own memories: for Marcus, of a sister; for Jake, of a friend, lover, wife – and for a short while, the mother of their unborn child.

'I need to see her,' said Marcus finally. 'Please come with me. I can't do this alone.'

'No,' said Jake firmly. He started the car, and set off for the airport.

Marcus disappointment was palpable.

'But I'll join you in London in a few days. That will give me a chance to try and fulfil a dying woman's last wish, and see if I bump into the man impersonating Arnold Wright, and get to the bottom of that.' Jake glanced at Marcus. 'By which time you will have had a chance to sort out that thing.' Jake was referring to the clearing in the woods and who in the Ross Corporation had given the go-ahead for something to be built there.

'I don't care about the business.'

'Don't give me that crap,' Jake said sharply. 'Of course you do. It's your life, and you know it.'

Marcus's mouth twitched in a knowing smile.

Jake pulled into the airport car park, switched off the engine, and turned to Marcus.

'If you want to stay in control of the company from here on out, you need to get in control of yourself, Marcus. I know what you're on. You need to stop – right now.'

Marcus frowned. 'I don't think I can. Besides, it's no big deal. Do you know how many execs are users in the city, to cope with the long hours and demands of their jobs?'

Jake wasn't interested in excuses. He folded his arms.

Marcus sighed. 'Honestly, I don't know any other way to keep myself going.'

'I do,' said Jake. 'Delegate.'

Marcus looked at him, aghast, as though he'd just suggested he hand over the reins to somebody else. He said, 'I don't trust anyone implicitly like I trust you – we were partners.'

'The best,' said Jake, remembering the cut and thrust of those business deals, the feel of elation at every new contract scored, the sense of achievement at each new ceremonial brick that was laid in the foundations at the start of a new project. 'I've got a new job now, a new life. It's where I belong, Marcus. You have to accept that.'

'I don't know how to delegate,' Marcus said miserably.

'Then learn,' said Jake. 'I know that since I left, you've been virtually doing both our jobs.'

'How on earth could you possibly know that?'

'Oh, let's just say I have my sources.' Jake let him stew a little before adding, 'It's those women from the London office that you keep setting me up on dates with. It's been very enlightening.'

Marcus opened his mouth to protest that it wasn't him, realised he'd been rumbled, and shut it again.

Jake continued, 'You think you've been keeping tabs on me? Marcus, I've been keeping tabs on you. I found out you've been working like no sane human being can – without some help of the chemical variety, that is. And with a little insider gossip coming my way about whose been hired, fired, and promoted, I made a very good bet about what was going on. And you know I'm not a betting man.'

Jake knew that no young blood had been hired or promoted since his impromptu departure, and that left a board of ancient directors who had been there since time immemorial. They turned up to board meetings like self-important hens, and they did bring with them years of accumulated business acumen to make critical decisions for the company. But who implemented them? Who saw the job through to completion?

Jake realised that for Marcus, the past few months must have been hell. Times had changed. Where once there had been three executive directors at the helm – William, Jake and Marcus – taking equal share in the day-to-day responsibilities, now there was one. And there was nothing Jake could do about that. He couldn't go back. But he was prepared to cut Marcus some slack, for old times' sake. 'Marcus, have you ever heard of rehab clinics?'

Marcus looked at him blankly.

'There's a luxury residential clinic in London. I looked it up online. It's the sort of place where celebrities go who are suffering from …' Jake chose his words carefully, 'exhaustion.' It was a familiar euphemism, which as far as most people were concerned, Jake included, meant attempting to kick their latest addiction, and having some very expensive therapy sessions thrown in.

'If you think for one second that I'm going to check myself in to some clinic with a bunch of—'

'People, Marcus. They're only people like you and me, trying to make sense of their lives, trying to make sense of the hands they've been dealt – that's all. If you just stopped to think about it for a moment, you'd know it makes sense. You need to sort yourself out, Marcus, and you need to do it now. But you can't do it on your own.'

Jake was playing the *you've got to be cruel to be kind* card. And he had another card up his sleeve, or at least he hoped the clinic did; it was called the therapy card. Jake secretly hoped that while they helped him kick his habit, the counsellors could help him face his demons; Marcus was suffering from denial. Perhaps, this way, Marcus would come to some sort of acceptance of his part in Eleanor's condition, and there would be closure for them both.

Marcus still had to deal with what had really happened on the ski slope when he'd found the two of them buried in the snow after the avalanche. There had been no one else up there, although Marcus had convinced himself there was. If only he could come to terms with the truth.

Jake would gladly have taken her place. The fact was that if Marcus had dug out Eleanor first, Jake would be in that hospital now rather than Eleanor, and maybe their baby would still be alive. Jake would never go so far as to tell Marcus what else they had lost that day when he'd made the decision to dig Jake out first instead of his sister. No one else knew about the baby. They'd never had a chance to make the announcement.

He studied Marcus. 'Good,' he said, detecting a hint of resignation in those dark eyes. 'I've still got plenty of holiday left, so what I propose …' Jake drew a long breath in the knowledge that once he'd said it, he couldn't go back on it. Was he sure he wanted to do this? Not in a million years. But what he was sure of was that it was time to help Marcus. He wished a fist in the face would bring Marcus to his senses, as Marcus's punch had done for him, but he knew it could never be that simple.

'What I propose is this. While you're out of the office for … oh, a week or so at rehab …' Jake wondered how long Marcus would need in the clinic. He really didn't want to spend the rest of the school holidays, which amounted to about six weeks, back at the Ross Corporation. But if he really had to, for Marcus to sort himself out once and for all, then so be it. He had the time. At least he could console himself with the thought that he'd be returning for the new school year in September.

Jake took a deep breath, and said, 'I'll hold the fort until—'

'You're coming back?' Marcus said eagerly.

'No, Marcus. It's just temporary – that's all. I'll make sure the board doesn't do anything else behind your back while you're away. I'll be your eyes and ears.'

'You'd do that for me?' Marcus wasn't stupid; he knew how hard it was for Jake to return.

'Of course I would, you idiot.' Jake smiled at him. 'But as soon as you're back, I'm history.' He wagged a finger at Marcus. 'Is that understood?'

❖

Marcus understood. Jake had found more than a new job these

past few months; he had found another woman that he loved, and the guilt was eating him alive. For Jake to move on with his life, it would have been better if Eleanor had died. Marcus understood this now. Jake had to believe – however insanely – that this was true. It was the only way to distance himself from her and continue to be a functioning human being.

But it was over. It had to be – this charade, this deceit. And what Marcus wanted now more than anything was for Jake to stop blaming him for Eleanor's fate. So he was going to check himself into the clinic Jake had suggested, if for no other reason than to give Jake an opportunity to take that step back into his old life. Maybe, just maybe, it would be like another fist in the face; the fist of reality forcing him to face the truth that it had been an accident, pure and simple; nobody could have done a thing to change the outcome. Her fate had been sealed the moment she had stepped out of that cable car onto the ski slopes with an insane idea in her head that would lead them all off-piste and into a living nightmare. Only time might heal some of the pain that her absence had left behind.

Marcus knew part of that healing process would be for them to visit Eleanor, to accept what had happened and move on. But neither of them were ready for that; not yet. Marcus knew he'd have to get through his little sojourn at the clinic first. And then he had someone to find – the other person who had been on that ski slope, and who had dug Jake out of the snow first after the avalanche. It wasn't him. He just had to convince Jake of that fact.

He knew what Jake was thinking: that he was in denial over what had really happened. Marcus knew better. He just had to find the person to prove it.

❖

Marcus got out of the car. 'You okay to drive?' he said, holding the driver's door open as Jake got in.

'Yes, yes,' said Jake, feeling a lot less confident than he sounded but impatient to get going, to find Martha's son, and to leave Scotland.

He did have the urge to return the car and leave with Marcus, but there was something he had to do before he left which had nothing to do with Arnold or Martha or the business with finding her son.

Marcus slammed the car door shut and disappeared around the back of the car. Jake watched in his rear-view mirror as Marcus opened the boot. He reappeared at the side of the car with his case and tapped on Jake's window.

Jake pressed the button to release the electric window as Marcus squatted down beside the car, resting an elbow on the window ledge. 'You're going to need ice for that.' Marcus lifted a finger and pointed at Jake.

Jake touched his temple near his right eye. It felt very tender. He winced. He was just thankful that Marcus hadn't broken the skin; he didn't need another bandage, courtesy of Marcus.

'Look, about that …' Marcus began.

Jake could tell Marcus was building up to a monumentally unnecessary apology, but feeling absurdly fragile all of a sudden, and just a little sorry for himself, Jake let him continue.

'I am so sorry. I really don't know what came over me.'

'I do.' Jake stared out of the front window. 'I've been a real jerk.' He turned to look at Marcus. 'I just wish you'd smacked me one months ago, before … before I put up that stupid …' He didn't have to say any more; the expression on Marcus's face said it all – he understood. And that was what he had to stay behind and do; put an end to this insanity so he could face her – finally. The memorial stone in the garden of The Lake House had to come down.

'You will come back to London – won't you?' Marcus searched his face.

Jake clasped a reassuring hand on Marcus's forearm. 'You know I will. I'll drive you there myself. Once you're settled in, I'm sure everything …'

'Jake.'

Something in Marcus's tone stopped him short.

'Jake, I'm not talking about the rehab clinic.'

'Oh.' Jake shifted nervously in his seat.

Marcus repeated the question. 'You will come with me to see Eleanor, won't you?'

Jake looked at him for a long moment. It wasn't that he didn't have the answer to that question. He could answer him in a heartbeat. He just couldn't quite believe he had come this far, made it to this point where he could even recognise the question for what it was – that Eleanor was still alive – let alone give an affirmative.

'Yes,' said Jake in answer to his question. 'As soon as I've cleared up things here, I'll fly down to London – you can count on me. Just check yourself into the clinic – when you are ready. I will cover for you at work as promised.'

Marcus smiled. 'I know you will. And I'll do something for you. I'm going to phone Faye, speak to her.'

Jake creased his brow. 'Why?'

'Look, I know it's none of my business, and I hope it's not because of me, but I get the feeling Faye is a bit … well … cheesed off with you.'

Jake wasn't in the mood to go into that. 'Yeah, she won't answer my calls.'

'Don't worry. I'll sort it out.'

'Will you?' Jake wondered what Marcus could possibly say to her to make Faye phone him back.

'Of course. What are best friends for?' Marcus squeezed his forearm affectionately and got up.

Jake realised, as he watched Marcus walking across the car park in the direction of the airport terminal, that he needed Marcus just as much as Marcus needed him. Neither could go and see Eleanor alone, yet had been denied any possibility of going together – Jake had made sure of that. They had each been locked in internal battles with their consciences, and in an external battle with each other; it was a hell hole of their own making which they had both been desperate to escape. They needed to free themselves from this burden of guilt of surviving the accident intact where she had not. Only then, perhaps, would they be able to move along the road to some semblance of normality, always careful to avoid those backward glances to what might have been.

49

Jake manoeuvred the car out of the car park, anticipating an altogether less eventful ride back from the airport than the one there. He was right. The journey was only enlivened by the occasional pothole in the road, which sent sharp darts of pain whipping through his temples and exploding behind his eyes. They only served to remind him, once again, what an idiot he'd been.

Shortly before the turn-off for Aviemore, Jake heard his mobile bleep with a text message. Jake raised his eyebrows. His heart leapt. Was it Faye?

He continued until he reached a lay-by and then pulled over. Jake was disappointed to discover it wasn't Faye. The text was from Lawrence at the care home, asking him to give him a call. Jake hoped to goodness it wasn't bad news; that Lawrence was going to tell him that Martha had passed away before he'd been able to find her long-lost son.

'Mr Campbell-Ross, Jake, so glad you got in touch, as I have some good news. I made a few enquiries after you left, and yes, Martha did have a visitor on the day you came. It was a friend of the late Arnold Wright. Apparently, he has been visiting at least twice a week since Arnold died. I spoke to him on the phone.

Arnold had been trying to trace Martha's son for quite some time before he died, so his friend took over the quest. Unfortunately, Martha often mistook Arnold's friend for Arnold himself. You see, she thought Arnold was still alive. So, on the day he phoned you to come and visit her, he didn't want to upset her by using his real name, so he pretended to be Arnold instead. Arnold had been such a good friend to her. He didn't see the harm. And it was the same when you visited. He thought, why upset Martha?'

Jake sighed. Another piece of the jigsaw had fallen into place – thank god.

He knew he'd been through the ringer, with what had happened to Eleanor. Jake realised that he must have had some sort of breakdown, convincing himself that she'd died up there. But to think that he'd been talking to a dead person had been the last straw. He'd thought he was losing his mind.

'By the way, he said his name is Brian, and he gave me a phone number if you want to give him a call. He wants to apologise for the deception. He rather got carried away with his little charade.'

Jake understood. He thought of Marcus, who'd never know he had nearly become an uncle. There were times to spare people the truth. Martha clearly didn't remember that her good friend, Arnold, was gone. Brian had done the right thing. Jake just wished he'd told him.

Lawrence said, 'Oh, and he was absolutely delighted to hear you're going to try and find Martha's son.' Lawrence paused. 'I didn't know she had a son. There was no mention of that in her notes.'

Jake remembered what Martha had said: *if only he'd married me, we could have been a family*. Jake guessed she'd been talking about her son's father. Jake had an idea that she'd given the baby up, and it had been a secret.

After thanking Lawrence, Jake ended the call. He set off once more and headed for Aviemore, anticipating that Gayle would be surprised to see him. He hoped that the additional night in the room he'd originally paid for was still available.

Jake arrived at Gayle's with three desperate wishes: a bucket of ice for his head, some headache tablets, and a warm bed. He felt so tired.

He was about to get out of the car when his mobile phone rang. He really hoped that Marcus hadn't missed his flight and was now angling for a lift back to Lark Lodge for the night. He looked at the number, shocked that it was Faye. Marcus had already put in a good word – he hoped.

Jake answered immediately.

'What's this about you returning to the Ross Corporation?'

Jake frowned. He'd forgotten to tell Marcus not to share that conversation with Faye. But it had had the desired effect – when he'd told Marcus that she wasn't returning his calls, he had said, *don't worry. I'll sort it out.* He certainly had. Jake managed a smile as he replied, 'It's only for one or two weeks, the summer at most. I'll be back at school in September. But I have to do it for Marcus.' He imagined Marcus hadn't shared the reason.

'While Marcus is in rehab.'

Jake raised his eyebrows. So he *had* shared the reason.

'Yes, so he can get his act together, and we can go and see Eleanor.' Jake instantly put his hand over his mouth.

'Go and see Eleanor? What are you talking about?' He could hear the concern in her voice. He imagined she thought he'd lost his mind, and it wasn't Marcus that needed to check himself into the clinic for therapy.

Jake sighed. He knew he'd have to tell her some time. He didn't want to do it over the phone, but it was too late for that now. 'There's something I didn't tell you about the accident last Christmas.'

Faye was quiet on the end of the line.

'Eleanor survived.'

❖

Jake put his phone down on the dashboard and sat in the car outside Lark Lodge pondering that phone call. He'd told Faye he didn't want to go into details; not over the phone. They'd talk when he got back the next day. He'd barely got a word in when he heard Natty in the background, haranguing her mum to let her speak to him.

Faye had acquiesced, but not before telling him she missed him terribly and that he'd better be heading back tomorrow.

Jake let out the biggest sigh of relief. He was back in her good books, back in their lives. He couldn't wait to return. However, his smile faded at the thought of that visit he'd promised he'd make with Marcus when he got out of rehab.

Jake sat for a moment, thinking of The Lake House as he stared at the Cairngorm mountains in the distance. He was reflecting on that conversation with Marcus at the airport. They had come a long way in the last couple of days. It was a huge step, confronting the pain, the loss, and finally deciding to go and see her. Jake couldn't have done it without Marcus. Marcus was right: they were best friends.

There was just something nagging away at him – a possibility he'd rather not confront: what if Marcus had been telling the truth? What if there had been someone else up there with them on

Christmas Day when they'd skied off-piste? But who? And why hadn't they come forward after the accident?

The more Jake thought about it, the more plausible Marcus's version of events sounded. Why hadn't he at least considered the possibility that Marcus was telling the truth? Jake knew the reason; he'd been so wrapped up in his own grief that he'd needed someone to blame.

Marcus. They were best friends, akin to brothers. But he wasn't Marcus's brother, and Jake knew in his heart that in an emergency, Marcus would have saved his own blood, his sister, first, if he could.

Jake stared up at the mountains, his eyes drifting down to Lark Lodge. He wasn't going to find the answers there. As he turned the car around, it dawned on him that he'd made promises he couldn't keep. He was meant to return to London. He was meant to head up the Ross Corporation, albeit temporarily. He'd promised to return to Faye and Natty. But there were secrets still to uncover, and he knew in his heart where he had to start.

It was time to return to The Lake House.

The Scottish Highlands Series continues in

The Boathouse by the Loch

Paperback and Kindle eBook coming soon.

If you enjoyed *Return to the Lake House* I would be grateful if you would leave a review on Amazon.

For further details about the author and her novels please visit the author's website.

www.elisedarcy.com

Also by Elise Darcy

The Living Apart Together Series

Living Apart Together

It Takes 2 to Tango

Dear John

Love on the Rooftop

The Sunrise Coast Series

New Beginnings at the Harbour Inn

The Secret of the Summerhouse

The Cottage by the Sea

The Guest House at Shingle Cove

The Houseboat by the Quay

Return to Willow Tree Cottage

The Bookshop of Memories

The Beach House

A Summer to Remember

Standalone books

A Mallorcan Affair

Lola & The Man

We'll Meet Again

The Villa in Sicily

Printed in Great Britain
by Amazon

57924934R00239